beautiful place by the sea

DANIELLE SMYTH

ASTRALUMEN
PRESS

Book cover design by Danielle Smyth.

Editing by Dan Smyth.

ISBN (Paperback): 979-8-9933163-7-6 | ISBN (Hardcover): 979-8-9933163-6-9 | ISBN (Kindle eBook): 979-8-9933163-8-3

Library of Congress Control Number: 2026931386

Publisher's Cataloging-in-Publication data

Smyth, Danielle, author.

Beautiful Place by the Sea / Danielle Smyth. — First edition. — Burnt Hills, NY: Astralumen Press, 2026.

Edited by Dan Smyth; cover design and illustration by Danielle Smyth.

LCCN: 2026931386

ISBN (Paperback): 979-8-9933163-7-6 | ISBN (Hardcover): 979-8-9933163-6-9 | ISBN (Kindle eBook): 979-8-9933163-8-3

LCSH: Romance fiction | Contemporary romance fiction | Couples—Fiction | Coastal fiction

Classification: LCC: PS3619.M66 G47 2026 | DDC: 813/.6–dc23

Visit the author's website at www.daniellesmythbooks.com

Printed in the U.S.A.

Published by Astralumen Press: www.astralumenpress.com

For my sweet daughter: may your life always feel as magical as a summer vacation.

one

The house stands like a beleaguered sand castle long forgotten along the shore. Its white paint is peeling, and the faded letters on a sign hung by the door spell out "Beach Haven." I'm sure it was impressive in its glory days, but now, like so much else just off Route 1 in New England, the rental cottage looks like it could use a facelift.

That's not to say I don't love being here. My family's been traveling to coastal Maine every summer of my life, and it's always been beyond amazing. Well, except for last year. That was when everything changed.

The whole town is rife with memories—mostly pleasant, some less so. Dripping vanilla soft serve onto the hot sand as the waves petered out against my toes. Chasing my cousin Laurel up and down the beach while my grandmother patiently embroidered from the comfort of her chair.

Growing into an awkward teenager and glowering at my mom behind my beach book. Sneaking out at night to the antiquated dance hall down the block with Laurel, hoping to impress cute boys.

Bringing my college boyfriend here to meet the family, then realizing he wasn't right for me when he was rude to my grandpa, who might have been the nicest person on Earth. Browsing quaint bookstores with my grandmother and daydreaming about having my own someday.

Then, when things got tougher, watching my parents' marriage break down before my eyes. And seeing my grandmother slip away right after our trip last year, before the family splintered into fragments and decided it would be too difficult to come back.

But I grew up on this beach, and something about the way the waves lap against the shore has permanently altered the rhythm of my heart, pouring itself into my very soul. I can't seem to stay away.

Plus, given what's happened at work, with Kyle, I felt even more motivated to come back. To flee my hometown. No matter how much I tried to convince myself I was a strong, independent woman, I just couldn't stomach an entire summer in Brookline.

Especially a summer with no one to hang out with because they all took his side, despite it being his fault in every way. Sitting around and remembering everything that went on, feeling trapped within the confines of my misguided faith and naïveté, didn't seem like a great time.

And that's how I find myself in the driveway behind Beach Haven on a sweltering July day with Laurel, rolling a battered purple carry-on toward the back door.

She tosses her strawberry blonde hair over her shoulder. "Geez. It's so humid today. I should have gone for a ponytail."

I nod in sympathy. "I think I have a hair tie in my purse somewhere, if you want it."

Laurel shrugs. "Eh, it's okay. I'm planning to run straight into those waves," she gestures toward the beach, just over a dune from the front yard of the rental, "when we're done settling in here."

I chuckle. "You and me both."

"I've missed it. I can't wait to get some vitamin sea."

The pun makes me grimace, but I shoot her a conciliatory smile. I definitely share her sentiments.

We're silent for a minute, and I'm sure we're both thinking the same thing. Ogunquit was our family's annual vacation spot since time immemorial, up until Grandma Eleanor passed away last September. Then it became a place that pulled on too many heartstrings; brought forth too many painful memories. No one else wanted to come back this year, but staying away felt wrong, too.

A pang of sadness fills my chest as I remember my grand-mother, reading on the beach while we played in the surf; sneaking us fudge at the rental cottage when our parents went out for the night; eyes sparkling, telling us stories of her misad-ventures up and down the shore with her sister, Janie, back when *she* was a teenager and used to come here, too.

It isn't going to be the same without her.

Clearing my throat, I fish my phone from my pocket. "The caretaker sent me a code for the door," I announce. "I'll check my messages; I've already forgotten what it is."

Laurel nods, coming out of what I'm pretty sure is a trance of family memories much like my own.

I scroll until I find "Maribel at Beach Haven" in my list of text messages. "Okay, it's 6-5-3-1." I type the numbers into the electronic lock and hear a satisfying click as it deems my entry acceptable.

"Ready?" Laurel asks, shouldering her duffel bag.

I nod. The minute I wheel my suitcase inside, I'm hit with a wall of stale air. "Ugh," I grimace. "When was this door last opened?"

Laurel waves her hand in front of her face, as if she can clear the musty smell in favor of the sea air from outside. "God, I don't know. I guess it's been closed up for a while." She drops her bag on the floor. "This is prime beachfront property. How is this not getting snapped up for rent left and right?"

"Maybe Simon's too busy to deal with it?" I start down the hallway, flipping on light switches and peeking through doorways to see what we're working with.

Beach Haven belongs to Simon Foster, a friend of our late grandparents. He had to move into a nursing home a few years back, but he hired a caretaker for the house. It seems like either the caretaker is cleaning less than she should, or perhaps Simon just doesn't do much in the way of advertising. The house has the general aura of a time capsule that hasn't been discovered yet.

"Do you want the room with the desk?" I ask Laurel over my shoulder. She's currently finishing her dissertation, but she was able to slip away from TA duties this summer because there wasn't enough interest in the women's lit classes she usually teaches. Her faculty advisor signed off on our trip but made it very clear that Laurel needed to make some serious writing progress before the fall semester.

"Sure, I'll take that one." Laurel swooshes her duffel past me and slides into the room at the end of the hallway.

It occurs to me that I'm going to need something to do

while Laurel works on her dissertation. The beach is amazing, but I only brought four books, and I'm a quick reader. I'll blast through those by the end of the week, especially if I'm sitting on the sand by myself every day. We've rented the cottage for a full six weeks, until the end of August.

"Want to hit up the bookstore in town later? I need to get a few more beach reads."

I hear Laurel's melodic laugh from the other room. "How many did you bring?"

"Only a couple." I pause. "Plus two."

She chuckles again, coming to lean against the doorframe of the all-blue bedroom I've selected for myself. "I'll admit, I expected this from you, Ivy. I'm surprised you didn't stop at the bookstore on the way *into* town."

I toss a pillow at her, but I know she's right. The bookstore here is among my favorite places on the planet.

Unfortunately, it was also my grandmother's favorite. And there are a lot of memories tied up among its mahogany shelves, so it's going to require effort not to cry when we visit later.

Laurel looks around us at the ancient scrolly bedroom set and the suspiciously flat mattress, the latter looking like it's been squished within an inch of its life through decades of use. "Wow. This is some room."

I chuckle. "So you see why I'll need something to do outside of it."

Laurel purses her lips and nods. "Sure, we can swing by the bookstore later. But not until we've hit up the beach."

"Oh, absolutely," I agree.

. . .

FIFTEEN MINUTES LATER, we're dropping our towels in the sand and jogging awkwardly toward the waves, silly smiles on our faces. It feels like our inner children want to break into an excited run at top speed, but we somehow think we shouldn't. After all, we're adults who should be long over the joy of splashing into the eddying bubbles at the edge of the shore.

When my feet hit the water, I realize that my inner child is alive and well. I don't even care that the water is only 62 degrees and is quickly making my toes feel like they don't exist.

Laurel turns toward me, a huge grin on her face. "This is awesome."

I'm pretty sure I'm reflecting her ballooning happiness back when I say, "It really is."

But we contain our excitement, walking reservedly along the edge of the ocean, letting the waves lap up against our numb feet. We don't say a whole lot, but we don't really have to. I know we're both feeling the same thing.

This is *our* place, the place where we grew up. The place where I can still see my grandparents, smiling at us while we play in the sand. My parents, holding hands on their towels when they think no one is looking. My heart lurches. These waves have watched the formation of our family, all the way from the beginning. And now they've watched it fall apart.

But somehow, standing here now, I feel like all of those timelines are mixed up, swirling together like the tiny waves that mix and reform on the edge of the beach. It's like my parents are still happy. Like Laurel and I are still young and carefree, and the world hasn't beaten us down yet. Like my grandparents are still here, sitting right behind us.

The waves are a constant heartbeat, no matter what's

happening on the shore. Steady, all-seeing, all-knowing. It makes the past feel like it's all around us. And I don't think I knew how much I needed that until this very moment.

WHEN THE SUN starts to dip in the sky and most of the beach-goers head out to ready themselves for hard-won dinner reservations, Laurel and I begrudgingly gather our towels and traipse back to the cottage.

"We're lucky this is so close," she remarks. "I actually can't feel my feet."

I nod. "I think mine lost sensation a good 20 minutes ago."

"Want to get cleaned up, then head to the bookstore?" Laurel punches in the security code, which I'm frankly shocked she remembers, and the smell of the past overtakes my nostrils as the door swings open.

"Sounds like a plan. Want the first shower?"

She nods eagerly. "Thanks. I need to remind my feet that I still love them."

Snorting, I head to my room. "The ocean isn't *cold*. It's *refreshing*." This is something Grandpa Charlie used to say.

I can hear her laughing as she heads into the bathroom.

While Laurel showers, I get unpacked. I toss the casual outfits I brought into the monstrous carved dresser, then hang several dresses and a jacket I hope I won't need in the closet. I line my makeup, toiletry bag, and bottles of shampoo and shower gel up on top of the bookshelf in the corner. Then, my hand stumbles on a small black book at the bottom of my suitcase.

Removing it gingerly, I take in a small breath. It's my grandmother's diary, and, while I *did* pack it, I'm somehow startled to find it. Like I'm not entirely ready to face what its presence means.

Seeing it on a day when the air is so thick with memories is making me feel things. Things that are also making my eyes more than a little bit foggy all of a sudden. I sink onto the edge of the bed, being careful to keep my sandy feet away from the dust ruffle.

I'd found the diary in a box of trash when we were cleaning out my grandparents' house after Eleanor died. It was just three short months after we'd been to the beach together for the last time.

I'd met my dad at the house after work, and I'd noticed right away that he seemed more rumpled and dejected than usual, even in this new world without either of his parents. I knew he and Mom had been fighting, but I didn't think much of it. I was too focused on powering through the evening without bursting into tears.

Stepping into my grandparents' house for the first time after their deaths was like entering a tomb. But in the weirdest possible way, because it didn't really feel like anything had changed. All of their belongings were exactly where they'd been left, as if Charlie or Eleanor might be back at any moment to return to their regularly scheduled programming.

That's the hardest part of losing someone, I think. Trying to make sense of the world without them, all while realizing the world is actually the same one they've just left. They're just not in it anymore.

What do you even do with someone's coat, or their favorite hat? The book on their nightstand? You donate them, of course, or find a family member who's the same size, or who likes the same types of novels. But in a more philosophical sense, what do you *do*? How do you come to terms with the fact that whoever you lost isn't coming back to shrug on their jacket? That they'll never again perch their hat jauntily atop their head?

Cleaning out the house was hard. I tried to keep myself busy finding things to shuffle into donation or keep piles. I think my dad was doing the same thing, but I wanted to give him space to grieve. At one point, while he was upstairs sorting through Grandpa's record collection, I needed a breather, so I took a bag of trash out to the can by the front porch.

It was there that I noticed a cardboard box filled with old books, sitting on the ground near the garbage cans. I'm such a sucker for novels, and my grandmother and I had always loved traipsing through bookstores together. It broke my heart in two to think about throwing away anything from her collection.

My great-aunt Janie was the only one who had been by the house to clean so far. I was a little bit surprised that she'd toss books, but I tried to give her the benefit of the doubt. This entire experience was extremely emotional for all of us; who knows what her reasoning was.

I started to browse through the box, pulling out a copy of *Little Women* that I figured I'd add to my shelf at home. Grandma also had a novel called *Fault Lines* that I remembered her grabbing at the bookstore in Ogunquit that last summer together.

The author, Will Pearson, was doing a book signing while we were in town. Always in awe of successful writers, Grandma stood in line for 45 minutes to get her copy signed. I waited with her, and we chatted about our latest reads the entire time. I grabbed that book out of the trash, too. I couldn't bear to part with the memories.

The day was chilly, and my hands were starting to protest the cold. I was about to go inside to warm up when I spotted the diary. It was a thin, black leather book with a stitched-in red ribbon to use as a bookmark. I flipped it open to see what was inside, then immediately closed it when I noticed my grandmother's handwriting. I wasn't ready to deal with that yet. Instead, I ran the three books to my car, stashing them under the front seat where my dad wouldn't notice.

And I haven't opened the diary yet. But today, here in this place, feels like it might be the right time. I'd brought it with me because I wanted my grandmother to be able to come back to the beach with us, just one more time. And I think that maybe, finally, I'm ready to face her loss.

I slide my finger under the cover and open to the first entry. *July 9, 1953.* My jaw drops. *Today* is July 9th. What are the chances that I would open this exactly 66 years after it was written?

It feels like a sign, somehow. I try to still my ragged breathing and wipe a stray tear from my eye. Then I steel myself and begin to read.

two

July 9, 1953
The sunset was pink the night we met. He was wearing blue.

I'd let my mother convince me to curl my hair, even though I didn't expect to be making a first impression on anyone new. I assumed it would be business as usual; just me and Janie, dancing, laughing, coming alive to the music.

The dance hall was packed to the brim, mostly with couples eager to get out from under their parents' critical gaze so they could cozy up a bit. With each swell of the band, I caught a glimpse of another girl, falling, doe-eyed, onto another jacketed guy's shoulder while they swayed gently to the music.

I was used to this; these weekend outings with my sister. It was comforting, if not a little bit depressing, to be here on the outside looking in. I was accustomed to getting all dolled up and pushing aside my own loneliness, watching other people fall in love.

I can't honestly say I ever expected to be one of them.

We spend every summer in Ogunquit. They call it "beautiful place by the sea," and I can certainly see why. The ocean is calm on the vast beach, glittering in the sun and welcoming you to sit down and stay awhile. In my favorite part of town, the waves crash against rocky cliffs, while I walk the thin strip of land far above, surrounded by flowers.

Here, our days are spent marveling at the tranquil expanse before us or sitting under the canopy at the top of the beach, where I work on my embroidery. I'm not much of a swimmer, so I prefer to admire the ocean from a respectful distance.

Janie and I love our quiet, contemplative moments watching the sun go down beyond the horizon, which always looks so vast, thanks to the swath of waves stretched as far as the eye can see. We spend our weeknights stargazing on the sand, and, on weekends, we somewhat begrudgingly leave the shore in favor of the dance hall.

I probably wouldn't have bothered going out dancing at all that first night if she hadn't pushed me. If my mother hadn't been worried that we were too isolated, spending all of our time together.

Crowds have never been my thing, and I have no idea how to talk to boys. Or men. We've met both here this summer. I would have preferred sitting in the back, sipping a cola, to introducing myself to any of the suited teenagers, or, worse, the lonely twenty-somethings who were desperate to find a girl.

But Janie was bubbly and bright, and she always knew what to do. The night I met him, she pulled me by the hand, dragging me onto the dance floor. Her curls bounced against her shoulders.

"Come on, Eleanor," she'd said, eyes sparkling. "Let's go introduce ourselves to those two over there."

I nodded slowly and followed her to two men in blazers, standing along the edge of the dance floor.

"Hello," Janie said loudly as we walked over. "I'm Janie. This is Eleanor."

The first man, blonde and blue-eyed, grinned at her. "Francis," he replied. He turned to the taller, darker man next to him. "And this here is—"

The other man raised his eyes to meet mine. "Eleanor, it's a pleasure to meet you." I felt like his gaze was piercing my soul, it was so intense. Butterflies flittered around my stomach. I'd never felt anything like it before.

It didn't even occur to me that he didn't introduce himself to Janie. I took his hand and let him lead me onto the dance floor. They were playing "Till I Waltz Again with You" by Teresa Brewer.

And that's how we met. And it's been a week now, and I can't stop thinking about it.

three

I don't tell Laurel about the diary. I figure I can bring it up some other time. Plus, I'm still feeling some kind of way about intruding on Eleanor's intimate reflections of her first time meeting my grandfather. I have to sit with this for a while, figure out how to process it, before I can bring myself to talk about it.

My cousin's shower is long and ostensibly luxurious. By the time it's my turn, there's very little hot water left, so I get ready quickly and we leave Beach Haven to set off into town.

"Want to hit the bookstore first, and then grab dinner?" Laurel asks as we head up the sidewalk toward the town square.

"Sounds good to me," I agree.

My heart flips in my chest a little as Shoreline Books comes into view. I have so many happy memories here with my grandmother, taking strolls off the beach and browsing for what felt like hours in the cool, air-conditioned shop.

She always let me pick out a new paperback to take back to

our rental, even when my parents told her not to. When I was younger, she'd read the stories to me before bedtime. As I got older, we still shopped together, but we'd coordinate to get two books we both wanted to read, and then we'd take turns.

We called it BOGO books, even though we were still paying for both. Well, she was. Even once I was an adult and had a job, Grandma never let me so much as pull out my own credit card.

"None of that, Ivy," she'd say, hands shaking as she unzipped her pocketbook. "This is my treat."

As I remember her now, gray hair always permed close to her head, dyed within an inch of its life, I feel tears forming behind my eyelids. I shake my head, willing them away. This summer is about loving the past, yes, but it's also about escaping it. Moving on and making new memories.

The wooden shingles of the bookshop are stained a slate blue that meshes perfectly with the blue hydrangeas out front. A pride flag flies next to the door, and a small white sign in the window says, "Help Wanted for the Summer. Ask for Maisie."

My heart thuds against my ribcage. Help wanted? Seasonally? Something like hope whirls around my chest. Maybe *this* is what I could do while Laurel's working on her dissertation. Pick up some hours at the bookshop, make some extra (much-needed) money, live in the memories of my grandmother, all while making new ones with every reader who comes through the door.

Eyes bright, I turn to my cousin. "Did you see that sign?"

"I knew you were going to bring that up," she teases.

"It's just...I could really use the money," I tell her, picking what feels like the most acceptable reason for wanting to work here. I'm subletting my condo while we're away, but that will just barely cover my share of the cost of Beach Haven.

Laurel nods. "I hear you. Also, you've been in love with this bookshop since we were kids."

I can't deny that she's right. In fact, coming here with my grandmother and falling in love with books the way I did is a big part of why I decided to become a school librarian. I didn't see myself as an author, and I wasn't sure I could handle the business side of running a bookshop, even though I would love nothing more. But guiding young minds and making a difference, all while surrounded by books? That seemed like an attainable goal. Much more realistic than the romantic notion of being a bookseller.

Sure, I'd always dreamed about a future where I ran a cute little bookstore like this one. Usually, the fantasies took place in a seaside town, too. And often, they involved an attractive rival bookstore owner, à la *You've Got Mail*, but that's neither here nor there.

For countless reasons, working at Shoreline Books for the summer feels like a great idea.

"I'm going to apply," I say to Laurel, sounding more confident than I feel.

"Of course you are." She grins over her shoulder and pushes open the door to the shop. A bell jingles behind us, the only sound in an otherwise silent space.

The cashier station is empty, and I don't see anyone giving off a worker vibe, reshelving books, or anything. In fact, aside from an elderly couple browsing the biographies in the back corner, and a thirty-something guy bent over a notebook in the little café area to our right, the bookstore appears to be empty.

"I don't think anyone's working here," I say quietly to Laurel.

"There has to be someone," Laurel replies, a little too loudly.

The writer glances inquisitively up from his notebook. "Are you looking for something?"

I wasn't expecting anyone to join our conversation, in no small part because we're at least 15 feet away from everyone else. "Oh, no," I answer, suddenly feeling flustered. "Someone, actually. Not something."

He raises a dark eyebrow. "Someone in particular?"

Laurel, always better-equipped for casual small talk with strangers than I am, walks closer to him and sticks out her hand.

He shakes it with a confused look on his face.

"Hi, I'm Laurel Montgomery-Parker. And this is Ivy Parker." She flashes a charming grin. I don't know why Laurel bothered with last names. Surely we're not going to be spending more time with this guy.

Seeing her like this reminds me why she was always the one boys gravitated toward when we snuck out to the dilapidated dance hall in town during our annual vacations here. The same one that my grandmother wrote about in her diary, I realize with a start.

"We're in town for the summer," Laurel continues. "Ivy's here to talk to Maisie about the job opening." She jerks her head toward the sign in the window.

"Oliver Clarke," the writer nods in introduction, running a hand through his hair. It's such a deep brown, it's almost black. "Are your parents gardeners, or something?" he asks, nodding between us.

"What?" I wrinkle my forehead.

He mirrors my facial expression, like it should be obvious. "*Laurel* and *Ivy*."

I guess it *is* obvious. I feel a flush creep up my cheeks. "Oh. That."

He's still looking at me like I might be a little slow, but Laurel saves the day with her typical enthusiasm. "I'm actually named after my great-grandma on my mom's side. Ivy and I are paternal cousins, so no obvious horticultural connection there."

Oliver doesn't react, but Laurel barrels on. "My great-grandmother was Laurel Rose, and her daughter was Rosemarie, so the garden thing runs pretty strong going back quite a ways." She beams a little too eagerly.

Oliver is, after all, a perfect stranger. He probably doesn't need to know this level of detail about her matrilineal naming history. And judging by the look on his face, he probably doesn't care very much, either.

"Huh," he replies noncommittally, then looks back down at his notebook.

"Do you know when Maisie will be back?" I ask, watching Oliver scrawling a sentence on his paper. The ink strokes sweep messily back and forth across the page like waves crashing onto the beach. Also like waves on the beach, I'm finding them oddly soothing.

He doesn't glance up from his notebook. "Should be here by six," he says.

I tear my eyes away from whatever he's writing, which I can't even read from where I'm standing. "Thanks." Turning to Laurel, I incline my head. "Shall we?"

She gives me a quizzical look. "It's 5:45. Wouldn't we just stay here?"

I can't quite explain why, but the idea of sitting in silence for 15 minutes while Oliver works feels very unappealing. And the notion of hanging around the bookstore and chatting loudly with my cousin (because that's the only way she knows how) seems even worse, because I'm pretty sure Oliver would still just be sitting there, silently judging us. Perhaps wishing we were quieter, so he could focus on writing what I assume is some sort of angsty Holden Caulfield-type novel.

"Let's go grab a coffee next door," I suggest. I realize there's a small coffee counter right here in the bookstore, but I want to leave as quickly as possible.

Laurel still looks confused, but she doesn't push me. "Okay, sounds good." She grabs her brown raffia bag off the café table where she'd set it down when she shook Oliver's hand and tosses it over her shoulder. "See you later, Oliver."

He barely lifts his head. "Bye."

"Bye," I mumble as we hustle out. The bell on the door jingles loudly as it swings shut behind us.

We're just a few steps down the sidewalk when Laurel rounds on me. "What was that about?"

I shake my head. "Something about Oliver's general disposition made me feel very judged."

Her tinkling laugh fills the air. "He was a little grumpy, huh?"

"Indeed," I chuckle. "Now, time for a latte."

WE GRAB a bench on the road to the beach and people-watch while sipping our coffees. At this time of day, most of the passers-by are heading back to their hotels and rentals, dragging beach wagons and cranky children behind them.

I marvel at the sheer amount of *stuff* some families seem to feel is required for a day along the shore: beach chairs worn as backpacks, wagons packed to the brim with umbrellas, boogie boards, buckets and sand toys, pop-up tents, coolers, bocce ball sets, blankets, towels.

I guess things probably change once you have kids, but, for me, a tote bag with a towel and my book has always been enough. Maybe a bottle of water and a tube of sunscreen, too. I'm coming to the beach to swim or read or just *be*; the experience feels like plenty without the addition of 50 cubic feet of sporting equipment. But to each their own, I suppose.

"So, what do you want to do tonight?" Laurel sips her Americano tentatively. The drinks are still pretty hot.

I shrug. "We could grab takeout on the way home, if you want. I think that new pizza place on Shore Road is supposed to be pretty good."

"Pizza would be lovely," she agrees. "I've been subsisting on ramen noodles for what feels like an eternity at this point."

"And just how *is* your dissertation going?" I grin teasingly.

"Oh, well, you know." She sighs. "It's certainly going."

I snort. "Sounds like a blast. But, hey! Only one more year and you'll be done!"

Laurel nods in mock seriousness. "At least I have something to look forward to." Her green eyes dance at the joke. "And what about you?"

"What about me?" I take a big gulp of my latte, which I immediately regret, because it scalds my throat all the way down.

Laurel gives me a look like *"you couldn't possibly* not *know what I'm talking about, Ivy,"* but she asks casually, "What's on the horizon for you?"

I cast my eyes downward, shaking my head. "I'm not really sure anymore, I guess."

She touches my hand gently. "I know things have been tough. I'm sorry; I didn't mean to bring up a sore subject."

"No, it's okay," I start.

"But it isn't," she returns. "You've had a hellish year. I want to make sure you're okay."

I consider her words. The year was, indeed, hellish. Though it didn't start off that way.

Last summer at this time, I was preparing for another standard school year, filled with excuses about lost library books and seminars about how to use the ChromeBooks in the lab.

And it was like that at first. Fall hit Boston, everything was adorably orange and pumpkin-spiced, and I hung out with my friends, all teachers at Farnsworth Middle School.

And Kyle. My boyfriend of just over two years, at that point. Kyle was a math teacher I'd met shortly after starting my job. He was everything I'd dreamed of in a man—intelligent, charming, and considerate. He seemed to love his job, especially the students.

We hit it off right away after our meet-cute in the teacher's lounge. I'd dropped my orange on the floor, mid-peel, and it rolled all the way under his table. He'd brought it over to me, making a truly terrible joke about runaway fruit, then gave me the orange he'd packed for his own lunch. We ate together that day, and that was it for me. We started dating two weeks later.

In the time that followed, all of my work friends became his, and vice versa. Even though I was living just two towns over from where I grew up in the Boston suburbs, I didn't have many friends left in the area. Laurel was busy with grad school in the city, and all of my high school crew had scattered across

New England, chasing better jobs (or, in the case of my best friend, Amie, a string of increasingly flawed men). Because my work friends, and Kyle's, were the only people in my orbit, it mattered to me tremendously that I keep them.

My coworker Alex, whom I'd been close with since day one at Farnsworth, was the only one not thrilled with the Kyle pairing. Alex knew Kyle already from working together on the same seventh-grade teaching team, and while he liked my boyfriend just fine, he insisted that things were going to end poorly.

"You can't date Kyle," Alex had told me when things started.

"Why not?" I'd been annoyed, but Alex was often sassy and opinionated, so I'd entertained the conversation.

Alex had sighed deeply. "You're going to ruin the friend group," he'd explained.

"You mean the friend group that Kyle and I have just created by starting to date, and introducing our friends to each other?"

He smirked. "Yes, that one. But it's going to end, and when it does, they're all going to pick him."

My jaw had dropped. "Excuse you?"

Alex threw his arm around my shoulders. "Of course, being your work bestie, I'm always going to pick you. But Kyle is charismatic, and he's been here longer than you. He's on committees; he knows everyone. He's *hot*. People are going to choose him, mark my words."

"Okay, please stop lusting after my boyfriend," I'd snapped at Alex, throwing his arm off of me. A silly little thrill went through me at the word "boyfriend," because the relationship was new, and I was still lost in that butterflies-in-your-stomach era. "And I think it will be fine. Not to mention, who's to say it's going to end?"

I'll never forget the look on Alex's face, somewhere between *"Come on, Ivy, you idiot"* and *"I feel bad for you, you pathetic fool."* But, to his credit, all he'd said was, "I'll be here for you no matter what. Just be careful."

As it turned out, when things went south, Alex was right. Everyone else *did* pick Kyle, as evidenced by the pitying yet awkward looks I started getting in the teacher's lounge and the whispers that haunted me when I walked down the hallway. The ghosting from friends I'd thought were mine for life; the suddenly-too-busy-to-hang-out group that I'd seen almost daily before the breakup.

And then there was Alex, who in the end didn't officially take sides, but who did tell me he couldn't "openly show favoritism" toward me, because Kyle was probably getting promoted to admin next year, and Alex might "need him." Alex, who also stopped talking to me at work when other people were around, just in case.

The horrible year went far beyond Kyle or work, of course. Grandma Eleanor died in September, right after we got back from Maine. And then in November, with seemingly no warning, my mom told my dad she wanted a trial separation. As if things weren't bad enough already.

Yes, the past year has been hellish. I'm not sure I'm ready to talk about it, though. Especially with Laurel, whose righteous fury on my behalf will get me worked up all over again. Besides, I've already given her the Cliff's Notes version in real time via text message. I'm not sure how much more detail she needs.

So I just say, "It *was* a really tough year. But we're here now, and I'm looking forward to some time away."

Laurel's known me too long to let it go. "Kyle treated you like trash, Ivy. You deserve way better."

I feel tears start, and I push my sunglasses higher up the bridge of my nose, hoping they'll catch any stray droplets before my cousin notices. "I know," I reply softly.

"And your so-called friends? Scumbags, all of them." Laurel waves her to-go cup around in the air while she talks, sloshing coffee on her pink t-shirt. "Damn it," she mumbles, digging through her purse for a napkin.

"I agree." I watch in amusement as she attempts to dab the stain away. "I have a Tide stick back at the rental," I offer.

"Thanks." She sighs deeply. "So what are you going to do?"

I tilt my head. "What do you mean?"

"Are you going back in the fall?"

I consider her question. *"No,"* I want to scream. I'm not sure I can handle being in that building, with those people, ever again. I'm all for not giving in to bullies, or whatever, but this was just too much for my heart to handle. And it's not like I'm in love with my job so much that I wouldn't consider going somewhere else. In fact, I've been pretty bored at work for the last couple of years.

But it hadn't really occurred to me before this moment that *not* going back was a possibility.

"Oh, I'm not sure," I say, trying to seem like I've considered it. "I haven't really looked elsewhere yet. But maybe I should."

Laurel nods emphatically. "You *definitely* should. Why put yourself in a position to be treated like crap again? Find another job and start fresh."

"You don't think it would be like letting them win?" I ask.

"They already lost when they treated you like you don't matter," she says, patting my arm reassuringly and sounding just like my mother. "And, anyway, who cares? Your happiness is all that you need to worry about."

"My happiness, but also my bank account," I respond wryly. "I do have tenure."

She shrugs. "Eh, you'll get it again. Somewhere else." Sipping her coffee, she considers my face. "And who knows, maybe this summer job will turn into something? You've always wanted to work in a bookstore and fall in love with Tom Hanks."

A snort escapes me before I can stop it. "It's not so much Tom Hanks, the person, as the essence of what he represents."

"Tom Hanks isn't exactly my ideal man, either," she admits.

"Right? Not enough edge."

Laurel nods. "Exactly. Too clean-cut."

"So it needs to be a dark, handsome, edgy lit nerd." I run my thumb over the plastic lid of my coffee cup, imagining how great it would be if such a man actually existed.

"Like Oliver from the bookstore?" Laurel's eyebrows rise suggestively.

I hit her arm. "Absolutely not like Oliver. He's *too* grumpy. We need to find someone closer to the middle of the bell curve."

"Yeah, but he's got the dark and handsome thing down," she retorts.

"I guess." It occurs to me that she's right, at least about part of it—maybe this summer job *could* turn into something more. My heart skips gleefully at the idea of moving to Ogunquit. I love it here. I always have. Sure, I'd miss Boston, but living in my favorite seaside retreat, working in a bookshop? That's like the stuff of a bibliophile's wildest dreams.

I check my phone and see it's almost six o'clock. "Well, anyway, Oliver doesn't own the bookstore. That discounts him from my *You've Got Mail*-style fantasies."

Laurel laughs. "I guess that's true."

I grab my bag and stand up, downing the last of my drink. "I'm going to head back over to talk to Maisie. Want to order the pizza? If you text me the details, I'll pick it up on my way home."

"Sounds good!" Laurel gets up, too, and starts to walk in the opposite direction. "I'll see you later. Give my regards to Oliver!"

"Absolutely not!" I yell cheerfully as I walk away.

four

W hen I get back to the bookstore, I'm not surprised to
see that Oliver's still sitting in the same place in the
café, pen scratching along his paper.

"Where's the other shrub?" he asks drily when I walk by.

I glare at him. "Seriously?"

I assume this is the point where someone trying to be
quippy would flash a grin, but his expression doesn't change.
"What?" he asks unflinchingly.

"I'm not sure what your problem is, exactly," I reply, then
immediately regret it. He's being a jerk, but I don't need to
mirror his attitude back at him.

He raises an eyebrow, and I swear the corner of his mouth
is twitching up. "What makes you think I have a problem?"

I can feel anger rising in my chest, but I try to quash it
down. He doesn't matter. *This* doesn't matter.

I'm here to talk to Maisie and hopefully get a job for the
summer. To take my mind off of what happened with Kyle. Off
how I've been feeling at work. Off the fact that all my child-

hood memories, so tied up in this place by the sea, are slipping further and further into the recesses of my mind.

"Look, it doesn't matter," I bite back, letting just a little bit of my frustration slip through. "Is Maisie back yet?"

He indicates the checkout with a slight inclination of his head. "She's over there." Oliver looks right at me, and I feel like his blue eyes are piercing my soul. "But don't you think you should save that job for someone who isn't going to leave in six weeks?"

I glare at him. "Let me guess: you grew up here, you feel like you're stuck in this dead-end town, and you hate tourists, even though our frivolous spending in July and August provides the bulk of your livelihood all through the long, cold New England winter?"

He snorts. "Good to see you have me all figured out after two minutes of conversation."

"It's not my fault if you're a walking cliché," I say.

He takes a beat, but I see his eyes recoil with something like offense. "Oh, is that so?" he replies quietly.

"Absolutely," I nod. "The tortured artist aesthetic? Writing in a notebook in a bookstore café, harassing tourists? Hating the world because of some deep-seated insecurity that you work out through the pretentious characters in your stories?"

Oliver just stares at me, then settles back in his chair, startling me with a sharp chuckle that feels out of place given the diatribe I just unleashed on him.

A rakish grin spreads across his face. "And I suppose you didn't grow up with an OGT sticker on the back of your family's car? Driving to the beach for a week or two every summer, crowding the restaurants and the roadways, dragging sand into all the little boutiques? Coming back here now in your..." he considers me carefully, "early thirties, chasing some sort of childhood nostalgia to quell the pain of living a mundane, WASP-y life somewhere 20 minutes outside of Boston?"

My mouth hangs open for a minute before I remember to close it. I hadn't wanted to give him the satisfaction of realizing he'd hit the nail on the head with his assessment, but, judging by the smug look on his face, I'm guessing it's too late.

I will myself to flash him my brightest grin. "I'm only 29."

He bursts out laughing. "That fact notwithstanding, I rest my case."

"Well, fortunately, it's up to Maisie whether I get to work here this summer." I smirk at him. "I can only imagine what *your* decision would be if *you* were in charge."

"You seem like you have a good imagination," he says, once again expressionless.

"Well, it was a pleasure," I reply, annoyed all over again. What a pretentious dick.

He offers a mock salute with his pen. "Good luck."

Giving him my bitchiest glare, I stomp off toward the checkout, where a short, gray-haired woman is jotting something down in a floral notebook. She looks up when she sees me coming.

"May I help you?" Her voice is quiet, but filled with warmth.

Anxiety rises in my chest, but I force it back down with a firm reminder that this is a low-stakes operation. If I don't get the job, I'm no worse off than when I got here six hours ago.

I take a deep breath and smile, aiming to mirror the woman's kind vibes. "Hi, I'm Ivy Parker." I stick out my hand, and she shakes it. "I'm interested in applying for the seasonal position you advertised."

"Maisie Lyons," she says. "It's a pleasure to meet you, Ivy."

"Likewise," I reply.

She sets her pen down and flips the notebook closed. "Would you care to join me in my office?"

"Certainly," I agree, following her to the back of the store and through a blue door. My insides are brimming with hope—this seems like an auspicious start.

"So, tell me a little bit about yourself, Ivy." Maisie sits behind a small antique desk, bare aside from a purple laptop and a corded telephone. She gestures for me to take the chair opposite her.

"Well, I grew up coming to Ogunquit, and I think it might be my favorite place on Earth," I begin, sitting down and smoothing my skirt over my legs. I'm suddenly self-conscious about my tank top, but there's nothing to be done about that now.

Maisie grins a little at hearing that I love her town. "I share your sentiments."

"Right? It's just so charming here." I take a deep breath. I need to do more than suck up to her by praising her zip code. "I'm a school librarian in Massachusetts," I continue. "I've been working there for five years so far. I love books more than anything in the world; there's truly nothing like the feeling of connecting a person to the story or the information that they need in any given moment."

She nods in agreement. "Very well put. I feel the same way."

I'm feeling better about this opportunity with every passing second. "I'm in town until the end of August. My cousin and I are renting a house—Beach Haven? It's north of the public beach a bit; if you follow Shore Road and then hang a right, then stick to the edge of the sand, or take the back road—"

"I know Beach Haven well." Maisie smiles kindly. "I've been friends with Simon Foster for years." Her smile fades. "Shame about his leg."

I let my face fall and try to look like I know what she's talking about. "He's a friend of my grandparents. Charlie and Eleanor Parker? Well, he was, I should say. They both...well, they both passed away within the last five years. But we would see him every summer when we came to town for our family vacation." *Get it together, Ivy,* I reprimand myself. *You're rambling.* "Anyway, we're renting his house for the season."

There's an expression on Maisie's face that I can't quite place, but she seems to snap out of it quickly. "I knew your grandfather," she says quietly.

Something about her response strikes me as odd, but I shake it off. Grandpa Charlie grew up here; it makes sense that people in town would know who he was. And Maisie is probably almost 15 years younger than my grandparents were, but she has to be at least 70. She could have crossed paths with him countless times over the years. Once the tourists leave, it's a very small town.

"Wow, that's amazing," I reply, not sure how to steer the conversation back to the job I'm hoping she'll give me.

"Charlie was a great man," Maisie says, then shakes her head as if clearing the memories. "In any case, the job is seasonal. I typically have a couple of folks who work the floor during open hours, and I try to pop in every day for an hour or two to take care of administrative tasks. Things get busy during high season, but we can usually handle it with just two or three workers." She pauses, running her hand through her wiry hair.

"Unfortunately, one of my best staffers recently moved to New Hampshire. Now it's just me and one other person. He's working overtime, and I've been here 50 hours a week myself so far this summer. I'm past my prime, so it's a little too much for me," she admits.

"Hence the job ad." I smile kindly. I don't know how else to respond to her comment about being past her prime.

Maisie nods. "Exactly. To be honest, I'd been hoping to step back even further. I'm getting too old for this." She sighs. "Anyway, having another person to pick up some shifts will have to be enough for now. I can look into other options once summer ends."

I wonder if she's ever been married or had a business partner, or if she's always run this bookshop on her own. It seems like a tremendous undertaking. I'm a little ashamed, meeting her now, that I'd always assumed I could never open my own bookstore because it would be too great a challenge.

"Well, it sounds amazing," I say honestly. "I'd love the opportunity to work here." I'm not sure how formal this interview is. I don't have a reference list or anything.

"Consider yourself hired." Maisie smiles kindly.

So I guess not very formal at all.

"Really?" My heart soars. This is just what I need right now. And having met Maisie, I'm excited to help her out, too.

"Absolutely. Stop by tomorrow with your ID—did you bring a passport on your trip, perchance? That'll satisfy the I-9 requirements."

"I did, actually." I mentally thank my father for impressing upon me the importance of always traveling with my passport.

"Great! We'll knock out all the standard employment paperwork when you drop in. It'll be five shifts a week, eight hours each, $20 an hour. We pay biweekly via paper check—will that be all right?"

I nod vigorously. "Yes, of course. Thank you."

Seeing her suddenly all businesslike, it's clear how she's been able to juggle this enterprise on her own. Shame hits me again—why did I allow self-limiting thoughts to convince me I couldn't accomplish something like this? It seems like Maisie just figures things out. I could probably do that, too.

"Perfect. Can you start Friday? I won't be in, but I'll have the other worker show you the ropes."

"Yes, of course. Thank you so much for the opportunity." I take a deep breath. "Honestly, I can't tell you how excited I am."

"Me too," Maisie says kindly. "It's always a pleasure to find others who love this town as much as I do. And you're a book lover to boot! It's kismet."

I grin, standing and reaching out to shake her hand again. "Thanks again. I'll see you tomorrow to complete those documents."

I STARE STRAIGHT AHEAD when I head toward the front of the bookstore, hoping to avoid further conversation with Oliver.

I hear his baritone at my back as I pass. "How'd it go?"

God, he's annoying. *Now* he wants to make friendly chit-chat? I whirl to face him. "It was fine," I say in what I hope is a measured tone.

"So does that mean you'll be working here?" He lays his pen down and surveys me with an expression I can't quite read.

Given his general demeanor, I assume I was correct earlier

that he'd prefer I not get the job, so I shoot him my most charming grin. "Sure will."

He nods. "Cool. I'll ask Maisie when she wants me to train you."

I think my jaw must be on the engineered hardwood floor. "I'm sorry, what?"

Oliver tilts his head. "I'm going to ask Maisie—"

"No, no," I interrupt him. "Why would *you* be training me?"

"Oh," he says slowly, leaning back in his seat. "Did I not mention that I work here?"

What in God's name have I done? "You most certainly did not," I return coolly. Is *he* the other person she mentioned? *Jesus.*

Now he smiles, reaching his elbows up to lean on the back rail of his chair. I try not to notice how sculpted his biceps are.

"I work here." His eyes are twinkling, like this is somehow hilarious.

"So you've said," I reply. "You didn't want to mention that before I went and talked my way into a job?"

He laughs. "Now, where would be the fun in that?"

"Okay," I say slowly, feeling lost in the simultaneous desires to curse him out for being a douchebag and to behave professionally around someone who is apparently my new coworker.

"I've been working here since I was in high school," Oliver explains, still smiling like he's incredibly pleased with himself. "Now that Maisie's trying to step back a little, she lets me run things when she's not around."

He runs things when she's not around? Like, a manager? Jesus freaking Christ.

I take a deep breath. "Am I to understand you're my boss, then?" I'm dead inside. This summer is going to be horrendous.

"Why?" He raises an eyebrow mockingly. "Would that upset you?"

I blink rapidly, not sure how to respond to this obnoxious man who seems intent on pushing all of my buttons for seemingly no reason.

When I don't answer, Oliver grins. "I'm not your boss. But I'll be happy to tell you what to do, if that would make you feel better."

My cheeks flush despite my overwhelming urge to smack his stupid face. Everything he just said sounded oddly suggestive, though I'm sure that wasn't his intent. At least, I hope not.

I clear my throat. "Well, Maisie said I should start on Friday," I manage. "So I guess I'll see you then?"

"Come by around eleven," he agrees. "It'll be easier to train you when there aren't many customers here."

I nod quickly. "Okay, I can do that."

"Excellent," he says. "Give my best to your cousin."

My eyes narrow. "What's *your* best, exactly?"

He bursts out laughing, so loudly that a couple of customers by the children's books turn around to stare.

"Friday's going to be fun," he drawls, grinning again.

My life is over. "I'll let you get back to your pretentious man drivel." I gesture to his notebook. "Good night, Oliver."

I can still hear him laughing when the door jingles shut behind me.

ON MY WAY back to the rental, I grab a pizza from Ruggerio's and hug it to my chest as I walk. I take the scenic route along the water, away from the throngs of sunburned tourists spiffed up in crisp white linen pants and nautical striped shirts after a full day of beach time.

One of the things I love most about Ogunquit is how everyone in town seems to have gotten the memo about maintaining lush gardens. Everywhere you look, stunning blue hydrangeas are fighting the jaw-droppingly gorgeous pink ones for your attention. Paths up to the bed-and-breakfasts are embellished with velvety roses in every color of the rainbow, and tall wildflowers act like homing beacons to fuzzy bumblebees and lacy butterflies along white picket fences. Annual beds filled with pansies, morning glories, and marigolds line the streets, split off from the sidewalks by flat gray stone walls. Even the grass itself is fluffy and verdant.

I hang a left and traipse across what might be the most magical footbridge on earth. It's flanked on one side by flowers so beautiful I think they must have been planted by fairies, and on the other by the Ogunquit River, with the Atlantic sparkling beyond it over the swell of the beach itself. The beach separates the river and the ocean, changing from a thin strip of sand at high tide to a tremendous swath of paradise when the waves retreat.

Laurel and I spent our childhoods getting to the beach at low tide and setting up for the day, skipping back and forth between sand castles and wave hopping as the sun shifted unnoticed in the sky. When the tide encroached on our home base, we would shriek with glee, furiously digging a moat around our sand toys. We'd watch with feigned terror as wave after wave increasingly threatened our defenses, until finally, one bigger than all the rest whooshed in and drenched our towels in seawater.

Only then did we begrudgingly drag our buckets and shovels back 20 feet or so closer to the shore. We continued in this vein all day, every day, until the beach was but a shadow of its former self, shrinking into the coastline like it was shivering and needed to share the warmth of the land.

Sometimes, when the tide was high, we'd gather up our things and follow our parents around the curve of the sand to the side facing the river. By then, the water would've filled the valley, and families on tubes would float eagerly under the Beach Road bridge to the sheltered area behind the heights of the beach.

Some days we would hit up the river side at low tide first, to look for tiny crabs in and amongst the moist rocks. Laurel liked to chase me with the crustaceans she found. When she caught me, I preferred to grab the crabs and set them free.

Even though we only spent two weeks here every summer, that time adds up. At a fortnight for each of the first 28 years of my life, that makes more than an entire year spent watching these waves crash against the shore. Laurel, three years my junior, has had just a bit less. But I know this place lives in her soul just as much as it does mine.

I take a deep breath. It's hard to be here without the rest of our family.

Because as much as this town means to me, I know it means even more to my dad. He and my uncle Gregory, Laurel's father, are twins who grew up coming to the beach every year with my grandparents. I know losing Grandpa Charlie, and then Grandma Eleanor just a few short years later, has been horrific for my dad. And then the conflict with my mom took so much out of him, it seems like he's a shell of his former self. But I just don't understand why he stayed away this summer.

The waves call to me. I know they must call to him, too.

A warm breeze whispers across the end of my nose, and I pause for a moment in the middle of the bridge, hefting the pizza box onto my right hip while I take it all in.

At low tide, this view is very different. The Ogunquit River all but disappears, rushing back out to join the waves on the front-facing side of the beach. But now, when the ocean has nestled against the shore, the river swirls around the jut of land that is the beach itself.

I can see my family there, laughing on borrowed floats, desperately trying to control the direction of our drifting. Laurel and I having a splash battle in the shallows, our grand-mother's eyes filled with joy as she watches us over the top of her embroidery. Me, running up and down the water's edge, arms outstretched like a tiny plane. Dashing straight into the arms of an elderly man who turns out not to be my grandfather, and being so embarrassed that I sprint away up the beach, refusing to leave our blanket for the rest of the day.

Snacking on soggy peanut butter and jelly sandwiches and blueberries, watching my grandmother's eyes water when she talks about how her parents could never afford them, so they foraged wild ones whenever they took her and her sister, Janie, here to Maine for a getaway. They'd stay with a friend in town to save money, but it sounds like they had the time of their lives here, all those years ago.

So much history. So many memories.

The smell of pepperoni brings me back to the present, and I realize I should get back to the house before the pizza gets cold. Laurel was so excited to eat it—I feel like she would be exceptionally disappointed if her first non-ramen meal in months turned out to be room temperature.

With a sigh, I push off the fence with my left hand and re-hoist the pizza box to my hip. "Sayonara," I whisper to the waves as I walk away.

WHEN I GET BACK to Beach Haven, Laurel is chopping vegetables in the kitchen, making a salad to what seems like an Alien Ant Farm playlist.

"Wow, that album takes me back," I say, sliding the pizza box onto the counter.

She flashes a bright grin. "I thought nostalgia was what this summer was all about."

My grandmother's face flashes before my eyes. "I guess it is," I agree.

"Lot of tourists clogging the sidewalks?" Laurel flips her hair over her shoulder as she turns to me.

I watch her tip the cutting board on edge and scrape quartered cucumber slices into the salad spinner.

"Nah," I answer in what I hope is a nonchalant tone. "Just stopped to take in the river from Bridge Lane."

She fixes me with a knowing look. "As I said, nostalgia's the theme here."

"So very true." I grab two plates from the cupboard and am accosted by a cloud of dust. "Jesus," I cough. "When do you think these things were last cleaned?"

"Who knows?" Laurel shrugs. "Simon's been in the nursing home for a few years, right? I feel like Grandma Ellie went to see him the last time she was here."

"I think you're right," I agree, a pang of grief hitting me low in the gut. I run hot water over the dishes, squirting them with the watermelon dish soap Laurel scored at the local Hannaford on her way into town.

"We should probably wash everything before we use it. I can pull all the dishes down and clean out the cabinets in the morning, if you want." I figure Laurel's going to be busy working on her dissertation tomorrow, so I might as well make myself useful. It should only take me an hour or so to head to the bookstore and fill out paperwork with Maisie.

Laurel considers me carefully. "Alternatively, you can enjoy your summer vacation. I'm getting the feeling you really need it."

"I'll have plenty of time to relax." I roll her concern off with a hitch of my shoulders. "I'll clean tomorrow, then head to the beach in the afternoon." I snag a piece of pizza and shove the box down the counter toward my cousin. The first bite is perfection.

"Okay, sounds good. I'd offer to help, but I really do need to make some headway on my writing." Laurel smiles apologetically. "I'm about 5,000 words behind where I wanted to be at this point in the game."

I visibly shudder. "You do what you need to. I can't imagine having to write 100,000 words on the intersection of feminism and the Pre-Raphaelites. I don't want to stand in your way."

She snorts. "What can I say, it's my passion." Taking a bite of her pizza, her eyes close a little. "This was absolutely worth the wait. Hey, how did it go with Maisie?"

"Great," I reply. "She's super sweet! We chatted for a bit, and then she offered me the job."

"Ahhh!" Laurel throws her arms around me and squeezes. "I'm so excited for you!"

Snickering, I hug her back. "Thanks, Laur. It'll be nice to

make a little extra cash so we can support your wine habit." I nod toward the bottle of rosé she was a good third of the way through already when I arrived with the pizza.

She sticks her tongue out at me. "I don't drink *that* much."

"Tell that to your favorite Pre-Raphaelite, Christina Rossetti," I joke. "I bet she sees you tipsy all the time when you're supposed to be writing."

"I *so* regret telling you that I talk to her when I'm working," Laurel moans, putting her hand on her head in mock desperation. "It was just a joke, you know."

"If you say so," I tease. The idea of Laurel chattering away to a bunch of dead artists while writing her dissertation is both hilarious and disturbing. "But I don't blame you for liking Christina the best. You can't really beat her writing. I mean, look at *Goblin Market*." I crack a grin. "Sexualized poems for kids with weird religious undertones? Sign me up."

"It's not my fault Grandma read us that poem. Honestly, I think she did it because the one girl's name is Laura, and then she has a sister named Lizzie. Sounds sort of like Laurel and Ivy."

I wrinkle my nose at her. "But not really, though."

She laughs. "But a little? Maybe she thought we'd like it. And I'm not sure she thought it through beyond that. I mean, how often does classic lit have such overt sexual undertones, or such terrifying imagery?"

"If you're paying attention, actually quite often," I point out. "But I forgive her."

A hush settles over us both as we're lost in memories of Eleanor reading to us from her *Norton Anthology* on the porch of our old summer rental.

"She was great," I say finally.

"She was the best." Laurel agrees, wiping the side of her right eye. "Anyway, I'm going to finish my wine, and then I think I should probably get to bed." She sighs, resigned to the fate of a newly minted adult with real responsibilities. "It's been a long day."

I nod. Because it *has* been a long day. A long month; a long year. My own glass of wine is swirling through me, pulling warmth in its wake, dragging me under. Things are feeling a little fuzzier than usual when I impulsively say, "I found Grandma's diary. At her house before the estate sale."

Laurel's eyes grow wide. "Whoa. Anything juicy?"

"I haven't read most of it yet," I admit. "It feels like an invasion of privacy."

"Then why'd you take it?"

I shake my head. "I don't really know. To feel closer to her, I guess."

Laurel lays her hand reassuringly on my forearm. "I think she'd be okay with you reading it. She loved you."

"Maybe," I concede. "But, for instance, I love my mom, and I still don't want her reading my innermost thoughts." Especially when it comes to how angry I am that she demanded space from my dad when he was at his lowest.

Laurel snorts. "Yeah, good point. I don't keep a diary anymore, but when I was a teenager, I definitely spent a fair amount of time detailing what Spencer Collins looked like without a shirt on." She shudders at the memories. "God, I was awkward."

"We both were," I reassure her.

"I think it's par for the course for teenagers," she says, taking a sip of her rosé. "Anyway, how old is this diary? Was Grandma Ellie a teenager when she wrote it?"

Nodding my head, I swallow the gulp of wine I just poured into my mouth. "It looks like it starts in summer 1953, so she would have been, what? About 18? Janie was 16."

"So it's harmless," Laurel decides. "She was so uptight anyway, and this is back when she was practically still a girl. There can't be anything bad in there." Her eyes grow brighter. "Do you have it here?"

I know she wants to see it. Suddenly, I wish I hadn't brought up the diary at all. "I do," I hedge. "But I thought you needed to get to bed?"

She snickers. "I do. But it feels like this is more important." She downs the last of her wine. "At the very least, it's more interesting."

Laurel settles onto the end of my bed while I fish around in my closed suitcase for the diary, which I'd put away after reading the first entry earlier. It had been more than enough for my heart at that point. My hand finally lands on the smooth leatherbound book, and I pull it free.

"Here," I say, handing it to her. "Take a look."

She runs a finger tentatively down the cover. "Are you sure? I'm suddenly understanding your hesitation. This feels real now, and I'm nervous."

"You can at least read the first entry," I tell her. "I've already read that one, and it's harmless. It's actually about the night she met Grandpa. It's really sweet."

Laurel's eyes light up. "Aw, that sounds adorable." She flips open the cover and slides her thumb to the right-hand page as she begins to read.

"Wow," she breathes when she's done. "That *was* sweet, you're right."

I nod. "He was quite a catch, our grandfather."

"But, wait," Laurel says, a confused look descending. "Didn't Grandma always say she knew Grandpa when he was a little boy? His parents lived here in town, or something?"

A memory tugs at the edge of my brain then, Laurel and I on either side of Grandma Ellie in the guest bed, cuddled in for stories during a sleepover. Something about a cute boy she met in a shop when they were both small.

"You're right," I nod, brows wrinkled together. "I vaguely recall that, now that you mention it."

"I remember it very clearly," Laurel says, never one to shy away from making herself seem superior if it suits the conversation. "Grandma told us the whole story of how they met." She mimics our grandmother's voice. *"He was the cutest little tow-headed boy,"* Laurel begins. *"His parents owned the grocery store at the end of Shore Road, and he liked to help run the register. I went in one day to window shop; I couldn't actually afford anything. But there he was, barely tall enough to see over the counter. And he asked me, 'Do you like blueberries?' I hadn't even known you could buy berries in a store; I assumed everyone foraged them. My parents had so little back then. We wouldn't have even been on vacation at all if we didn't have friends we could stay with for free. But Charlie pulled a bowl of blueberries he was eating out from under the counter and offered me some. And we became friends instantly."*

I nod slowly. "You're right. I do remember her saying that."

"But then, who is she talking about in this diary entry?" Laurel asks the question already on my mind.

"No idea." I shake my head. "She and Grandpa got married in 1953, didn't they?"

"Yeah, in November." Laurel looks as puzzled as I feel. "This guy must not have been a keeper."

"I guess not," I reply. It could be that she met someone that summer and things didn't work out, and then she fell in love with my grandfather. But something about the way she described her night out with Janie, and the man who swept her off her feet, strikes me as odd. Eleanor was never one to waste words, and she made her feelings sound none too subtle.

"I'm going to head to bed. Night, love." Laurel wraps me in a quick hug, then heads for the door of my bedroom.

"Goodnight, Laur."

After she leaves, I'm left sitting on the end of my hard-as-a-rock mattress, wondering who the guy was, if my grandfather ever knew about him, and if the next entry in my grandmother's diary might reveal the answer.

But it's been a long day, and I'm exhausted. The wine is pulling me even further toward sleep, and I let myself lie back on the bed. I must drift off there, because the next thing I know, it's pitch black, and I can see stars sparkling out the window. Rather than get up and close the shades or bother to go brush my teeth, I just roll over and pull the comforter over my street clothes and go back to sleep.

five

I wake up earlier than I'd like the next day, thanks to last night's Ivy refusing to close the blinds. The sunlight is aggressively cheery, beckoning me to the day like there are great things in store for me.

At least at first, those things are two cabinets full of dusty china.

I pull everything out, immediately regretting I didn't change into an old t-shirt first. I'm covered in filth from the dishes almost instantly. Spreading everything next to the sink, I count eleven dinner plates, twelve salad bowls, eight teacups, and ten saucers. I imagine the set originally had twelve of each and things broke over the years. I grab all the silverware from the drawer, too. Who knows when it was last washed.

Throwing some music on my iPhone, I set about filling the sink with hot water and dish soap. It smells heavenly, frankly. Normally, I hate washing the dishes, but this watermelon-scented stuff Laurel found really is a cut above the rest. I make a mental note to look for it when I get back home.

Home. The word sends a flurry of emotions racing through my mind. Yesterday's conversation with Laurel flashes back to me. What *am* I going to do when summer ends? Deep down, leaving my job still feels a little like giving up; giving in to bullies who don't deserve to dictate my future. And to a certain extent, I suppose that *is* true.

But isn't my mental health more important? I think so. I mean, with time, I'm sure I could move past what happened with Kyle. How everyone else treated me afterwards. Is it worth it, though? I'm no longer sure.

Maybe I'll start looking for other work. It might be a hassle to sell my condo back in Brookline, but perhaps other opportunities near home would be comparable to where I work now. I guess I'd be willing to go anywhere in New England for the right job.

Especially if it meant being rid of Farnsworth.

The dishes take me the better part of an hour, but seeing them laid out on three mismatched dish towels, glinting in the light, is pretty satisfying. I feel fairly disgusting because of all the dust, though. I decide to grab a shower before I head out to the bookstore to meet with Maisie.

When I'm done getting cleaned up, I notice warm, domestic smells wafting from the kitchen. I quickly get dressed and head in to find a solid third of the dishes I just washed already soiled, plus a quarter-cup of batter spilled next to the stove.

"Waffle for your thoughts?" Laurel holds out a plate.

I nod gratefully, choosing to ignore the mess she's made. I haven't eaten yet today, and it smells amazing. "Honestly? I'm not looking forward to this."

"The waffles?" At my scowl, she corrects, "Ohhh! The

job?" Concern washes over her face. "Is this because of that guy?"

"I'm ashamed to admit that it is."

"But working in a bookstore! It's your dream!" She pours syrup on the plate and shoves it toward me across the kitchen island.

"Well, it was. But maybe this will be the kick in the ass I need to appreciate the job I already have." I grab a fork from the dish rack and sit down to eat.

Laurel is surveying me over a carton of orange juice. She shakes her head slowly. "I don't know, Ivy. He didn't seem *that* bad."

I narrow my eyes at her. "He was a total dick."

Her laugh twinkles through the air. "Okay, so he was a *bit* grumpy." She takes a sip of her juice. "But hey, at least he was hot. You can just tune him out and enjoy his face."

My eyebrows shoot up. "If you think he's so hot, maybe *you* can do this training with him on Friday. I'm not sure we'll both make it out of there alive if I have to spend all summer with him."

Laurel's eyes are bright as she downs the rest of her coffee. "You *also* thought he was hot."

I practically choke on my waffle. "I most certainly did not."

"Oh, please," she says. "You *so* did. And anyway," she stands up and heads to the sink with her plate, "it's not up for debate. He's hot. And he's grumpy, but you'll survive. Plus, you're going to be around books all day, so it won't be as bad as you're imagining."

She's right. About the books, that is.

As for Oliver? I'm not so sure.

· · ·

49

IT'S eleven by the time the bell is jingling behind me on the door of Shoreline Books. There are a few college-aged girls, halter bikinis tied around their necks under sundresses, browsing the New Adult section, but the bookstore is otherwise deserted. It occurs to me that Maisie didn't say where I should meet her. Did she want me to go right to her office?

I shake my head as if I'm having this conversation with someone else. It might be a little presumptuous to assume I should go back to a staff area when I haven't even filled out employment paperwork yet.

Kyle would tell me I'm overthinking this. His gentle smile flashes through my mind. "Don't be so nervous, Ive," he would have said. "Everything's going to be okay. Just go to the office; she's expecting you."

I used to love how he shrugged off my anxious thoughts like they weren't worth my time. And how he called me "Ive," which makes no sense as a nickname, really, since it doesn't actually shorten the spelling of my name at all. But it felt endearing. Today, I resent him popping into my mind uninvited.

Because fuck that guy.

I decide to head toward the cash register and ask for help from whoever's working rather than head back to Maisie's office, just to spite the Kyle in my mind. Even though I realize he probably would have been right—I know my anxiety tends to get the better of me when I'm in uncharted scenarios.

It seems that the universe wants to continue punishing me, because Oliver, rather than Maisie, walks back behind the counter just as I get there. I hadn't noticed him in the store before.

He's wearing dark jeans and a gray t-shirt, which feels a

little too casual for work, but Maisie must not mind. It's an outfit that might look sloppy on some guys, but it's just tight enough that it accentuates his obviously very toned body in a way I feel obligated to ignore.

He fixes me with a smile that seems a little bit too friendly. For him, that is. "Can I help you?"

I don't bother with niceties. "I'm here to meet with Maisie."

Oliver nods slowly, assessing. "She stepped out for a moment to run some online orders to the post office, but she should be back shortly."

I'm suddenly struck by how many hours Oliver must be working if Maisie is off-site so often. Something close to sympathy pangs in my chest, but I shove it away as quickly as it arrives.

"Do you want a coffee?"

I'm startled by the question, largely because it's coming from Oliver, who I definitely thought was a colossal jerk. But there he is, looking at me like he understands social convention and is trying to be polite.

"Um, sure," I say, still a little shaken by his behaving like a normal human.

"Come on." Oliver gestures to me to follow, then crosses to the café area and lifts the hinged counter next to the gleaming silver espresso machine. "What can I get you?"

"A latte, I suppose? Thank you." I reach into my purse to find cash, but he shakes his head.

"Don't worry about it. On the house."

I raise an amused brow. "Is this that kind of place?"

"What kind of place?" He looks at me quizzically.

"You make it sound like the local watering hole, and yourself its congenial barkeep." I try to fight the smile tugging at the corners of my lips.

"I mean, basically," he jokes, starting the machine, then leaning forward on his elbows. "So are you headed to the beach after this?"

I'm continuing to feel very confused about how nice he's being to me right now. And it's been a long time since a man offered me a hot beverage in any scenario, on a date or otherwise. *Is he trying to flirt with me?* No, Oliver would never.

I nod, both to acknowledge his question and to clear my mind of the possibility that he's coming on to me. "Yeah, I think so. Laurel has to work on her dissertation this summer, so I'll probably have a lot of time to myself."

"Hence the job." He pulls a steaming ceramic cup from the espresso machine and hands it to me.

"Thank you. And yeah, basically. But I wanted the job for other reasons, too."

He doesn't even look up from where he's wiping off the chrome espresso spigot. "To get a free trial on books you're considering purchasing for your school library, I assume."

I snort in surprise. "I hadn't thought of that, but that's a great idea." Maybe on my breaks, I can gently flip through some YA fiction and make a list of what I want to order for Farnsworth. If I decide to go back, that is.

Oliver's mouth twitches. "Well, I tend to have those from time to time."

I smile in spite of myself, and I'm starting to wonder what, exactly, I'd thought was so bad about his guy. It certainly wasn't this physical appearance, which Laurel was more than a little bit right about. His hair is thick and just a little too long, like he's overdue for a haircut, but the way it curls around his ears is making me feel some kind of way. And his eyes might just be the brightest blue I've ever seen, as if the ocean itself is mirrored there.

I snap out of my trance. "Hey, wait a second. How did you know what I do for work?" I realize we hadn't covered that during any of our antagonistic chats yesterday.

He shrugs. "Maisie told me this morning."

Of course she did. I make a mental note to be careful what I say around Oliver. He and Maisie are obviously quite close.

"And anyway," Oliver continues before I have a chance to respond, "I know you must have an ulterior motive for being here."

And there it is. We're back to the obnoxious behavior. I curse my lonely hormones for lusting after his hair.

"Why is that, exactly?"

"Come on, Ivy." Oliver's eyes are intense on my face, and I want to look away, but I decide that would be letting him win. "This job doesn't pay very well. You're here on vacation. No one gets a part-time job on their vacation without a reason."

I have a reason, I want to scream. Sure, the money will be nice. And it'll give me something to do when Laurel is writing.

But more than anything, I need a distraction. I need to forget about the events of the last year and slip away into a fugue state. Keep myself busy with something that tethers me to my past while I push through the grieving process.

I'm debating between some sort of simple explanation that even an emotionless drone like Oliver might understand or simply telling him to fuck off when I hear the bell on the door jingle.

A genuine smile overtakes his face. "Hi, Maisie," he says warmly.

I turn around and wave.

"Oliver and Ivy! My two favorite people." Maisie grins at us.

My insides heat at the notion that I, who she just met yesterday, might be one of Maisie's favorite people. But she seems like a sweetheart, so she's probably just being nice.

"Shall we?" Maisie touches my arm and gestures toward her office.

"Absolutely. Bye, Oliver." I shoot him a saccharine look and follow my new boss out of the room.

"SO, I see Oliver got you a coffee," Maisie says brightly, bustling about her office and pulling several folders out of a drawer.

I start. Was he not supposed to do that? "I'm sorry if that wasn't okay," I say quickly. "I offered to pay, but..."

She laughs then, a bright chuckle that puts me immediately at ease. "No, I'm glad he did. Coffee's always free for the team."

"That's very kind of you. Thank you." He could have made it clear that it was Maisie's gesture, rather than his own. What a tool.

"So, here's some paperwork." Maisie slides a pile of forms and a blue pen across the desk to me. "It includes rates, pay schedule, employment contract, the whole nine. Take your time filling it out, and let me know if you have any questions, okay?"

"Thanks." I start with the I-9.

"I hope you don't mind that I won't be the one training you," Maisie says, watching me write. "I'm so overextended these days. I used to do all the management myself, but..." She shakes her head. "It's just too much for me now."

"I understand," I reply with what I hope sounds like copious empathy. "Did you start the bookstore yourself?"

She nods. "I did, back when I was young and convinced I was invincible." A slight chuckle, and then: "Funny how those feelings evaporate over time."

I smile. "You seem pretty invincible to me."

"You have to say that, dear." She's definitely teasing, but I blush anyway.

"I always dreamed of opening a bookstore," I rush before I can think better of it.

Maisie raises an eyebrow. "Oh?"

The heat creeping up my cheeks intensifies. God, now it makes it sound like I'm clamoring for her job. Or worse, her business. But I incline my head. "My grandmother and I shared a love of reading, and she used to bring me here whenever we were in town. I love the bookstore aesthetic." I try to fight the awkwardness I'm feeling with self-deprecation. "But I don't think it's something I'd be able to do." I look down at my signature looping across the employment documents. "I'm just glad I get a chance to work here. That's a dream come true on its own."

When I look up, I see Maisie assessing me with interest. "Why don't you think you could do it?"

"I just...it seems like a lot of work, is all."

She smiles like that's the understatement of the century. "It really is."

"And like there would be a lot of ebbs and flows. Especially here, with the end of tourist season."

"It does involve a lot of careful budgeting."

I offer a self-effacing smile. "Well, I tend to get very anxious when dealing with uncertainty. And overwhelmed with large projects."

Maisie runs her hand through her hair, which still looks a bit windswept from her trip to the post office. "You and me both."

I stare at her. "But you've run Shoreline for, what? Forty years?"

"Forty-three." Her face lights up with pride. "And I've been terrified almost every day." I must look shocked, because she pats my hand reassuringly. "Don't let assumptions of how you'll feel scare you off from pursuing something that's written on your heart, Ivy."

"Wow. Are you sure you weren't a writer in another life?"

Maisie smiles. "Oh, I've dabbled in this one."

Of course she has. Is there nothing this woman can't do?

"But, as you've noticed, running a business is more than a full-time job. So I've never really gotten very far. Not like our Oliver."

I raise an eyebrow. Oliver's messy notebook of misogyny, or whatever it is, cannot possibly be what she's holding up as an example of successful writing.

But I really like Maisie, so I say nothing.

"Anyway, I've distracted you too much. You're not even working today!" She waves her hand in the air. "Get back to those papers, and I'll leave you alone. And grab something off the New Release shelf for yourself when you leave. I want you to have something to read when you go to the beach later."

I start to protest, but she cuts me off. "No, I insist. I've taken up too much of your time already. Let me give you this."

I want to remind her that I work for her, that she's hired me without a glance at my résumé or any sort of employment verification whatsoever. That she, by way of Oliver, already gave me a free hot beverage today.

But she stands up from her desk and grabs her purse. "I forgot that I need to pick up some signs for a book signing we're hosting next week. They're ready at the copy center. When you head out, let Oliver know where I went, would you?"

I nod in agreement, though why she couldn't do that herself is a bit puzzling. "I will. Thank you so much!"

"Have fun at the beach, dear!" She bustles out.

I FINISH up with the paperwork, then head back to the shop, closing the office door carefully behind me. Oliver has taken up residence at the register again and is ringing out the three college girls I'd seen when I first came in. They're giggling a little too much, which makes me think they're either finding him very enthralling or perhaps buying smut.

"What's your name?" one of the girls asks coquettishly.

Oliver seems taken aback, and I laugh out loud from my vantage at the New Release shelf. He looks up and glares at me.

"Oliver," he mumbles in response to the girls, busying himself with the screen in front of him.

"I'm Rachel," the first girl answers, leaning over the counter to show off her cleavage. "And these are my friends, Emily and Maddie." She nods to the two brunettes on her right.

"Cool." He's making every effort not to look at them, and I have no qualms about continuing to stare and cackle.

"Do you ever go to the beach?" Maddie is mirroring her friend, leaning her chin in her hand near where Oliver is desperately trying to bag their paperbacks as quickly as humanly possible.

"Never," he says sarcastically.

"Would you like to?" Emily asks, clearly missing his tone.

"I have to work." Oliver slides the bag toward the trio, looking over their shoulders as if he can will them to disappear by refusing eye contact. "Have a good one."

Maddie is persistent. "Maybe after work?" She twirls a curl around her finger and attempts to look older than she is.

They seem like they're of majority age, though maybe only just. But I think Oliver deserves a little grief, so I stride towards the register with a grin. "Oliver gets off work at eight o'clock tonight."

If looks could kill, I'd be sprawled on the floor without a pulse right now.

"Oh, awesome!" Rachel playfully hits Oliver's arm. "We'll swing by then. Maybe we can go for a walk on the beach."

"But—"

Grinning at the girls, I interrupt Oliver's attempts to excuse himself from their invitation. "I'll make sure he's ready."

They head out in a swarm of giggles. He's shooting daggers at me from the cash register. "What in the everloving hell, Ivy?"

I flash him my sweetest smile. "I'm so glad you made some new friends."

"They're *children*. Do you want me to get arrested?"

"Nah, they had to be at least 18. They probably just look young to you because you're past your prime." I shake my head as he continues to glare. "You'll be fine. Besides, I checked the weather earlier, and it's supposed to be a gorgeous night. Perfect for a beach stroll."

He mumbles something incomprehensible and storms out from behind the counter.

"What was that?" I ask, following him across the store precisely because I know he doesn't want me to.

He whirls around to face me so quickly that I almost drop the employee badge Maisie gave me. "I said, 'This is the thanks I get for making you coffee.'"

Trying to still my heartbeat, which is still raging at being startled, I purse my lips. "About that coffee, actually. It seems like maybe it wasn't really from you."

"What are you talking about?" Now he seems less angry than just plain confused.

"Well, Maisie told me everyone on the team can get free coffee whenever they want to."

His eyes hold mine, unreadable even under the harsh fluorescents of the store. "Yes, and?"

"You made it seem like it was your treat."

"Did I not make you coffee?" Oliver continues to stare at me, unflinching.

I'm losing ground here. "Yes, but—"

"Was it not free to you?"

I squirm a little, then hate myself for doing so. "Well, yes, but—"

He crosses his arms, declaring victory. "Then I don't see what the problem is."

"You maybe misrepresented who the coffee was from, is all." I counter, most of my steam boiled off into the atmosphere.

He blinks twice. "Do you want me to *buy* you coffee?"

Heat rushes up my cheeks. That wasn't what I meant. At least not consciously. But I suppose it *was* what I'd been implying.

I swallow hard, then shoot my last shot. "I appreciate the offer, but I believe your evening is already filled, thanks to your new friends."

A hint of a smile starts to hit the corner of his lips, but he quashes it back down immediately. "I think you and I both know what I'll be doing at eight o'clock tonight." He turns to walk toward the children's section.

"Sneaking out the back door like a criminal?" I joke.

"See, I knew you got me," he quips over his shoulder.

I try to shove the smile off my face. I need to stop bantering with Oliver and head out.

"Well, anyway," I follow him past a colorful archway that says "EXPLORE A WORLD OF STORIES" in whimsical block letters. "Maisie wanted me to let you know that she had to run to the copy center to pick up signs for that author event."

"Thanks." Oliver's just pulled a box cutter out of his pocket and is slicing open a carton of books.

I grimace. "Should you really be keeping that in your pocket?"

"Eh," he shrugs. "Probably not." He raises an eyebrow. "Why? Are you worried about me?"

My face falls at his mocking expression. "Definitely not. But I bet if you tell Rachel and her friends about it later, they'll be very concerned about the parts of your body the box cutter might injure."

I think he visibly shudders. "Very funny." Oliver starts pulling copies of *Ella Enchanted* out of the box and stacking them on a nearby shelf.

"Oh my God!" I exclaim, grabbing a copy and hugging it to my chest. "This is my favorite book of all time!"

His eyebrows wrinkle over his nose, like he's baffled by someone loving the best children's book ever written. "Really?"

I nod emphatically. "I love everything about it. My grandma bought it for me. Here, actually. On our vacation when I was ten." I blink back the tears I feel forming behind my lids. "We went back to our rental and devoured it in a day. I've probably read it 50 times since."

It looks like his eyes soften a little. Like maybe he's set down the mantle of trying to piss me off, if just for a moment, since I've exposed my humanity a bit.

"I haven't read it," he admits.

I hand him the copy I'm holding. "You have to."

He shoots me a wry smile. "Well, thanks to your meddling, I'm not sure my night's free."

"Sorry," I say, not feeling very sorry at all. Then an idea strikes me. "Hey, Maisie told me to pick out a free book to take to the beach with me. But I'm hereby passing my freebie off to you. Take Ella with you when you leave tonight. I promise, you won't regret it."

Oliver looks like he thinks he may regret it very much, but he nods. "Okay, fine. As long as you also promise to stop trying to get me arrested for hanging out with teenagers."

I snort. "You can't get arrested just for talking to them, weirdo."

"Point taken." He goes back to lifting stacks of books out of the box.

I really need to leave. "Okay, I'm going to head out. I'll call the store at 7:45 or so to make sure you're ready for Rachel and company."

"Screw you, Ivy," Oliver says, but he grins rakishly, so I

know he's at least kind of joking. My heart jumps a little at how he looks when he's pretending to be angry with me.

I tell that part of my heart to STFU.

"See you Friday," I reply cheerfully, waving over my shoulder as I make my way out of Shoreline.

Thank God my back's to him so he can't see my cheeks flush at the sound of his gravelly "Can't wait," which sounds not entirely sarcastic. It's almost a little earnest, even.

I shake my head in time with the bell on the door as it swings shut behind me. I'm just lonely, and he's a jerk. I definitely shouldn't be having these thoughts about him.

six

W hen I get back to Beach Haven, I warm up some leftover pizza and grab the first of my new paperbacks, *Ghost Writing* by Callie Sheffield. It just came out and has been getting a lot of hype, so I'm really excited to start. Balancing my plate on top of the book, I head to the front porch to eat.

It would probably be an unpleasantly warm day if not for the ocean breeze, but thanks to the wind, it's perfect. I can feel my soul relax as I inhale a seemingly never-ending string of cheese. Food, a new book, and an ocean view: what could be better?

Occasionally, my peace is interrupted by various profanities being hurled from Laurel's room and making their way out the open windows to me. "You okay in there?" I yell after the fifth such exclamation.

"Why did you let me enter a PhD program?" she whines loudly.

"Would you have listened to me if I told you not to?"

"No," she admits.

I grin, then toss a bookmark between pages 84 and 85. I should get to the beach.

Poking my head around Laurel's doorway, I say, "I'm going to take a dip and then read on my towel. You're welcome to come, if you want to."

She pouts up at me from beneath long lashes, clearly losing a mind-numbing battle with her laptop. "You know I can't. Have double the fun for me, okay?"

I nod and go to grab my suit. It's a pale pink one-piece that's covered in strawberries, and I think it might be the most delightful piece of clothing I own.

Sliding my feet into an old pair of Birkenstocks (I shop for comfort, not style), I head out the front door. "See you later!" I shout to Laurel, who responds with a loud groan.

The beach isn't very crowded, probably thanks in large part to it being a weekday. Still, it's July, which is high season for Ogunquit. I'm sure if I tried to find a hotel room for tonight, pickings would be slim. Anything that did exist would probably cost triple what I'd be able to afford.

Thank God for Simon Foster, I think to myself, kicking off my sandals and jogging toward the waves. I pick a spot near a few kids playing on boogie boards, their parents watching with amusement from 15 feet away. If I start to drown, someone will probably notice.

That's one of the first things my grandmother ever taught me. "Never swim alone," she liked to say. She was right, of course. But she repeated herself every summer, and I did grow a little weary of the advice. Eleanor wasn't a proficient swimmer, and I think that gave her an unnatural fear of the water.

Even still, I knew she was right, at least to an extent. So I've always tried to be as careful as possible.

The water feels frigid today, but I wait a minute and let my feet go numb. It doesn't take long after that before the waves start to feel refreshing. That's a trick I picked up from my dad. He was one of the only ones who braved the water for more than 15-minute intervals, always heading out to chest depth to jump the waves.

In Ogunquit, that meant wading out a good 50 yards from shore at low tide, since the beach was so large, and the slope where the waves broke so gradual.

Out there, bobbing up and down in the sea, was one of the only places I ever saw his inner child on full, vibrant display. My mom and I loved to watch him.

"He's crazy," she'd say from the comfort of our beach blanket, words dripping with affection.

"I know. It's so cold!" I'd glance up at him, then go back to my book.

It's weird, the things you remember. The things you take for granted. If you'd told me, the last time my grandmother warned me not to swim alone, that I'd never hear her say it again, I don't think I would've believed you. And if someone said my mother would stop appreciating my dad's joy, I probably would have laughed in their face.

But here I am, Eleanor gone, my parents separated and unlikely to ever be on a beach together again. Swimming all by myself.

Life can be surprising like that.

After ten minutes or so of letting waves slosh up against my hips, I head back to my towel to warm up. Wrapping it around my waist, I dig my toes into the sand and crack open *Ghost*

Writing again. It's a love story, set at about the same time my grandparents would have met. I'm loving the book, but it's getting a little heavy for me, given all the fraught emotions hanging in the air here, in my real life.

I check my phone—it's only 3:45. I wish I'd let my grand-mother teach me to embroider so I'd have a second activity to do on the beach. She was always asking Laurel and me if we wanted to try, but we were typically too busy trying to rescue our sand castle from impending destruction to be bothered with what we secretly called "old person hobbies."

There are a lot of things I wish I'd done when my grand-mother was still alive. Listen more attentively to her stories, for one. It's still bothering me that Laurel remembers how my grandparents met in such great detail and, before she recounted the tale the other day, it had completely slipped my mind. Reading Eleanor's diary has opened up a gaping hole in my heart, leaving me wanting more—more stories, more wisdom imparted. Mostly just more days with her.

It also hit me, reading about her youthful escapades, that Eleanor was a complete person before she became a mother. *Long* before she became a grandmother. A person with hopes and dreams and love and lust and longing. I know how absurd that sounds, because *of course* everyone is a complete person, regardless of their age. But I think we all tend to view our grandparents, and our parents, to some extent, as stodgy carica-tures, rather than real, full people who've already lived the youth we're now enjoying.

I suppose I saw some snatches of that humanity in Eleanor when she and my grandfather would get together with their friends, here at the beach. There were a few couples in town they'd invite for picnics, and my grandmother always had a huge grin on her face when they were sipping wine and swapping stories. Even though she was about as introverted as they come, Eleanor was a commanding storyteller, and she definitely seemed to come alive when she was sharing some misadventure or other with their friends.

My grandparents were always particularly close with Simon Foster, who seemed like a constant fixture at our beach rental every summer. He would come over for dinner or to play cards nearly every night, always bringing a bouquet of fresh flowers for the table and a kind smile for me.

When my parents went out for the evening with Laurel's mom and dad, Eleanor and Charlie would watch Laurel and me. Simon often came over for dinner on those nights, then retreated to the porch with my grandfather to sip scotch while my grandmother put us to bed. Occasionally, Eleanor would join them after she'd read Laurel and me a bedtime story. Other nights, she fell asleep in the chair beside us, a book open in her lap.

It was comforting to hear the gentle mumbling of Charlie and Simon, talking and laughing outside long into the night. It kept me awake at times, trying to eavesdrop and figure out what they were saying, but it was rare that I could.

On the nights Eleanor joined them on the porch, all I remember is hearing her genuine laughter pealing high above their baritones. When I was younger, I felt surprised by her mirth, because she was a grandmother—what could she possibly be laughing about? Bundt pans or vile-sounding aspics?

But I understand now that they were probably reminiscing about esoteric jokes or mocking ridiculous swimsuits they'd seen on the beach. Doing the things that everyone does.

How incredibly daft I used to be.

And now I know also that Eleanor had been in love, not only with Charlie, but at least once before that, with some mystery man. I just wish she were still here, so I could ask her, among countless other things, how it felt to fall in love to the rhythm of the Atlantic.

AT EXACTLY 7:45, I dial Shoreline Books from my vantage on a porch chair. I hadn't really been serious when I told Rachel and her friends I would make sure Oliver was ready for their beach stroll, but I'm still exceptionally bored.

I'd borrowed Laurel's laptop when she took a shower earlier and applied to several librarian jobs, then aggressively cleaned the entire living room at Beach Haven. I'm fresh out of ideas for entertainment, and Laurel's closed the door to her room so she can focus on her work.

The phone rings twice before Oliver picks up. "Shoreline Books." He sounds about as enthused as a teenager at Sunday dinner with their grandparents.

"You really should try to seem more excited. It would be good for business," I respond snarkily.

There's a beat, then he asks, "Who is this?"

"This is Ivy."

"Jesus—"

"What? I promised I'd call."

"Goodnight, Ivy."

This conversation was not nearly long enough to rid me of my boredom. "Wait!" I stall.

"What's up?"

Shit. Now I have to think of something else to say. "Um, are they there yet?"

"I don't know, Ivy." He draws my name out in the most patronizing way I've ever heard. "But I'm not going to the beach with them. So if you don't mind, I'm going to hang up so I can finish my work and leave, before the children who should be at home and in bed swing by to harass me further."

I snort. "You're such a baby."

"Don't even get me started on what *you* are," he mutters. "Oh, shit—"

In the background, I hear a bell jingle and a cacophony of giggles. "Jesus. Are they actually there?" Somehow, I wasn't actually expecting the trio to make good on their threat of showing Oliver a good time.

"I have to go," Oliver says quickly. I hear a click and realize he's hung up on me.

I cackle to myself, then immediately feel guilty. While Oliver is ostensibly a dick, he did seem genuinely uncomfortable earlier.

Before I can talk myself out of it, I fire off a quick text to Laurel. *Going for a walk.* I don't want to interrupt her. She was deep in Rossetti land when I'd asked if she wanted to go get ice cream earlier, but she declined. If she's at the point of turning down soft serve, I know better than to bother her again.

Hopping off the porch, I walk through the sand to Beach Street. The shops are all lit up, hoping for tourists high on sunburn and libations to drop in for some impulse purchases. I hear loud music coming out of a karaoke bar, and lots of families are strolling around, licking ice cream and paying very little attention to the cars trying to inch their way through town.

I see more than one near-accident, and I marvel at how the

proper use of crosswalks seems to elude tourists. I guess I see, just a little bit, why someone like Oliver might not appreciate his town being taken over by vacationers who don't watch where they're going for a full third of every year.

It only takes me ten minutes to get to Shoreline Books. Oliver's wiping down a café table, his back to a group of four girls and three college-aged guys. I guess the trio from earlier found a few more friends.

The girls are clearly having the time of their lives, flirting with this (admittedly very attractive) older man. They're probably here on summer vacation with parents too drunk to pay attention to where they're sneaking out for the night.

It doesn't escape my attention that, with the addition of Oliver, the group now has enough people to pair off into four couples capable of wreaking quite a bit of inappropriate havoc. From the way he's avoiding any eye contact whatsoever, I'm guessing it hasn't slipped Oliver's attention, either.

Taking a deep breath, I push open the door. At the bell, Oliver looks up. I think he's about to announce that the shop is closed, but a wave of confusion passes over his face when he sees it's me.

I paste on a smile. "There you are!" I sidle up to him and wrap him in a hug. I can't help but notice how warm his chest is under my cheek. I definitely should have brought a sweater; it's much cooler outside now that the sun's setting. A classic tourist mistake I should *not* have made, given my many years of familiarity with Maine's summer evenings.

Oliver's confusion only deepens. "Um. Hi?"

"I told you I'd come by tonight."

He continues to stare at me blankly.

"For our walk?" I raise both eyebrows to covertly indicate the ruse.

Rachel glares at me out of the corner of her eye. I'm throwing off their ratio, and I know it. But I don't care. It's partially my fault that Oliver's in this mess. It's the least I can do to help him out of it.

"Oh," he says finally, understanding hitting. "Right. Thanks."

"Let me finish up with this table," I offer. "You go close up, and then we'll all meet you outside." I turn toward the others. "Right, guys?" They nod awkwardly.

He hands me the cloth he's using, fingers brushing mine in the process. I try to ignore the way my heart leaps at the contact.

I make a few more aimless passes across the table, then I head through the front door. Rachel and company are already huddled just outside, looking more than a little uncomfortable.

Oliver joins us a minute later, flicking off the remaining light switches and locking the door behind us.

"Shall we?" I address the group, but I'm only looking at him.

Everyone starts to walk down the sidewalk toward the beach. Maddie is telling a raucous story about a time when she got sick from too much champagne. She keeps stealing glances at Oliver, oblivious to the fact that one of the younger guys is eating up her every word.

"Do you like champagne?" She leans in toward Oliver's face, way too close.

Before he can respond, I grab his arm and wrap it around my shoulder, holding his hand against my bare skin. "Oh, he loves it. You should have seen him back in college."

The girls are staring at me. I'm pretty sure Oliver is, too, but he doesn't move his arm.

Their energy drops significantly, and they start whispering amongst themselves. One of the other guys, who looks like he wrote the book on yachting apparel, drapes his arm tentatively around Maddie's waist.

"Ivy," Oliver whispers in my ear. "What exactly are you doing?"

"Helping?" I turn my head to face him, but all I can really see are his eyes glittering in the twilight. The sun has dropped much lower in the sky since I left Beach Haven, and my vision is still adjusting from the bookstore's fluorescents.

"I see."

"I mean, it's sort of my fault you're in this situation."

He leans toward my ear. "At least you're willing to admit it."

I snicker, attracting attention from Rachel, who turns around and glares at me again. I lower my voice even more. "It seemed like you needed an out."

"I had a plan," he retorts.

"Right," I nod. "Sneaking out the back like a criminal."

I think he's about to toss a smartass retort my way when Maddie pivots and looks at us expectantly. "Hey, we're going to go to the dance hall. Harbor Lights? Ben has a flask in his pocket." She indicates Mr. Yachting Apparel. "Want to come?"

"Nah." Oliver shakes his head. "I'm just going to head home with my girlfriend. See you around."

My heart executes a perfect triplet of palpitations. His *what now?* I can't see him very well in the encroaching darkness, but I'm almost certain he's smirking at me.

The others wave their goodbyes and split off, heading along

Shore Road toward the dance hall. It's probably the only club-like place in town that they can get into, being below legal drinking age.

As soon as they're out of sight, I throw Oliver's arm off my shoulder.

He bursts out laughing. "I'm sorry touching me was so horrible for you."

"It was." My skin cries out for his warmth as the frigid night air sweeps in to take its place. I tell myself I'm a strong, modern woman who doesn't need a man to keep me warm.

I probably do need a sweater, though.

"Also, way to take the ruse to the next level and pretend I'm your girlfriend."

"I thought that was the point?"

I shake my head. "No way. I was just another woman, lusting after your particular brand of grumpy snark."

"Oh, well, if that's all." I can't really tell in the low light, but I think he's smiling.

"Well, I should head home. I'm just down the beach." I gesture over my shoulder.

He looks concerned. "Do you want me to walk you home?"

Something in my chest lurches at the surprising concern he's exhibiting for my well-being. "No, that's okay. Thank you."

"You sure?"

I nod. "Would it make you feel better if I texted you to let you know I got there okay?"

"I mean, a little," he shrugs.

"How shockingly chivalrous of you." I grab my phone and click to create a new contact, then hand it to him. "Go ahead and add your number."

He types it in quickly, then passes the iPhone back to me. "So what have we learned tonight?"

"Hmm," I muse, digging my toe into the sand at the edge of the sidewalk. "That we shouldn't encourage debaucherous street youths?"

"Damn straight." He sounds grumpy, but I don't think he's actually angry. At least, I hope not. He's annoying, but we're going to be working together all summer. I don't want to upset him too much.

At least not right away.

"Well, thanks for the walk," I say, hovering somewhere between earnest and coy. "Night, Oliver."

"Goodnight," he replies.

I don't turn around until I get back to Beach Haven, but when I slip into my porch chair and look back toward town, I think I see him still standing at the edge of the street, watching me walk home.

You didn't need to wait there, I text the number he's added to my phone.

Okay, it's definitely him. The person I saw has started walking away now, but is digging something out of their pocket.

A moment later, my phone buzzes. *There's a gang of unruly street youths out tonight. I did what I had to do.*

I snort. *Well, thank you for your service.*

Anytime. See you Friday.

I set my phone down on the porch table and turn to look out at the ocean. It's too dark to see much right now, but lights from shore occasionally pick up a whitecap or two as they roll in. I close my eyes and breathe deep to the sound of the waves, whooshing their way onto the sand.

With each one, I feel my body start to relax. I pretend the

departing waves are taking my worries out to sea, where I'll be free of them. Free of heartbreak, free of grief.

I imagine the new waves are carrying hope, and love, and my whole future, washing it up onto the sand like a seashell I can wear. Like I'm a hermit crab who can abandon my now-outgrown house and pick up a new one, carried ashore just for me.

Like maybe, here in this place, it's actually possible to start over.

seven

I spend most of Thursday cleaning around Beach Haven and reading the books I brought. I finish *Ghost Writing*, which is delightful but makes me cry at least once per chapter, then start *Flowers in the Cove*, a new Scarlett Sinclair book I've been eagerly anticipating. It's lush and dramatic, and it keeps me on the edge of my seat (and, at times, my beach towel) all the way until its sappy conclusion.

I start my third novel just before dinner, cursing my decision to gift Oliver my free book from Maisie. I'm going to be done with this one in a matter of days, and then I'll only have one left to get me through the next five-and-a-half weeks.

Let's be real, I'll have to buy something after work on Friday. There's no way I can go all summer with just one more beach read in my stash. I laugh to myself, imagining asking Oliver for a recommendation. He'd probably suggest something by Jack Kerouac. Or whatever's most like the pretentious nonsense he's been writing when he takes his breaks in the café.

Laurel and I make turkey sandwiches for dinner, because it's hot and neither of us feels like cooking.

"I'd love to order takeout, but I don't think I can do that every night, plus sit around all day writing, and still maintain this smoking hot bod," she jokes.

I cackle into my sandwich. "I understand your dilemma. Besides, we need to reserve our money for going to bars with cute lobstermen."

"I'm sorry, with whom?"

"You know, the strapping young sailors who supply all the restaurants in town. I'm sure they hit up the bars here at night."

Laurel purses her lips. "You realize this is not the song 'Brandy,' right?"

"But their love and their lady probably *is* the sea."

She shakes her head dramatically, her topknot flopping from side to side as she does so. "Ivy, Ivy, Ivy. What am I going to do with you?"

"I'm not sure what you can do, really," I say in mock seriousness. "It'll be good when I'm at work tomorrow so you can get me out of your hair."

"Oh, absolutely. I've been counting down the hours."

"Thanks a lot." I grab a second pickle out of the jar. "How goes the dissertation?"

Laurel sighs loudly. "I mean, I'm making progress. My advisor actually emailed me today to check in, and I was happy to be able to say I'm on track, for once. I sent her what I have so far to prove it. She's kind of a raging asshole, and I'm not sure she'd believe me without receipts. But I have such a long way to go. And I'm getting sick of staying in this house."

"You could work on the porch from now on," I suggest, crunching loudly into my kosher dill. "You can't beat the view."

"Good idea," Laurel agrees. "The only view that would be better would be the one you're in for tomorrow."

"Huh?"

"You know, at work." She waggles an eyebrow at me.

"I mean, I do love a carefully curated bookshelf, but I'd still rather look at the ocean."

"No, dummy," she says, like we're still kids. "Your new coworker."

I nearly spit out my food. "Are you talking about Oliver again?"

She nods.

"Give it a rest, Laur. He's annoying. It's just not going to happen." I poke her shoulder. "Besides, if you're so interested, why don't you try to snatch him up for yourself?"

I think she considers it, but then she shakes her head. "Nah. Not my type."

"And who *is* your type, exactly?" Come to think of it, it's been a year or two since Laurel's really dated anyone. At least, anyone that she's mentioned.

"I'm partial to John Everett Millais," she replies, a gleam in her eye.

"Laurel. He's dead." If she's cracking jokes about being romantically linked to nineteenth-century painters, she needs to get away from Beach Haven even more than I thought.

She grins. "When you spend as much time writing about him and his artistic brethren as I do, it really doesn't feel like it."

"Okay," I say, patting her head patronizingly. "That's it. We need to get you out of this house. This weekend, you and I are going to a bar. We're going to meet other people—friends, lovers, whatever. You need to socialize with someone besides me, and *certainly* besides the imaginary Pre-Raphaelites I'm starting to wonder if you've been talking to when your door is closed."

"I can neither confirm nor deny these allegations," Laurel says, still smiling. "But I will agree to a night out. Especially if I can eat something really bad for me." Her eyes light up. "Ooh, like nachos!"

"Sure thing," I promise. "We'll get you some nachos."

I'm pretty sure her grin could illuminate all of Maine.

AFTER DINNER, I let Laurel get back to work, and I head to my room to read. I get a few more chapters into my third book, but I'm not in the mood for a thriller. The fourth novel I brought is a mystery, and I don't think I want to read that right now, either.

I stand and stretch, looking aimlessly around my room, desperate for something to do. I really should have packed my laptop. I was so hellbent on creating a perfect getaway, free of any semblance of responsibility, that I defiantly left it sitting on my desk at home. It has my Netflix login, though, and I definitely overestimated how much time I'd want to spend just sitting on the beach, alone with my thoughts.

It occurs to me I could keep working through Eleanor's diary. I peek out my door, but Laurel's is closed. I can hear her blasting Black Sabbath in her room, so I know she's in deep-focus mode. I've always thought her heavy metal obsession was pretty weird, but I guess it does do a good job at masking the noise in your head. Maybe it helps her think more about the work at hand.

Damn it, now I want to listen to Ozzy, too. I throw some music on my phone and grab my grandmother's diary from my dresser drawer. Now that Laurel knows about it, I don't feel the need to keep it hidden.

I flip past the first entry and find the second, which is dated July 22, 1953. Almost two weeks after she first wrote.

I never expected the whirlwind that's descended upon me these last weeks. Ever since I met him at Harbor Lights, we've spent nearly every evening together. He's charming and sweet, and I'm completely swept away, possibly beyond the point of recovery.

Janie has been so supportive, helping me sneak out once our parents turn in for the night. She usually comes with me, and we meet him at a prearranged spot on the beach or on the footpath overlooking the cliffs. He brings his friend, the one we met that first night, so Janie has someone to talk with. Sometimes, Charlie comes with us, too.

I don't want to use either of their names here, just in case Mama reads this. She claims she would never invade my privacy, but I've seen her read Janie's diary. More than once.

If she knew his name, she might start asking around town to see about inviting him for supper or some such. Since we're staying with the Blackburns, I would be so mortified to have my mother invite a man over on my behalf. And besides, people talk. If Mama mentioned him to Charlie's mother, for instance, it would certainly get around. Everyone here goes to the Parkers' grocery store; that's where the best gossip is sold.

We're only here until the end of the summer. I don't want to become the talk of the town.

Instead, I'd like to just live in my magical dream world a little longer. As long as I can. Just him and me and the ocean, stretching out before us like the possibilities of our future.

God, my grandmother had a way with words. *Must have been all that reading she did,* I muse with a smile. I'm so curious who this mysterious gentleman caller was. It really seems like she was at the very least infatuated with him. Maybe even in love for real.

How is it that just four months later, she was married to someone else?

Grandpa Charlie *was* incredibly charming, I admit. And, based on old photos I'd seen of him, he was pretty handsome, too. I guess it's possible that this mystery guy didn't stick around, or broke her heart, and Grandpa was there to pick up the pieces. It just feels...quick.

I wish my grandparents were here. To ask them for this story; to hear all of their stories. Even just to hug them, one last time.

With a sigh, I flip to the next page. This entry is dated July 26, 1953.

Tonight, Janie helped me sneak out to my favorite place—the bench on the cliff overlooking the cove. It's the perfect vantage to see it all—sea, sky, the distant horizon. That part of the footpath is in a circle of pine trees, so it's mostly secluded from prying eyes.

Charlie got me a bottle of wine and some fruit and cheese from his parents' shop, and I brought a blanket for a picnic. He's such a good friend. We have fun together, Charlie and I. Sometimes I wish he could be the one I have these feelings for, but it just doesn't work that way, I suppose.

The man who makes my heart beat faster met me along the foot-path, and then Janie went off to the dance hall with some girl-friends. My parents thought I was with her, but I stayed behind and had a magical evening instead. I hesitate to say so, but the way my soul soars whenever he and I are together makes me think we are falling in love.

In fact, he told me as much, even going so far as to suggest he would be talking to my father about his intentions in the near future.

I won't speak to the more intimate specifics of the evening, but suffice it to say, it was more than I could have hoped for.

My eyebrows jump up my forehead. Was Eleanor referring to...sex? I'm both intrigued, as a reader, and disgusted, as a granddaughter must be when faced with a reminder that her departed relative was once a sexual being.

God. I'm pretty sure I know the place along the footpath that she's talking about. Not only can I not imagine *her* having sex, period, but I can't fathom doing so safely on the edge of a rocky outcropping, 20 feet above the Atlantic. I didn't give my grandmother enough credit for being a badass, apparently.

Shaking my head, I turn the page.

November 3, 1953

Charlie and I were married today. There wasn't a cloud in the sky, and the weather was unseasonably warm. It was like the universe was smiling down on us, giving us the gift of a beautiful day to start our lives together.

I look down at the journal in confusion. How did we skip from debauchery at the tide pools in July to marrying my grandfather in November, with nothing else in between?

It's then that I notice a frayed edge in the very inner crease of the book. Almost like...no, it couldn't be.

I run my finger along the middle of the diary, then pull it apart as far as I can without damaging it.

No, I'm definitely not imagining things. Several pages have been ripped out.

My heart starts racing, like this is a poorly executed mystery that I'm living in my actual life. Who would do this?

Maybe it was just my grandmother, I muse, later regretting some detailed descriptions of what she and Mr. Summer Romance did by the shore? Perhaps she was too embarrassed for my grandfather, or worse, one of her sons, to ever read a lurid entry about teenaged passion?

I shake my head. But she already basically admitted to the sex. If she'd wanted to remove mentions of anything incriminating like that, wouldn't she have pulled out the July 26th entry, too?

I guess I could ask my dad, but that feels like it would be a more awkward conversation than I'm willing to have. I'll have to run it by Laurel. But I hear "Iron Man" emanating from her room, so sharing my grandmother's intimate encounters with my cousin will have to wait.

It's getting late, anyway, and I have to work in the morning. And deal with Oliver. For that, I'm going to need all the rest I can get.

If I go to bed now, I can probably even make time for a leisurely jog on the beach before it gets too crowded. Maybe I can puzzle through this mystery a little more then.

eight

When I get to Shoreline at eleven o'clock on the dot on Friday, the sign on the door is flipped to open, but it doesn't look like anyone is inside.

Anyone, that is, except Oliver, who is unpacking a cardboard box of books and shelving them in the children's section. Taking a deep breath, I walk up behind him.

I'm greeted by the sound of Andrew W.K. blasting through his noise-cancelling headphones.

"Hi!" I say, hoping my voice is loud enough for Oliver to hear over the sound of his party anthems.

Apparently it isn't.

I start to walk around him so he'll notice I'm there at the precise moment he turns to face the shelf at his back.

He collides into my chest, dropping an armful of *Frog and Toad* books all over the floor when he throws his arms up to stop his momentum.

"Fuck!" he swears, instinctively grabbing my shoulders to

steady himself. His cerulean eyes are inches from mine when it seems like he finally registers what's happened.

My voice catches in my throat with the feeling of his warm breath on my cheek. "Hey," I finally manage.

"Sorry about that," he mutters, looking down and stepping backward.

"No, *I'm* sorry," I say, bending down to help him pick up the books that are all over the floor. My legs, sore from my run this morning, protest the squat the whole way down. I definitely need to exercise more.

I almost bump into him again when I stand up, easy readers piled in my arms.

"Shit." Now it's my turn to swear. "I promise, I don't usually cause so many collisions."

Oliver shoots me a wry smile. "I certainly hope not."

Okay, maybe Laurel was right. This isn't so bad.

Maybe she was also right that Oliver is just a little bit hot. My chest dips as I take in his dark eyelashes and the moody stubble that's growing in across his cheeks.

"You can finish shelving these." He nods toward the box and turns as if to leave.

I furrow my brow. "I thought you were *training* me."

Now it's his turn to look confused. "Do you need me to teach you how to put these books on the shelf?"

Okay, maybe Laurel was wrong. He's still a douche.

Shaking my head, I reach down to grab another pile of paperbacks. "No, I think I've got it."

"Awesome," Oliver says, checking his watch. "I'm going to go pack up some online orders."

"Okay," I reply, and I watch, puzzled, as he walks away.

· · ·

MOST OF THE afternoon continues in this vein, with Oliver finding menial tasks for me and then rushing off to do other things. While I'm glad he isn't hanging over my shoulder, being a jerk, I also feel like I'm not really learning a whole lot.

I reshelve books and muse about the diary entries I read last night. I'm probably overthinking things. A lot can happen to a book in 66 years. Maybe the pages were removed by accident. Perhaps the journal was damaged, or something.

Most likely, it really *was* just my grandmother, deciding she was too embarrassed about some sort of unholy thing she wrote about in there, and deciding to tear the pages out so nosy granddaughters like me would never read them.

I'm amused, both at the knowledge that she was doing unholy things at all, and that she was savvy enough to make sure no one ever found out.

And that's about where my amusement runs out in the bookstore today. I quickly grow weary of picking things up and moving them around. Even though it gets very busy in the shop for most of the afternoon, I only get a chance to talk to three customers, and none of them are looking for a reading recommendation.

I'd really been looking forward to showing off my knowledge of literature and pointing tourists toward their perfect beach read. I'll be honest, I thrive on feeling like I'm so good with books that other people notice.

Maybe another day, I tell myself. *Today is just about getting oriented.*

At 2:30, Oliver saunters over to where I'm wiping down the tables in the café, the latest in a string of tasks I would prefer not to be doing. "I need to run an errand. Can you watch the register for me?"

I'm taken aback. "You haven't even shown me how to use it yet."

He shakes his head. "There's nobody in here. I'll only be gone a minute."

"Um. Okay." I don't know what else to say. So he's going to do nothing whatsoever to train me and then expect me to be in charge? Is this some sort of weird power thing? An attempt to set me up for failure so he can get rid of me?

"Be right back." He doesn't wait for me to reply, instead crossing to the door in long strides. It jingles shut behind him.

This is not at all what I expected when Maisie told me I had the job.

I go back to wiping the tables, thinking about how Meg Ryan seemed much happier in *You've Got Mail* than I am right now, and how, at this point, I might even flirt with a guy who looked like Tom Hanks if he were to come through the door, just to take the edge off my boredom.

In any case, Oliver wasn't lying—he comes back in less than five minutes, carrying a coffee.

"That was your errand?" I say in disbelief. "Getting a drink?"

Wordlessly, he hands me the cup.

I wrinkle my eyebrows. "What...what is this?" The words stick in my throat on the way up.

Oliver surveys me with mock concern. "It's a to-go cup, Ivy. Surely you have these in Boston."

I narrow my eyes. "Yes, we have them."

He nods with finality. "Great. Want to take a break?"

I'm still standing there, staring at him like an idiot. Finally, I manage, "A break from cleaning these already perfectly clean tables?"

He crosses his arms and leans back against the table next to me. "Would you prefer I make you seal 500 envelopes? Because that's what *I'm* doing next."

"I'll take a break," I mutter quickly.

"Okay, I'll sit with you." He pulls out a chair and gestures for me to take it, then sits down across the table.

My brain is still having trouble processing.

"What?" he asks, completely earnestly.

"I didn't think we'd be taking a break *together*." I ease my way into the chair, trying not to notice how tight his black t-shirt is against his pectorals.

He frowns. "You don't have to sound so disappointed."

"Sorry," I reply, not bothering to seem at all apologetic.

"Aren't you going to drink your coffee?"

I look back at the cup in my hand. "We have coffee *here*."

Oliver nods. "We do."

"I could have gotten some myself." *Jesus*. It hits me all of a sudden. Is this because of the other day?

As if reading my mind, he responds, "True. But you seemed upset the other day when I didn't buy you a coffee."

Heat shoots up my cheeks. "I didn't mean you had to..." I start to mumble.

"I mean," he begins slowly, drawing a line on the table with his pointer finger, "I *am* training you. I figured I should try to make you feel comfortable."

Embarrassed and not sure how to feel about this display of kindness, which somehow seems like it's edging on flirtation, I choose violence.

"Speaking of that, actually," I pull my lips taut. "Why haven't you been? Training me, that is?"

Oliver's eyebrows rise quizzically. "What do you mean?"

"Well, you've been giving me intern-level tasks all day and then running away in the opposite direction."

"This isn't a biochem lab," he replies. "I figured you could handle basic things like shelving or cleaning without me showing you how." His eyes rove over my face. "Was I wrong?"

I glare at him. "No, you weren't wrong."

He nods. "Okay, then. So what's the problem?"

I don't know, really. What *is* the problem, exactly? That he's trusting me too much? That he seems to want nothing to do with me? That the work is much less interesting than I'd hoped?

That maybe, just maybe, working in a bookstore isn't for me, despite my daydreaming about it my entire life?

I shake my head. "I don't know."

Oliver's mouth tips up into a smirk. "If you want me to insult your intelligence and follow you around for a little micro-management after this, I can."

"No, thank you." I glower at him, then take a sip of my drink. It's a latte, so I guess he remembered my order from the other day. And, because I really want to hate him right now, it just *has* to be beyond delicious. I think he knows I'm enjoying it, too, because he looks awfully smug.

"That's what I thought," he says in a self-satisfied way that makes me want to punch him in the face. Even if he did just go out and buy me a drink.

"Jerk," I mutter under my breath, almost immediately regretting it.

Something like hurt flashes over his face, but it's fleeting. "And besides," he adds, narrowing his eyes, "why bother training you when you're going to leave soon and I'll just have to train somebody else?"

"Wow," I reply. "Still hung up on that, are you?"

He shrugs. "I wouldn't say I'm hung up on it. I just don't think there's much point."

"Much point in training me?"

His eyes flick down. "Much point in you being here."

I draw in a sharp breath. "Are you kidding me?"

"Sorry," he says. "It just seems inefficient." At the vitriol I'm pretty sure is displayed all over my face, his own softens a bit. "But, hey, clearly Maisie's okay with it, so who cares what I think, right?"

He's right, of course. I shouldn't care what he thinks.

But for some reason, I think I do.

"It's ridiculous for you to hate me just because I don't live here," I retort. "I've been coming here every summer of my life. I love this town, and my family has deep ties here." I glare at him. "I'm not some oblivious tourist who rapes the environment and abuses the locals."

He's staring at me, and I can't read his expression, so I barrel on. "And anyway, I have just as much right to a job here as you do. I'm a hard worker, and I need the money. I've been through a lot this year, and..." I pause, wondering how far to go with my explanation of my year.

On the one hand, I might garner some major sympathy points if I open up and explain how my charming ex-boyfriend cheated on me with one of our colleagues for five months, then refused to do the right thing and just dump me, instead publicly stringing me along for the next two. Even though pretty much everyone in the entire school knew about the affair by that point, aside from me.

Or about how my grandmother, who has always been my role model, had died suddenly, right before my parents' equally unexpected and messy separation, so I couldn't even grieve either her loss or their splitting up in my own way.

On the other hand, Oliver's face is still impassive, and I don't trust that he'll have the reaction a normal person might if I were to share my story.

"I've had a tough time of late," I finally manage.

I think maybe his face softens a little, but all he says is, "Fine."

My eyes narrow. "What exactly is your problem? Why do you hate me?"

Now it's his turn to look upset. "Why do you keep assuming that I hate you? Or that I have a problem?" He shakes his head three times, like he's brushing my absurdities away with each movement. "Is it so hard for you to understand that perhaps my life might also have its challenges? That you might be misreading my reactions, because I'm a mere human and can't always carefully curate how my face is going to look at any given moment? That maybe I have reasons for my feelings, which I'm equally entitled to?"

"Obviously you're entitled to your feelings."

"Then I don't think we have anything else to discuss." His eyes are intense on me from across the table.

I blink rapidly. He may claim he doesn't have a problem, but his behavior is a bit of a head-scratcher. The latte notwithstanding, he's acting like he detests every second he has to spend in my presence. And it's pissing me off, so I decide to push his buttons. "Hey, what was up with the party rock earlier?"

He quirks up an eyebrow. "What?"

"The Andrew W.K." I set my lips in a firm line, trying to look as bitchy as possible.

"Oh, you heard that, did you?"

"Oliver, I think that the baristas in the café next door heard that."

He shrugs. "I like to listen to music when it's slow. Helps me focus." His eyes flick down to the table, where he's still drawing a line across a divot with his index finger. "Keeps me from thinking too much."

I choose to ignore the humanity in his statement. He's got me too riled up to ask what he's trying not to think about, or if everything's okay. "Would you even hear a customer if they came in?"

"Sure," he says noncommittally.

"You didn't hear *me*," I counter.

His mouth tips up. "I don't *need* to hear you. I figure you'll knock a bunch of things over when you want to make your presence known."

I glare at him. "I could hear your music. I don't think the WASPs who shop here want to listen to lyrics about jizzing on somebody's face."

It's brief, but I think I catch a blush creep up his cheeks.

He recovers quickly. "I'm going to be honest, I didn't have you talking about ejaculate on my bingo card for work today." He leans back in his chair, lacing his fingers together behind his head, an amused expression on his face.

Now it's my turn to blush. "Whatever. It just doesn't seem appropriate."

"I'm sorry if I offended you with my music, Ivy." Oliver smirks in a way that makes me want to slap his stupid face all over again. "What do you like to listen to when you work? Taylor Swift?"

I snort. "Do I look like I listen to Taylor Swift?"

His eyes rove over me as he tips backward in his chair, its two front legs off the ground. "I mean, kind of."

"Way to reduce me to a stereotype."

He grins. "Is that a yes, then?"

I sigh without meaning to. "It's a no. Not that there's anything wrong with her," I add quickly, trying to avoid the type of pick-me behavior that drives me insane, "but I actually prefer rock. Usually alt, sometimes classic."

Oliver's mouth twists in feigned affront. "Yet you mocked my Andrew W.K."

"If you must know, I was listening to Jimmy Eat World on the walk over here."

"What is this, 2004?"

I frown at him. "I like what I like, okay? Also, that's three years more current than *I Get Wet*."

Oliver's surprise at me casually dropping Andrew W.K. album trivia is apparent, and I take great pleasure in a moment of his stunned silence. "That's fair," he finally agrees, letting his chair settle back onto the floor. "*Futures* was a pretty solid album, anyway."

Now my jaw drops. "You don't strike me as an alt-rock guy."

He shrugs, yet again. His trapezius muscles must get one hell of a workout every day.

I try not to look too closely at his shoulders, which are spectacularly well-defined in the t-shirt he's wearing.

"Well, anyway. Now that you're *training* me," I emphasize the word brattily, since he's doing absolutely nothing to show me the ropes, "maybe you can reserve your party anthems for after work? So you can, you know, actually pay attention to me?"

Oliver leans across the table, eyes glittering. "You want me to pay attention to you, Ivy?"

My breath catches in my throat. I hadn't meant it in the way he seems to be implying. Although now that he brings it up, I feel like maybe I *do* want that.

"I'm not sure you'd like the attention," he says in a low voice, still staring at me.

Okay, maybe I *don't* want that.

"Dick," I mutter under my breath.

A surprised laugh escapes his throat. "Wow! Thanks a lot."

"Whatever," I say, tossing my hair with a flourish and standing up from the table. "I'm going to get back to work. I'll leave you to your jerk-off anthems." I push in my chair, then mumble awkwardly. "Oh, and thank you for the latte."

He grins. "Happy to brighten your day."

His sudden sarcasm has me about to burst out laughing, so I hurry away before he notices.

THE REST of my shift goes fairly smoothly. I avoid Oliver as much as I can, and he doesn't do anything to stop me. When seven-thirty rolls around, he comes to find me in the children's area, where I'm shelf-reading to ensure everything's in alphabetical order.

I'm actually surprised at how many books have been shoved haphazardly into the wrong spot on the shelves, apparently by rather sticky fingers. I keep a wipe handy so I can rub spots off the covers as I go.

"Time to close up," Oliver says over his shoulder as he flips off three light switches in one motion. The children's area goes dark.

"You couldn't have waited until I was out of the room?"

"Nope," he says, striding back to the checkout without so much as a smile, but I can tell he thinks he's hilarious. "Want to learn how to shut down the register?"

"Wow, you're actually going to teach me something?" I follow him.

"Well, I figured that might make you stop calling me a dick."

I smile sweetly. "Oh, I very much doubt that."

"I knew you were reliable." He punches a few buttons on the computer, and the register drawer pops open. "So, this is the cash drawer," he gestures. "It's got the money."

"Enthralling."

"Yep." He ignores my sarcasm. "So at the end of the day, we count it. And then we make sure it matches the total here." He points to the computer screen, then looks over at me and seems to notice I'm still standing 15 feet away. "Aren't you going to come look?"

I sigh. "I suppose so." The area behind the desk seems very small, and I'm not in the mood to be stuck with him in a confined space.

"And here I thought you wanted me to train you," he says in mock exasperation while I walk to join him behind the desk.

"Please just show me how to do this so we can get out of here."

Oliver leans back against the counter next to me. "You can start by counting the money." He nods at the drawer. "Just make sure there aren't any customers around when you do it."

"I certainly wouldn't want the good people of Ogunquit to know we have..." my eyes roll quickly over the cash before me, "just north of $100 here."

"I don't want you to get held up at gunpoint, or anything."

"Aw, you do care," I joke, working my way through the bills. "Looks like $113," I say after a minute.

"Don't forget the coins."

"Right." I don't know why, but I'm suddenly feeling very flustered. This is easy—anybody can count change in a drawer. I don't want to seem incompetent. I pile the coins on the desk next to me and count in my head to regain some sense of self.

"Looks like another $1.42 in change, so $114.42 total."

Oliver nods. "Cool. So then, you want to go here," he points to the computer screen again, "and just make sure things match up."

I follow his gaze. "Looks like they do."

"I'm glad to see your math skills align with those of the students you teach." He's fighting a smile; I can tell.

"I don't really teach them," I counter. "Well, I guess sometimes. Like when I have to talk about writing bibliographies or show them how to use the Chromebooks."

"See? I know what I'm talking about."

He's still leaning against the counter, looking at me sideways. Everything about it feels intimate, from the way his eyes are reading mine at just six inches away to how I can feel the heat from his body radiating across the space between us. I'm not happy with how it's making me want to move closer.

I clear my throat. "So, what happens next? With the drawer, that is?"

He shakes his head, as if extricating himself from a trance, much like I did just a moment ago. "We take the entire drawer out and put it in the safe in Maisie's office. Come on, I'll show you."

Oliver shuts down the register, removes the drawer, and

heads for the back. I follow like a confused puppy, my mind still reeling from the heat from his leg next to mine, his gaze on my cheek.

We finish the closing protocols quickly, and before I know it, I'm standing outside the shop while Oliver locks the door.

"So now you know how to close up," he says. "Was it everything you hoped it would be?"

"And then some," I confirm drily.

"That's what I thought."

An awkward silence stretches between us, filling the night air with questions I'm not ready to ask.

"Well, I should get home," I say finally.

Oliver nods. "Sounds good. I'll be in at nine tomorrow."

It's been a long time since I had to work on a Saturday, but I'm hoping I'll have more opportunities to help customers during a weekend shift. "Maisie asked me to come at noon. So I guess I'll see you then." I take a few steps backward.

For a second, I swear Oliver's going to follow me, but he takes a beat, then bids me goodnight. As we walk our separate ways, I'm left pondering a whole host of things, but the thing that floats to the top of the mix is the expression on his face when he handed me the latte.

nine

I'm ready for work far too early on Saturday. The sky's the charming blue of a postcard, and the shore is dotted with colorful umbrellas. Laurel's holed up in her room, writing again. I remind her she'd promised me on the soul of her parents' new corgi that she wouldn't work this weekend, and that we'd get some beach time together before I had to go to the bookshop.

"I'm sorry," she wails. "I'm in a flow state. I want to harness that as much as possible."

I pat her on the shoulder, trying to be reassuring. "It's okay. I get it."

And I do. But I've also been hoping she'll take a break, because she's starting to look pale from too much time in front of her computer. Is that even possible, after less than a week? Maybe she just looks white against my arms, which are darkening quite quickly from all the time I've been spending outside reading.

In any case, while I'm not a medical professional, I'm pretty sure you can't get the requisite vitamin D from your laptop's blue light.

"We wouldn't have had much time before my shift, anyway," I add, because she clearly feels guilty about breaking her promise. "Just make sure you save some time for fun tomorrow, okay?"

She assures me that she will, and, not sure what else to do with myself, I leave Beach Haven early. I figure I'll walk around town for a bit, but the sidewalks are crowded with tourists, and I'm not able to relax as much as I'd hoped.

I consider heading to the Marginal Way, the breathtaking cliffside walk Eleanor was always talking about in her diary, but a quick check of my phone's clock puts the kibosh on that plan. I don't have enough time to get there and back before noon.

Anyway, that's how I end up at Shoreline a full 30 minutes before I'm supposed to start work.

"What are you doing here?" Oliver asks the second I walk through the door.

I shrug, trying to seem nonchalant, like I actually *do* have important things going on and just *felt like* coming in early. "Had a little extra time," I say.

He looks like he's going to question my motivations further, but he blinks away whatever quip he'd been preparing and nods instead. "Cool. Well, I'll be back here," he gestures toward the bargain bins at the rear of the store, "but come find me at noon, and I'll give you something to do."

"Okay," I agree. I'd sort of been expecting him to ask me to immediately start scrubbing the floor with a toothbrush, or sorting paperclips by size, or something. I don't know why I'm surprised that he's not making me violate labor law and work off the clock.

As he walks away, I'm momentarily distracted by his gray Henley and dark jeans, both of which are extremely flattering. For someone who seems to do nothing but log hours in this store, he certainly does know how to dress.

I decide to peruse the fiction section. Even without the free book from Maisie, I know my bank account can survive me splurging on a few novels. I'm definitely going to need something to keep this summer from dragging any more than it already is.

Shoreline has a great selection, but there's a lot here that I've already read. I have a shocking amount of downtime at Farnsworth, so I always keep a paperback in my purse. It's pretty easy to pop into my office and read 50 pages or so in between meetings.

And with the way my time freed up unexpectedly due to the loss of both my relationship and my social life, I found myself speeding through my to-be-read list faster than ever this past year.

I don't really know what I'm looking for, walking up and down the rows of crisp paperbacks and proud hardcovers. I think I'm just waiting to be inspired. It occurs to me that this is true in more parts of my life than I'd care to admit at the moment.

A dark blue paperback, *Ugly Love* by Colleen Hoover, catches my eye. My heart suddenly feels like it's twisting around in my chest, wringing the breath out of me like water from a sponge.

Kyle bought me that book for Christmas last year. He'd wrapped it in brown kraft paper, which he knew was my favorite. "You're like a little Maria von Trapp," he'd joked when I first told him. But there was just something so wholesome, so classic about a gift in brown paper. An unassuming statement—just, here is this gift—its contents matter far more than its presentation. The thought behind it is what matters. My love for you is what matters.

I guess I should have been put off by the title of the novel, since it was coming from Kyle, but I didn't think anything of it. I'm always up for discovering new authors. "Thanks," I'd said, giving him a peck on the cheek and handing him a similarly wrapped book on the history of the Olympics that I thought he'd like.

He hadn't seemed as excited about it as I'd expected, which stung a bit. Little did I know, his affair with Melinda had already started. Maybe that's why his smile looked so uncomfortable that day; a little bit guilty, even. I'd assumed it was because I also got him tickets to the NFC championship football game, plus a hotel room for the weekend, and the reservation alone almost certainly cost four times as much as the matching cashmere gloves and scarf he got me to go with my book.

But it was much worse than that.

In the end, we didn't even end up going to the game. Kyle had gotten sick, and I gave the tickets and the reservation at a ritzy 4-star hotel in the city to Alex. Alex took some "incredibly hot" guy he'd met at a cooking class, but apparently it wasn't enough to impress his love interest du jour. They broke up a few weeks later.

Standing here now, I'm struck by the realization that Kyle probably wasn't even sick. Maybe he was with Melinda that weekend, curled up beside her in bed, watching the football game on TV. How have I never thought of this before?

God, I think I'm going to be sick.

Even though I want nothing more than to shift my focus, my mind races back over the day it all started. The day my world was shattered. I'd ignored signs that were perhaps overly obvious for far too long; Kyle kept gently laughing things off, telling me it was all in my head.

I honestly wish it had been.

It began one evening after work at McCreary's, the bar all the teachers from Farnsworth frequented. Kyle saw his friend Zack, the boys' track coach, come through the front door.

"I'm just going to go congratulate him on winning the meet last week," he'd said, hopping off his stool.

Almost as soon as he'd gotten up, his phone lit up with a text. I glanced down instinctually and saw the words "come to your apartment" before I realized I shouldn't be looking at his messages.

But who was coming to his apartment? Usually, we left the bar together and I spent the night with him, since his place was within walking distance.

I dared another quick peek and saw that the message was from Melinda, the nurse at our school. *That's odd*, I'd thought. *Why could she possibly need to come to his apartment?*

Then I noticed the words "to blow you."

I think my eyes just about bulged out of their sockets. *What?* My heart started skittering around my chest at the realization that Kyle was almost certainly cheating on me.

I pulled my eyes away from his phone and turned to see Kyle talking with Zack. Kyle's blonde hair was perfectly combed, his eyes crinkling at the corners while he laughed at something Zack was saying. I took in his button-down, rolled up to the elbows, his jeans that perfectly accentuated his toned legs from exactly one hour in the gym each morning. All the things that usually made me swell with pride that this was *my* boyfriend of almost three years. I'd been head over heels for him for so long. But right then, I felt like I was going to vomit up my Manhattan.

When Kyle finally came back to the bar, I found it hard to look at him. "We need to talk," I'd mumbled.

He looked taken aback, but he said, "Of course. What's up?"

I remember shaking my head, like, how could he not know? But I managed to say, "Outside."

So we retreated to the parking lot, where I confronted him. And he seemed surprised, and confused, and then I showed him the message on his phone. His eyes had gone wide.

Kyle shook his head intensely. "I honestly have no idea what this is about, Ivy," he'd insisted.

And he had truly looked completely blindsided. I wanted to believe him, so, so badly.

But I'm not a moron, so I pushed him on it. "I don't understand why a colleague would think it's acceptable to send a message like that if there wasn't something going on."

Kyle looked about as upset as I felt. "I don't know," he'd said. "I took a student down to see her a few weeks back," he explained. "Melinda was a little flirty. And I've been dealing with her on the Student Safety Committee." He was the faculty liaison to the committee, and she was a member in her official medical capacity to the school. "But I didn't engage, I swear. I don't know where she gets off thinking she can talk to me like that."

I'd considered him carefully. His eyes were earnest, and he looked upset. But angry, not upset like I'd just caught him in a lie.

"It seems like *you* getting off is more what she's concerned about," I'd joked grimly.

He had smiled faintly then. "I'm really sorry, Ivy. I don't know what she's talking about."

The ice in my chest was thawing a bit. Maybe this was all just an awkward misunderstanding. "You're going to have to go to HR."

I'll never forget how he shook his head then. "I'll just talk to her," he shrugged. "I'm sure we can clear things up."

I'd been horrified. "Kyle, this is sexual harassment."

Kyle snorted. "Who's going to believe me?"

"You have it in writing." I glared at him. "What are you talking about?"

He shook his head. "No, but I mean, guys don't go to HR for stuff like that. Who's going to believe I care that a woman is threatening to blow me?" He said it like I was being ridiculous.

I couldn't even believe what I was hearing. "It's still harassment, and she could get fired."

"I'm going to deal with it. I don't want anybody getting fired. It was probably just a misunderstanding."

I hadn't known what to say. I wanted him to be as upset as I was. Why didn't he care about this glaring professional misstep?

Obviously now I know why. But I was somehow blind to it then. Or at least willing to convince myself it wasn't true.

Kyle must have sensed how distraught I was. He'd put his arm around my shoulders. "I promise, babe, I'm going to deal with it, okay?"

I didn't know what to do, so I just nodded. I wanted everything to go back to the way it was before I saw the text message.

So I let him lead me back into McCreary's, finished my

drink, and went back to his apartment afterward. It was only when I heard his breathing grow slower behind me and I knew he was asleep that I let myself cry.

There were other signs, too. Like when he started staying out late whenever he had a Student Safety Committee meeting. When we spent time with our friends and he turned away every time I tried to kiss him. When he was too busy to meet up for two full weeks, and I spent every night at home, alternately crying and desperately trying to figure out what was going on; what I should do.

Or when, at the end of that lonely fortnight, I finally decided to be more direct, so I texted him about getting together and he didn't reply. After talking myself through a panic attack, I resolved to confront him the next day. But when I called him out on it, he'd said he'd lost his phone.

"It's in your front pocket," I'd replied, fury rising in my chest as I looked at the outline of his phone in his khakis.

He didn't blink. "I'll call you tonight, okay?"

That's when I knew it was over. I just didn't know why.

That night, Kyle didn't call, so I called him. "What's going on, exactly?"

"Sorry, I got caught up at work."

"Kyle, you're obviously avoiding me. And lying."

There was silence on the other end.

I took a deep breath. "Do you want to try to talk things through? Or should we just end this? Because I'm not okay with being treated this way. I don't even understand what's going on."

"I think we should end things." His voice was quiet, but the wind whipping through the hole his words ripped in my chest might be the loudest thing I've ever heard.

It was another month before I got the full story. I was in the bathroom after a faculty meeting when Melinda came in to touch up her lip gloss. Like, who even wears lip gloss in their thirties? At work? I guess my ex's new lover, that's who.

"Hey," she'd said, looking nervous as she turned toward me.

"Hi," I'd said cautiously, knowing she had sent him inappropriate texts, but not knowing the full extent of her involvement in my breakup.

"Look, Ivy. I just wanted to say that I'm sorry."

I turned to face her, somehow still so oblivious. "What do you mean?"

"I'm sorry about what happened with Kyle."

My mind flashed to the night at McCreary's and the text messages. "Oh. I mean, it seems like my relationship with Kyle was doomed to fail regardless." I'd taken a deep breath. "But thank you."

She shook her head. "It's my fault it ended."

That's when it started to sink in. My pulse raced. "Are you two...together?"

She nodded, so slightly that I probably would have missed it if I wasn't in full fight-or-flight mode, senses on high alert as I stared at her face.

"Shit," I'd said, sinking back against the wall of the bathroom. A desperate attempt to support my now-floundering soul, which I never would have considered if not under duress. Bathrooms are vile, and I usually try not to touch *anything*. To the extent that I open the door with a paper towel, then awkwardly twist around backwards, propping it with my shoulder as I try to make a three-point shot with the paper towel into the bathroom garbage.

Melinda, to her credit, looked like she was going to cry, too.

"I'm so sorry," she'd said again. "When it started, I didn't know he was with you. And then I found out, but I didn't want to stop. But when you and I both chaperoned the winter dance, I felt like we hit it off."

I remember that night, passing time with Melinda in the cafeteria because none of my other teacher friends had been at the event. I wouldn't exactly say that we'd hit it off, but it was well before the night of the blow job text message, so I'd had no reason to hate her. She seemed pleasant enough.

"I've felt horrible about it ever since," she continued. "I hope we can still be friends."

She felt horrible, but not horrible enough to stop it. And we definitely weren't friends. Not at the dance, and especially not here in this bathroom.

But somehow, at my core, I realized that she wasn't really the one to blame. Even in the depths of my broken heart, I knew that it was Kyle I should be angry with.

So I'd said, "It's okay."

Even though it wasn't.

And then I'd dried my hands and gone back to my office like my entire world hadn't just been turned upside down. Again.

I'm lost in remembering how I sat in the dark and sobbed when I got home from work that night when a shadow falls over the shelf in front of me.

Turning around, I see Oliver looking expectantly at me. His hair is curling around his ears again, and his eyes are so intense, I have to shift my gaze to the side.

"Yes?" I ask, wondering what he wants. I cast a quick look toward the clock. It's not noon yet.

"I wanted to tell you," he says, apparently missing the

memo that we aren't doing eye contact, "I read *Ella Enchanted.*"

I notice that he's got the book in his hands. "Really?" I grin in surprise. I can't believe he actually read it. And so quickly, too.

Oliver nods. "Yep."

"And?" I ask expectantly.

His eyes twinkle a bit. "I liked it."

"You *liked* it?" It comes out much more accusingly than I intend, but come on. "Like" is too weak a word for what is surely the greatest children's book of all time.

"I did," he chuckles. "It's not my usual genre, but it was really well-written." He runs his hand through his hair as if to neaten it, but it settles back down like he never touched it. "I can see why you like it. It suits you."

"It suits me?"

Oliver tilts his head appraisingly. "It does. It has the same witty, twist-on-a-classic vibe that you do."

It's like my brain has stalled and I need to turn the key in the ignition to restart it. When I manage to get things humming again and can process what he's said, I'm not actually sure how to respond.

"Anyway, here you go." He holds the book out to me.

I don't reach for it. "That's yours."

He shakes his head. "I know how much you love it. Plus, it was your free book from Maisie. You should have it."

I'm still struggling to justify *this* Oliver with the grumpy loner I met the first day I came in here this summer. Which was somehow only earlier this week, even though it feels like a month ago already.

"That's okay," I say softly, pushing the book back toward

his chest. "Trust me, now that you've met Ella, you're going to want to visit her in the future."

His mouth curves up. "I trust you."

I smile, too. "Awesome. So, what's on my task list for today? Cleaning the dust from the vacuum rollers? Pulling all the books to the very edge of their shelves so they're in perfect rows? Organizing the espresso pods by color?"

"Actually," he begins, holding back a laugh, "I was hoping you could help me with something. But it's not quite noon yet. Go grab a coffee and sit, or something."

"I thought you weren't my boss?" I tease.

"Is anyone?"

"Ha! What's that supposed to mean?"

He shrugs, shooting me a mocking look. "Just seems like you don't take kindly to being told what to do."

I nod dramatically. "Fine, I see how it is. In that case, show me to this task you can't handle on your own."

Oliver rolls his eyes. "So demanding. Geez."

Snickering, I follow him to the front desk. "But you wouldn't expect anything less from me, right?"

"You haven't disappointed me yet," he says over his shoulder.

I haven't disappointed him yet? Now what exactly is *that* supposed to mean? And why does it make my insides feel like they're melting?

I join Oliver in front of a row of four-by-six notecards with the Shoreline logo printed in the top right corner, laid out carefully across the front of the desk. "Behold," he says. "Our task."

"I'm going to need you to be a little bit more specific," I reply.

One side of his mouth tips up. "Maisie asked me to write

out a new set of staff picks for the store. And I thought, who better to help me with this project than a literary expert?"

I've never disappointed him, and now I'm a literary expert? I don't know what was in Oliver's coffee today, but I can't say I mind this shift in his attitude where I'm concerned.

"Wow, high praise." I flash him a grin. "I didn't know you felt that way about me, Oliver." I realize too late that I seem like I'm flirting. That I probably just straight up *am*. That wasn't my intention, at least not consciously, but with the way feelings are fluttering around my chest like butterflies in a bed of cone-flowers, I guess maybe it makes sense.

He doesn't look up, but I'm pretty sure he's blushing. What in God's name is going on today?

Oliver clears his throat. "I mean, you *are* a librarian, after all."

For now, I think, before I can stop myself. But all I say is, "This is true."

Now he makes eye contact, which continues to be too intense for me because of how bright his blue eyes are. *This is a professional setting*, I remind myself. *It's okay to look at him. Professionally.* I take a deep breath and try, but it's still making my stomach flip-flop.

"Typically, we do about 20 staff picks at a time. Obviously, it would be better if we had more staff; it might add to the legitimacy of the whole endeavor." He casts me a rueful glance. "But I figured if you and I each did half, that would work pretty well." Oliver surveys my face hopefully. "What do you think?"

I nod. "Sounds great. There's nothing I love more than raving to people about great books."

Oliver's eyes shine even brighter when he smiles at me. "I've noticed that."

Now it's my turn to blush. Whatever coffee he drank this morning, it seems like I drank it, too. "So, should we each take ten?" I gesture to the papers on the desk.

"You can take ten. I've already done one of mine." He grabs two pens and hands me one.

"Oh? And which book caught your attention this month?"

He's looking at me like I might be a little slow, and when he says *"Ella Enchanted,"* I realize that I probably am. He *did* just finish it. Of course it would be top-of-mind.

I'm also feeling a very particular way about this adult man being confident enough to endorse a preteen fairy tale on a note card. Especially when I was the one who recommended it to him, and when he read it in just two days. Like he actually liked it. Like he actually values my opinion.

How close we're standing behind the counter, staring at these notecards, is definitely not helping, either. I'm leaning on my elbows, one of which is just inches away from his Henleyed arm, and I'm very distracted by the warmth that's radiating my way.

I really, really need to get a grip.

"Wow," I manage. "I'm glad it made such an impression."

Oliver tosses me a smile that I think a romance author would call "roguishly charming" and says, "I thought you'd like that."

What. Is. Happening.

I decide to ask.

"Hey," I hedge. "It seems like you're being...nicer to me today. Than when we met."

He stares at me blankly. To be fair, I guess I didn't really ask him a question.

"I just..." I'm scrambling for purchase and failing miserably. "It's nice, that's all."

"Being nice *is* nice," he agrees, clearly mocking me.

"Did something change?" My heart is racing like this is an actual conversation that matters.

Oliver shrugs. "Not sure what you're talking about. Come on, let's go check the New Releases for books to review." And with that, he brushes past me, turning back to grab my arm. He leads me out from behind the counter.

I'm working very hard not to notice that his hand lingered on my sleeve a good 15 seconds longer than it needed to when he says, "So, what other books do you recommend?"

And that's when my mind goes utterly blank, because honestly, there's nothing more attractive to me than a cute guy asking for book advice.

I'm fully aware of how incredibly nerdy that sounds.

"Um," I begin, willing my brain to start functioning normally. "I really love anything by Jane Austen, but I'm assuming you haven't read those."

"Ivy," Oliver fixes me with an amused look, "I spend about 75 percent of my waking hours alone in this bookstore, especially during the wintertime, when we get an average of two customers per day. I've read every single Jane Austen novel. *Persuasion*, twice." He shakes his head. "Don't like *Pride and Prejudice*, though."

"Interesting," I muse. "How about *Gone with the Wind*? That's one of my favorites."

"You *would* like that," he replies, pulling a hardcover off the shelf and scanning the back cover.

"Because I'm a literary expert?"

Oliver shakes his head, still bent over the book he grabbed.

"Nah. Because Scarlett's sassy as hell, and you seem like you'd enjoy it."

"Oh really?"

He turns and looks directly at me, a smirk overtaking his face. "Very much so."

"I see how it is, Oliver." I shake my head in mock frustration, grabbing a book of my own to look at. I need to shift my focus away from wherever this banter we have going on might be headed.

Fortunately, a customer comes over then, asking for help with a book on local history, and Oliver rushes off to assist. It takes a full minute and a half before I realize I'm staring at him. I'm caught up watching the quiet, confident way he pulls books off the shelves, flipping them open and pointing to salient information, smiling when the customer does, and just generally seeming fully at ease here.

I shake my head rapidly as if to clear my thoughts. This can't happen. I'm pretty sure Oliver hates me, and besides, I'm leaving at the end of August. There's no point in entertaining this kind of daydream.

Taking a deep breath, I turn back to the counter and will my brain to focus on writing the staff picks. I only get through one before my eyes are dragged, as if by a magnet, back to his face across the room.

ten

I don't have to work on Sunday, and I manage to pull Laurel away from her computer for a walk on the Marginal Way. The fact that we've been here almost a week already and haven't yet made it to my favorite place in town has me very antsy.

The sun is high above us, inviting little beads of sweat to race down the back of my neck as we stroll. But the flowers are luscious, the bees and butterflies flitting excitedly from bloom to bloom. I can't say I blame them. Between the gardens and the sweeping oceanscape stretching out before us, I suspect we may have unwittingly stepped onto another plane entirely.

We walk mostly in silence, slipping into a single-file formation every 60 seconds or so as joggers and overwhelmed parents with strollers pass by on the narrow path. Between the constant need to move over and the steep, curving hills on parts of the walkway, it's challenging to carry on a conversation.

"It's hot," Laurel moans, turning to face me when we're

about a quarter-mile from the end of the path. "Can we sit down?" She indicates a nearby bench.

My breath catches in my throat when I realize it's surrounded by a ring of pine trees, set out on a rock jutting over the ocean. This is *the* spot. The place Eleanor wrote about in her diary.

My gaze flits over to Laurel's perfectly made-up face, now marred by a sheen of sweat. I should tell her what I read. But I remember the feelings sharing Eleanor's first journal entry dredged up for me, and I decide to sit with the information on my own a little bit longer.

"Absolutely. Let's take a break." We sink wearily onto the bench, and the temperature immediately drops at least five degrees thanks to the shade of the pines. *The breeze is nice here*, I think, looking out at the waves as they crash against the rocks.

To my right, just a little further down the path, is Perkins Cove, a perfect postcard of a place connected to Ogunquit's main drag via the Marginal Way. It's small; so small you probably could almost miss it, and it juts out into the water like the letter L, as if desperate to prove it belongs to the land.

A few restaurants dot the ocean side of the strip, just behind a calm patch of the Atlantic that's technically called Oarweed Cove. The walking path continues in a loop around a minuscule fishing village made up of tiny shops, selling mostly fudge and high-end artisan wares.

On the back side of the village is a small harbor called the Basin, featuring several lobstering boats that take visitors on guided tours of their traps. On any given day, you might also spot a few sailboats that offer sunset trips out to Nubble Light down in York, plus a smattering of family-owned crafts. Spanning the harbor is a drawbridge that delights small children and adults alike when it breaks apart to let tall ships disembark for the open sea.

"I've missed it." Laurel's eyes are trained on a small sailboat bobbing over the waves south of us.

She doesn't have to clarify. "So have I. Water?" I take a swig from the bottle I brought in my backpack, then pass it to her.

"Thanks." We're quiet for a moment as she drinks, and I get lost in my thoughts. I'm imagining Charlie and Eleanor, hovering like ghosts on the very rocks around us, setting up for a picnic. Grandpa's eyes crinkling with joy when he looked at Grandma, as they always did; her smile bright as the midday sun. Him casually waving goodbye when her paramour arrived, heart twanging with his longing to stay. Her soul not yet aware of the future in store for her; distracted by this powerful, yet temporary love affair.

Then my mind flicks back to last summer, when my parents and I walked to Perkins Cove and stopped in this very spot. They'd been snippy with each other all morning, and by the time we'd found an available bench to take a breather, I'd had about enough.

"So, should we go out for lobster tonight?" I'd asked, hoping to lighten the tension in the air.

"I don't care what we do," Dad said quietly.

My mother had rolled her eyes. "Do you care about anything anymore?"

I remember shooting her a shocked glare. "Mom! Would you ever say that to a patient?"

She shook her head. "Of course not. I'd like to think no psychologist would."

"Then why are you saying it to someone you love?"

I saw guilt, shame, and sorrow swimming through her eyes then, but I didn't know what to make of them at the time.

Dad spoke next. "I appreciate your attempts at mediation, Ivy, but I think this is a lost cause."

"It's not a lost cause," Mom had practically shouted. "That's the whole point."

My father stood up from the bench. "I'm going to head back. You two enjoy your walk."

Mom didn't reply; she just watched him leave with a sad look on her face. I wasn't sure who to be angry at, or what had caused the argument in the first place. It felt like it was about something deeper than Dad buying the wrong milk, which was what started their bickering this morning.

So I'd just pasted on a fake smile and asked, "Should we go into town and window shop?"

"That sounds like the perfect way to spend the afternoon," my mother had replied, forcing a smile of her own.

By the time we'd gotten back to the rental cottage after browsing jewelry and pottery for hours on end, Dad had left a note saying he went for dinner with Uncle Greg, and that we shouldn't wait up.

I couldn't quite put my finger on it at the time, but I had the sense that something big was coming. Little did I know that in a few short months, my parents' marriage would essentially be over. Hell, maybe it was over already that day in July.

"How was work this week?" Laurel's voice breaks through my rumination.

"Not bad," I reply. "Got Oliver to read *Ella Enchanted*."

Laurel's brows fly up. "Seriously?"

"Yep." My mouth twitches with a smile I can't fight.

"I'm just going to say I called this," she says with an obnoxious grin.

"Called what?" I run my finger over the "A + G" carved into the bench next to my leg.

She smirks. "You and Oliver."

"There is no 'me and Oliver.'"

"If you say so." Laurel rolls her eyes.

"I do."

"Fine. Should we keep walking? I can smell the fudge in Perkins Cove from here."

I snort. "Let's pack it up, Montgomery-Parker."

But later, when we're eating the fudge on yet another bench overlooking the cove, I find myself thinking maybe she did, in fact, call it. Call *something*. Because the words "me and Oliver" won't stop flashing through my mind.

I SPEND most of Monday reading, toes buried in the sand. I'd managed to find several intriguing books in the bargain bin at work on Friday, so I'm all set for many a peaceful afternoon at Beach Haven.

I'd asked Oliver to check me out at the register when there was a lull, and he'd made a joke about me spending the entirety of my paycheck on novels.

"This is why I'm shopping the bargain bin," I'd smiled.

"You should let me take you to the library," he countered. "If you promise not to get sand all over the books, I'll let you use my card."

The idea of Oliver checking out books for me, like we were *together*, was, quite frankly, a little hard to take. I don't think Kyle even *had* a library card. And until that moment, I hadn't realized a man bankrolling my library holds was on my list of fantasies.

I'm pretty sure Oliver noticed the flush of my cheeks and how it had taken me an extra moment to respond, because he grinned to himself and muttered something about how I could buy him ice cream as payment.

The image of his face when I agreed to go to the library with him after work on Tuesday flashes through my mind more times than I care to admit while I'm reading today.

Halfway through the second novel, my mind starts wandering even more, traversing the distant horizon rather than swimming through the words on the page. Working at Shoreline is a pleasant surprise; I wasn't expecting any kind of income this summer. I'm excited to help Maisie and to get to talk about books with customers.

It's a far cry from a tenured job with benefits, but there's something about the bookstore that intrigues me. No two shifts at Shoreline seem alike. It's a refreshing change from what I'm used to at Farnsworth, where time crawls by in exactly the same monotonous pattern every day. At the bookstore, the customers and their preferences vary by the hour. The tasks of operating a small business are many, but that means plenty of things to do, and time seems to fly by. Granted, I've only worked two shifts so far, but I'm excited to see where the summer takes me. I think my boredom on the first day was just a fluke, my mind flustered by whatever was going on with Oliver.

I don't head back to Beach Haven until the sun sets. Laurel's still working on her dissertation, so I cook some pasta and jarred sauce and settle in with a magazine she let me borrow. 50 Sexy Looks for Summer, screams the hot pink cover.

Not my usual preferred vertical, but in the absence of anything better, I'll take it.

While I'm eating, I feel my phone go off. I think my brows wrinkle of their own volition when I see it's Oliver.

Still want to go to the library tomorrow?

It's like he's in my head. *It depends. How much is your ice cream going to cost me?*

How many books are you going to make me carry?

I snort. *It's not 1950. I can carry my own books.*

His response comes immediately. *Okay, I'll order a reasonable amount of ice cream, then.*

Will you also be browsing for books while we're there?

Could be.

I try to imagine Oliver in the library. I wonder which section he visits first; how long he browses before selecting things to check out. If, like me, he tends to amass a pile too unwieldy to carry comfortably without even realizing what's happened.

I probably shouldn't be imagining Oliver anywhere. *Especially* in a library.

This magazine is boring, and Laurel's still blasting Black Sabbath with the door closed. Continuing this conversation is the best entertainment I've got right now. *What kinds of books are you going to check out?*

Erotica, probably.

My face heats. He's joking, I'm sure. Do public libraries even have that kind of thing? I shake my head to clear the smoky thoughts brewing there. *Wow, this is some library.*

You've no idea.

I raise both brows, struggling to wrap my mind around how

this conversation is making me feel. Amused, yes, and entertained. And aroused?

Yeah, definitely that, too.

Can't wait to explore the library with you, I reply before I realize it sounds awfully suggestive, given his jokes about erotic literature.

I'm sure you can't, he sends back. A minute later, he adds a winky face.

It's hard to focus on anything after that.

eleven

S horeline is packed all day Tuesday, and I barely have a chance to notice Oliver, much less speak to him, until Maisie's shooing us out the door at the end of our shift.

"Have fun at the library!" She grins like something about our impending outing is vastly amusing to her.

"Thanks, Maisie." Oliver turns to me. "Ready?"

I nod, but I don't speak. My words have turned to mush in my throat, thanks to a poorly timed flash of Oliver's "*Erotica, probably*" text that wipes out all coherent thought.

"It's not far," he says, taking the lead and heading up Shore Road, away from the beach.

I've noticed the little library every time my family's vacationed here, but I've never visited. Going inside, especially given the circumstances and the company, is going to be surreal. I feel like someone's welcoming me into the smoky back room of Ogunquit, where tourists aren't allowed.

Between working here and checking out library books, I

suppose I *am* becoming something of a local. Or maybe it's more like being a groupie? A poser who wants so badly to belong that they walk around doing the work of the tourism board for free?

I'm so caught up in this bizarre string of thoughts that I don't even notice Oliver talking to me at first.

"Ivy?"

"Hmm?"

His eyes are bright on my face. "I asked how your day was."

"Oh." I hate that I'm so flustered. "You were with me all day. You know how it was."

"Shoreline was slammed," he counters. "We barely spoke."

He's right, of course. "It was fine. I met a very nice lady who wanted recommendations for spicy romantasy."

Oliver smirks. "Don't you love that so many *New York Times* Best Sellers are basically porn?"

There goes the blood, rushing to my cheeks again. I can feel it. "I mean, I guess that's one way of looking at it."

"So which one did you tell her to buy?" He looks so smug, I can't stand it.

"I suggested a few." I swipe my eyes covertly to the left and see his self-satisfied grin.

"Ivy, you don't seem the type," he says sardonically.

I turn to face him now. "I'm just giving the customers what they want."

"I'm sure." His voice drips with amusement.

Shooting him my best glare, I decide to shift the conversation elsewhere. "I also got to listen to the most adorable little boy read all of *Green Eggs and Ham* aloud. He was so excited; he was running up to everyone in the children's area and asking if we'd be his audience."

Oliver's smile is genuine now. "That does sound adorable. I love it when kids are excited about reading." He considers me carefully. "I suppose that might be part of what led you to work as a school librarian."

The reminder of Farnsworth hits like a gut punch, but I nod. "Pretty much."

We're at the library now, and Oliver holds the heavy wooden door open for me. "After you," he offers. My heart skips a beat when his hand briefly comes to rest on my shoulder as he guides me inside.

The library is an old Cape Cod-style house that's been lovingly treated to a series of boxy additions over the years. It's packed to the brim with books, but everything seems orderly and exceptionally clean. The air is thick with the smell of paper and leather and time, the appeal of which only a true lit nerd can appreciate.

"I'll meet you back here in 20 minutes?" Oliver's baritone breaks me out of my book trance.

"Oh." I'd assumed we'd be browsing together. "Um, okay?"

"I need to go look for something over there." He gestures over his shoulder to where the nonfiction is kept. "I assume you're seeking fiction today."

I incline my head. "Yeah, probably."

"See you in a bit." He walks away quickly, almost too quickly, like he's extremely averse to the notion of me following him.

Is he *actually* going to look at erotic literature?

No way, the librarian in me protests. *That wouldn't be shelved in the nonfiction section.*

I manage to find eight novels I want to borrow. Several are part of a romantasy series I'd started before leaving for vacation, and the rest catch my eye on the New Releases endcap.

When I'm done, I find that Oliver's waiting for me near the circulation desk just like he promised, three books shoved in the crook of his arm.

"What do you have there?" I lean closer to inspect their spines.

He lurches away. "Just some reference stuff."

My brows knit together. *What the hell is going on?* I force a smile. "Is this the erotic lit you were talking about?"

A surprised laugh tumbles from his throat. "Something like that. Come on, let's go."

Oliver strides to the circulation desk like he owns the place, shoving his books across the counter before I can get a great look at them. "I'll take those," he offers, grabbing my pile, too. He's so distracted with worrying about whether I'll see what he's borrowing that he doesn't even crack a joke about the spicy picks in my stack.

"Hey, Sam," he greets the library clerk. She's a curvy redhead with green glasses and even greener eyes.

Sam grins coquettishly. "Hi, Oliver. How's it going?"

He smiles back, an expression that feels exceptionally *familiar*, and my stomach lurches. "I'm good. Just getting some books for my coworker. Sam, Ivy. Ivy, Sam."

I mumble a greeting at the introduction, and Sam returns it in what seems an equally perfunctory manner. For some reason, Oliver calling me his coworker feels like a slight.

"Will you be at McGarrity's on Saturday?" Sam's eyes are bright on Oliver's face.

Just check out the books, I want to mutter. I imagine tacking on any number of rude words that start with "s" and insult Sam's right to a sex life, but the feminist in me chokes out the thought before it escalates.

"Not sure," Oliver's saying, grabbing his secret books from Sam and shoving them back under his arm before I can fully read their titles. Did one of them say "Poetry?"

"Well, I'll be there." She slides her glasses up her nose and winks at him. God, I want to vomit.

"Cool." He seems uncomfortable, but I can't help noticing that he keeps darting looks at me out of the corner of his eye. A smug warmth floods my torso. Is he squirming because Sam's flirting with him in front of *me*?

Sam's sizing me up now, jealousy scrawled across her face. I fix her with my sweetest smile. "It was a pleasure to meet you." I grab my books, which she's finished with, and touch Oliver's arm with my other hand. "Shall we?"

He looks like he wants to laugh, but he just nods. "Sure, Ivy. Let's go." Oliver offers Sam the most attractive grin I think I've ever seen. "Maybe I'll see you this weekend, Sam." Then he smirks at me, like this whole thing is hilarious.

I swear, I'm going to punch him in the face.

Once we're outside the library, I force myself to rein it in. Oliver doesn't owe me anything. And, as much as I've been feeling more and more assimilated into this town that I love so much, I don't actually live here. I'm not staying. What Oliver does, and who he spends his time with, is none of my business.

"Thanks for the use of your library card." My voice sounds stiff; more formal than usual.

The clipped words seem to confuse him, also. "You're welcome. Everything okay?"

Nodding, I try to sound flippant. "Absolutely. Still not going to tell me why you're sneaking books about poetry like they're porn?"

A guilty expression flashes across his face. "I just need them. For a project."

I suppose my poetry guess was spot-on, then. "You know, when women say they like mysterious men, I don't think this is typically what they mean."

He takes a step toward me, a dangerous glint in his eye. "What do *you* like?"

My breath catches in my throat at the blind intent in his tone, but I recover quickly. "What does *Sam* like?"

"I'm not interested in what Sam likes," he retorts.

The urge I'm fighting is no longer related to punching him.

"Well, don't tell her that," I manage quietly. "You might break her heart."

Oliver snorts. "I think she'll survive."

"Well," I draw in a shaky breath, deciding to forget I promised to take Oliver out for ice cream, "I should probably get home. Laurel's cooking us dinner, and I don't want it to get cold."

Laurel texted me earlier that she's making egg salad sandwiches for us tonight, but Oliver certainly doesn't need to know that.

He nods slowly, as if coming to terms with the fact that this tense conversation isn't going to go any further. "Okay. See you tomorrow?"

"Yep. Thanks again."

I spin on my heel before I can let my heart fixate on how crestfallen he looks right now.

I just can't. I can't do whatever *this* is. It's a bad, bad idea.

The way sparring with Oliver makes me feel isn't compatible with the duration of my tenure here, nor with our status as coworkers.

And besides, I don't need him. I have egg salad and several smutty romantasy books to get me through the night.

twelve

The rest of the week flies by, thanks to the seemingly endless throngs of vacationers eager to find their perfect beach reads. I'm loving every minute of working at Shoreline now, maybe even more than I adore the languid afternoons I've been enjoying on my days off, stretched out on the beach with my books.

The shop is almost always busy, and my mind rarely has time to feel stagnant. It's just me and the challenge of reading people and matching them to their literary soulmates, over and over and over again.

I can't get enough of it.

On Saturday, Oliver and I are finishing our project with the staff pick recommendations when the bell on the door rings. I straighten up, ducking out of the New Release shelves so whoever just came in can see that there's help to be had, if they need it.

It's Laurel.

"Ivy!" she shouts, as if we haven't seen each other since

college and we just happened to show up at the same restaurant.

"Laurel?" I'm puzzled. She'd been so focused on her work this week that I've barely seen her, but she'd made it quite clear that she couldn't take the time to do anything else.

Not to mention, she looks more than a little disheveled at the moment. Usually, Laurel is very concerned about curling her hair and applying several coats of mascara before she goes out in public.

Right now, though, her Venetian blonde locks are gathered loosely in a ponytail, and she's wearing an oversized Brookline Youth Soccer t-shirt that features at least four stains of dubious origins. Her neon purple yoga pants clash with her orange running shoes, and it doesn't even appear that she has her purse.

"Just taking a little break." She grins, and I can't help but notice that she looks a little bit deranged. If you're allowed to say such things about your beloved relatives, that is.

I assess her face for some indication of what made her change her mind about having to work all day today, but I find none. "I'm glad," I reply honestly. She really seems like she needs some time away from her laptop.

"Also, I've finalized our plans for the evening," she continues.

My brow quirks up. "Oh?" Because she'd blown me off last weekend, other than our Marginal Way walk, I'd made her swear she would pick something recreational for this weekend instead.

Just then, Oliver strides out from between the bookshelves, carrying the most recent James Patterson novel. "You'd think he'd be ready for a break by now," he's saying, clearly expecting me to be somewhere besides in the entryway of the shop, talking with my cousin.

"Oh," Oliver says. "Hey, Laurel."

"Hi, Oliver!" Laurel beams. "You're just in time to hear about Ivy's evening plans!"

"Alleged plans," I mutter.

"See, I knew you were sassy," Oliver jokes.

"No one asked your opinion," I shoot back.

He waves a staff pick notecard in my face. "True, but I was kind enough to ask yours."

I smirk. "Let me guess—now you're starting to regret it?"

"Is there no mystery left?" He shakes his head in mock exasperation.

Laurel is watching us, an intrigued look on her face. She tries very hard to make eye contact with me, presumably to communicate some sort of subtext about how I'm flirting with Oliver. I purposely ignore her and stare at the book that's still in my hand.

She clears her throat. "I've decided that we're going to the dance hall tonight."

She's talking to me, but Oliver answers her. "The dance hall? Is this 1950?"

"Clearly not," I respond. "Rachel and her friends love it there, and you said they're only children. Thus, the dance hall is ageless."

Laurel's face is rapt on us as we banter; she's obviously feeding off this drama, bereft of any social interaction whatsoever as she's been of late.

"We're going to the dance hall," Laurel repeats. "To see what it was like for Grandma Ellie."

I nod slowly. "Okay. That could be interesting." I'm not

really a big dancer, but I can handle going out, listening to some music, and socializing my cousin with others until she stops behaving like she's never been around humans before. I think she needs this.

Plus, the idea of walking where my grandmother walked, even if it happens to be where she met her hot summer fling, is intriguing, too. It seems like it could be soothing, somehow, to see the world through her eyes.

Who knows, maybe I'll even meet a charming gentleman who can take me up to the cliffs for a sultry evening.

"Good." Laurel twirls the end of her ponytail around her finger. "Oliver, you should come, too." Her eyes glint mischievously when she sees the horrified look on my face.

"Oh," he starts, clearly uncomfortable. "I don't know about that."

"Yeah, Laur, Oliver doesn't like to go places where he has to exhibit proper etiquette." I flash him my sweetest grin.

She lets her face fall to an innocent mask. "But we don't really know anyone else in town, and I fully intend to meet some eligible bachelors tonight and leave Ivy behind. Who will she hang out with while I'm off being my charming self?"

"Hey! Who's to say *I* won't be *my* charming self and attract just as many eligible bachelors?"

"Come on, Ivy." Laurel shakes her head, a few more times than I think is really necessary given what she's protesting. "We both know you're not going to strike up a conversation with guys at a club."

Oliver makes a face. "It's not a club. It's a *dance hall*."

"Where plenty of modern street youths go for debauchery," I remind him.

"So?" Laurel's looking at me expectantly.

"So?" I parrot.

"So?" Oliver says, ostensibly just to be a jerk.

I sigh loudly. "Okay, fine. Oliver's invited."

"I think I was already invited," he retorts. "Your cousin invited me."

Laurel nods brightly. "It's true. I did."

I turn toward him, putting my back to Laurel so she knows to butt out of the conversation. "You really don't have to entertain this," I say under my breath.

"Do you not want me there?" His eyes are intense on my face.

I blink quickly, trying to still my heart, which is pounding again. I paste on a grin that hopefully exudes far more confidence than I'm currently feeling. "If you want to save me from whatever's making Laurel seem like she's been bitten by a rabid dog," I say, "I want you there."

"Then I'll be there."

I force down my blush and quip, "What about your date with Sam at McGarrity's?"

"I already told you," Oliver replies, looking at me in a way that makes my knees weak, "I've got my sights set elsewhere."

In fact, he hadn't said that. Not really. His self-attested lack of interest in Sam didn't necessarily mean he was interested in someone else. But apparently he is, and I can't help but notice that his sights are, quite literally, fixed tightly on me. I feel the flush running up my cheeks deepen.

For a moment, I forget Laurel's behind us.

"Excellent!" she exclaims, shattering the illusion of a private conversation. "Then we're all set for tonight! Oliver, meet us at the Hall of Debauchery at nine." She pokes me in the shoulder. "I'll see *you* at home after your shift. I'll help you do your hair." She surveys me with pity, like *I'm* the one who currently looks as if they don't own a hairbrush.

"I promise, I'll buy you a drink later to make up for this," I mutter to Oliver.

He nods solemnly. "Maybe even two."

"Cheerio, darlings!" Laurel yells vibrantly, like she's Cruella De Vil, but without the Dalmatians. She waves over her shoulder, then lets the door swing shut roughly behind her.

It feels like her chaotic energy whooshes right out of the room at her exit. And now it's way, way too quiet.

"Maybe even two," I echo, looking after Laurel as she zig-zags down the sidewalk.

"Is she drunk *now*?" Oliver wonders.

"I truly have no idea what's going on with her." I inhale sharply. "I'm a little worried, to be honest."

Oliver takes a step toward me. "I don't blame you. Do you need to go check on her?"

I process his look of concern, his eyes poring over my face like I'm the next book he's going to slap an index card on. "No, thanks. I'll talk to her when I get home." I shake my head quickly. "Well, when I get to Beach Haven, that is."

"Okay. Let me know if you change your mind. And Ivy?"

"Yeah?" I meet his gaze.

Oliver's mouth ticks up a bit at the corner. "You really should tell Laurel that a dogskin coat is a nonstarter. She should definitely try the green curtains instead."

A smile tugs at my lips. "So I take it you've read *Gone with the Wind*, then?"

"You may be a literary expert," he replies, "but I can assure you, I know my way around the Penguin Classics catalogue."

"Oliver," I say, hugging the book I'm holding to my chest, "you might just give me a run for my money."

He grins. "Oh, I plan to."

Just then, the phone at the front desk rings, and he goes to answer it, taking long strides across the entryway. I watch him walk away, swept up in a wave of confusion—for how he's treating me today, like he's enjoying my company; for how his eyes are making my stomach lurch; for how it's been such an incredibly long time since I smiled so much; and wondering what, exactly, it is about him that's making me feel like maybe everything's going to be okay after all.

MAISIE STOPS by the bookstore at 4:30. "I'm sorry, I'm sorry," she apologizes as she bustles in. She's carrying three tote bags and a sandwich board, plus a pile of flyers for the upcoming author visit. "I've been running all over tarnation today, trying to get ready for this event next week. I wanted to get in here sooner to help you two out on the floor, but nothing has gone smoothly today."

Oliver lays a gentle hand on Maisie's shoulder. "Hey, it's okay. We have it more than under control here."

"Absolutely," I add, flashing her what I hope is a reassuring smile. "Oliver's done a great job showing me the ropes the last couple weeks, and we were able to manage just fine, even during a big rush of customers around two o'clock." Oliver's face descends into shock at the praise, which almost makes me chuckle, but I manage to restrain myself.

"I'm so glad to hear it," she says, sounding more than a little relieved. "I'm not surprised, of course. I knew you two could handle it."

"We even got the staff picks situated," Oliver adds, grabbing the flyers and sandwich board from Maisie and setting them on the front counter.

"What would I do without you?" Maisie's smiling at Oliver like he's her beloved grandson. It's an adorable dynamic, most especially because their personalities clash so majestically.

"Cry, probably," he teases.

Maisie chuckles. "Oh, there's no 'probably' about it. Say, after the author event next week, I'd like to invite you both to my house for dinner. We're going to be working extra hard between now and then to get everything ready, and I really want to do something special to thank you for all your hard work. Maybe Thursday night?"

She might be the sweetest person on the face of the planet. "That's so incredibly kind of you, but you don't have to do that. You have so much on your plate already." I gesture to the bags and the pile of flyers.

"And I'd like to put something on *your* plate." She's clearly pleased with her joke, so Oliver and I both laugh.

"I accept, but only if you let me bring something," Oliver tells her.

Maisie throws up her hands in mock surrender. "Okay, I concede. You may bring something. But only if that something is your unbeatable chocolate raspberry cheesecake."

I do a double-take. Oliver makes unbeatable chocolate raspberry cheesecake?

"Gladly," he's telling her, like making a cheesecake is a straightforward task he tackles every day.

"What can I bring?" No way am I showing up empty-handed to this gathering.

"Oh, whatever you want, dear," Maisie says. "Surprise us with your favorite dish!"

I smile, but I actually have no idea what that dish would even be. I don't cook much, in large part because cooking for one is among the more depressing adult tasks I've faced thus far. And Kyle usually picked up takeout for us after work (I would Venmo him for my share), or insisted on preparing various combinations of grilled meats if we were trying to save money. I'll have to brainstorm some recipe ideas. Maybe Laurel can help.

Alternatively, Laurel may be too busy worshipping her furs to assist. Simon must have a cookbook in his house somewhere. I'll have to find it later.

I set the sandwich board up out front so passers-by will keep the author event on their radar. Oliver unpacks Maisie's tote bags, which it turns out are filled with signed bookplates and other goodies to hand out after the reading.

"I need to get these flyers hung up around town, too," Maisie says. "My knee is bothering me from all the running around I did earlier. Do you think you two could take care of that for me?"

"I'm not sure we both need to go." Oliver shoots Maisie a concerned look. "Why don't I stay here and work the store so you can sit down?"

She waves her hand in the air like his suggestion is the most absurd thing she's ever heard. "Nonsense, Oliver. I'll sit in my chair at the register. It's been too long since I've had a chance to speak to any of our customers." She grins from ear to ear. "You know how much I love that."

I smile back. "I totally understand the sentiment."

Oliver leans toward Maisie and whispers loudly enough for

me to hear, "It turns out that Ivy's actually a bit of a literature exhibitionist."

I laugh once, a shocked "Ha!" that takes even me by surprise.

Maisie rolls her eyes. "Ivy just knows what's worth reading." She pats my arm. "I knew you were a great hire, dear."

"I'm happy to distribute the flyers on my own, Maisie. It's really no trouble." I share Oliver's concern about her being left alone here.

She gesticulates wildly in the air again, shoving away our worries. "I promise, I'll be fine here. I've been doing this for 43 years, remember?"

Oliver looks like he's about to protest again, but Maisie shakes her head firmly. "Oliver, take these flyers and some tape. Show Ivy the secret spots only locals know about." Her tone is furtive, like there are actually some things the town keeps hidden for itself. "Don't you dare come back here before it's time to close up. I want you to get some fresh air."

Oliver rolls his eyes. "Okay, if you insist. I'll grab the tape." He looks to me. "Meet you outside?"

"Sure thing." I pick up the flyers and start to head for the door.

"Ivy?" Maisie calls from her spot at the desk.

I turn back to face her.

"Make sure you keep him in line," she says with a smile.

"Hey, I heard that," Oliver mutters, coming back out of the office.

Maisie and I both laugh loudly. He just rolls his eyes.

. . .

139

WE SPEND two hours walking around town, hanging flyers. Oliver knows all of the business owners and is somehow charming enough that no one turns down his request to leave behind an ad for the author reading. I'm still having a little trouble justifying this version of Oliver with the one I thought I'd met earlier this week.

Funny how he doesn't like *Pride and Prejudice*, because I feel rather like I might be living it.

"So, what do you think of Shoreline so far?" he asks as we head down Beach Street, our pile of flyers depleted almost to zero.

"It's great. Maisie's really amazing, and you know I love the books." I turn to grin at him.

He returns the expression. "I do know that."

"And it's nice, you know, to learn that I *could* be doing something else if I wanted to." I realize as soon as I've said it that he's not going to have any idea what I'm talking about.

Oliver raises an eyebrow. "Something else?"

I nod slowly and scuff my shoe over a pile of sand on the sidewalk. "Yeah. Besides working as a librarian."

"I hate to be the one to tell you this, Ivy, but you're leaving in a little over a month to go back to that job."

I shrug, desperately trying to seem nonchalant, rather than the emotionally demolished mess I am inside right now. "I might. Or I might try something else next year."

He stops walking. "Something else like what?"

Damn it, Ivy, I berate myself. I shouldn't be telling him this. I stop, too, and turn around to face him. "Maybe another librarian job. Or something like this." I point in the direction of the bookstore, which is only a couple of blocks away.

Oliver sits down on a wrought iron bench shockingly

devoid of tourists and gestures for me to follow. I hesitate, both because I don't want to leave Maisie hanging, and because I'm not sure I want to go into more detail with him about my vocational woes.

But he's looking up at me like he's actually invested in this conversation, and my feet are feeling a little sore from all the walking, so I drop down beside him, being careful to leave several inches between us. Because of his eyes, and all.

I break the silence. "I haven't been happy at work." How insane is it that Oliver, whom I just met, is the first person aside from Laurel I've bothered to discuss this with?

He offers a measured nod. "I'm sorry to hear that."

"Thanks. It's been...a tough year. And even beyond that, I've had a lot of downtime at work, and I think I might want something a little more...challenging."

I don't think I was fully aware that I was craving a challenge until I said it. But now that it's out there, it does make a lot of sense. How many days last year did I sit idly at my desk, or read books I smuggled in from home, just to make the hours pass?

I'd gone to administration a number of times asking if I could start book clubs, literacy programs, and computer classes, but they shot down all of my ideas. No funding, they'd said. No time. No resources. And my insides slowly shriveled up with nothing to ignite my passions. To make me feel like I'm moving the needle forward, both for the kids at school and for myself.

"You do seem like you'd thrive on a challenge." Oliver turns his gaze my way, and my heart dashes through my chest like the stones my dad used to skip across the Ogunquit River.

I smile, looking down in an attempt to stop whatever's happening in my body right now. Whenever he looks at me, actually. "I've been applying to jobs. Well, I've just started, really. We'll see what happens." I dare to make eye contact. "What about you?"

He seems startled. "What about me?"

"Do you plan on working at Shoreline indefinitely?" I'm curious, both because I want to learn more about Oliver, who is becoming more interesting to me with every passing moment, and because I'm dying to know what's going to happen to the store, since Maisie's itching to retire.

Oliver shrugs. "Might be stuck here for a while."

Before I can ask what he means, my phone buzzes in my pocket. I grab it and see it's my mom calling. Low-level rage starts to simmer in my belly. We haven't really talked much since my parents' separation. I've been finding it hard not to let the way she dropped everything and ran color every interaction we have.

"Do you need to take that?" Oliver's looking at me questioningly.

I click the button on the side of my phone to turn the screen off. "Nah. I'll call her back later."

"It's your mom?" He must have seen the caller ID.

"Affirmative."

"Huh," he says, running his finger over the scrollwork on the bench seat between us.

"What?"

His hand brushes against the side of my leg. We both tense up, and he pulls away like he's been stung by a jellyfish. Oliver clears his throat. "You just seem like the kind of woman who would always answer a call from her mom."

A sharp laugh forces its way out of the base of my throat. Not because he'd been joking, but because of the cruel twist of fate that made me this kind of daughter. I swish my head back and forth. "I think I was that person, once upon a time."

"But not anymore?"

"Not anymore." I swallow down my grief. "Are you close with your mom?"

Now it's his turn to scoff. "Not even a little bit."

He doesn't offer additional information, and I decide I don't want to press him. "So, what are you going to wear later?"

Oliver wrinkles his nose. "I don't know, a sport coat and some saddle shoes? Maybe a bowler hat?"

"Oliver."

He snorts. "I'm not sure. This?" He gestures up and down at his current outfit.

My chest dips again as my eyes follow his hands. How is he this built? He spends all of his time inside, surrounded by words. I guess he *does* have to carry a lot of heavy boxes.

The notion of Oliver hefting cartons of books around is making it challenging for me to look away from his chest. I clear my throat. "Well, that's a very nice outfit." I blush despite my best efforts to play it cool.

"What are *you* going to wear?" He's gazing intently at me in a way that's *really* not helping me brush away the thoughts humming through my mind.

"Um. Maybe a dress?"

His mouth sweeps up into a smile. "Curtains?"

I giggle. "Maybe."

He's still looking at me like he's really eager to see my curtain dress tonight, and I think his knee has moved ever so slightly closer to mine on the bench. I'm pretty sure this isn't what Maisie had in mind when she sent us out together to hang up flyers.

Or...God, maybe it was. *"Show Ivy around town, Oliver. Show her all the secret spots, Oliver."* He *is* basically like her grandson. Is she trying to set us up?

"Should we get going?" My head is spinning, and I need to remove myself from this situation before I spiral further into a pit of wanting. Or into a pit of embarrassment, since I've evidently allowed myself to be wholly manipulated by a septuagenarian matchmaker.

Oliver slides the sleeve of his Henley back to reveal a silver watch, then he nods. "Yeah, it's almost seven. I think we've adequately obeyed the 'Don't come back for at least two hours' rule."

"You think *I'm* sassy," I joke as we stand up. "But what about Maisie?"

"Oh, she's definitely the worst offender," he returns.

Our conversation turns to the best flavor at a local ice cream shop we're passing (Oliver says it's blueberry pie; I insist it's cookies and cream; he retaliates by reminding me that I owe him ice cream for the library books), and then we're back at Shoreline.

We help Maisie ring out the last few customers, then start the closing protocol. Oliver looks positively triumphant when I remember how to shut down the register on my own.

"See?" he says. "I knew you could do it."

I rebuff him with, "I just had a good teacher."

Maisie sits in her chair, grinning maniacally over the top of the James Patterson book Oliver mocked earlier in the day.

Okay, now I'm fairly certain that she's trying to set us up.

When the shop's all set for the night, Oliver and I head for the door.

"I'm going to hang around and finish this Patterson," Maisie says, still sitting behind the front desk. "Have a good night!"

The air feels thick when it's just Oliver and me outside the store.

"I'll see you in a bit?" I shove my hands in the pockets of my sweater. I mentally pat myself on the back for remembering to bring one this morning.

"Yup." Oliver runs his hand through his hair. "Good luck with Cruella."

I crack a grin. "I thank you. I'll need that luck."

"Later, Ivy."

thirteen

As it turns out, I need Oliver's luck more than I realized. Though things don't appear all that bad, at first.

Laurel's deeply focused on giving herself a hot pink manicure when I get home.

"Hey," I say cautiously, setting my bag down next to her. "Can we talk?"

"Sure," she replies, without looking up.

"I'm a little worried about you, Laur."

She raises her eyes to mine, then looks down again to blow air across her nails. "Why's that?"

"You know why."

She shakes her head indignantly. "I really don't."

"Okay," I begin. "How about because you showed up to the bookstore today looking like you just rolled out of bed? Which you know *I* am more than fine with, but *you* never go anywhere unless you've primped for at least an hour."

She scowls at me, but I barrel on. "Or how about because you simply couldn't bear to pull yourself away from your dissertation, then, suddenly, you had to drop everything in the middle of the day to arrange a bizarre night out between us and my coworker? Or—"

Laurel cuts me off. "He's more than your coworker."

"He isn't," I snap.

She examines her nails. "Whatever. But he's a friend-type person that you can talk to tonight, so I don't see the harm."

I'm not understanding what's going on with her. "No harm," I continue a bit more gently. "Although the Cruella de Vil quote was a bit of a head-scratcher."

"I'm nothing if not whimsical," Laurel says with a grin.

"Be that as it may—"

"Oh, it may."

I laugh in spite of myself. "Yes, fine. You're very whimsical. But you also seemed more than a little insane today." She looks like she's about to protest, but she looks down in silence. "Can you tell me what's going on?

Laurel examines her nails so intensely, I wonder if she's forgotten our conversation entirely.

"Laur?"

Finally, she sighs and looks up. "I got a call from my advisor today."

"About your draft?"

She inclines her head ever so slightly.

"And?"

Her eyes fill with tears. "She hates it."

If you'd given me a thousand guesses, I never would have imagined that Laurel, always a teacher's pet to an extent that was, frankly, extremely irritating, would displease her PhD advisor.

"Are you sure?" I put my arm around her shoulders and

squeeze her toward me. "There must be some kind of mistake, right?"

Laurel shakes her head back and forth despondently. "No. No, there isn't. She says my conclusions are 'subpar' and 'irredeemably derivative.' And she wants to meet with me in person as soon as possible to go over next steps."

My jaw drops. "Next steps?"

Her chin wavers. "If I can't get things back on track, I may get kicked out of the program."

"What?" I explode. "But you're their best student! The university practically begged you to enroll after the way you crushed your Master's thesis. They can't just do that!"

"Oh, but they can," she says ruefully. "And unfortunately, I have to shape my draft to Dr. Spillinger's whims, because she's my advisor, and she's the one who has to talk me up to the other profs when it's time to defend this bad boy next spring."

"I just don't understand. You've been working so hard. And you're so goddamn smart. What's not to like?"

Laurel refuses to meet my eyes. "It's possible this is actually just about my draft. But also...there may have been...an incident. At school, last April."

"An incident?"

She gives a meek nod.

"Laurel, what happened?"

"It doesn't matter, okay? I'm just going to meet with Spillinger and straighten this out next week."

"No, that's not good enough. If something happened, I want to know what it was."

She laughs bitterly. "You're not my mother, okay, Ivy? And even if you were, you couldn't do anything to intervene. I'm 26 years old; I have to handle this on my own." She takes a deep breath, as if convincing herself. "I'm *going* to handle this."

"Fine," I say, reclaiming my arm and draping it across my bent knees. "But as your super cool older cousin, I'd love to know what's going on regardless."

Laurel smirks. "I'm sure you would."

I wait patiently. I'm not breaking this silence, because I want her to spill the beans.

"Okay, fine," she concedes. "There was a guy."

"And there it is."

She looks confused. "Huh?"

"It's always a guy in these stories, isn't it?" I shrug.

Laurel tightens her lips. "I guess so, yes. In this case, it was a very cute guy in the history department. We started seeing each other, and things were going really well. Until it turned out that I wasn't the only one who'd dated him."

I gasp when it hits me what she's implying. "No! Spillinger was sleeping with a student?"

"Right? I was as disgusted as you are when I found out. And Nick—that was his name, Nick—insisted everything with her was over. But I guess it wasn't over for her. As soon as she found out Nick and I were together, she started getting really nasty toward me."

"Laurel, that has to be a violation of every HR rule your university has."

"Oh, absolutely." She holds up her hand to admire her manicure. "And I'd report it, but she's been tenured for quite some time, and I very much doubt they're going to fire her. She hasn't actually done anything wrong, see? Spillinger's actually an evil genius. Nick was never *her* student, and they declared their relationship through some formal university process. And she isn't even that much older. She might be 35? So the court of public opinion won't even judge her all that harshly. Rule of half plus seven, and all that." Laurel sighs deeply. "I still need her to like me so I can finish my dissertation and get out of there. So I'm holding off on reporting her, at least for now."

"But what about Nick?"

Laurel shrugs. "That fizzled out after a few months anyway; Nick's great, but I was just so focused on school. Unfortunately, I think Spillinger is still holding a grudge. She used to love me, but it's been extremely awkward ever since the first day she saw Nick and me holding hands outside the mailroom."

"God, what drama! This is entirely insane. You realize that, right?"

"Of course I do."

"But you're kind of loving the drama, yes?"

Laurel sticks out her tongue. "You suck."

"Look, even if you like being the center of a forbidden love triangle, it's not fair for you to have to jump through hoops with your dissertation because of it. You should tell someone. Or at the very least, be straight with Spillinger about it."

I can tell from her face that she's considering my suggestion. "I guess I could level with her when we meet next week."

"I really think you should try. Remember what Grandpa always used to say?"

She nods. "There's always another way."

"Exactly. Don't suffer in silence." I crack a smile. "Hey, maybe you can appeal to her feminist side. Show up there and bitch about how Nick is an evil man who broke your heart. That's probably an experience she can get behind."

Laurel snorts loudly. "Have I ever told you that you might be a genius?"

Shaking my head somberly, I hop off the floor and grab my bag. "Nope, but it's never too late. I'm going to grab a shower, okay?"

"Sounds good. When you get out, we can start on your hair."

I roll my eyes as I walk away. Is she serious? My hair is the least of our collective worries right now.

"Oh, and Ivy?" she calls after me.

"Yes?"

Laurel shoots me a genuine smile. "Thanks for being so eager to defend my honor. I know it's not the same, but...sometimes I imagine this is what it would be like to have a sister."

My face softens. "I think maybe this is exactly what it's like."

WE LEAVE Beach Haven at 9:05. Laurel couldn't make up her mind about whether to curl or straighten her hair. She ultimately settled on the former, strongly urging me to do the same. I figured she'd had a pretty shitty day already, and it had been a while since I did anything fun with my own admittedly dull waves, so I decided to take her advice.

To her credit, when I looked in the mirror before we left, I was pretty pleased with the results. My hair shone a little more than usual, thanks to some sort of cream Laurel had glopped all through it, and the curls were soft around my face. I went a little darker than usual with my makeup, and I opted for a dark green midi dress that I thought would be especially perfect given all of the *Gone with the Wind* jokes getting tossed around today.

As we're heading out the door, Laurel is kind enough to tell me that if I were hoping to pick up guys tonight, it wouldn't be my looks that would keep them away. And even though she repeatedly tries to counsel me on appropriate bar conversation because she "knows how [I] am with men," there's only one person I'm thinking about.

When we arrive at Harbor Lights *much* more than fashionably late, Oliver is leaning against the building, reading a curled paperback.

"Do not even tell me he isn't your ideal man," Laurel mutters under her breath as we approach.

"Depends on which book it is," I return.

Oliver looks up over his novel. "For a second there, I thought maybe you two stood me up." He unrolls himself from the wall and tucks the book into his back pocket.

"We would never," Laurel trills, leaning in to give him a hug that I'm pretty sure he was not anticipating.

I flash him a mischievous grin. "She wouldn't. But maybe I would."

"Oh, I know you would." He's smiling, too, but I notice his eyes sweep me up and down none too covertly. He swallows a little harder than usual. "Curtain dress?"

"Aw, you noticed." I reach out and squeeze his forearm, which is delightfully warm under my fingers. "I like your outfit, too."

He's wearing the same thing he had on at work today.

He grins rakishly. "I thought you might."

"Shall we?" Laurel is standing impatiently at the door,

probably imagining all the men inside getting snapped up by lesser women with every passing second.

"Sucks to be kept waiting, doesn't it?" Oliver quips smugly as he strides past her.

I snicker.

"Your boyfriend," Laurel whispers under her breath, "is a jerk."

Heat creeps up my cheeks as I follow her into the building. "He is no such thing."

Her eyebrows jump up her forehead. "Which part?"

"Either, I guess." It hadn't been my intention to defend Oliver against her name-calling, but he really doesn't seem like a jerk to me anymore. Not even a little bit.

Oliver pays the bored woman sitting at the ticket counter for all three of us to enter.

"You didn't have to do that," I protest.

He shakes his head. "Word on the literal street has it that you may not have a job come fall. And this one—" he indicates Laurel, who has run off to claim a high-top table, "might lack the emotional stability to even hold a job."

I snort. "Well, I appreciate it. Especially since we're the ones who invited you out."

"Well, Laurel did," he reminds me. "But I didn't see her offering to pay." His shoulder brushes mine as he leans down to speak quietly into my ear. "Did you ever find out what's going on with her?"

I hesitate. It feels like a betrayal of Laurel's confidence to provide many details, so I settle for a vague reply. "I did. It's something with her dissertation. But I think she's got it figured out." Because if I know my cousin, she is absolutely going to find a way to get this Spillinger woman on her side somehow.

"Well, that's a relief." Oliver guides me to the opposite side of the large dance floor, which is flanked by 20 or so bar-height tables where revelers ranging in age from 16 to 55 are standing around, drinking and talking. There's one couple dancing, but I don't fault everyone else for holding out—the DJ is playing a poorly executed Queen cover that never should have seen the light of day.

"Want a drink?" Laurel asks us when we join her at a cock-tail table.

I nod. "Sure. I thought that was sort of the point of the evening."

She sighs in mock exasperation. "No, Ivy. The point of the evening is to find a nice man to take my mind off John Everett Millais."

Oliver quirks a brow. "Did she just say—"

I lean into him and whisper, "It's probably better if you pretend you didn't hear that."

He nods solemnly, but his eyes are full of mirth. It makes my stomach lurch, how amused he looks, how warm he was when we just touched. I'm either extremely lonely or very horny, because there's no way I'm falling for Oliver.

"So I brought a book, just in case we get bored," he says into my ear.

Okay, maybe there is a way after all. Is it possible to be turned on by hearing that someone brought a book to a club?

"Excuse me, lit nerds." Laurel snaps her fingers near my face. "What do you want from the bar?"

"Whiskey, if they have it," I say. "Preferably Jameson."

She nods. "Oliver?"

"I can get my own drink."

"I'm aware that you *can,* but this is my treat." She smiles sweetly.

Oliver pulls a five-dollar bill out of his pocket and shoves it at her. "You can at least let me leave the tip. And Jameson is good for me, too. Thank you."

"My pleasure." Laurel leaves his money lying on the table and practically skips away.

"God, she's annoying," I say as soon as she's out of earshot.

Oliver snickers and puts the cash back into his wallet. "I'm glad you're the one who said it."

"So, what book is it?" I gesture to the paperback that he's pulled back out of his jeans to lay on the table beside us.

He shrugs. "Just something I picked up at work from an author reading a while back. It's called *Fault Lines.*"

I inhale shakily. "By William S. Pearson, right?"

He grins. "Oh, you know it?"

"I was at that reading, actually. With my grandmother."

Now he looks a little shaken, too, but he recovers quickly. "Wow, we were in the same place and didn't even know it."

Nodding slowly, I say, "My grandmother got that book signed. I found it in her collection when she died and took it home. I..." I trail off, stumbling over the memories. Over the notion that Oliver and I have probably met before without realizing it. Or at least been in the same place at the same time. Over the fact that my grandmother found this book important, so I made sure to save it from the trash, and now Oliver's here, noticing my green dress, with the same book in his hands.

"It's okay," he says. "You don't have to—"

"No, I want to. It's just hard."

He waits patiently, eyes roving over my face in a familiar way that feels like a caress.

"I couldn't bring myself to part with something that mattered to her," I manage finally, my eyes wet with tears that will almost certainly ruin my mascara if I let them fall. "She and I waited in line for almost an hour that day. We met the author; got the book signed. I think she read it that night. She was a big reader, my grandmother."

Oliver's continuing to regard me like I'm the most interesting person in the room. If only all the timelines of history could blur together in this space and Eleanor were here, too—then, surely, he'd realize that she was far worthier of that designation.

I try to shake off the idea that my grandmother could ever be here in this bar with us. I've been noticing the heat from Oliver's arm a little too much to want Eleanor looking in on me. "Anyway, I also found her diary at her house when we were getting it ready to sell. Thank God for *Fault Lines*; I probably would never have looked closer at the pile it was in if I didn't recognize the book on top."

Oliver nods. "A happy accident, then."

I consider how both the book, and all the ways it's starting to get tangled up with my present, are indeed happy accidents. "You could say that." I smile softly. "I've been reading her diary here this summer. I wanted to feel like I could bring her back with me, just one more time."

"Did she like it here?"

"We used to come as a family," I reply. "Every year of my life, in fact. Last summer, I had no idea...I didn't know she was so sick. She'd had COPD for years, but I guess it had progressed more than anyone realized. After we got home from our trip, it was only a matter of weeks, and then she was gone." My eyes well up again. "And my parents' marriage imploded at about the same time. That was also unexpected. And it just about killed my father."

"Let me guess," he says. "Your mom's the one who wanted to end things?"

I nod slowly. "Yep. She requested a trial separation last fall. But the trial period is starting to seem indefinite."

"I'm understanding a little bit more why you ignored her call earlier."

"I really want to forgive her," I start, then realize it isn't true. "I wish I wanted to, anyway. But between losing my grandmother, and trying to help my dad, and then...some stuff at work, it's just been a whole lot to deal with." I grin wryly. "I guess you could say I'm not handling it well."

Just then, Laurel arrives back at our table with two whiskeys and a fruity pink cocktail that looks like it's straight off of Pinterest.

"And then there was alcohol," Oliver says into my ear, tipping his glass toward me in salute. "Makes everything better."

I quirk an eyebrow at him. "Does it?"

He snorts. "Nope. But it helps you forget it for a while."

Laurel takes a delicate sip of her drink. "I'm trying to figure out which guy I should go talk to."

"I'm not good enough for you?" Oliver feigns offense.

She rolls her eyes. "With all due respect, Oliver, you're not at all my type. And besides," she grins maniacally, "I think Ivy would kill me if I took the only sardonic, obnoxious book nerd in town away from her."

I'm torn between angrily rebuffing her implication and ignoring her completely, but Oliver reaches over and pats my hand. "Fear not, Ivy. I could never be with a woman who makes coats out of puppies."

Now it's Laurel's turn to be lost for words. At least for a moment. Then, she sets her drink down on the table a little too forcefully, sloshing some over the sides. "I'm going to do a lap. I'll see you shortly."

IT ONLY TAKES Laurel five minutes to locate a guy dressed entirely in Dockers, like he thinks the bar is a middle-class yacht. They're huddled together over another cocktail table, her pink drink long forgotten at ours.

"Looks like she's making waves with that ship's captain over there," Oliver quips.

I spit out my drink. "You don't strike me as the type to enjoy puns."

He shrugs. "A well-timed pun is always appropriate. Especially where bad coastal fashion is concerned."

"I hope you're feeling *ferry* good about that one." I'm pretty pleased with my own joke, but I'm trying to hide my smile until he laughs.

He does, and it reverberates through my chest in a way that makes me feel more than a little bit glad Laurel left us alone here.

"Glad we're in the same boat," he replies.

"Oh, Oliver." I shake my head. "Does Maisie know about this side of you?"

He takes a long sip of his Jameson. "Maisie loves puns more than anybody."

Just as I'm about to reply with another boat pun, "Days Like This" by Van Morrison comes on, and the mood in the room shifts. All the singles flee the dance floor, heading back to the bar to top off their drinks.

I catch Oliver looking at me out of the corner of my eye.

"What?" I ask.

"Interested suitor, nine o'clock," he says, nodding to my left.

I follow his gaze and see a frumpy twenty-something in a red polo shirt and stained khakis staring at me as he crosses the room in our direction.

I am *not* in the mood to be polite to some guy who looks like he's never heard of laundry detergent.

"Oh, God," I groan, casting my eyes desperately around the room for Laurel. She and Mr. Boat Shoes have sidled into a corner and are whispering softly to one another.

Damn it. She looks happy. I can't make her leave; not after the day she's had. And I'm sure as hell not going to abandon her here when she's with a stranger.

But if this other guy is headed my way, I need a diversion. Quickly.

"Time for you to repay a favor. Come here." Without thinking, I grab Oliver's hand and yank him toward the dance floor.

Surprise flashes across his face, but he doesn't pull away.

His hand is really soft, and the fact that I'm noticing makes me blush.

"What favor is that, exactly?" he asks quietly, blue eyes intent on my face.

I stand on tiptoe and whisper in his ear, partially just to avoid the eye contact that's making the room lurch. "I saved you from Rachel and her friends. After partially causing the problem in the first place, but still. Now it's your turn to help me."

Realization hits, and he closes the remaining distance

between us, putting his other hand on my waist as he pulls me against his chest.

My breath catches in my throat.

"There you go," he murmurs next to my cheek. "Now that guy's checking his phone in the middle of the dance floor, trying to look busy."

My free hand slides up to Oliver's shoulder. "Thanks," I breathe, all too aware that we've started dancing, that his hand is on the low of my back now, that his cheek is touching mine.

"This has always been my favorite Van Morrison song," he says after a minute.

I pull back to look at him. "Mine too, actually."

But it's too tight a space, here in the inches between our faces, to have a conversation. His eyes are right there, and I accidentally look into them before I remember I shouldn't. I tear my gaze away and look down, inadvertently lingering on his mouth.

I think he notices, because he shifts uncomfortably. "So, tell me more about your job search."

I will my brain to come back to earth and remember who I'm dancing with, and why this isn't the time to be getting flustered. "Um, I applied to something in Springfield the other day."

"Nice," he says, offering a measured nod. "School librarian?"

I shake my head. "Nah, city library. Head of children's services."

"That seems like the perfect job for you," he replies.

"I guess so." I shrug a little.

"You guess?" He pulls back a little so he can peer into my face.

I manage a wry smile. "I'm surprised you don't think it's a problem for me to take a job away from a native Springfieldian."

"Ivy, look," he begins, but I cut him off.

"It's okay. I get it. It's a tale as old as time. Tourists are the necessary evil, right?"

Oliver gives me a surprisingly earnest look. "No, it isn't that. I shouldn't have...it's about me, not you."

I've never heard him flustered before. "Well, your hatred of me certainly seemed to be about you, and not anything *I* did. I know I'm annoying, but no way am I *that* bad." I grin.

He shakes his head. "How many times do I have to tell you I don't hate you?"

I take in his bright eyes, stark against the somber expression he's now wearing. "Maybe just one more," I say quietly.

"I don't hate you," he repeats, his arm tightening against my back.

"Okay," I nod, suddenly feeling a little dizzy, like there's not enough oxygen in the room.

"And I don't hate tourists."

I start to interrupt, to remind him that he definitely does, but he shakes his head. "I think we might have miscommunicated a bit, that day in the bookstore. It's just that I love Maisie, and I hate to see her investing in someone who's going to bail as soon as summer ends. She works so hard already. I worry about her, you know?"

"I do," I nod. "She said she was hoping to scale back quite a bit."

"Exactly," Oliver says. "I promise, if you read anything in my reaction as derision because you're from out of town, that was never my intention."

He's looking down at me with a tenderness that is making my heart skitter about wildly. I scramble to take a clarifying breath. "And here I was, thinking you just couldn't stand Massholes."

Oliver snorts. "It's true that I'm not a fan of the drivers on I-90 outside Boston," he admits.

"That's more than fair."

"I also might have been a little grumpy when we first met," he adds, a thoughtful look on his face. "I was dealing with a family matter that was pissing me off."

I raise a curious brow. "Oh?"

"You're not the only one who has issues with their mother," he says with a wry grin.

"Want to talk about it?" I try to sound interested rather than pushy.

He takes a deep breath. "My mom wanted to let me know that she's getting remarried. She asked if I'd like to come to the ceremony."

"And would you?" I can barely handle how dejected he looks right now.

"I told her no. I just don't want to deal with her, you know? She left when I was five. Moved to Boston to climb the corporate ladder. Promised she'd make it big and then come back for us." He looks down. "But she never did."

I stare at him in stunned silence. I certainly wasn't expecting this.

"And my parents tried to make it work for a while, long-distance. But my dad grew up in a lobstering family, and he couldn't up and leave to go work somewhere else. He loved what he did, and he didn't want to give it up, either. Eventually, the conflict became too big to overcome, and they just gave up on each other."

"I'm really sorry, Oliver."

He purses his lips. "They dragged it out for years. It was hard, growing up like that. It only ended for good when my dad got us a hotel room in the city for Christmas week so we could surprise her, and we caught her kissing another man on the front step of her brownstone when we got there."

My eyebrows go up. "Jesus. That's horrible."

"It wasn't great," he acknowledges with a grim smile. "They had it out right there in the street. She admitted she'd been sleeping with Brody—that was his name, Brody—for three years. My dad filed for divorce the next day."

"Wow. That's incredibly shitty." I think back over how I felt when I found out about Kyle's philandering. Marital infidelity is even worse, especially when children are impacted. I squeeze the hand he's holding in solidarity. "No kid should have to deal with that." I think of my own parents' separation, which shook the foundation of who I am. And I was 28 when it happened. The instability Oliver's describing would have made life extremely challenging for a child.

"I haven't seen her since that Christmas," he admits. "We talk on the phone from time to time, but that's been it. And to be honest, I haven't missed her at all; I'm too angry. The only time I wished she would come back was when my dad hurt his back."

My eyes go wide. "This story gets worse?"

He nods quickly. "When I was 17, my dad slipped fixing our roof and fell."

I gasp. "Off the roof?"

"Yep. I'd asked him to let me spot him, but he insisted I

work on my college applications." He glares bitterly into memories of the past. "He's lucky he wasn't paralyzed. Or killed." He sighs deeply. "He managed to walk away with a thoracic spine fracture and several herniated discs, but it's made lobstering impossible for him. He's been on disability ever since."

Realization hits, and I say softly, "So you never left."

Oliver blinks twice, and his eyes look a little glassy. "I never left."

The song ends, but we're still standing there, holding onto each other.

I clear my throat. "Did you get to go to college?"

"It didn't feel fiscally responsible," he says quietly, "but my dad insisted I apply anyway. I did manage to get a scholarship to the University of New England, so I commuted there and got my degree. Things were really hard. I started working for Maisie shortly after the accident while we were waiting on the disability payments to start, and I kept that up all through school." He smiles slightly. "And Maisie's just so sweet, you know? So I never left."

I return his smile. "She is indeed very sweet."

"My degree is in English," he says, "which was fairly ill-advised. But I pick up freelance writing assignments whenever I can, and between that and the bookstore, it's been enough to pay the bills."

"Because you're so talented?" I joke.

He smirks. "Something like that."

Suddenly acutely aware that I'm still tangled up in him, I blush. "Anyway," I mumble, dropping his hand and stepping back, "thank you for helping me avoid that guy." I gesture to the right with my head.

"Anytime," Oliver says in a low voice, his hand slipping off the small of my back while his gaze slides down my face and catches on my lips.

I feel my breath shudder in my throat. "Should we go find Laurel and her boat-shoed gentleman friend?"

Oliver cracks a grin. "I'm on board with that plan."

"So many boat puns." I roll my eyes at him. "Let's go." I grab his hand and pull him off the dance floor.

fourteen

"So, I think I'm going to leave with Porter," Laurel whispers in my ear a few minutes later.

"On principle, I feel like I have to stop you from leaving with a man named Porter," I murmur back, hiding my mouth with a hand so no one else can pick up what I'm saying.

She snorts. "He's really sweet. And it turns out we both went to BU. He actually lives in Brookline now, so there's a chance we could go out after we get home, too."

I raise an eyebrow. "Aren't you getting ahead of yourself a little bit?"

"I guess I'm just excited to meet someone cute," Laurel pouts. "It's been a really long time."

"I know what that's like," I say wistfully.

"Shit. Sorry," she replies. "I wasn't thinking."

"It's okay." I pat her on the shoulder. "You should definitely go home with Porter. And also text me immediately when you get there, and before you go to sleep, so I don't have to stay up worrying about you."

"You sure?" She looks concerned with the notion of leaving my dowagered ass alone in this antiquated club.

"It's fine." I shrug. "I'll make Oliver walk me home."

"Hey," Laurel nudges me with a grin. "I saw you guys dancing." Her eyes twinkle mischievously. "Something brewing there?"

"Oh, God no," I shake my head vehemently. "He was just helping me deter an interested weirdo."

"If you say so," she replies with an annoyingly *knowing* glance.

"Get out of here." I playfully shove her with my hip. "Be safe. Have fun."

"Okay, Mom," she jokes cheerfully. "Ready?" She slips her arm over Porter's shoulder. He nods emphatically, the "ready" of a man who knows he's about to get some.

Porter takes one last swig of his beer, then wipes foam off his mouth with the side of his hand. "Nice meeting you," he says to Oliver, who he'd been regaling with talk about his job at a hedge fund, then throws his arm around Laurel and waves goodbye to me.

"See ya." I wave at their retreating backs. "Well, shall we?" I ask Oliver.

"Shall we what?" He stares at me blankly.

"Shall we go?" I raise an eyebrow. "Unless you want to stay."

He shrugs. "If you're ready to go, I can walk you home."

"Oliver," I grin, trying to make sense of the disappointed look on his face, "do you want to stay?"

He gestures toward the cocktail table where Laurel and Porter had been canoodling while we danced. "I mean, they left behind a perfectly good plate of nachos." He shakes his head in mock disgust. "I don't think they even ate any."

I laugh loudly. Laurel had wanted those nachos so badly. "Okay, nachos it is."

He holds up his glass with a pout. "And my whiskey is empty."

"I guess I did promise you a drink," I say with a small smile. "I'll be right back."

I get myself another whiskey, too, because there are a lot of nachos, and I figure we may be here a while.

"So tell me something," I say, swirling the amber liquid in my glass. "What did you really think of me when I came into the bookstore that first day?"

Oliver looks at me seriously. "You reminded me of my ex."

I choke on my drink. "Are you serious?"

He nods slowly. "Bethany also had light brown hair and exuded nervous energy." He takes a sip of his Jameson, but I see the snicker he's trying to hide before the glass covers it up.

"You're such a jerk," I say, throwing a chip at him.

"Guilty," he replies, catching it in his right hand and then eating it.

"So, tell me about Bethany. She must have been quite the woman to be able to tolerate your angst." Two can play at this game.

Oliver snorts. "She didn't tolerate it. I just hid it from her for as long as I could. And then, when she got to know me better, she decided I was 'too grumpy' for her, and she left." He lowers his fingers from the sarcastic air quotes he just drew.

My face falls. "I'm sorry. I didn't mean to bring up a sore subject."

"It's okay," he shrugs. "I met her at NEU, and she moved to

New York City after graduation. It wouldn't have worked out anyway."

I nod slowly. "So if I'm understanding you correctly, I remind you of your ex, whom you couldn't be yourself around?"

Oliver shoots me a rakish grin. "Nah, I take it back. I'm comfortable being my true dickish self around you."

Now it's my turn to snort. "You're something else." I down the rest of my whiskey. It burns all the way to my stomach, but I like it. I haven't been drunk since the night I found out about Kyle and Melinda, and I think I'm due.

"Likewise," he returns. "Are you in a hurry to leave, or something?" He gestures toward my glass.

"Oliver," I say as if making an important announcement, "I think I'd like to get drunk tonight."

His eyebrows go up. "Oh, really?"

I incline my head in affirmation. "That's my new plan for the evening. Want that second drink I promised you?"

"This was already our second drink."

"Yes, but the first one was from Laurel. This would be the second one from me."

He pauses for a moment, then nods. "Sure, why not?"

FORTY-FIVE MINUTES LATER, the volume at our table has risen several decibels, as we're down another whiskey and a half each. The nachos are gone, but they've been replaced by a platter of mozzarella sticks.

"Did I tell you why I came here this summer?" I ask, far too loudly.

"Was it to fulfill your lifelong dream of working in a bookshop?"

"No, weirdo," I respond. "That was just a fringe benefit." I grab a mozzarella stick and wave it around in the air. "Actually, it's because of a man."

Oliver nods. "Me?"

I snicker. "Definitely not. It's because of Kyle."

"Kyle?" He wrinkles his nose. "He sounds like a douche."

"You have no idea," I nod sagely. "He *cheated* on me. With the school nurse."

"Wow, those jokes just write themselves," he says, dipping a mozzarella stick in marinara.

"As it turns out, everyone at work knew but me. Apparently," I slur a little, "he wasn't as into me as I'd thought."

Oliver's considering me thoughtfully, leaning his elbows on the edge of the table.

"What?" I'm suddenly self-conscious. "Do I have food on my face, or something?"

"Nah," he says. "Just thinking."

"About what?"

He shakes his head. "Don't worry about it."

"But I want to know!" I whine.

"Just not understanding how someone could do that to you," he says quietly.

My heart skips in my chest. "What do you mean?"

His eyes settle on mine. "You're too good a person for that."

"Evidently not." I smile wryly. "Alternatively, that might have been the exact problem. I'm too good, and that's boring, and so I got taken advantage of."

Oliver shakes his head. "Nope. There's no excuse. Kyle's scum, and you deserve better." He leans toward me over the table. "Perhaps like the weirdo with the red polo?" His mouth twitches.

"Ew, no," I say, once again very loudly.

"Shh," he whispers. "Don't look now, but he's making another pass."

"You've got to be kidding me," I reply. I shoot a glance over my shoulder and see the guy, who looks like a Sperry's Docksiders ad that got trampled under a park bench, walking with intention toward our table once more.

"Let's go," Oliver says, grabbing my hand and pulling me away from the table.

"Go where?"

"To dance," he says, like he couldn't possibly have meant anything else. "It worked earlier," he shrugs.

I follow him back to the dance floor. Our hands find each other again, a little clumsier than before, thanks to the booze. His arm slides around my back, pulling me against his chest a little more tightly than when we danced earlier. I feel my breath catch in my throat.

"Wow," I chuckle awkwardly, "you saved me twice in one night."

His body is warm against mine, and I'm acutely aware of every shift of his fingers on my hand.

He chuckles softly. "Well, that guy is still staring at you from about ten feet away. I'm not sure you're in the clear just yet."

"Damn it," I whisper. "I'm so not in the mood to deal with a creeper."

Oliver grins in a way that makes me feel a little weak in the knees. What in God's name is happening to me tonight?

He's looking right at me now, but we're so close. If I fall into his gaze, I'm not sure I'll be able to get back out. I pick a spot on the far wall and stare at it for a second, trying to get my bearings.

"To be fair," he muses, "the first time I saved you was just payback for you helping me with Rachel. So maybe that one doesn't count. They cancel each other out."

"Maybe." I tap his shoulder with my pointer finger, considering. "But you wouldn't have been in that situation if I hadn't encouraged the depraved street youths in the first place."

"Hmm." Oliver's chest is firm against mine, and I sink into him a little further. He doesn't pull away. "So what you're saying is that, really, helping me with Rachel was just fixing your own mistake? And thus, I really did save you twice in one night?"

"Exactly."

"So therefore, you really do still owe me. Twice."

"Hey!" I swat playfully at his shoulder with my free hand. "Way to back me into a corner, there."

I feel his laughter vibrate against my chest.

"Fortunately, I'm very solutions-minded."

"Oh, are you?" I tease.

He nods in mock seriousness. "Absolutely. And I think we can take care of the afore-mentioned debt *and* make Mr. Red Polo go away, all with one simple act."

I dare to meet his eyes. "Oh?"

He doesn't look away. "Can I kiss you?"

I can't breathe. I don't know if it's the song, or the alcohol, or how good it feels to be held after months of heartbreak, or if it's because of how safe Oliver is making me feel right now. But my heart is palpitating like it's never beat steadily in my life, and I nod before I can talk myself out of it.

"Go ahead," I whisper.

He raises an eyebrow, then a small smile flashes across his face. He weaves his fingers through the hair on the back of my head, tips me backwards, and leans in to cover my lips with his.

I see stars. His kiss is firm, and warm, and it makes my heart pound. I don't even think; I just kiss him back, opening my lips to him and slipping my tongue inside his mouth. I'm lost in the feeling of Oliver—something I didn't anticipate, but now that I've found it, I can't imagine I ever lived without. It's like everything before this moment was a foreword, and this is the story itself.

Before I can muster a coherent thought, he pulls my face toward him more tightly as he gently guides us back to a standing position.

I realize the bit is probably supposed to be over by now, but I'm lost in a whirling eddy of emotions, and I'm not ready to stop. I slide my free hand over Oliver's cheek, down his shoulder, around his neck, pulling him to me.

God, this feels so good.

"Ivy?" he finally murmurs, breaking free.

"Mmm?" My eyelids flutter open.

He gestures with his head. "He's gone."

I nod quickly. "Thanks." I can barely catch my breath, and I don't even realize I'm staring at him until he clears his throat.

"I should probably get you home."

He probably should. But I desperately want to stay.

"Okay," I say quietly.

THE WALK back to the rental is mostly quiet. We take Bridge Lane out of town, even though the streets are pretty deserted at this point. But I'll leap at any opportunity to see the moon reflected over the ocean, so I suggest the back way.

"Nice house," Oliver says when we get to Beach Haven.

"Right?" I feel awkward now, the heat from his body radiating through the crisp night air, reminding me of the kiss we shared back at the dance hall. I'm met with the overwhelming urge to reach out and touch him again. I try to shake it off.

"Beach Haven belongs to a friend of my late grandparents. He transitioned to a nursing home a few years back, but he hired a caretaker for the house." I shift my purse on my shoulder. "Evidently she doesn't do much cleaning, but we got a great price on the rental."

Oliver laughs, offering his arm as we walk up the porch steps, which don't have a handrail. "A little dusty inside?"

"You've no idea how much." I accept his offer of help, and my stomach flip-flops at the contact. As soon as we're on the porch, I quickly let go of his arm. I can't let myself get swept up in this. Whatever *this* is.

"Well, thanks for a very...*interesting* evening," I say, leaning against the front door.

Oliver smirks. "I'm starting to get the feeling it's always a very interesting evening when you're involved."

My heart flutters like a butterfly emerging from its cocoon. "Are you suggesting *I'm* very interesting?" I ask coyly.

His pupils are huge in the dark. "Something like that," he breathes next to my cheek. He reaches out and tucks a strand of hair behind my ear.

My breath catches in my throat. I meet his gaze, pretty sure my eyes look just as inky as his do.

"Hey," I whisper. My resolve to ignore the feelings swirling through my drunken brain is unraveling rapidly.

"Hmm?" His eyes drop to my mouth.

Okay, I definitely can't breathe.

"I'm glad red polo guy was there tonight," I finally manage.

He slides his hands onto my hips and presses against me, closing the space between us. "Oh yeah? Why's that?" he murmurs against my neck, sweeping his lips along my cheek.

My hands find his shoulders. "You're a good dancer," I say through increasingly rapid breaths.

"So are you," he replies, grazing my lips with his.

I moan a little into his mouth without meaning to. That seems to encourage him, because he pushes me up against the door and slips his tongue into my mouth.

I kiss him back, running my fingers through his hair. He's sliding his fingers along the hem of my dress, then skimming up my waist over the fabric. I can feel him harden against my thigh, and it makes me long to invite him inside, to see where the night could go.

But Kyle's face flashes through my mind, the worst kind of poorly timed intrusive thought. The truth settles like lead in my chest. I can't get involved with someone at work again. Thanks to Kyle, I don't even know if I want to return to my high-paying, tenured job.

God, if I slept with Oliver, how awkward might things get at the bookstore? That dalliance would almost certainly implode, because we actually can't stand each other. Today was just a fluke.

Even worse, what if Maisie found out? I like her too much to risk the humiliation and judgment that would surely follow.

Would I even want to come back to this place that I love so much if it became tainted by memories of a hookup-gone-wrong?

"Oliver," I murmur against his skin. "We can't do this." I shake my head and push him backwards, away from me. The night air feels cold in the void he's left behind.

He raises a brow in amusement. "Do what?"

"This." I gesture between us. "Whatever is happening right now. We can't." I shake my head again, as if convincing myself. "We work together."

Oliver's eyes sweep across my face, assessing. "Okay."

"Okay?" I ask.

He looks at me quizzically, still breathing quicker than usual from the fervor of our brief makeout session. "I'm trying to respect your boundaries. Isn't that what you want?"

Words catch in my throat as I'm about to respond. Yes, I want my boundaries to be respected. And we definitely can't do this.

But some not-so-small part of me really wishes that we could, and it hurts a little to see him agree so readily.

So I settle for, "Yes, thank you." And then, "Thanks for coming out with us tonight." I force a smile. "It was fun."

He returns the grin. "It was. Surprisingly so."

A door slams shut in my mind. "And there it is."

Oliver looks taken aback. "What exactly is that supposed to mean?"

I roll my eyes. "The insults, the cynical banter. It was missing this evening. But now it's back, with your suggestion that it was a shock to enjoy my company."

"I already told you I enjoy your company." His face is impassive.

"That was when you wanted to get in my pants," I joke.

"You're not wearing pants," he teases.

"Oliver."

He wrinkles his eyebrows over his nose. "So you think I'm the kind of person who would lie to a woman just to seduce her?"

"I didn't mean it like that," I say quickly.

He takes a step backward toward the porch stairs and crosses his arms. "Then what did you mean, exactly?

"I don't know. I'm sorry. It's been a long night, and I'm pretty drunk." The high from whatever was happening between us a few moments ago is rapidly disintegrating.

"I may be a lot of things, but I'm not a liar," Oliver says earnestly. "I enjoyed spending time with you tonight, and I kissed you just now because it felt like what we both wanted, not because I was trying to trick you into bed with me."

"Okay, fine," I reply, swiping a damp curl off my forehead and wishing this conversation were over.

He's looking at me intently now, as if trying to determine whether I believe him. I guess he finds what he's looking for, because he takes another step away from me and toward the walkway. "I'm going to head home," he says.

My heart lurches a little. He looks genuinely sad that I thought the worst of him. "I really am sorry," I promise. "I had a nice time with you tonight, too."

Oliver shoots me a small smile. "Of course you did. I'm a great dancer."

I snort. "You've got that right." I want to wipe away the lingering look on his face that suggests I've deeply insulted him, but I don't know how. I settle for uptight courtesy instead. "Good night, Oliver."

"Good night, Ivy."

I watch him walk away, thinking about how good it felt to kiss him, how nice it was to be held again after being alone for so long. After being rejected, made to feel like I don't matter.

How bad it would be if I'd let him continue and things went south. How I can't afford to mess things up at the bookshop; how my heart can't take another humiliation like what happened with Kyle. And how I don't want to sully my love of this beautiful place with a mangled hookup.

I nod as Oliver fades into the night, reassuring myself that I made the right decision. And then I unlock the door and go inside, feeling surprisingly hollow despite it all.

fifteen

I wake up to my phone ringing on my nightstand. Cracking open one eye, I see that it's my mother calling.

"Damn it," I mutter blearily. I never acknowledged her message from yesterday afternoon. I got too distracted by my walk with Oliver.

Oliver. His name shoots like fire through my chest. After he left Beach Haven, my night had been restless, filled with lots of self-doubt and questioning and strange longing sensations. I'd hoped that the morning would bring some relief.

Apparently not.

My mom's voicemail yesterday was pleasant enough, but her gentle, "Hey, Ivy, thinking about you and Laurel. I had something to ask you. Please call me back," was tinged with something that sounded a lot like desperation.

I haven't spoken to her since the middle of June, when she called to wish me a happy birthday. I'd told her about my plans to go to Ogunquit with Laurel, and that was about it. She generally tries to give me the space to call her when I'm available, never wanting to get in the way of what she seems to view as my very important, busy life.

Ever since she broke my father's heart, I haven't found much of that space at all.

But I'm feeling more than a little broken inside myself, and there's just something about taking a call from my mother that seems like the right move. Aren't we all programmed to want our parents when the world beats us down or we've lost our way? Even if it's tremendously subliminal and buried deep in our psyche, I think that biological tendency is always there.

And besides, she and I have never actually acknowledged that I'm angry with her. Not out loud. Sure, we used to talk almost every day, and that stopped abruptly after November when she asked my dad to find an apartment. She must suspect there's a reason I don't call anymore, but it's not like I've ever told her I'm furious that she's ripped our family apart for seemingly no reason.

Still, I know I can't ignore her forever, no matter how wounded and confused she's made me feel over the last year. At some point, we're going to have to work through this.

I answer on the last ring.

"Hey, Mom."

"Ivy."

Guilt slices through me at the relief in her voice. She didn't think I was going to answer.

"What's up?" I'm trying to modulate my tone to sound more cheerful, and less like it's partially her fault that my insides have turned into a raw, aching mess.

She swallows hard. "I was cleaning in the basement and found a box of your old artwork. I was curious if you wanted it."

Mom's been working through the countless piles of ephemera in the damp basement of our Dover house. It's where I was raised, and, up until last fall, I thought it was where my parents were going to grow old together.

After my mother told my dad she wanted a trial separation, he got an apartment ten minutes down the road, like he was resisting the idea of giving her up with every fiber of his being. Mom stayed in the house, but she's made it clear, with no reconciliation on the horizon, that she's cleaning it out with the intent to sell.

I close my eyes, fighting back the urge to cry. "I'll take it, sure."

"Thanks. I can bring it by your condo when you get back from Maine." It's a statement, but she makes it sound like a question. Like she's unsure whether she'll be welcome.

I'm not sure, either. But I just say, "Thanks."

There's an awkward silence, and I want to fill it by asking her why. Why she was suddenly so unhappy that she had to break up our family. Why it had to happen just as Dad was dealing with the loss of his mother, with closing out her estate. Cleaning out his childhood home and ridding himself of the memories. Couldn't she have left him with some shred of his former life, rather than ripping the last vestiges of it out from under him all at once?

But I'm not certain I'm ready, either to ask the question or to understand the answer. So instead I say, "I got a job at a bookstore."

I can practically hear her smile through the phone. Her heart, so tentative, brightening back up a little with the promise that maybe I don't hate her after all.

"Ivy, that's wonderful! Tell me all about it!"

So I tell her about Shoreline, which she remembers immediately from our many trips to Maine, and Maisie, who she says sounds lovely. I don't mention Oliver, because I'm not even sure what I would say.

"Are you going to work there until you go back to school?" Mom asks.

I haven't told her much about what happened at Farnsworth; just the high-level stuff. She knows Kyle and I are broken up, and that I was feeling a little lonely, but that's about it. Taking a deep breath, I reply, "Possibly. I'm actually applying to other jobs for the fall."

"Oh! I had no idea."

Of course she didn't, because I didn't tell her. "Yep. Just thinking that maybe it's time to move on. I want more of a challenge."

"You always were a go-getter," she responds, voice full of pride.

The front door opens and shuts. I cast a quick glance at the clock—10:15. Laurel must have had quite the night.

"I try," I say. "I actually have to go. Laurel needs my help making breakfast." This may or may not be true; Laurel is probably extremely hungover, and she may actually just need some black coffee in an IV. But I'm also desperate to hear about her night with Porter and escape from my own reality a little.

"Okay, honey. Thanks for chatting!" Mom hesitates. "Call me soon, okay? I miss you."

My voice breaks. "I miss you, too."

Hanging up the phone, I slip out of bed and hurry into the kitchen, where Laurel's bent over the island, head in hands.

"Fun night, huh?"

She doesn't look up. "My head is going to split in half."

"Let me start the coffee," I offer.

OVER STRONG COFFEE and two Excedrin, Laurel regales me with tales of her evening. Porter's family owns a condo in Perkins Cove, and he's using it this summer to get a break from the city. At the moment, his parents and two sisters are back in Boston.

Laurel describes the unit as "beyond luxurious" and explains that it's up a bit of a hill, overlooking both the cove and the ocean. The unit has a fully stocked bar, and it sounds like Porter and Laurel had several more drinks each before making out a little and then falling asleep.

"I'm not even disappointed that there was no sex," she admits, sipping slowly from a chipped blue mug. "I'm glad, actually."

I raise an eyebrow. "Because you like him?"

She blushes a little. "I think I do, yeah."

"Well, that's something, right there." I pour myself a second cup of coffee. I know I should stop at one, especially given the effect caffeine tends to have on my anxiety, but I need a little more oomph to get me through this day. Too many emotions are swirling around my head.

"He's going to call me later," Laurel continues. "I think it'll be good for me to have a nice man to distract me from my dissertation."

"You have no idea how badly you need this," I reply.

She playfully hits me. "Thanks a lot."

"Hey, not to raise a sore subject," I hedge, "but when are you going to Boston to talk to Spillinger?"

She sighs. "Thursday. I'll leave early, but I think I'm going to spend the night with my parents. I plan to head back here at some point on Friday."

"Sounds good." I'll be out Thursday evening anyway for the dinner at Maisie's.

We're silent for a moment while Laurel stares off into space, probably rehashing her magical evening with Porter. I worry I might have judged him a little too harshly. I suppose just because he was dressed like a fraternity brother and works for a hedge fund doesn't mean he's a douchebag.

Suddenly, Laurel practically shouts, "Oh my God! I never asked you about your night with Oliver!"

Heat rushes up my cheeks. "There was no 'night with Oliver.'"

"Why does that blush make me doubt you?"

I squirm in my chair. If I tell Laurel what happened last night, she's going to have some opinions, with a capital O. And I'm not sure I'm ready to hear them.

On the other hand, it would be good to get some of this off my chest.

"We hung out at Harbor Lights for a while after you guys left," I say finally. "Had some drinks. Ate your nachos." I grin.

"Mmm. Were they divine?" She closes her eyes, as if imagining the taste.

"So good." I smile. "Then, we danced a little more. And then..." She's watching me expectantly, but I need a minute to consider my words. "He kissed me. Um, to scare off that guy who was coming to our table that other time?"

Her brows are almost to her hairline. "He WHAT?"

If I wasn't blushing before, I would be now. "He kissed me," I say quietly.

"OH MY GOD!" Laurel's never been great about control-ling her volume. She hits the counter for emphasis. "How did you not lead with this?"

I shake my head. "It's not going anywhere. I told him we can't...we work together. I can't do that again."

"Because of Kyle?" She scoffs when I nod. "Ivy, come on. That was a really shitty, really unique situation. That's not going to happen again."

"I can't go down that road a second time. No matter how unlikely it ending the same way might seem."

"But you're leaving at the end of the summer. Even if things went bad, it wouldn't matter."

"Exactly." I nod once for emphasis. "I'm leaving. So even if things *didn't* go bad, what's the point?"

She surveys me carefully, then asks, "But what if they were great?"

And for that, I don't really have an answer. If I leave Farnsworth, who's to say that I can't leave *for* somewhere specific? Somewhere like Ogunquit? I don't need to run away to just anywhere that will have me. I can pick the place where I want to spend my life.

And what if I *did* move here? I could date Oliver, maybe rent this cottage a while longer, and work at the bookstore. Maisie did say she'd need to find someone else in the fall, and that she wanted to step back even further.

The idea hits me all at once and is so appealing, makes so much *sense*, that the logical side of my brain immediately slams on the brakes. My head starts to shake violently as if of its own accord. No. No, no, no. I'm not quitting my job to work retail at the beach with a guy I've only kissed once. Well, a few times. A guy who probably hates me now that I've rejected him. Even if his was the best kiss of my life.

"They wouldn't be," I say quietly, putting my mug in the sink and leaving the room as quickly as I can.

LAUREL and I spend most of Sunday on the beach. The weather is perfect, with a warm breeze and just enough sunshine that the water feels shockingly comfortable. We splash in the waves, read our books, and even dig around in the sand a little with a red shovel another family accidentally left behind near our towels.

"This brings back a lot of memories," Laurel notes with a smile when the waves start encroaching on the moat we've built.

"It sure does. In the old days, we'd be scrambling backwards, trying to build a new moat in a hurry right now." I look at her questioningly, but she wrinkles her nose.

"I don't think I have it in me to scramble anywhere today."

"I don't blame you."

As recollections of our mutual pasts continue to run through my mind like a film reel, it occurs to me that I still haven't told Laurel about the few diary entries of Eleanor's I read the other day. Or about the missing pages. It's been bothering me, not knowing why the pages are gone, or what happened to the man who won our grandmother's heart at the dance hall. Why she married my grandfather if she was in love with someone else.

And I'm not sure I can really discuss this with anyone besides Laurel. At least not while my dad is still mired in grief.

I decide to go for it. "I read some more of Eleanor's diary," I begin.

"Oh?" Laurel waggles her eyebrows suggestively. "Anything juicy?"

"Well, actually," I shift up on my elbow so I'm facing her, "it seems like she might have enjoyed a physical relationship with her Prince Charming from the dance hall."

"Must run in the family." She grins smugly.

Comparing Porter to anyone my grandmother might have loved feels wrong to me, but I don't want to insult my cousin. "It sounded like Grandpa actually helped set up a picnic on the Marginal Way for Eleanor and her paramour. And she and that guy maybe...consummated their relationship there when her parents thought she was out with Janie."

Laurel gasps. "Wow, Grandma was a badass!"

I giggle a little. "Evidently."

Laurel's lying back on her towel, one arm draped over her sunglasses to block any light that might worsen her hangover. "What else happened?"

"Well, she cuts from the juicy stuff to her wedding in November. But there's actually something weird—some pages are missing in between. Almost like someone ripped them out."

My cousin doesn't react. "The binding was probably just old."

"Yeah, maybe." I've been around books long enough to know how damaging time can be. But something about *which* pages are missing still strikes me as odd. It feels like they must contain critical pieces of the story. "Doesn't it seem weird to you, though? She's falling in love with this guy, she sleeps with him, and then she marries somebody else? And all the details in between are gone?"

"Maybe." Laurel shrugs.

I drag my fingers through the sand between our towels. Grains swirl around my pink manicured nails, slipping away before I can hope to grab them. "I really want to know what happened. Maybe I'll ask Janie."

Janie still lives at home with her husband, Peter, a few minutes away from my grandparents' old house. She's fairly sharp, especially for her 80s, and she might remember what precipitated my grandparents' apparently abrupt nuptials.

Now Laurel sits up and looks right at me. "I don't think you should do that."

"Why not?"

She shakes her head once, twice, three times. "You're always complaining about how grief-stricken your dad is. How do you think Janie is feeling?"

Her words cut like the dullest knife in the drawer. The pain lingers, slicing through me slowly and leaving plenty of jagged edges.

"I'm not 'always complaining' about my dad," I retort, still reeling at the implication that I've been whining about my father. That his grief is somehow not real and it's just something I've made up for attention.

She looks like maybe she's going to apologize, but she just shakes her head again. "Please don't bother Janie with this. Everybody is working hard to heal. And at the end of the day, it doesn't matter what happened. Grandma and Grandpa fell in love and had a wonderful life together. Who cares about that other guy?"

I stare at her for a beat. It had certainly seemed like *she* cared, not even two minutes ago, when she was wildly entertained by the idea of my grandmother having sex on a cliff with some guy she met at a club.

I consider telling her I'll let it go. But deep down, I know I won't. I can't.

So I brush off my hands. "I'm going to head back and grab a shower. I'll see you later." I stab the shovel into the sand and walk away before she has a chance to respond.

sixteen

The work week flies by. Maisie is right—we are incredibly busy, both with customers and with preparations for the author event on Wednesday.

I'm a little nervous to see Oliver on Monday, given what happened at Harbor Lights. When I get to work, he's carrying five folding chairs in each arm like it's nothing to the children's story area where the book reading is going to take place. "I left a list for you on the counter," he says over his shoulder as he passes.

I stash my cardigan and a protein bar in the break room and go check out the tasks he's scrawled on a Shoreline notecard next to the register. *Set up display of signed books, stock cookies in the café, call Ruggerio's to ensure delivery of footlong subs,* and on and on and on. The list is long, but I'm comfortable tackling everything on it.

The work keeps me busy for most of the day. At 2:30, Oliver stops running around the store like a madman and swings past the register, where I've just finished checking out a very polite teenaged boy who was buying the entire *Eragon* series.

"How's it going?" Oliver's gaze is inscrutable beneath the dark fringe of his eyelashes.

I'm pretty sure mine is not. Now that he's standing before me, I want nothing more than to rehash the events of the weekend, to try to fix the mess I've made of things. I've never had a very good poker face, but I try to mask my feelings as much as possible. "So far so good," I muster. "Lots to do, but we'll be fine."

He nods. "Maisie should be in soon. She had to go to the doctor this morning about her knee."

"Oh no! I'm worried about her."

"Me too," he agrees. "She needs to take it easy. That's why I'm trying to get as much done as possible before she gets here."

"Of course." My eyes sweep over his face, desperate for some indication that he's still remembering what it felt like to kiss me. Because ever since I saw him this morning, that's basically all I can think about.

"I should get back to work," he says quietly, dropping his gaze to my lips for just a fraction of a second.

But it's long enough that I notice. Long enough that it sends a wave of warmth through my entire body. A wave of hope, and of something a lot like lust.

"Sounds good," I murmur.

TUESDAY'S MUCH THE SAME. I manage to have several amazing conversations with customers who are looking for very specific sorts of beach reads. It gives me no small amount of joy when they all tell me my suggestions are "just right."

Maisie's hobbling around Shoreline all day, her knee in a brace. Oliver and I try to shoo her away about three thousand times, but she insists on helping get everything ready for Wednesday. Oliver reminds her that scrubbing the windows and dusting the tops of the bookshelves won't matter for the reading, but Maisie is committed to everything being absolutely perfect. He and I exchange a look, then we grab the rags and cleaning solutions from her and get to work on it ourselves.

"Can you hand me that bottle?" I ask, teetering on tiptoe atop a stepladder that's just a bit too short for me to comfortably reach the top shelf of the New Release section.

"How about I just switch with you?"

I glare down at him. "I'm fine." He'd already tried repeatedly to get me to do the lower shelves, but I don't know if I can handle watching his extremely toned body while he cleans right next to me, so I told him I'd be fine on the stepladder.

He hands me the bottle wordlessly, and I almost fall again. I guess letting go of the bookshelf to turn and grab the cleaning solution wasn't the best idea. My arms flail stupidly around in the air while I try to regain my balance.

Oliver must have the world's quickest reflexes, because his hands are on my waist before I even know what's happening. And thank God, because right after he grabs me, I lose my battle with gravity and fall backwards against his chest.

He lowers me to the ground with an amused laugh. "You're fine, huh?"

I hate how good it feels to be held by him. I whirl to face him. "I would have been fine."

He smirks. "What you would have been is laid out on the floor with a concussion."

He's right, and I know it, so I just say, "Fine. You clean the top shelves."

We stand there staring at each other for a moment. His face is only inches away, and the image of his slight smile before he kissed me on Saturday night flashes through my mind. My heart starts galloping around inside my chest.

I don't know what Oliver's thinking about, exactly, but it looks like he's blushing. He clears his throat. "I'll, uh. I'll dust the top shelves." He crosses in front of me to climb the stepladder.

Let's just say I don't get much cleaning done after that.

MAISIE ASKS us both to come in early on Wednesday to get ready for the reading, which is at noon. When I drop off my cardigan, she's in the back chatting with the author, Sue Brinkman.

Sue writes children's books about a teddy bear who has misadventures all around the globe. She's got a bit of a cult following, so being able to book her when countless families are in town for summer vacation is a dream come true for Maisie. We're anticipating a lot of sales after the reading.

Maisie introduces me to Sue, then tells me to go ask Oliver how I can help him get ready. I find him making coffee for a few middle-aged women who look like they fell asleep in the sun. I wait patiently off to the side to see what he needs me to do first.

"Here," he says when the customers walk away, sliding a latte toward me.

"Oh." My voice catches in my throat. "Thank you." I try to smile, but it feels stilted because of how hard it is to breathe right now.

He quirks up a brow. "You okay?"

I nod, maybe a little too emphatically. "Fine."

"Is this the same way you were fine yesterday?"

I glower. "Shut up."

Oliver swings out from behind the counter, then closes the distance between us, shooting me a roguish smile. He leans forward, lips against my ear, and whispers, "Still thinking about my tongue in your mouth?"

My grip on the mug loosens and it slips out of my hands, shattering on the floor in a cacophony of ceramic and froth. The women with lobster tans turn around to see what the noise was.

I throw my hand over my face, which I'm pretty sure is the same color as their skin. "Oh my God," I moan.

Oliver looks torn between laughing and consoling me, but instead, he jumps back to the espresso machine and grabs a few rags. "It's okay," he says quietly, handing me one. "I think that was my fault."

I try to erase my mortified look and glare at him instead, but I'm guessing my expression comes across as a jumble of idiocy. "I don't even have words."

He's wiping up the floor on his hands and knees, trying to gingerly sweep the broken mug pieces into a pile with his rag. I figure I should probably help, so I squat down and start running my cloth over the floor, too.

His mouth tips up on one side. "That's a first."

I raise my eyes to him, jaw dropping. "Are you kidding me?"

"What?" His eyes are full of mirth. I both love and hate how amusing he's finding this.

I inch a little closer to him so no one can overhear. "First, you make me a latte, then you mock me, then you toss a provocative image my way and make me spill said beverage, and *now* you're going to make fun of me further?"

"What I'm taking from this is that you find me provocative."

I groan in frustration. "I'm going to get the broom." And I stomp away before he can figure out that I am absolutely, 100 percent, still thinking about his tongue in my mouth.

THE BOOK READING GOES SMOOTHLY. We get around 60 attendees, 25 of whom are children. I love how animated Sue is when she tells her story, and how comfortable she is with the kids. They're completely invested, hanging on her every word—shouting warnings to the bear in the story when he's about to fall into a honey pot, cheering when he saves his friend, Bunny, from the top of a tree.

Maisie sits next to Sue up front, grinning from ear to ear the entire time. I can only imagine what it must mean to her, after 43 years of running this shop on her own, to be able to sit back and watch people enjoy a universe of stories under her roof. It makes me a little teary to think about making the world brighter like that.

Oliver and I sit in the back, on two folding chairs we set up off to the side. We need to keep an eye on the register in case other customers come in. The display of Sue's books that I'd set up on Monday is blocking my view, so I have to peer around Oliver to see if anyone's at the counter.

On the third such occasion, he leans toward me. "What are you doing?" he asks in a low voice.

"Just making sure there's no one at the counter," I whisper.

A smile starts. "The bell will jingle if anyone comes in."

"I just want to be sure."

The smile hits his eyes now, and he reaches out to pat my knee. "You're adorable. But don't worry about it; I can see the register from where I'm sitting. I've got it covered."

My brain tries to process the feeling of his hand on my leg. It tries to process the smile on his face. But instead, I spend the rest of the reading sitting there, the words "you're adorable" running endlessly through my mind like the stock ticker in Times Square.

seventeen

Things at Beach Haven have been weird since Laurel asked me not to call Janie, and I'm not ashamed to admit I've been looking forward to today. First and foremost, because it's the day Laurel's heading back to Boston, so I can call Janie without her knowing.

And besides, I need some space from my cousin, who's been giving me major attitude. I think our argument, plus the stress of her dissertation drama, has been getting to her in a big way.

I've also been excited for today because of the dinner at Maisie's, which I'm pretty sure is going to be adorable.

You're adorable. Oliver's face flashes through my mind. I shake my head, trying to clear the image.

"Good luck with Spillinger," I tell Laurel as she shoulders her purse and her pink duffel bag.

"Thanks." She slides on her sunglasses and spins her keys around her finger. "I'll see you late tomorrow sometime."

I nod and walk her to the door. As soon as the sound of her

car's engine fades, I grab my phone off the counter and head to my room to get Eleanor's diary.

There's only the briefest of moments where doubt flashes through my mind, but I brush it away. I have to know. I *have* to.

Sinking onto the mattress, I find Janie in my contacts and box breathe while I wait for her to pick up. *One two three four, one two three four.* This is far more nerve-wracking than I expected.

"Hello?" Janie sounds surprised to be answering her phone, but I suppose she probably doesn't get many calls. She and Peter never had any children, and I know many of their friends have passed away in the last few years.

I think my dad and my Uncle Gregory try to visit her a couple of times a month, but Janie's probably pretty isolated. Suddenly, I feel very guilty for not calling more. For only calling now, when I want something. Something she may not be prepared to offer.

"Hi, Aunt Janie," I say, smiling even though she can't see me. "It's Ivy, Eleanor's granddaughter." I assume she'll know who I am, but, out of context, just "Ivy" might not be enough.

"Oh, hello, Ivy." Her voice warms. "It's wonderful to hear from you."

Guilt continues shoving against the edges of my mind, vying for an opening. I do my best to clear it and focus on the task at hand.

"How are you?" It's the least I can do to make pleasant conversation before getting to the tough stuff.

"Oh, you know. I'm all right. I've got a new medication for my diabetes that's giving me some trouble. And Peter hurt his hip. But, all things considered, I can't really complain."

I know when people Janie's age say they can't really

complain, what they actually mean is that they're lucky to be alive at all. "I'm glad you're doing pretty well, all things considered." I echo her words, hoping that's the right response.

"And how are you, dear? Your father told me that you and Laurel were going to the beach for the summer?"

So I guess my dad is keeping up with his familial obligations. If only my mother could do the same. Where he's concerned, that is.

"Yes, we are. Renting a house from Simon Foster until the end of August. It's been lovely so far."

The other line is silent for a moment, then Janie says, "Simon Foster. Well, I'll be."

Now it's my turn to be at a loss for words. What's so surprising about Simon Foster, I wonder? Thankfully, Janie speaks again, so I don't need to come up with a reply.

"It's been a long time since I've heard from Simon. How's he doing?"

Between this line of questioning and Maisie's comment about Simon's leg, I'm feeling like I might be the worst person on Earth for not visiting Simon to check in. "I think he's okay," I reply. "I guess he hurt his leg." At least that's an honest reply.

"Oh, that's too bad."

"He's in an assisted living facility now. Out near Wells." Before I can reconsider, I add, "I'm planning to visit him while we're in town."

"That's wonderful," Janie answers. "That would make your grandparents so happy. Especially Charlie. They were so close."

I feel my opening fading away with every passing second. "So, I have a strange question for you." I close my eyes tightly, willing myself to keep going. "I've been reading Eleanor's diary.

Um, we found it during the cleanout. And it looks like there might be some pages missing."

Silence. Complete and utter silence.

"Um." I try again. "It could just be damage from 66 years of use and storage, of course. But the diary mentions some things that I think the missing pages might resolve. And I'm just..." My voice breaks a little. "I'm just trying to get to know her better." I rub my thumb over the book in my hands.

Janie is quieter now. "What do you want to know?"

I'm not sure I expected this to be so easy. "Well," I begin, voice growing stronger. "It sounds like she met a gentleman at Harbor Lights, the dance hall. Maybe the summer you were 16, and she was 18?"

Janie chuckles. "Oh, she certainly did."

I knew I was onto something here. "Do you know his name?"

"It was George. George Marlowe."

My mind hurries to mash the name onto the blurry image it's painted of a tall, handsome man in a blue blazer. "It sounds like Grandma Ellie really loved him."

Janie coughs. "She did, yes."

I'm definitely not going to ask her about the sex. That would be far too weird. "It seems like she married my grandfather a few months after she met George. I just...I found it surprising, given how she described her..." The words "torrid love affair" flash through my mind, but I tame them into "summer romance" before I let them leave my lips.

"George was charming, and Eleanor loved him dearly. But things fell apart very quickly there. Thank God for Charlie. He saved her from a very difficult life."

A very difficult life? "What do you mean, exactly?"

Janie sighs. "Some things are better left in the past."

I want to bang my head against the wall. I'm so close; I can't give up now. "Did George...did he hurt her?"

"I think he hurt her very much," Janie says softly.

My chest pangs at the thought of *anyone* hurting my sweet, gentle grandmother, never mind someone she cared about. At the image of my grandfather, heroic and romantic, swooping in and saving her. Making her believe in love again.

"Do you know what George did?" I ask quietly.

"It's best left in the past," Janie says again. "Thank you so much for calling, Ivy. Let's catch up again soon, okay?"

No, I want to shout! This conversation can't be over! Not when I've come so close to finding answers.

But Laurel's words flash through my mind. *Everybody is working hard to heal,* she'd said. And Janie clearly isn't willing to relive these painful memories. At least not today.

So I thank Janie for chatting, then I let her go. And I don't bother trying to stop the tears of frustration when they fall.

eighteen

After my disappointing call with Janie, I lick my wounds for a bit, then I remember I need to make something to bring to Maisie's house tonight. In addition to cooking dinner for us, she insisted that both Oliver and I take today off. There's no way I'm showing up empty-handed.

I scour the kitchen cabinets for cookbooks, but I come up woefully short. I try to google various recipes, but I don't have great cell service today. The meteorologists are calling for pretty major storms tonight and tomorrow, and there's an awful lot of cloud cover.

There has to be some sort of cookbook in this house. It occurs to me that I could check the attic. Laurel and I had noticed the pull-down stairs above the hallway our first day at Beach Haven. If I use the step stool from the kitchen, I can probably reach.

Shielding my head with one arm just in case a mountain of dust is about to fall on me, I pull the stairs down and gently test them with my foot. They feel a little wobbly, but I think they're solid enough for me to make my ascent.

The attic is sweltering, to the point that I can barely breathe. I desperately look around for a window I can crack open for a few minutes. Spying one on the far side of the room, I skirt around boxes covered in years of accumulated dust, sashaying my way across. The window, unsurprisingly, is almost impossible to budge, but I finally get it open with a shove the likes of which I never thought I was capable.

Sticking my head out the window as far as it will go, I gasp in the muggy outdoor air, which feels refreshing in contrast to the attic. I run my hands through my hair, trying to get it off my neck, which is already slick with sweat.

Most of the boxes up here are labeled in elegant script. *Christmas decorations*, one proclaims. *Winter blankets*, says another. *Photo albums*, declares a third.

I know I'm here to look for a cookbook, but the photo albums box calls to me. I wonder if Simon has any pictures of my grandparents.

When I slide the interlocking flaps of the carton open, they fling another cloud of dust into the air. Coughing, I fan my hands in front of my face in an attempt to filter it. I'm not sure it works very well, because I sneeze several times in rapid succession when particulate flies up my nose.

The albums inside the box vary in size, but they're all black, and every last one has a white label on the spine with a date. I start rummaging through the box, pulling out albums as I go. 1945 is the earliest one I see. 1946 to 1948. 1951.

I wasn't really sure what I was looking for when I started, but when my eye snags on the volume from 1953, I grab it immediately. This is the year of George and whatever heart-break he brought along with him. Shifting to the wooden planks beneath the open window, I settle in for a journey to the past.

Simon has several photos of Beach Haven standing proud along the dunes. One such picture features a middle-aged couple, who I assume must be his parents. It hits me that this house has likely been in their family for several generations.

There are photos of gulls on the beach, and one of a skittering crab trying to make off with part of a sandwich in its claw. I see a young man who resembles the Simon I knew from dinners past, before the years gifted him wisdom and wrinkles.

And then there's a face that's very familiar: Grandpa Charlie. My breath catches in my throat. He's smiling widely at the camera, a very familiar expression on his lips. I rack my brain for where I've seen that look, but it doesn't immediately hit me.

Flipping the page, I see several more photos of Charlie dressed in the same outfit, probably all taken on one day. His pictures give the vibe of test shots an excited photographer takes with their best friend upon getting a new camera.

About two-thirds of the way through the album, I spot a picture of my grandmother. She's lithe and gorgeous, hair gleaming in the sunshine, laughing at the edge of the shore. A stunningly handsome man in striped swim trunks rests his arm on her shoulder, a grin on his own face indicating that he was the one to make her laugh. Could this be George?

And next to them, so far off to the side that he was almost out of the picture, was my grandfather, smiling at the camera in that same secret way.

Something's tugging at the edge of my brain, but it flickers so faintly I can't make it out. Shaking my head, I shut the album and lay it gently on the floor under the window. I need to keep looking for a cookbook if there's any hope of making something before I have to get ready for Maisie's.

Fortunately, it's not long before I find a box labeled "Kitchen," and a red-and-white checkered cookbook is lying right on top. "Bingo," I say to myself. I grab the book and race back down the stairs, eager to get away from the must and memories in the attic.

After wiping the cookbook with a damp paper towel to rid it of any lingering dust, I lay it out on the counter and run a finger down the contents page. Appetizers, canning, candy; something called "jiffy recipes." Sounds like the perfect main course to pair with an aspic. "How old is this cookbook?" I muse out loud. Quick breads, pies. Then, an idea hits me. We *are* in Maine, after all.

Digging through the fridge, I find two pints of blueberries that Laurel and I had grabbed at the farmer's market over the weekend, plus milk and butter. I know we have flour, salt, and sugar. And it looks like Simon has a pie plate under the stove. I think a blueberry pie would be perfect.

The cookbook offers instructions for giving your fruit pie a lattice top, and I'm struck by an uncharacteristic desire to make art through pastry. I'm not a particularly good chef, and I've never attempted to make food pretty before, but impressing Maisie feels very important to me. She's the sweetest person on earth, and she deserves something delicious and beautiful as a thank you for inviting us into her home.

Rising to the level of Oliver's "unbeatable" chocolate raspberry cheesecake is only a small part of my sudden resolve to accomplish this.

Impressing him with my latticework? That may be a slightly larger part.

. . .

WHIPPING up the filling is a cinch, and rolling out the pie crust is only slightly more challenging. Where I really start to falter is with the latticework, which requires precision and a steady hand. And apparently I have neither.

I'm not thrilled with how everything looks when I'm done, but it will have to do. I barely have enough time to bake the pie and let it cool before I'm due at Maisie's.

Just as I lay my last piece of protective aluminum foil over the lattice, my phone buzzes in my pocket. *Are you wearing your curtain dress tonight?*

I snort. Leave it to Oliver to refuse to let a joke die. *It depends. What are you wearing?*

Well, if you're dressing up, I guess I will, too.

Gray or black Henley? I imagine his eyes crinkling in amusement as he reads my text.

Black seems fancier.

I actually hadn't been planning on dressing up tonight, but now that Oliver's mentioned my green dress, I sort of want to wear it. *I'm sure we'll impress Maisie with our sense of style.*

Oh, indubitably, he texts back.

I'll probably have to throw on a sweater for modesty's sake, but I can curl my hair like I did last weekend.

I can't believe I'm excitedly planning an outfit to wear to dinner at my boss's house. Funny how life changes you over time.

My phone vibrates again just as I slide the pie into the oven. *Did you need a ride?*

At the notion of getting picked up and driven somewhere by Oliver, my heart flip-flops a little. The idea feels a little date-like, even though I know it isn't. But I want it to be, and that's why I probably need to say no. Besides, if I didn't feel like walking, I could take my own car, anyway.

Oh, it's not far; I'll walk. But thank you.

Cool. See you later.

STANDING before the mirror in my green dress and a white cardigan, blueberry pie in hand, I feel pretty confident. My hair looks amazing, even without Laurel's intervention. I wish I'd done it on my own last Saturday; it might have gone a long way toward wiping the smug look off her face.

The sky's a little green when I leave for Maisie's house. She lives just outside of town along Route 1, but she told me it's only about a mile from Beach Haven. I figure it'll take me about 25 minutes at the most to walk there. I'd say less, but I'm carrying a liquidy pie covered in cling wrap that doesn't seem to want to stick, so I want to be sure my steps are as even as possible.

When I arrive at Maisie's adorable gray bungalow exactly 22 minutes later, I see two vehicles in the driveway: her blue Subaru hatchback and a black truck that looks like it's seen better days. Oliver typically walks to Shoreline, but given his offer of a ride earlier, I realize the truck must be his.

I'm thinking that he doesn't strike me as a truck guy when the door swings open. Maisie peeks at the sky nervously, then waves me over. "Ivy, come inside! It's looking rather stormy out here."

I don't think I'm going to be swept away by gale-force winds in the 20 feet from here to her front door, but I hurry anyway, glancing anxiously down at the pie with every step.

Thankfully, the filling stays within my novice latticework without issue.

Maisie greets me with a warm hug. "Thank you so much for bringing that pie! It looks delicious!"

I hand it to her, and she swooshes away into the kitchen.

"Oliver, grab Ivy a drink, would you? I need to check on the roast."

It's then that I notice him, hovering in the corner of the room. He's wearing a black Henley and jeans. I hide a snicker.

"Laughing at my outfit?" His eyes twinkle just like I imagined earlier.

I smirk. "Nope."

His eyes trail down my body. "Well, I like yours. A lot."

"Oliver!" Our conversation from last weekend about closing the door on an *us* seems so distant. It's been slipping away bit by bit all week, with every quip, every look, every touch. I'm starting to forget why I thought he and I together was such a bad idea.

"My sincerest apologies," he offers with a rakish grin. He definitely doesn't look sorry. "What can I get you to drink?"

"What are my options?"

"Maisie has everything," he says, putting his arm around my shoulders and guiding me gently into the dining room. "Provided you want water, seltzer, or gin."

I chuckle. "Gin it is."

Oliver runs off to fetch my drink, and I look around Maisie's dining room. She has a triptych of black-and-white photos on the wall above a sideboard. It looks like the center one is of Shoreline, a much younger Maisie standing out front.

The picture on the right shows two kids on the beach; I assume the short, curly-haired girl is also Maisie. Then, on the left, there's a formal family portrait, with the same two children and their parents.

The whole dining room plays off the black and white theme, actually. The table is stained black, with white cushions on the matching Shaker-style chairs. There are three place settings, one at the head of the table, and two on either side, all featuring white bone china and crisp linen napkins. The chandelier above casts sparkles across the glaze on the plates.

The hand-knotted rug under the table is black and white, also, with dashes of blue here and there. A cream-colored vase with blue hydrangeas that look just like the ones outside of Shoreline takes a place of honor at the center of the table.

Oliver returns with my drink a couple of minutes later. "I wasn't sure how you took it," he says apologetically.

I take a small sip. "This way's fine."

He gives me a questioning glance. "You didn't know until just now that there were different ways to serve it, right?"

"Well, there's a gin and tonic," I say, hoping to convince him I know my way around a cocktail bar.

"Very good." His mouth is tipping up. "What else?"

"Um. With ice? On the rocks?"

He fights a good-natured chuckle. "Yes, those are the same thing."

I nod. "I knew that." I most assuredly did not. "Then there's neat, and um...messy?"

He raises an amused eyebrow. "Messy gin?"

"Yeah, you know. Like a dirty martini." I grin broadly at how silly I'm being. I know nothing about drinks.

Oliver laughs out loud. "Oh, Ivy."

"What?" I pretend to glower at him, just to make a point.

"Nothing. You make me laugh."

Just then, Maisie hobbles back in. I notice she's still wearing her knee brace.

"Now, who's making who laugh?"

I'm pretty sure my face is the color of a beet.

Oliver swoops in with, "Oh, Ivy was just telling me a joke."

"I want to hear your joke, Ivy. Shall we head to the living room to wait for the roast? It still needs a bit."

We troop behind Maisie, Oliver hiding a snicker. I have no joke. Now I have to think of one or seem like a fool. And I don't think well on my feet.

When we get to the living room, Maisie plops down into a blue floral armchair. "You two take the couch," she gestures.

What she calls a couch is most definitely a loveseat. But not the kind they make in the twenty-first century; the old colonial-looking ones that are basically only big enough for one.

I stand awkwardly in front of it, waiting for Oliver to say something. Something like, "No, Maisie, we can't both sit here, because Ivy will essentially be in my lap, and ever since I repeatedly stuck my tongue down her throat, we cannot be in close proximity to one another."

But instead, Oliver sits down, then pats the cushion next to him. "Plenty of room for you, Ivy. Have a seat. Then you can tell Maisie your joke."

nineteen

Maisie doesn't stop trying to throw Oliver and me together for the rest of the night. She asks him to pull out my chair before I sit down, then shares stories of all the times he's been a "true hero" and gotten her out of a bind at the bookshop. He entertains the stories with a blush and a smile, rolling the praise away like it's nothing. She compliments my dress and asks what he thinks, which elicits *quite* the look on his end. Then, she tells me about the time he took her out on his father's boat to lift her spirits when her vacation was cancelled.

"And you should see his writing," Maisie is saying as we sip after-dinner tea. "He's really got a way with words."

Oliver's eyes are downcast with embarrassment. "Oh, I don't know about that."

She nods emphatically. "It's true! You should see the poems he writes in that notebook of his when he takes his breaks, Ivy. It's the stuff of laureates."

My brows go all the way to my hairline. Suddenly, the

library books he secreted away make a lot more sense. "I didn't know you were a poet, Oliver." I try not to sound like I'm teasing him, because I'm actually shocked. But then again, there have been a lot of layers of Oliver that have surprised me as I've gotten to know him better.

"I just dabble," he shrugs. Something in my chest swells.

"But that isn't true," Maisie insists. "You've won all those contests!" She turns to me, shaking her head earnestly. "And he even had a column in a poetry journal for a while."

"I picked it back up again a few months ago, actually," Oliver says, taking a sip of his tea.

"Oh! That's wonderful," Maisie replies. "I had no idea. You just let me know if you need more time away from the shop so you can do that work, won't you?"

Oliver smiles gently. "I don't think you could afford to have me away from the store, Maisie."

"Like I couldn't handle it on my own?"

"Well, your knee is proving a bit of a hindrance."

Maisie leans toward me conspiratorially. "Ivy and I could handle it, right?"

I grin. "Oh, definitely. Anything to let you get back to your writing, Oliver."

He scowls. "Why do I feel like the two of you are ganging up on me?"

"That's because we are, dear," Maisie says, trying not to smile over the top of her teacup.

I snicker. "But it's for your own good. Sounds like you need time to pursue your true passion."

Before Oliver can reply, Maisie jumps in her seat. "Oh! I just realized I have one of his poems here. I'll get it so you can take a gander."

"Oh, I don't think that's nec..." he begins, but she cuts him off.

"Nonsense, Oliver. Ivy needs to read it! Your piece in *The Fountain* is pure magic." She jumps out of her chair, swears loudly, mumbles "Forgot about the knee," and then hobbles as quickly as her short legs can carry her down the hallway. "I'll be right back!"

"So you write beautiful poetry, huh?" From across the table, I take in Oliver's dark edges, his masculine wit, his smug stoicism. And somehow he's also got the soul of a poet? I don't think I've ever found him more attractive than right at this moment. But I can't let him know that, so I'm trying to mask it with snark.

He's looking at me with a glint in his eye. "Try to restrain yourself, Ivy."

My jaw drops. "Excuse me?"

"You're practically salivating." He smirks. "And besides, Maisie's basically my grandmother. Just because she says my poetry is beautiful doesn't mean it actually is."

I guess my poker face has failed me once again. "I'll be the judge of that," I say quietly.

Maisie bustles back into the room. "Here it is, I found it!" She holds up a cream-colored magazine triumphantly. "He's right near the beginning, on page seven." She passes the periodical to me and reclaims her seat at the head of the table.

Casting an amused glance at Oliver, who suddenly looks more than a little nervous, I open to page seven and smooth the paper down on the table. Then I begin to read.

Safe Harbor
by Oliver Clarke

The cove beckons along the shore,
Promising halcyon days and respite—
From the past,
From the terror of the open sea,
From the unknown.

It welcomes ships that sail on uneven keels;
Vessels that are no longer seaworthy.
Its lighthouse a beacon, steadfast in its oath:
Of help, of shelter, of harbor.
Safe harbor.

For the shores are rocky,
And the waves are deep,
And the open ocean brings a host
Of uncertainties.

In the cove, troubles are few.
In the cove, adventures are few.
The hulls of the ships rot at their docks,
Starved for the waves that will set them free.
Safe harbor.

I CLEAR my throat and raise my eyes back to Oliver, who is watching me intently. "This is spectacular."

His expression relaxes, but almost imperceptibly. "I'm glad you like it."

I wouldn't even say I like it. It's heartbreaking. Completely, utterly heartbreaking. Because as much as one could assume this is just the brainchild of a man raised near the ocean, I know better. This poem is both a love letter, and a warning. To the idea of staying put, of growing roots, but never wings. Of never living life on your terms for fear of the unknown.

I had no idea Oliver felt so trapped.

So I smile gently and tell him he's truly talented. And Maisie grins, and then says it's time for dessert. We ooh and ahh over Oliver's cheesecake, which is without question far better than Maisie let on, and they pretend my pie is even remotely in the same league. Then we retire to the living room with gin (Maisie and me) and tea (Oliver), laughing and talking as if something huge wasn't laid out here tonight.

Because now I know the truth. Beneath his sarcastic exterior, Oliver is terrified. Terrified, and desperate to leave this town behind and harness agency over his own life. I don't know what it means that I feel my heart breaking for him.

"NOW, OLIVER," Maisie says an hour later, her brown eyes glinting. "I want you to drive Ivy home."

"Oh, that's okay," I start to protest. "I can—"

"It's after dark, and I won't have you wandering around by yourself." She shakes her head rapidly. "You'd be surprised how crazy the drunks in town get."

Oliver shoots me a furtive glance. "I think we've encountered some of those."

I laugh, thinking of Rachel and her friends. "A ride would be great," I say, both to pacify Maisie and because the idea of riding home on the bench seat of Oliver's truck is strangely appealing.

Oliver nods, slipping his pointer finger through his key ring. "No problem. Maisie, thank you so much for dinner."

"Yes, it was wonderful," I echo.

She hugs us both, then hustles us toward the door. "I want you to get home before the storm hits."

Once we're outside, Oliver opens the passenger-side door and offers me a hand up into his truck.

"Thank you," I mumble, taking his hand and stepping up. Just like at Harbor Lights, I'm struck by how soft his skin is.

We don't say much at first as Oliver navigates expertly down Ogunquit's back roads, carefully avoiding any of the main streets that might be clogged with late-night revelers.

"That was an interesting evening," I offer finally.

It's too dark to tell, but I'm pretty sure his eyes are twinkling by the way he says, "Whatever do you mean?"

"Oliver."

"Are you perhaps referring to the way Maisie attempted to throw us together at every possible turn?

I chuckle. "You know I am."

He clears his throat a little uncomfortably. "Yeah. I'm sorry about that."

"Don't be."

"It's just that I'm probably the closest thing to family Maisie's got. She's very...*invested* in my happiness."

"Or at least what she perceives would make you happy," I retort.

He doesn't respond, and I worry I've offended him somehow. Insulted his relationship with Maisie, maybe, by suggesting that she doesn't actually know him well enough to gauge what he wants.

Or is he hesitating because being with me would, in fact,

make him happy? My palms start to shake at the thought, so I splay my fingers and press my hands against my thighs, willing them to stay still.

Oliver throws on his directional to turn down the side street where Beach Haven is waiting, stoic beneath the stormy sky.

I need to break this awkward silence somehow. "See, I told Maisie I could have walked home. It's only about a mile."

He shrugs, pulling up to the house and turning off the engine. "I really didn't mind."

The only sound then is the wind, which is picking up its tempo rather impressively outside the truck. Oliver's looking over at me, shadows clinging to his face like they're old friends, and it occurs to me that I don't want to go inside.

"That cheesecake was divine, by the way," I say with a grin. "You're clearly a man of many talents."

Oliver smiles in the darkness, so broadly you'd think I just confessed my undying affection. It does something to me, knowing that my praise has that effect on him.

"What are these other talents of which you speak?" he asks with a magnetism I'm struggling to fight.

"Okay, now you're just fishing for compliments," I tease.

He smirks. "Maybe."

"Well," I begin, willing to take the bait, "you're also a brilliant writer."

Now I know he's blushing. "I don't know if I'd say that."

"No, but I would. And anyway, I'm the literary expert."

His hand is only an inch away from mine on the bench seat. It's calling to me, a beacon of warmth that I want to submit to so badly.

"That's true," he admits. "You are definitely the last word in great writing."

"Your poem was heartbreaking," I admit. I could say more, but I'm not sure where to begin.

He breathes deeply. "No one's ever perceived it that way before."

"No?"

"Nope." He shakes his head. "But it broke my heart to write it, so I think it must mean something that you picked up on the feelings beneath the surface."

My heart thuds in my chest. *It must mean something?* What is he implying? The air in the truck is too hot; too thick. I feel like I can't breathe. "Well, it's that whole literary expert thing," I finally manage.

We stare at each other in the dark. The moment is heavily charged, and I simultaneously want to taste him and to wrap my arms around the damaged pieces of his heart and make them whole again.

Oliver breaks the tension with a grin. "So, what are my other talents?"

I laugh out loud. "Um. Well, I like your shirt," I tentatively run my finger along the sleeve of his Henley, wondering if this is too far, but wanting it so badly. "It's very...flattering." I've been hardly able to keep my eyes off it all night. Both because of how he looks, and because of how his chest felt against mine last weekend.

I can practically see the wheels turning in his mind, but he doesn't budge. "My shirt is not a talent," he finally returns.

"No, but your ability to wear it just might be." I flash him a flirtatious grin and reach out to squeeze his hand.

"Ivy," Oliver says quietly, peeling my hand off his. "What are you doing?"

My face falls. "What do you mean?"

He looks directly into my eyes then. "You know exactly what I mean. You were very clear that this couldn't happen." He gestures between us, just like I had when he kissed me after Harbor Lights.

"What if I changed my mind?"

He shakes his head. "You had a lot of gin at Maisie's tonight. On the rocks," he adds with a twist of his lips, as if I still might not remember.

I don't acknowledge his joke. "I changed my mind before the gin. And you've been flirting with me all week."

Oliver looks more than a little sad. "There's a difference between flirting and acting on it."

I swallow a little harder than usual. "I know. I'm sorry."

"Look," he begins. "Just because Maisie likes to meddle doesn't mean you need to force something you're not comfortable with."

"I—" I'm not sure what to say. I don't think the molten lava flowing from my heart all the way down to between my thighs whenever Oliver's around has anything to do with something Maisie said. Nor does the way reading his poem makes me want to learn everything there is to know about him.

But Oliver's still just sitting there, staring at me from the shadows. Respecting my boundaries. Letting me direct the conversation. Waiting for me to decide.

And in that moment, it occurs to me that maybe he deserves a little better than my jumble of emotions. Maybe he deserves someone who knows what they want and is ready to commit. Someone who doesn't oscillate between ready and not in the space of just a week.

Maybe I owe myself that, too.

"I'm sorry," I say again, taking a shaky breath. I grab

Simon's pie plate and pop the handle on the truck door. "Thank you for the ride. I appreciate it."

He looks a little surprised at how abruptly I'm backing off, but he just repeats that he was happy to do it.

"Night, Oliver." I sneak one last glance at him as I hop down to the ground. There's a heaviness about him now, like he's being pulled beneath the waves by a lifetime of unspoken wants and burdens and responsibilities.

But he manages a small smile, one that makes me feel weak in the knees, it's so tender. And when he says, "Good night, Ivy," there's nothing I want more than to crawl back into the truck and throw my arms around him.

Instead, I wave and walk away, the wind whipping through my hair like the violent torrent of feelings whipping around my chest. It isn't until I get inside and close the door to Beach Haven that I allow myself to cry.

twenty

Maisie has an afternoon appointment with an orthopedist on Friday, so she opens the shop herself and asks Oliver and me to both work a closing shift.

My nerves are a wreck the entire walk from Beach Haven. I had a hard time sleeping last night, my mind full of what-ifs and regret. Oliver was right, of course, that I'm the one who put a stop to the *us* that seemed to be coalescing after Harbor Lights. And I think I had good reasons when I first did so.

Maybe those reasons are still valid. I haven't heard a peep from any of the other libraries I've applied to, and I can't very well quit Farnsworth with nothing to replace my salary. It's looking increasingly like I'll be back in my dimly lit office off the library come September, desperately hoping to be *anywhere* else. Hiding from Kyle and Alex and all of my erstwhile friends, wishing I could do more. Be more. Be *anything*.

What's the point of pursuing Oliver if it's just going to end in less than a month when I go back to Brookline?

But there's his poem, and the way my skin comes alive

every time we touch. How he looked at me when he bought me the latte. How his eyes rival the sunlight reflecting on the ocean when he laughs. The way he makes me feel safe. The way I desperately want to explore the possibilities of what could happen if we tried.

I have a hard time looking at him when I get to work, even though I feel starved for time with him. He's ditched his Henleys for a white t-shirt that says, "A book must be the axe for the frozen sea within us." I recognize it as a Kafka quote, and it feels oddly perfect for him. For us. And besides, I'm not sure I've ever seen a guy wear anything I find so uniquely attractive. If it were any other day, I'd be salivating at his feet.

But I'm trying to give him space. To give us both space. So I throw myself into organizing the New Release shelves, switching anything that's over six months old into the general fiction section, and unpacking cartons of the latest novels to hit the *New York Times'* Best Seller List to put in their place.

When it's time for my break, I tell Maisie I'm going to take a walk. I can't sit in the café with Oliver and his Kafka shirt in my field of vision. I need to get out of here.

The sun never came back out after yesterday's stormy overture, but it hasn't actually rained yet. The sky's still foreboding, though, and I don't want to get too far from Shoreline—it looks like it could downpour at any minute.

I find a bench in front of one of the many creameries that dot Shore Road and pull out my phone. There's a new text from Laurel.

I'm going to hang around Boston one more night.

I wonder if she's still mad at me. I can't imagine why else she would decide to stay at home. I type out, *Is everything okay?*, but I don't hit send. My fingers swirl over the delete button. I'm not sure everything *is* okay. And if she's choosing to hang out with her parents instead of coming back to Beach Haven, maybe she's not ready to discuss it with me.

Finally, I opt for a more measured, *Sounds good. Hope everything went well with Spillinger.*

Oh, it went.

I snort. *I can't wait to hear what that's all about.*

The streets are eerily empty right now. Presumably, most tourists are clinging to the safety of their rentals or hotel rooms. I only saw a few umbrellas out on the beach when I left for work, which is unheard of here on Fridays in July. If I had to guess, I'd bet that the outlets down in Kittery and the tiny movie theater in Wells are packed with tourists anticipating the storms.

I check the time—still 20 minutes left on my break. I have no idea what to do with myself. I had lunch before work, and I'm not particularly hungry right now, or in general lately. The swirling eddy of emotions in my gut has been making it hard to eat.

Suddenly, I'm hit with the urge to talk to my mother. I'm so surprised by the feeling that I actually say "What the hell?" out loud, garnering a glare from an old woman riding by on a motorized scooter.

But things are messy right now, and Mom was always my safe space. Besides, she *did* ask me to call again soon when we spoke the other day. Even though I'm mad at her, it might help just to have someone to distract me from what's happening in my head.

My mom has Fridays off from her psychology practice. Her office is situated in downtown Boston, and she mostly sees students, so she works a lot of evenings. Friday was always the day she took for herself, to balance what I think she felt was an overstep into her personal time.

The phone only rings twice before she answers. She sounds cautiously thrilled when she greets me.

"Hey," I say, trying to seem casual.

"I'm so glad to hear from you, Ivy."

My eyes well up with tears, the way they always do when you've been struggling in silence and you're finally with the person who makes you feel safe enough to let it all out. The person who will hold you until you heal.

I didn't have a game plan for this discussion. I don't actually want to talk about Oliver, just distract myself from thinking too much. Maybe low-key family gossip is a good place to start. "Did you hear that Uncle Peter hurt his hip?"

Mom might see right through this filler conversation, but if she does, she doesn't say so. "I did," she replies.

So she must be talking to my dad. That's interesting. Since she brought it up, sort of, I decide to pry. "Did Dad tell you about it?"

"He did," she says cautiously. "Why?"

"I didn't know you two were still in touch."

She laughs. "Ivy. Your father and I have been together for 35 years. I don't think there'll ever come a time when we're not in touch."

Warmed by the present tense in her response, I push forward. "So, how's Dad doing?"

"He's doing well. You can call him, too, you know." It sounds like she's smiling. Maybe amusement at the flagrant *Parent Trap* I'm trying to pull, or maybe because she likes talking about my father. I'll take either, frankly. Both feel like a far cry from wanting to divorce him.

"I should. I'll call him soon."

"If you haven't talked to your dad, how did *you* know about Peter's hip?"

Oops. Now I have to explain that I was talking to Janie, which *definitely* is out of the ordinary. I don't need Mom pulling a Laurel and getting upset with me for trying to reinvigorate decades-old secrets. "I talked with Janie the other day," I hedge. "I just had a couple of questions for her."

"Color me intrigued."

I think I've divulged too much to back out now, so I forge ahead. "I've been reading Grandma's diary."

Radio silence from my mother.

I go on. "There's some pretty juicy stuff in there. And some conspicuous omissions."

"Conspicuous omissions?"

"Several pages are missing."

"Interesting," she replies after a second, like this isn't news to her.

"Mom."

"Mmm?"

"What do you know?"

She laughs, but it's hollow. "Why do you assume I know something?"

"Come on."

My mother sighs. "You're going to need to talk to your father about this."

"Did Dad rip up Eleanor's diary?"

"Ivy, I can't. I'm sorry."

I don't understand what could possibly be so bad about a teenager's journal that all of these fully grown adults are so upset about it, 66 years after the fact.

Was she a Soviet spy, or something? Did she single-handedly orchestrate the death of King George VI? Invent the hydrogen bomb and go into witness protection? The 1950s were a crazy time, to be sure, but I don't think anything my grandmother might have done back then could be all *that* bad.

"I'm not sure I'm understanding what's happening here," I say finally.

"I'm sorry," Mom repeats. "Please call your father."

AFTER TALKING TO MY MOM, I wouldn't say I feel any better, but I'm *definitely* distracted. From that perspective, the conversation was a roaring success.

I'm so distracted, in fact, that I walk straight into Oliver the instant I enter Shoreline a few minutes later.

"Not again," he groans, hands flying instinctively to the side of his face, which my head has just hit. Hard.

"Oh my God! I'm so sorry," I cry, reaching for his cheek without thinking. "Are you okay?"

He catches my hand in his but doesn't let go right away. "Careful. That's a little sore at the moment." His right cheek does look pretty red from the impact. It also looks like it might bruise.

I pull my hand back. "I'm so, so sorry."

"I'll be fine. But *you* hit your head. I think that's the bigger concern right now."

"Oh, I'm okay," I reassure him. But the room is spinning a little, and my right temple is starting to throb. "I might just...I think I'll go sit." I take a wobbly step, then throw my arms out for balance as I start to fall. "Or maybe not. I don't feel so well."

"Come on." Oliver puts his arm gently around my shoulders. "I'm going to help you sit down." He guides me to the café and hovers against me as he lowers my body into a chair. "I'll get you some ice."

"Get some for yourself while you're at it." I tighten my lips into a line and gesture toward his cheek. "You've got quite a bruise forming there."

He heads behind the counter and comes back a few moments later with two plastic bags filled with cubed ice. When he hands me one, I'm struck by the look of concern on his face.

"The bag is a nice touch. My mom always gave me ice in a dish towel, and then it would melt all over the place."

He nods in agreement. "Nothing worse than a soggy towel against your skin."

"Hey, where's Maisie?" I ask, suddenly realizing we're both incapacitated and there's no one at the register.

"She had to leave for the doctor. But don't worry." He must notice my anxious expression. "There's nobody else in here. I think they all fled because of the storms."

"Yeah." I press the ice harder against my aching head. "There really wasn't anyone out when I went for my walk."

He's surveying me with an expression I can't quite place. "You've never taken a walk on your break before."

Don't move, I command the muscles in my face. I don't want to give anything away. "I just felt like getting some fresh air."

Oliver blinks. "Okay."

"Don't you ever have the urge to flee the artificial lighting in here?" I paste on a smile that I hope obfuscates every ounce of how I'm feeling right now.

"Sometimes." He's still staring at me like I'm a puzzle he can't crack.

The only sounds in the bookstore are the ice quietly popping; the plastic bags crinkling against our skin.

I can't deal with how tenderly he's watching me, so I hurry to break the tension. "So, I called my mom today."

"Wow. How was that?"

"It was..." I rack my brain for the right adjective. "Weird. It was really weird."

Oliver tilts his head, inviting me to continue. "Weird how?"

"I don't know," I reply, toying with my skirt under the table. "Good, I guess. I've got a lot on my mind, and I really needed someone to talk to. The call was pleasant enough. But she said something that confused me." I haven't mentioned the contents of Eleanor's diary to Oliver yet, just that I'd read it. I'm curious if he'll ask for more details.

"Can I help?"

My heart leaps at the offer; at the way his eyes are still tight on me across the table. But I shake my head. "I don't think so. But thanks. I'm just dealing with a bit of a family mystery that I can't seem to solve."

He shoots me a wry grin. "I've read every Sherlock Holmes story there is. Multiple times, in fact. I might be better-equipped to help you than you think."

After I laugh, I consider it. Laurel's mad at me; Janie and Mom won't discuss what they know. I realize I need to harness my inner moxie and ask my dad for the truth, but I'm scared. Afraid to open up a vat of grief that neither of us is ready to deal with just yet.

But here's Oliver, with no skin in the game whatsoever, looking at me like he cares. Offering to help me, even though, in the last week, I've both rejected his romantic advances and damaged his truly spectacular face. Why *can't* I open up to him? If he's willing, which it seems he is. And besides, I'll do just about anything to keep him sitting here, making my heart feel as warm as the beach sand at midday.

"Okay," I agree at last. "So, there's something strange about my grandmother's diary." And I tell him everything.

WHEN I'M DONE UNLOADING the story on Oliver, he sits there puzzling it over for a few minutes. He's so focused, his dark brows tight over his nose, that I lose myself in watching him.

"Well," he says finally, shattering my perfect daydream of reading while cuddled next to him on a beach blanket, "that's certainly quite the mystery."

"Right?"

He nods. "And you're probably going to hate me for saying this, but your mom is right. I think you need to talk to your dad."

"Oliver," I whine. "You tempted me with hype talk about your detective skills."

His face settles into a self-satisfied grin. "I did. And I stand by that assessment of my abilities."

"So?" I lean toward him, elbows sliding across the table.

He does the same, stopping just shy of colliding with my face again. "So?" he breathes, making my heart flutter.

"So tell me what you think."

Oliver sweeps his gaze across my cheeks, my eyes, my lips. Probably also the ice pack I'm still holding to the side of my head. I'm sure I've never been sexier. He's so close I can almost feel the breeze from his eyelashes when he blinks. "I don't think I should do that," he says quietly.

"Why not?" I sit back in annoyance.

He shakes his head. "I could come up with any number of plausible explanations, but it sounds like the only one who can give you the truth is your father. And you don't need a thousand possibilities swirling around in your mind, stressing you out. Seems to me you've got plenty to worry about as it is."

I blink slowly, the tension dissipating from my body as I consider his words. He's right, of course—I would definitely become a great big ball of anxious energy with all the possibilities in mind until I learned the truth. I both love and hate how well he was able to intuit that.

And I absolutely *do* have enough on my mind outside of this issue. Work. Grief. Loneliness. The existential dread leaching out of my vocational misalignment. The overwhelming urge, growing by the second, to reach across the table and put my hands all over Oliver.

"Okay," I whisper.

"But, hey," he grins. "Let me know once you talk to your dad. I want to see if any of my guesses were right."

"No way." I scowl and stand up from my chair. "You lost the right to show off when you refused to play the game."

"Ivy." His fingers close over my wrist as I walk away. I freeze, letting the warmth of his attention soak through me.

"Yeah?"

His face is serious now. "I'm here if you need to talk."

"Thanks," I manage shakily.

"Can I check your head?"

I think I probably do need my head checked, but not for the reason he's suggesting. I nod anyway.

Oliver stands in front of me, then puts one hand on either side of my face. "I just want to make sure you don't have a bump," he explains, but the logic of his statement does nothing to slow the pounding of my heart. He runs his thumbs gently over my temples, so tenderly that I can barely feel it. I'm not sure I'm breathing.

The moment stretches into an eternity, just Oliver, holding my head in his hands and looking at me like I'm the most precious thing in his orbit. I feel like the room is spinning, but it has nothing to do with the mild concussion I'm probably suffering from.

"I think you're going to make a full recovery," he says finally, trailing his thumbs down my cheeks, stopping right beside my mouth.

I swallow hard. "Well, that's a relief." Without really meaning to, I take a step toward him, stopped only by the warmth of his chest against mine.

Oliver runs one thumb over my lower lip, and it's the single most sensual moment of my life. We're so close now, I can feel his heartbeat quicken in his chest.

"I really like your shirt," I breathe against his cheek.

The corner of his mouth curls up. "I thought you might."

"I do. So much." And then I can't take it anymore. Throwing my arms around his neck, I pull myself against him until I can't tell where he stops and I begin. I press my lips to his, pouring all of my want and longing into the kiss; needing him to know how badly I want this. How badly I want him.

His fingers thread through my hair, tilting my head to just the right angle, so incredibly gently. He deepens the kiss, sweeping his tongue against mine, and I practically die from the pleasure. I'm ravenous for him; I don't think I'll ever get enough.

I've just started running my hands over his immaculately toned pectoral muscles when the bell on the front door jingles. We spring apart, the tension that's been building between us since we met flinging us to opposite ends of the room with brutal force.

"Storm's brewing," mumbles the elderly man who interrupted us as he toddles off to the military history section. I have no idea if he saw us or not; he gives no indication either way.

In the context of the larger situation, his words strike me as irredeemably hilarious. I start giggling uncontrollably, smothering my mouth with my hands and running behind the espresso machine to regain my composure. Oliver raises an amused eyebrow, then takes up a position at the register.

I watch him as I catch my breath, attempting to orient my brain to the reality of what just occurred. He's pulled his notebook out of his back pocket and is hunched over the counter, scrawling across the page. I devour his look of deep concentration, my brain rolling over all the permutations of thoughts that might be spilling out of his mind and onto the page right now. And when he looks up at me and smiles shyly, I can barely control the beating of my heart.

twenty-one

I f it seemed like it was going to rain earlier, there's no doubt about it by the time we close up Shoreline at eight o'clock. The wind has picked up quite a bit, and the air is thick with the promise of petrichor. I'm sure all the crusty local fishermen are warning anyone who'll listen that we're in for a powerful lashing because their bum knees are acting up.

"Do you want a ride home?" Oliver looks worried.

I hesitate. I want nothing more than to hop into his truck and see where the evening goes, but I would also hate for him to get stuck in the storm. If I leave now, I should be able to get back to Beach Haven before I get drenched. Probably.

"I don't want to keep you out any longer than you need to be," I reply.

My eyes must be telling a different story, because Oliver doesn't seem convinced. "You said it yourself the other day—it's a short trip. We're not even as far away as Maisie's." He reaches for my hand, which turns over automatically as he laces his fingers through mine. "Let me drive you."

Between the bruise I noticed on my temple when I looked in the mirror earlier and the maniacal grin I'm pretty sure is on my face now, I must be a real sight. "Okay," I agree, unable to stop beaming at him.

He smirks. "You're much easier to please than I expected."

"Hey!" I bump him with my hip in feigned frustration. "Rude."

"Sorry," he says gently, dragging his lips across my cheek. My stomach flips over, under, and over again.

"I don't think you're sorry at all," I joke as he leads me to his pickup.

"Nope." His lips turn up at the corners. "I'm not."

"So, let me ask you," I say as we pull out of the tiny parking lot next to Shoreline. "Why the truck? Something about your tortured artist aesthetic doesn't quite mesh with the yee-haw archetype."

"Is that an official literary trope?" he teases.

I nod solemnly. "Oh, absolutely."

Oliver snorts. "If I had to choose, I'd probably just walk everywhere. Or buy some sort of hybrid. But the truck is my dad's, and it came at a price I couldn't refuse."

"Free?"

"Affirmative."

If his dad's on disability, he probably can't drive anymore. I wonder how long they've had this truck. If Oliver's had to chauffeur his father around since the accident; if he ever had the chance to be free to come and go as he pleased.

"So, what does your dad do while you're at work?"

A pained expression flashes over his face, but it's gone before I can interpret it further. "Not a whole lot. Puts away the dishes. Reads. Sits at the window, waiting for me to come home."

"That last part makes him sound like a dog."

He grins sardonically. "Yep."

I laugh, but I'm still feeling guilty that his life has turned out this way. That he feels trapped here, in a place quite literally called "Vacationland." And most of all, that I misjudged him so horribly. I actually can't believe what a terrible judge of character I've turned out to be.

Before I know what's happening, Oliver's pulled into the driveway behind Beach Haven. "See? Super quick trip."

Just then, a tremendous clap of thunder rattles the windows of the pickup. Instinctively, I grab for Oliver's hand. "Whoa."

"I bet that felt good reverberating through your aching head," Oliver says sarcastically. He doesn't let go.

"It wasn't the best," I admit, though any pain signals were largely ignored in favor of the sensation of his hand in mine. "How's your face?"

"Eh," he shrugs. "I've had worse."

"Pick a lot of fights with rival poets?"

"All the time." He turns off the motor and grabs his keys from the ignition. "Let me walk you to your door."

I shake my head. "You should stay here, where the sky isn't trying to kill you."

Oliver snorts. "I think I'll survive."

The rain has begun to fall now, starting quickly and only growing in intensity. By the time we're halfway to the porch, it's coming down in angry sheets, waved this way and that as the wind commands. In just a matter of seconds, our clothes are drenched.

"Well, that wasn't great," I remark as we huddle under the overhang.

He pretends to wring out the bottom of my dress. "You might need to change."

A genuine laugh bursts forth from deep within my chest. I can't believe how easy it is, being with him. How I almost walked away from it without knowing. What a mistake that would have been.

I reach out and squeeze his hand. "You're funny." We're standing so close together, my wet hair is dripping onto his shoulder. Based on his expression, I wouldn't say he minds.

We're quiet for a moment, communicating some sort of new understanding without any words whatsoever.

"Hey," he says finally, his breath warm on my cheek.

"Hey," I reply, swept away in the current of his eyes. They're so like the Ogunquit River: safe, sheltered. Breathtaking.

A creaking noise breaks my focus. Over Oliver's shoulder, I spy the culprit: an old pine leaning precariously toward the roof.

Oliver turns and follows my gaze. "I don't think that'll fall."

He may know nothing whatsoever about trees, but the confidence with which he reassures me is enough to convince me he's a world-class arborist.

Suddenly, my eye catches on something adjacent to the tree. The attic window.

The one I left standing wide open yesterday. The one that's probably now welcoming torrents of water into the house, right on top of Simon's photo album.

"Shit!" I turn away from Oliver and hurriedly key in the door code.

"What's wrong?"

"I left an attic window open. Hold on." I start to run inside, then spin back toward him. "Or, well, you don't have to hold on; I should let you go. But I need to take care of this. Thanks for the ride." I'm caught between the violent urge to race upstairs and survey the damage and the frenzied need to keep Oliver from leaving. I don't even have the mental bandwidth to be embarrassed by my gibberish, I'm so caught up in my racing thoughts.

Oliver's looking at me like perhaps I hit my head harder than he thought earlier. "That's okay. I'll stay and make sure you don't need any help."

"Okay," I agree. "Thanks. It's just this way."

My heart's racing with fear that I've destroyed both Simon's home and his irreplaceable personal effects. It's also racing when I realize Oliver goddamn Clarke and I are alone in my house. Well, my rental.

I pull down the attic stairs, and Oliver attempts to steady them as I head up. He follows close behind. As soon as I flip on the lights, I groan. There's a massive puddle of water on the attic floor, with more streaming through the open window every second.

"Seriously?" I say out loud. I can't believe I forgot to close the window. Granted, I was fairly overwhelmed yesterday, looking at photos of my grandparents in their youth, then baking the most mediocre blueberry pie of all time. I'd had a lot to think about, and it makes sense that closing the window would slip my mind. But given the weather, and the fact that this is someone else's house, I really needed to do better.

I tear toward the puddle as fast as I can amidst the forest of boxes, then reach up on tiptoe to yank the window down.

Leveraging my weight forward, I pull with as much force as I can muster. The window taunts me by offering no movement whatsoever.

"You've got to be kidding," I mutter under my breath. I pull again, my hands slippery from the water that's blowing in all over the sill plate as the wind rages outside.

Oliver catches up to me then, reaching his arms over my shoulders to grab the head jamb. He must be pushing pretty hard, because I can see his biceps bulging out of the corner of my eye as he shoves the window down the track. Even in this moment of crisis, I'm not immune to a little thrill that he's pressed up behind me.

"It might be a little easier if I could get closer," he says apologetically after a minute. He's managed to narrow the gap, but the window looks crooked on its track and won't concede further progress.

"Sorry." I duck out from under his arm and watch as he wrestles it back toward the sill. All things considered, I'm enjoying the show—Oliver's face is determined, his damp hair is curling around his forehead, and his wet clothes are clinging to his muscular frame.

Finally, with one last shove, the window slams shut.

"You made that look easy," I say coquettishly.

"Did I? That window gave me a run for my money."

I shoot him an easy grin. "Well, you did a lot better than I did."

"I do have the advantage of several inches on you," he replies, starting to wipe his wet hands on his jeans, then realizing his pants are utterly drenched.

I laugh at his dismayed expression. "I'm so sorry," I shake my head. "Your face was just funny."

He purses his lips in mock offense. "Gee, thanks."

"You know what I mean." Stooping to the ground, I survey the damage. The floorboards are pretty wet, as is the photo album and the boxes closest to the window.

"I see a couple of box fans over there," Oliver gestures to the far wall. "I'll set them up for you. I bet that'll be enough to dry everything out."

My mind is melting a little at the way he's knocking out tasks around the house like some sort of insanely attractive handyman. "Thanks," I breathe, watching him lift both fans at once and carry them back to me.

After he's plugged them in and aimed them at the mess, he meets my gaze. "I should probably get home so I can change."

A clap of thunder that sounds like the apocalypse itself rattles the walls, followed immediately by a blinding flash of lightning. The storm must be close, because even though I rarely paid attention in Earth Science class, I know that order is backwards.

As if to prove that theory, another roll of thunder shakes the house just seconds later.

"You were saying?"

Oliver leans toward the window. The dark shapes of trees bend and flail wildly outside in the storm's angry gusts. "I'm sure it'll be fine." He doesn't sound convinced.

"Hey," I begin, not wanting to seem forward, but equally terrified he's going to get electrocuted the minute he steps out on Simon's porch. "Why don't you just hang out here until the storm passes?"

His eyes light up, but he says, "I don't want to get in the way of your time with Laurel."

"She's out, actually. Went home to Boston for a couple of days."

"To deal with the dissertation issue?"

"Exactly." As attractive as Oliver looks right now, soaking wet, he must be freezing. If he's going to stay, he'll need something else to wear. "I have a hoodie and some sweats downstairs, if you want dry clothes."

He bursts out laughing. "I don't think your pants will fit me."

My face flushes. "They were, um. They were Kyle's."

Something shifts in his face. "I see."

"Just didn't feel like meeting up with him to return them." I shrug. "Never wanted to see the prick again, in fact. Come on." I grab his arm and pull him toward the stairs.

Just as we've stepped back down into the main hallway, a tremendous crash echoes through Beach Haven, and the lights flicker menacingly.

"Uh oh," Oliver says.

A moment later, the house is plunged into darkness.

twenty-two

"I think there are some flashlights in the kitchen," I say over my shoulder. I remember seeing at least two above the stove, along with some matches. Living on the coast, I bet Simon's witnessed many a storm like this. I'm not surprised that he's stocked Beach Haven for bad weather.

Oliver follows close behind me, one hand on the side of my shoulder. "I don't want you to bump the wall," he explains when he sets it there.

We find the flashlights, but the batteries in both are long dead and have oozed acid all over the place. So much for Simon's impressive doomsday preparation skills. Fortunately, there's a cinnamon-scented jar candle in the cabinet, too.

I strike a match and the candle flickers to life. "Behold," I grin, positioning it below my chin. It casts strange shadows across Oliver's face, just a few inches away. He returns my smile.

"Now, let's get warm." I lead the way to my bedroom, acutely aware the whole time how we're about to strip our clothes off in each other's presence. I blame nerves for making me flip on the light switch as I enter the room, momentarily forgetting the power's off.

The candle casts just enough light to see. I use it to dig out two hoodies, my pajama pants, and Kyle's sweats, which I kept not for the memories but because they fit me well if I cinch the drawstring.

"Here." I hand Oliver one of the outfits, suddenly nervous. "I'll just go over here to change." I gesture to the far corner of the room, where the shadows are deeper.

I can't see him, but I can hear the amusement in his voice. "What, afraid I'm going to see you naked?"

My stomach flips. "I wouldn't say I'm *afraid*, exactly." I shimmy out of my wet clothes and almost gasp in relief as I slip into the dry fleece. The temperature dropped quite a bit with the rain, and I didn't realize how chilled I was.

"Well, I don't want to read too much into this, but Kyle's pants fit me shockingly well."

I turn around, and my heart skips a beat. Oliver's changed his pants, but he's currently standing shirtless next to my bed. As far as the pants go, he's right—they do fit. Actually, they fit him much better than they did Kyle, who was toned enough, but in an almost boyish way. He wasn't particularly muscular or masculine. Not like Oliver.

"Did you do that on purpose?" I cross the room to throw my wet clothes in the laundry bag hanging off the doorknob.

"Do what?"

I narrow my eyes. "Say something about the pants so I'd turn around and see you half naked?"

"Now, Ivy," he grins, "why would I do something like that?"

"Mmhmm. That's what I thought."

He throws the hoodie over his head, mumbling from inside it, "I'm sorry to have offended you with my pectorals."

"Oh, there was no offense taken, I promise."

It's weird, seeing Oliver standing in my room, wearing my clothes. It's making me a little dizzy, actually, so I ask, "Want some food?"

"Sure," he says, hair mussed from its trip through the hood of my sweatshirt. "Let me just call my dad real quick and let him know I've not been lost to the sea."

I snort at his turn of phrase. "I guess that *is* a legitimate concern around here." I want to give him privacy for his call, but it's too dark to leave without the candle. I'm hoping to conserve my phone's battery in case of an emergency, or I'd use it as a flashlight. "Is it okay if I stay while you talk? It's so dark."

"Yeah, totally." He rustles through the pile of his wet clothes and grabs his phone, then dials.

His dad must pick up right away. "Hey, Dad. Just wanted to let you know I'm fine, but I'm waiting out the storm with Ivy."

My breath catches in my throat. The familiarity in his use of my name suggests he's talked to his father about me. My brain starts tearing through all of the things he might have said.

"Yeah, we're good," he's saying. "No power over here, though. You?" He pauses. "Okay, well, you be careful. Call Dale if you need anything; he's right next door." Oliver grimaces. "Yes, Dad, we will. See you soon."

He hangs up. "Sorry about that."

"No need to be sorry." I flash him a flirty grin. The fact that he's such an attentive caregiver is, quite frankly, blindingly hot. "So, what have you told your dad about me?

"Hmm." His lips turn up in amusement, and his eyes sweep over my face, landing on my mouth. "I bet you'd like to know."

"Yes, obviously. That's why I asked." I take a step closer.

His features flicker in the candlelight. "I told him you're a little bossy sometimes."

I feign offense. "Gee, thanks."

He laughs, then tentatively reaches for my hand. "And I told him you have great taste in books."

My heart starts skittering around my chest like it's never beat steadily before. I squeeze his fingers in mine. "If you knew how much that sort of praise goes straight to my head, I'm not sure you'd offer it."

"Maybe," he replies, quieter now.

"Anything else?" My voice comes out in a whisper.

His eyes flick up to meet mine. They're dark, surrounded by shadows. I've never seen anything more sensual in my entire life.

"I told him that you're gorgeous, and that you like my poetry." He swallows harder than usual.

I'm pretty sure his flattery has sucked all the air out of the room. "I do like your poetry," I manage. "You told your dad I'm gorgeous?"

He nods once, twice, three times. The air between us is thick, heavy with words we haven't spoken. I no longer care if the lights ever come back on; there's more than enough electricity zinging from his eyes to mine and back again to power an entire city.

I inhale shakily, then place my palm against his chest. His pupils are huge on mine in the candlelight. "Can I kiss you?" I echo his words from the night at the dance hall.

He smirks. "I knew you were still thinking about my tongue in your mouth."

"Oh my God, enough already!" I laugh, then lean forward on tiptoe, wrapping my arms around his neck and dragging him into me. I crush my lips to his, and I'm lost. Lost in the warmth of his skin, his arms pulling me close, the way he's kissing me back like he can't get enough, either.

My fingers thread through his hair, run over his powerful shoulders, caress the sides of his face. He breathes my name, then drags his lips down my neck, paying homage to my collarbone.

God, he's good. Everything he's doing is sending lava coursing through my body, from my heart to my belly and lower. When he runs his hand over my chest and palms my breasts through my sweatshirt, I can't help but moan into his lips.

He chuckles, then slips his mouth over mine again, brushing my hair over my forehead and rubbing my cheek with his thumb. He parts my lips with his tongue, and I wonder if he's laughing inside at how badly he knows I want this.

I'm assuming the ideomotor effect is coming into play now, like we're the planchette from a Ouija board, because Oliver and I have drifted from the middle of the room toward the bed. When the backs of his knees hit the side, I gently lean against him. He gives me a questioning glance.

"It's okay," I nod breathlessly.

"As long as you're sure," he says, lying back on the mattress and letting me crawl over him. I straddle his hips, leaning on my forearms and resuming my explorations of his face with my lips.

Oliver's hands skirt up my sweatshirt, and the lava shoots

directly between my thighs. I think I shiver a little, but there's not a square inch of my body that isn't burning hot.

He must notice the movement, because he stops his meandering immediately. "You okay?"

"Yeah. That just felt nice."

He gives me a wicked grin.

"I regret that we bothered to put these on," I joke, gesturing between our hoodies.

"Well, we needed them to prolong the illusion that we weren't going to end up in your bed."

Now it's my turn to grin coyly. "Are you suggesting this was an inevitability?

"I'd be lying if I said I didn't want it to be." His fingers smooth my hair. "But I need to be sure you want this also." Oliver's gazing up at me earnestly. He looks so good on my bed in the flickering light, his damp hair flung every which way. He's warm beneath me, all hard lines and pure masculinity. I don't think I've ever wanted someone so much.

So I tell him exactly that, and his blush is apparent even in the darkness.

My hands skim under his shirt as if of their own accord. His chest is firm beneath my touch, and his muscles ripple in the most tantalizing way.

"May I?" I ask, gesturing to the hoodie. He nods, helping me ease it over his head. I toss it onto the foot of the bed. I don't want it to fall on the floor, because I have no idea when this room was last vacuumed.

Leaning forward, I press my lips against his collarbone, his pecs, his abdominals. The curve of his pelvic bone; the edge of his waistband. My hands follow as if in hot pursuit, sending warmth and affection deep into his skin. I could spend all day doing this. Hell, I could spend an entire lifetime doing this.

"You didn't tell me you were so good at this," Oliver says in a low gravel, like he's struggling to think straight.

"It's a secret I share with only a select few," I wink.

"I'm going to have to be extremely jealous of anyone else in said group," he returns.

"Don't worry." I pepper his neck with kisses. "It's very exclusive."

"Oh yeah?" He grins.

"Yeah." I smile back, warmth washing over me at how happy he looks; at how uncomplicated this feels. "Just you."

He reaches up and pulls my face to his, kissing me passionately. I'm caught up in playing with his hair when he slips his hands under the back of my hoodie, drawing me down against him. He begins to slide it up, and I shimmy to the side so he can pull it off.

I'm wearing a lacy black bra, which seems to capture his attention. He slips his hand under one cup and thrums a finger over my nipple, then slides both straps down my shoulders and peels the cups away from my breasts. My nipples immediately peak, and he seems to take that as a challenge. He licks each one, then alternates pulling each breast more fully into his mouth.

I'm struggling to maintain, straddling him while he devours me. I think I might involuntarily grind my hips against him a few times before I even realize I'm doing it.

"You like that, Ivy?" he asks, grinning at me from around the nipple he's currently licking.

I moan in pleasure rather than respond with words. What use are words in times like these, anyway?

He unhooks my bra and tosses it aside as I skim my fingers under the waistband of his pants, wanting more. Needing him in every way. He reaches for my hands and helps me slide the sweats down his hips. I run my fingers down the length of him as he springs free. It hadn't occurred to me he'd be naked underneath the pants, but I realize then I obviously didn't have dry underwear to give him.

"God, Ivy," he moans. I laugh greedily. I could definitely get used to being with him like this.

I move my lips to his hips and lower, taking him in my mouth. His eyelids flutter shut, and he groans, deep and almost inhuman. "You don't have to," he manages.

"I want to." And I do. This wasn't something I did with Kyle very often; sex was perfunctory and pleasurable, but it never felt like an activity in its own right. It was more a means to an end. But with Oliver? I want to take my time.

Oliver lets me ravish him for a few minutes, then he sits up and kisses my forehead. "Okay. My turn."

I slide out of my pants and lie down next to him. He wraps his arms around me, pulling me close. Being completely naked with Oliver is one of the most erotic things I've ever experienced. I guess there's something to that enemies-to-lovers trope after all. Seems like constantly bickering with someone is the best way to build sexual tension.

We get lost in each other again, kissing, touching, letting the world fall further and further away. When he lifts my knee and positions his face between my thighs, I think I'm going to die from the pleasure. And he hasn't even started yet.

I'm pretty sure I go to another plane entirely while he works otherworldly magic with his tongue. This is insane, what he's doing, how he's making me feel. It doesn't take me long to slip over the edge, my body finding its epiphany against his mouth.

"More," I say, pulling him up to me and pressing a kiss to his cheek.

He looks oddly sheepish. "I don't have anything. I wasn't exactly expecting..."

Of course. And I don't have anything, either, because I was pretty sure the chances of me getting lucky this summer were about zero. I think quickly. "I bet Laurel has something. Hold on." I hop off the bed and grab the candle, then cross to Laurel's room at the end of the hallway. She's much more worldly than I am, but I know she's responsible. I'm guessing she didn't go to Porter's house empty-handed last week, and I think she'd be supportive of my stealing condoms from her, given the circumstances.

"She emerges victorious," I say a minute later, coming back to my room and shutting the door behind me. I toss the condom I found in Laurel's toiletry bag onto the bed and set the candle back on my dresser.

Oliver's giving me a strange look. "Why did you shut the door?"

I laugh louder than I mean to when I realize the absurdity of shutting the door in an empty house. "I have no idea. To keep out the ghosts that Laurel's talking to all the time, maybe."

He snorts. "Can't say I blame you there."

I hop back into bed and rub up against him. "Sorry for the interruption."

"I missed you," he murmurs against my lips.

"I was only gone for a minute," I tease.

"I missed you regardless."

God, the smiles are nonstop today. "Where was this charming behavior at Shoreline?"

"I'm always charming." His mouth tips up roguishly as his hands slide to my waist. He hauls me against him and starts playing a very dangerous game with his fingers between my thighs.

"Hmm," I say, feeling myself slipping away thanks to what he's doing with his hands. "Because sometimes, it seemed like you were being a little bit...difficult." It's an effort to get words out at this point.

His eyes glint in the darkness. "When have I ever been difficult?" He plunges two fingers inside me.

I gasp, despite my best efforts to hold it together. "Okay, now you're being *very* accommodating."

His chuckle is low in his throat. "That's what I thought."

"Oliver."

"Mmm?" His voice is heavy with want.

"No more, okay?" I kiss his cheek and grab the condom. "That feels way too good."

"I don't mind making you feel good," he replies. "In fact, that's exactly what I want to do."

Is it possible for something to be both incredibly sexy and incredibly endearing? Because my body and my heart are battling it out for which one is falling harder for Oliver right now.

"There's the charm," I grin. I let him continue, shattering around his fingers in all of 15 seconds. "Now?" I ask when I catch my breath.

"Absolutely," he agrees.

Let me tell you, there's never been a better feeling than having Oliver between my thighs, lying over me and pressing kiss after kiss to my lips. His hard lines plus my curves plus this mattress is the formula for ecstasy, I'm pretty sure. With every push of his hips, every quickening of my breath, every moment I catch him looking at me like he's never seen anything more beautiful, I'm creeping closer to losing myself forever.

In the end, when neither of us can take it anymore, he drags my hands above my head and laces his fingers through mine, then leans down for the best kiss of my life. And then we lose ourselves completely in each other. It's an explosive conclusion to the most unexpected evening I've ever had.

Afterwards, he wraps his arms around me and draws me to his chest. I lay my head against his beating heart.

"Sorry about the food," I say at last.

He chuckles. "I promise, I was fine with the alternative."

"Are you hungry, though?"

I've been oblivious to the sounds of the storm thanks to our romp, but I hear the wind thrashing the sides of the house again. I don't want him to leave. Because of the weather, and because I want to fall asleep wrapped in his arms.

"I could eat," he agrees. "We won't be able to cook anything, though."

"Are you okay with sandwiches? That's all Laurel and I have been eating recently, anyway."

"Sure." Oliver stands up and slips my sweatpants back on, then reaches for my hand. I throw my hoodie over my head and accept it.

"Right this way," I tell him. And we walk hand in hand to the kitchen.

twenty-three

An hour later, we're laughing over a delightful dinner of peanut butter and jelly sandwiches. Oliver's been regaling me with stories of hilarious customers he's helped over the years at Shoreline. Like the woman looking for a cookbook with only potato recipes, or the man who came in every day for a year to read romance novels aloud to himself in the café, but never bought anything.

"I wish I could have seen that," I say of the latter customer.

"Hang around long enough, and I'm sure you'll meet lots of people just as ridiculous."

His words hover in the air between us, pulling me down from the cloud I've been sitting on since we kissed in the bookstore earlier. Because I won't be here much longer. And with every passing moment, that's killing me a little bit more.

"I can imagine," I finally answer.

Oliver sweeps his eyes over my face as if reading my thoughts. "Any movement on the job search?"

I shake my head quickly. "Not a peep." I'd spent some time

last Sunday applying to more jobs on Laurel's laptop while she FaceTimed with her parents, but so far, I haven't heard anything back.

He tucks my hair behind my ear with the ease of a long-time partner. "You could always stay here, you know."

There's a lump in my throat, because I know he's right. Maisie *did* say she'd need more help for the fall, and given what's happening with her knee, I suspect she may be even more desperate than she previously expected.

But I can't uproot my life for a guy. Imagine if I'd done that with Kyle. Moved away from my family, the place where I grew up, only to have my heart ripped from my chest, my every work day mired with humiliation. I'd be stuck in a new place with nothing but the grief and trauma he left behind.

Not that Oliver would ever do something like sleep with our mutual coworker. There isn't even a parallel in this scenario, since our only colleague is Maisie, who is not only our boss, but is also about 40 years Oliver's senior. Regardless, I doubt he'd stoop so low.

Still, though. I need to learn from my past. I can't rely on anyone's commitment to me. Can't count on the affection he's showing me today to stand the test of time, to be enough to warrant me giving up everything.

What would I have left if it all went wrong?

But he's looking at me now like his heart's screaming my name with every beat, just like mine is his. And I don't want to ruin this perfect, blissfully unexpected evening.

So I smile and say, "I could." And then I lean forward and kiss him, because I want him to know how good that dream sounds to me. Even though I can't let myself chase it.

· · ·

AT ELEVEN, Oliver calls his dad to say he's going to stay over. It's still stormy outside, but Beach Haven is feeling awfully cozy. Oliver was a little hesitant about sleeping over at first, but when I repeatedly assured him I didn't mind, he finally caved.

"How's your father?" I ask when he hangs up.

"Good," he replies, walking back to the bed to sit beside me. "He stays up late watching TV most nights, but he said he's going to get ready for bed now since there's nothing to do without the electricity." He smirks. "I told him he sounds like a petulant teenager."

I laugh. "He does, a little bit. He's definitely okay on his own?" I really want Oliver to spend the night, but not at the expense of his dad's medical needs.

Oliver nods. "He's pretty capable. He can get around the house on his own and everything. Just can't drive anymore without a lot of pain. No yardwork, or anything like that."

"Has he ever thought about getting a remote job?" I'm not trying to pry; I just want to learn everything there is to know about what life is like for Oliver.

"It's funny you mention that. He's actually been talking about taking some online classes so he can learn bookkeeping." Oliver offers a wry smile. "He says he's tired of being a burden and wants me to have my own life."

"It must be awful for him to be stuck at home, needing you for everything." I quickly realize how insulting that must have sounded. "Not that needing you is bad, obviously. You know what I mean."

Oliver leans over and kisses my cheek. "I know what you mean." His eyes on mine send my stomach lurching. "And yes, I think it's been pretty hard on him. Especially now that I'm 32.

It was one thing when I was in college and figuring things out, but he doesn't want me to be stuck taking care of him for the rest of his life." His gaze drops to his lap. "Although, to be honest, I'm going to be doing that to a certain extent no matter what. His mobility issues are pretty severe as it is, and they're not going to get better as he ages."

I squeeze his hand. "I'm sorry to hear that."

Oliver shrugs. "Eh. We all end up taking care of our parents eventually, right?"

I consider him in the candlelight. "I don't know if that's universal."

"I suppose that's true." He runs his pointer finger down my forearm, making me shiver. "I've been thinking about that a lot lately, actually. With my mom."

"Oh?"

"Just not sure what I'll do when the time comes that she needs me."

His face looks darker now in the shadows. I catch his hand in mine. "What do you *want* to do?"

"What I want," he says sorrowfully, "is to change what's already come to pass. To go back to the day she took the Boston job and make my dad follow her. Then he'd never have gotten hurt; she wouldn't have cheated. I would have had a normal life."

"Maybe," I say quietly. "It's hard to say what might have happened."

He drags in a deep breath. "You're right. And I've started thinking about maybe trying to call her, once in a while. To see if there's anything there worth fixing."

"What changed your mind?" He'd seemed so set against

any kind of relationship whatsoever when he first mentioned his mother.

His answer is immediate. "You."

My eyes widen. "Me?"

Oliver smiles at me. "Even though it was hard, you talked to your mom. And it made me realize that maybe I'm part of the problem."

I'd been telling him about the first call with my mother when there was a lull at work on Tuesday. We'd stood between the New Release shelves where no one could see us, Oliver leaning toward me and listening intently as I decompressed. Talking to her had been a lot; he was right. Telling him about it had made me feel much better.

I didn't think much of the conversation at the time, and I certainly wasn't trying to send some sort of message about the importance of family ties, or anything. I shake my head. "Our situations aren't the same. We aren't the same. You don't need to do something just because I do."

"I know. But I still think maybe I want to." He looks into my eyes. "I like that you don't give up on people."

My heart flutters in my chest, and I lose the ability to speak for a moment. "Well," I respond finally, not breaking his gaze, "I've been fortunate to have a family that never gave up on me."

He inclines his head. "If it goes well, do you want to be my date to her wedding?"

I'm so surprised, a sharp laugh escapes my throat. "Is this all some sort of excuse to show me off to extraneous relatives?"

One corner of his mouth tips up, and he bends to kiss my shoulder. "It wasn't, but now that you mention it, that would be quite the bonus."

I nudge him playfully with my side. "If you decide you

want to work things out with your mom, I would happily be your date to her wedding."

Oliver presses his lips to mine then, tasting of raspberry jam and possibility. I let myself fall back onto the rumpled sheets beneath him as he leans over me, taking my breath away and making me wish with my whole heart that this summer never had to end.

twenty-four

I wake up curled against Oliver's chest on Saturday morning. We both have to work today, and I'd set an alarm for 9, but my eyelids flutter open when the lights flick back on at 6:45 instead.

Taking in his rumpled hair, his powerful shoulders just visible above my blanket, and the peaceful expression on his face, I actually sigh out loud. I could definitely get used to this.

Oliver stirs next to me when I roll over to turn off my alarm. "I'm sorry," I whisper. "You can go back to sleep."

"But you're here," he says against my cheek. "I don't want to go back to sleep."

"I'll still be here if you're sleeping," I giggle.

"But I can't see you if I'm sleeping." He smiles, then pulls me to him more tightly.

If you'd told me three weeks ago that my summer beach vacation was going to involve all these squishy feelings with an irredeemably hot bookstore clerk, I'd have laughed in your face.

That goes double for the quasi-reconciliation that's

happening with my mother, the maybe-fighting with Laurel, and the scandalous secrets Eleanor was apparently keeping for most of her life. Whatever they were.

But at least the chaos and unpredictability that's plagued me for the last year has started heading in a better direction. I mean, it's still chaos. But my heart doesn't feel like it's shattered into a million little pieces today, and the respite is refreshing.

Plus, I'm sure I'll reconcile with Laurel at some point, so I'm not too worried. And besides, awful as it sounds, whatever's happening with Oliver more than makes up for sparring with my cousin. In terms of my emotional well-being, that is.

It doesn't escape my attention that Oliver's still shirtless, or that I'm not wearing any pants. I press a row of kisses to his chest, warm beneath the ancient coverlet. Our legs tangle together as he adjusts so we're more fully aligned. Everywhere I'm soft and accommodating, he's hard and enticing. I thank the gods of romance that we don't have to be at work for several hours.

"Last night was *extremely* enjoyable," he says against my neck, where he's started kissing me in an increasingly fervent way.

I raise an amused brow. "The understatement of the century, perhaps?"

He snickers. "Perhaps."

His roving hands are battling with my sympathetic nervous system, goading my breaths to come shallower, faster.

"It would be a shame for that to be a one-time occurrence," I manage as his tongue finds my nipple again.

"I'm solutions-oriented, remember?"

Seeing him grin up at me with his mouth around my breast is, frankly, more than I can take. "Oh, yeah?" My hands slip under the waistband of his pants, where he's more than ready for me.

"Extremely," he assures me, moving down the bed to spread my thighs, to tease me with his tongue.

"Oliver," I moan, digging my fingers into his hair.

"Mmm?"

"I like this solution."

His laugh is deep in his chest, and it's only a matter of moments before I'm jumping out of bed and raiding Laurel's stash of prophylactics again. Then I run back and throw myself under the covers beside him, giggling and grinning and behaving like a much younger, more effervescent version of myself who I quite frankly thought was lost forever.

When Oliver's deep inside me, both of us practically at the edge, we make eye contact, and it's electric—the look conveys raw emotion I've never felt before, much less seen reflected back at me by someone else.

"Ivy," he whispers, gaze rocketing around my face like he can't decide where to let it linger; like his brain is swirling with words he isn't ready to say. Then he's pressing his lips to mine like he needs me as desperately as I need him, and we both explode in a final moment of pure ecstasy.

And while I realize that sounds like some sort of extreme hyperbole, that's exactly how it feels.

OLIVER and I eat blueberry pie leftover from our dinner with Maisie straight out of the pie plate, sitting cross-legged on my bed. We're still not dressed, and, though I haven't dared a glance in the mirror, I'm assuming my hair is as unruly as his. Probably even more so.

Even though we've spent the past 12 hours worshipping at the altar of each other's bodies, I'm not sure I've ever felt more naked. But it's a good sort of exposure, both in paucity of garments and the way we seem to be wearing our hearts on our nonexistent sleeves. Seeing Oliver, rumpled and lean and vulnerable, staring at me and my mediocre blueberry pie like he can't get enough of either, is an otherworldly feeling.

"At the risk of launching another of your erotic 'solutions,' I wanted to tell you how incredibly hot you look right now." I grin at him under my lashes.

He raises both eyebrows. "Ivy Parker, are you coming on to me?"

I wrinkle my nose. "Right, because the repeated orgasms you've treated me to since yesterday evening didn't pave the way for a little flirtation?"

Oliver cracks a smile. "I guess I did leave myself open to that kind of coquetry."

"Hey." I swat his knee, a more serious expression on my face. "Is this going to make things weird at work?"

He shrugs, swallowing a mouthful of pie. "Probably not any weirder than before, when I spent most of the day thinking about shoving you up against a bookshelf."

My jaw drops. "Wow, you had that one ready to go, huh?"

I see the glimmer in his eye before he speaks. "It's just the truth."

"Honestly, that's tamer than what *I* was imagining," I admit.

"See? Then it won't be a problem." He leans over to kiss my cheek.

"Um," I begin, "we aren't going to let Maisie find out, right?"

Oliver shakes his head vehemently. "About this? No way. But she's pretty sharp; she may pick up on something eventually. Especially if you suddenly stop giving me a hard time."

I consider whether Maisie knowing that Oliver and I are... well, *something*, would be a problem. Given how she's been coaxing us together at every possible opportunity, I suppose maybe not. Hell, she'd probably be delighted. But for now, when all that's technically happened is sex, I think it's best to keep things to ourselves. Even if the sex was astronomically mind-blowing.

"Then I promise to keep teasing you and playing hard to get. For as long as it takes."

His pupils are growing again. "I like the sound of that. A lot."

"You're ridiculous." I lean forward to kiss him. "But I like it, too."

AT 11:15, we begrudgingly get dressed. Oliver has to go back to his house to get a change of clothes for work, but he says it will only take a minute. We leave together in his truck, a surreal bookend to last night's arrival.

A few minutes later, Oliver pulls up to a tiny red Cape Cod two blocks off the beach. "I'll be right back," he says, leaving the truck's air conditioning running so I don't get too warm.

Leaning my head against the window, I look out over his world. The yard is well-groomed, with a small garden near the front steps. I catch a glimpse of a picnic table in the backyard and a shed by the tree line. I wonder when Oliver has time to do all of the yardwork, what with his hours at Shoreline and his freelance writing projects. Not to mention all the chauffeuring he has to do for his father.

He comes back a few minutes later in his gray Henley and dark jeans, his hair combed into submission. "So, my dad wants to meet you," he mumbles a bit apologetically.

"Oh." I'm taken aback, because I wouldn't think we would be at the point of meeting each other's parents yet. Not because I'm not invested in whatever's brewing between us. Quite the contrary. In fact, I realize with a start, I've never felt more invested in a relationship in my life.

Instead, it's because people don't usually do this so soon. Definitely not when it's just a hook-up, and probably not even when feelings are involved if nothing's been defined. I'm wondering what he's told his dad to make meeting me feel so imperative.

Alternatively, maybe his dad's just really, really bored. Or nosy. Or both.

"If you don't want to, it's really okay," Oliver says. He looks nervous, and that just about breaks my heart.

"I want to," I promise. He helps me hop down out of the truck, fingers warm against mine, one arm reaching up to steady my waist. I think I surprise us both when I don't let go of his hand the whole way to the front door.

Oliver's dad is sitting on a brown microfiber couch, reading the newspaper. His long legs are sprawled out before him on the hardwood, and I can tell he was probably built like his son before his accident rendered him largely immobile. He looks tired, worn out by life, but his blue eyes are bright—so much like Oliver's that it's actually a little eerie.

"You must be Ivy," he says in a charming baritone. A flash

of pain on his face is the only indication of his limitations when he moves to stand, but he grins broadly to hide it.

I cross the room to shake his hand. "It's a pleasure to meet you."

"Robert," he introduces himself. "Thanks for letting Oliver ride out the storm with you. It was a rough night."

I will my face to stay as stoic as humanly possible. My night was anything but rough; it was divine. Out of the corner of my eye, I see Oliver trying not to laugh.

"It's been a while since I was on the coast in weather like that," I manage, looking away from Oliver so I don't start chuckling, too.

"Oh, do you come here often?"

I nod. "My family rented a place here every summer of my life. This year, it's just my cousin and me."

"You've probably eaten some of my lobsters, then." Robert appears pleased with himself.

Oliver looks like he wants to disappear into the wall. "Dad, that's a really weird thing to say to someone you've just met."

His father's laugh echoes around the small living room. "Just trying to make conversation with your lovely friend."

"We should get to work." Oliver shifts from one foot to the other.

Robert inclines his head. "Okay, you two have a good day. And Ivy, don't be a stranger. It's not often Oliver bothers introducing me to the girls he's seeing." His eyes twinkle. "You should let him take you out on the boat sometime."

"I'd love that," I reply earnestly.

"Consider it done." Oliver grins at me. "Shall we?" He gestures toward the door, holding an arm against the small of my back as I wave my way out of the house.

"Your dad's nice," I remark as we walk away.

"He really liked you."

I furrow my brow. "How do you know?"

"I could tell," he shrugs, then tosses me an obnoxiously charming smile. "And Robert Clarke isn't always an easy guy to please. You must be something special."

"I think I like you." I stop next to the truck and throw my arms around his neck.

When he smiles down at me, my heart plays a triumphant bass line. "I *know* I like you."

"You always have to one-up me, huh?"

His only response is a kiss that takes my breath away.

BEING at work is the ultimate test of my patience after the 24 hours I've had. Fortunately, now that the storms have finally passed, the tourists are back out in force, and Shoreline stays quite busy. Thank God for that distraction; I don't know if I'd be able to keep my hands off Oliver otherwise.

He and I exchange secret smiles whenever our eyes meet across the shop. I catch him staring affectionately when I recommend some books to a woman who reminds me of Eleanor. I'm pretty sure I return the expression when he takes his notebook out of his back pocket during a brief lull and starts scribbling his thoughts on a blank page.

Because she's missed so much work this week, Maisie decides to come in for a few hours to take care of some administrative tasks and check in with us. She must catch more than a few of our lovestruck exchanges, because I notice her laughing to herself several times when she seems to think we aren't looking.

Before she shoos us both outside to take a break (together, at her insistence), Maisie asks if we can join her in her office. I shoot Oliver a worried glance. I can't imagine what she wants to discuss is good news, given how many doctor appointments she's had recently.

Maisie doesn't bury the lede. "I need surgery."

"Oh, Maisie," I shake my head. "I'm so sorry."

She waves her hand through the air, pushing my apology aside. "Don't be. Once I recover, things are going to get a lot easier around here."

"When's your surgery?" Oliver asks. I see the wheels spinning in his mind. I know he's already thinking about how he's going to drive her to the hospital, shop for her, and take care of everything at Shoreline. My heart swells.

"Amazingly, they had an opening in a week and a half. Cancellation." She grins. "I snapped that up right away, let me tell you. I need to get this dealt with."

"What can we do to help?" I'm not sure how long her recovery will take, but I imagine she's going to be out of commission for quite some time.

"Well," Maisie begins, "I'll be out for a few days with the surgery itself, between pre-op and the procedure and the fun-filled anesthesia fever dream afterward." Her face falls a little. "Then, I'll be stuck at home for about six weeks. But I can handle administrative tasks remotely during that time. I may need your help getting my technology situated, though," she says to Oliver.

He nods. "Of course. And Ivy and I will take care of everything here."

"I can pick up as many hours as you need, Maisie."

Her eyes fill with tears then. "I know you will, dear. And I appreciate it. I just don't know what I'm going to do when you leave."

The office goes quiet. I hear Oliver swallow hard next to me. I can't say I blame him; I don't want to think about the end of summer, either. And Maisie's six weeks of recovery will last well beyond the time when I need to be back in Brookline.

"Let's talk," I say before I can think better of it. "Maybe I can extend my stay."

Oliver's head snaps toward me. I smile at him gently, reveling in the hope displayed all over his face.

Maisie's brows go up at the wordless conversation Oliver and I are having, but she just asks, "What about your work at the library?"

I look down. "I'm not sure what my plans are with regard to that job."

"Interesting," she replies, looking none-too-subtly at Oliver to gauge his reaction. I'm pretty sure he's blushing. "Okay. Why don't you finalize your plans, Ivy, and then circle back with me. Will that work?"

"Absolutely."

Her lips turn up. "Perfect. Now you two go get some sunshine."

"HOW WOULD you be able to stay?" Oliver asks me the moment we step outside.

"I haven't really thought that through," I admit as we sit down on a nearby bench.

He considers me carefully. "Could you take that much time off? Right at the beginning of the school year?"

"Maybe?" I'm not so sure my boss would be okay with it, honestly. Shaking my head, I quickly correct. "Probably not."

Oliver seems confused; understandably so. I clear my throat. "I'm wondering if I might just...not go back."

He raises an eyebrow. "Are you going to ask Maisie if you can work here indefinitely?"

I don't know. *Am* I going to ask her that? This is all a little too convenient, given what's happening with Oliver. I'd pretty much talked myself out of uprooting my life for him. Moving here for him feels like it could end so, so badly. And what good is recovering from the trauma of all things Kyle if I don't learn from my mistakes?

I can't help but wonder, though, if maybe I wrote off the idea too quickly. It's sort of hard to ignore the way the obstacles are starting to fall like dominoes.

My brain is swinging wildly back and forth between scenarios like the flipper in a pinball machine, and I'm struggling to keep up. As my thoughts accelerate into a whirling crescendo, I feel my anxiety whoosh into its usual spot, clenching my sternal notch and making my heart race.

I take a deep breath, desperate to seem unaffected. "Maybe? I need some time to think it over."

Oliver looks concerned. "Are you okay?"

Can he see the wild look behind my eyes, the fluttering in my chest? I normally pride myself on how well I hide my anxiety, but the worry plastered on his face suggests he sees all of me.

Taking another shaky breath, I nod. "I'll be okay. Just feeling a little panicky."

He puts his arm around my shoulders and pulls me close. "What can I do?" he asks against my hair.

"This is enough," I whisper.

We sit together for several minutes in silence, Oliver running his hand up and down my arm in soothing strokes, until the storm in my head has made way for the sun. "I feel better now. Thank you."

He peers into my face. "Are you sure?"

God, he's making it really hard to fathom leaving here and going back to Farnsworth. "I'm sure." I kiss him, tentatively at first, then with more emotion, like I can channel my gratitude straight into his lips. Aside from my parents, no one has ever intuited my anxiety so well before. Or bothered to helped me through it when it attacks.

When I break away from the kiss, I clear my throat. "I struggle with anxiety, and sometimes panic attacks. Typically I can manage them on my own, but it's always nice to have someone to wait it out with me. So, thank you."

He's looking at me dubiously. "How could I let you go through that alone?"

My heart melts into a puddle at the base of my torso. "Not everyone understands what it's like to feel trapped in a whirlwind of their own thoughts," I shrug. "I've always assumed they don't realize how appreciated their help would be."

"I might understand the feeling of being trapped more than most."

My mind flashes back to his poem. "I think you probably do."

"I didn't mean to cause you anxiety," Oliver offers. "Or force you to make a choice about staying here."

"No," I say, shaking my head. "You didn't. It's just that a part of me is terrified to make such a major change. And another part of me," I look knowingly into his eyes, "wants nothing more."

Oliver's clearly trying to remain neutral, but the hope written all over his face gives him away. "You sure you're okay?"

"I really am, now." I snuggle in tighter.

He grins. "Well, I don't want to sway your decision one way or the other, but Ogunquit's really gorgeous in the fall."

"You seem exceptionally unbiased," I tease.

"No opinion whatsoever." His eyes crinkle at the corners. "If you decide to leave, I'm sure I can find another girl to help me write the September staff picks."

I lean against his shoulder. "There's no way she'd do as good a job."

He kisses my forehead. "No way in hell."

twenty-five

The more I consider the possibility of staying in Ogunquit, at least until Maisie's back from surgery, the better the idea feels. At first, I hate that I'm using this opportunity as an excuse to run from something. After endless rumination, however, I come to terms with the truth—Farnsworth isn't the right fit for me. Certainly not anymore, even if it was once.

I'm bored there. The administration doesn't care enough to let me make changes, to make things better. The programs I run are stagnant, and worse still, I feel stagnant. I don't think I'm doing justice to the kids, and there's nothing I can do to remedy the situation.

And then there's Kyle, and Alex, and that whole mess. I don't know how I'm going to manage it, but I need to give myself permission to run away. Laurel was right when she suggested leaving Farnsworth in the first place. I realize it more with every passing day. I just hope someday I'll stop feeling like leaving is giving up on something, rather than allowing myself to chase the future I deserve.

I think through the logistics of the situation. If I'm going to hang around Ogunquit longer, I'll need somewhere to stay. And if that place is going to be Beach Haven, I'll need to talk to Simon.

Sunday's my day off, but I think Simon's cleaning lady is working. She'd stumbled into Beach Haven with a mop last Sunday, scaring Laurel and me about half to death while we were eating breakfast. I send a text to the number I have stored in my phone for her, asking for Simon's contact information.

She provides it almost immediately, warning me that Simon plays pinochle at noon, so I'd best try to catch him before that.

My heart's pounding in my chest when I dial, even though I freely admit there's no reason I should be nervous. No legitimate one, anyway.

"Hello?" A bright tenor, only slightly shaky with age, answers on the first ring.

"Hi, is this Simon Foster?" There's a brief pause, during which I assume he's trying to figure out if I'm a serial killer, so I rush out with, "This is Ivy Parker. Charlie and Eleanor's granddaughter."

"Oh, hello." From the relief in his tone, I guess that I did unsettle him a bit with my questioning-before-self-identification. "How are you, Ivy?"

"I'm doing well, thank you. And you? I heard that you were having trouble with your leg." As soon as it's out, I wish I hadn't added that last bit. Maisie probably shouldn't be gossiping about his medical challenges.

"Ah, it's been a bit of a struggle, but I'm managing. Tore my ACL on the pickleball court. I had surgery, but I'm stuck in a wheelchair for the time being."

Simon was a few years younger than my grandparents, but he must be at least 80 by now. I'm amazed that he's still involved in athletics of any kind. "I give you a lot of credit for staying fit," I reply. "I'm ashamed to admit I haven't been getting out for my morning runs most days this summer."

"Do you still take your jogs on the beach?"

I'm touched that he remembers this habit of mine, which I've treasured since back when Laurel and I were teens and desperately needed something to do out from under the cloying gaze of our parents. We used to go running, then rest in the sand at the farthest point of our jog, about three miles down the beach. We'd people-watch and mock what we viewed as our parents' overbearing rules until we got hungry and had to run back.

"I do," I smile. "It brings back a lot of memories."

Simon is silent for a moment. "I understand the allure of memories."

I swallow hard. It's probably difficult for him to talk to me without reliving the loss of his best friends. I decide to change the subject. "So, I've been working at Shoreline Books this summer. Just for something to do, and for a little extra cash."

"Oh, Shoreline is lovely! Give my regards to Maisie the next time you're in, won't you?"

"I definitely will. That's actually partly why I'm calling." It's pretty much the only reason I'm calling, but I feel guilty that I haven't bothered to check in with him yet this summer. Simon has no one; it's the least I can do to be social. "Maisie's actually going to be having surgery," I continue. "She'll need some help in the shop this fall, and I'm hoping to stay in town a little longer. I have to check with my job back home to see if that will be a possibility, but I wanted to speak with you first in case renting Beach Haven a little longer wasn't an option."

Simon sounds elated. "Of course it's an option! Anything for Charlie's granddaughter. He and Eleanor did so much for me over the years; I'm happy to help."

"Thank you so much; that's very kind of you."

"Of course. Check with your job, and let me know what you decide."

My chest is full of nervous energy. Is this actually happening? With another domino in the pile on the floor, I'm running out of excuses *not* to call my boss at Farnsworth.

"I'll do that, thank you. And, Simon?"

"Yes?"

I take a deep breath, seeing my grandparents' smiles in my mind. "Could I come visit you sometime? While I'm here?"

I'm pretty sure he's smiling, too. "I'd love it if you did," he replies.

When we hang up, everything inside me feels tingly and energized. Thanks to my ever-simmering anxiety, tough conversations take up a lot of space in my mind before I have them. Once they're in the rearview, I'm usually hit with a sense of elation—that I've tackled the challenge, that it's in the past. It's a bit of a high, if I'm being honest. Still, I could live without the racing heart and queasiness that typically precedes a situation I'm nervous about.

Right now, though, I'm high on the possibilities. Simon's beach house with a view is apparently at my disposal. I need a new challenge, and Maisie wants me to stay. Hell, I think *I* want to stay. Not just as something to do to get away from Farnsworth. But as something worth leaving for.

And then there's Oliver. I close my eyes, painting a picture of his smile against my cheek. The way his hand feels in mine; how he held me when we danced. How his body moved over mine in the flickering candlelight. The way he teases; the pride in his expression when he introduced me to his father.

I'm struggling to keep the elation inside now. I can't think of another time in my life when things have lined up quite this seamlessly for me. I feel like the universe is trying to tell me something, and I'm pretty sure I owe it to myself to listen.

The joy bubbling in my chest is threatening to boil over. Shaking my head roughly, I attempt to bring myself back down to earth. I drop my phone on the bed, then grab my workout clothes from the dresser. I'm going to deal with this excitement the best way I know how—running on the beach.

twenty-six

Laurel doesn't come back to Beach Haven until late Sunday afternoon. "Got caught up with some stuff," she explains, barely looking at me when I meet her at the door.

Are we still fighting? Or maybe something happened? I think I have a duty to her, and our relationship, to try to be there for her and repair whatever schism seems to be forming between us.

So I follow her down the hallway. "Is everything okay?" My thoughts immediately jump to Uncle Gregory, who's a Type 1 diabetic, or to Janie, whom Laurel might have gone to see while she was home.

Something could have gone wrong with Dr. Spillinger, also. When Laurel said "it went" about their conversation, I'd assumed she meant things shifted in her favor. But maybe that was the wrong conclusion to draw.

Laurel tosses her duffel on the floor of her bedroom and turns to face me. "It's fine. How was your weekend?"

I take a beat, wondering how to explain the last few days.

So much has happened that I'm not really sure where to start. "Great," I say finally. "We had some bad storms on Friday. Maisie's having surgery. I might stay here a little longer to help her out."

My eyes dart over to the toiletry bag Laurel left here when she went home. I wonder how long it will take her to notice that several condoms are missing.

She's barely paying attention right now, though, wavy hair falling over her face as she bends to unzip her bag. "How much longer?"

"Possibly a few weeks. Maybe more."

Her head whips toward me then, a wicked grin on her face. "Something happened with Oliver, didn't it?"

I curse whatever bond we share for making me so transparent. "Yes, something happened." Narrowing my eyes at the *"I told you so"* reflected in her smirk, I add, "But I would help Maisie out regardless."

Laurel nods slowly, still much more amused than I'd prefer. "Well, that's very noble of you."

"I guess. It seemed like a nice way to test the idea of not going back to Farnsworth, too."

A serious expression moves in. "Have you told your parents?"

Shaking my head, I plop down on her bed. "Not yet. I need to call my boss first to see how long they'll let me take leave."

"Gotcha. My lips are sealed." She throws several shirts into her dresser.

"So, what happened with Spillinger?"

Laurel sighs deeply. "We chatted. It wasn't great, at first. She didn't want to admit that her feedback had been colored by her feelings toward me. I eventually dragged a half-confession out of her. Then I tried the whole, 'an evil man broke my heart' technique that you suggested, and she seemed to buy that. She even started offering genuine feedback about my paper, most of which was fairly positive."

"That's great, Laur!"

"Yeah," her voice is quiet. "It was. Until she happened upon Nick and I in the quad almost immediately afterward."

"Wait, what?"

"After my meeting, I was headed to grab coffee with some friends. I ran into Nick on the way."

"When you say ran into him, you mean...?" I'm not sure I've ever seen Laurel embarrassed before, but she's definitely most of the way there now.

"He hugged me, and we sat down and started talking. He told me that he misses me, and he wanted to take me out to dinner."

"Okay, so Spillinger came upon you while you were discussing dinner plans. So what?"

Laurel shakes her head. "Nick kissed me. And I...I more than kissed him back. A lot."

My eyes are definitely bulging out of my head now. "I'm sorry, what? I thought things with Nick were over? And what about Porter?"

She slaps her hand to her forehead as if beside herself. "I know, I know! I mean, Porter and I left things very open. He's seeing other people, too. And there's just something about Nick. I'd come to terms with everything being over, especially because of all the drama surrounding my dissertation, but...I can't help myself when he's around."

"Okay," I begin slowly. "So, what then? Spillinger got pissed?"

"Yeah, she started screaming at me in the middle of the quad."

My brows shoot all the way up to my widow's peak. "She did not."

Laurel nods emphatically. "She did. Then she and Nick got into it."

"Oh my GOD, Laurel. This is the stuff of bad rom-coms! So melodramatic!"

"Believe me, I know. Anyway, they yelled at each other for a few minutes, then she told me she thinks it would be best if she recuses herself from my dissertation defense. She said she'll go to the dean and request that they find me a new advisor. So at least that's dealt with."

"*At least.*" I'm not trying to sound like I'm mocking her, but *come on.*

Now it's her turn to shoot me an evil glare. "I think you're just jealous that you don't have this kind of drama in your life."

My mind flashes over the last school year: keeping my eyes down every time I walked down the hallway, hearing snickers and catching sympathetic looks when I entered faculty meetings. The charming grin Kyle would give me every time we were forced to share airspace, like nothing had ever happened; the way I wanted to punch him directly in the face whenever he did.

"No, I think I've had enough drama for a lifetime," I assure her. "How did you leave things with Nick?"

"Well, you know." She shoots me a furtive look.

"Laurel!" I shout. "You *slept* with him?"

"Not right away," she scoffs, like waiting a day or so made the whole situation any less insane. "We went out to dinner on

Friday night. And one thing led to another, and...it just happened."

I shake my head. "I raise my glass to you, living the life so many women dream of."

"Do many women dream of academic ruin and disastrous love triangles?" She quirks a brow.

"I think so," I say matter-of-factly. "That's the premise of nearly every teen drama ever aired. At least, the second part is."

"Hmm." She pretends to consider this, then flips the script. "So, what happened with Oliver?"

"Oh. Um, he brought me home the night of the storm. And then he had to stay because of the weather."

"Here we go!" She honestly looks deranged, she's so excited. At least she doesn't seem angry with me anymore. "Tell me all about it."

I think of Oliver's warm chest and his kisses in the dim light; the way I screamed his name and then fell asleep in his arms. The way the peanut butter and jelly sandwiches we ate tasted like a gourmet meal; how his tone about *us* shifted to future tense almost immediately. Because he wants me to stay. Because *I* want to stay.

I don't know that I'm ready to share any of it. It feels too intimate, too sacred a thing to just blab about like it's merely locker room talk.

Suddenly, Eleanor's reticence to go into detail in her diary makes a lot more sense to me.

I decide to go for brevity. "We borrowed several of your condoms," I shrug. "I'll buy you more."

Laurel's jaw drops. "Ivy, you harlot."

I snort. "That's pretty rich, coming from you."

"It's true," she agrees, throwing her arm around my shoulders. "We're just a couple of crazy women-about-town."

We decide to go for a walk where the waves meet the sand, and that keeps us occupied until dinnertime. I'm meeting Oliver for ice cream after his shift, so I keep things simple with an egg salad sandwich. Laurel updates me on her parents' laundry room renovation, and I tell her more about Maisie's surgery.

The topic of Simon, or of my discussions with my mom about Eleanor's diary, don't come up at all. Things are feeling a little bit better between Laurel and I, and I'm afraid to tempt fate by reintroducing my quest to unravel the hidden mysteries of the past. When and if I'm able to figure out what happened all those years ago, I'll have to decide whether to share it with Laurel. But that's a worry for another day.

"YOU HAVE TO TRY THIS," Oliver insists, holding out a spoonful of blueberry pie ice cream.

"Only if you try the cookies and cream."

"You drive a hard bargain." He leans forward and licks the edge of the cone I've shoved next to his mouth.

Watching his tongue dart along the ice cream is, frankly, a religious experience for me. But we're in public, so I shove thoughts of his head between my thighs out of my mind for the moment. Instead, I take his spoon and am overwhelmed by how deliciously bright and fruity the blueberry pie flavor is.

"Okay, so, I don't often do this," I say once I swallow, "but I'm going to admit I was wrong. That's definitely the best ice cream I've ever had."

His eyes glint with victory. "I'm honored to be on the receiving end of one of your rare concessions."

"This just means you're going to have to let me take you out for ice cream again so I can order this flavor for myself."

We'd haggled a bit over who got to pay for tonight's dessert, but I ultimately won the battle, reminding him I owed him for his help with the library books.

"Taking you to the library benefited me, also, you realize," he'd teased.

"Why? Did you enjoy watching me verbally spar with another woman with you as the prize?"

"Maybe," he'd smirked.

"Well, I've got news for you," I'd whispered close to his ear. "Next time, I'm going to let her win. She can deal with all *this*." I gesticulated wildly like he was exuding an aura of absurdity.

"Oh yeah?"

I'd taken one look at him and then shook my head. "Never mind. I want you all to myself."

The kiss he'd given me then was one of the best of my life.

We're sitting on a bench now, watching tourists scuff sand along the sidewalks in the setting sun. The air is humming with the heat of the day, but there's an underlying chill starting to creep in. I'm grateful to have both my cardigan and the warmth of Oliver's arm around my shoulders. Between the ice cream and the company, my soul is glowing so bright I'm surprised passers-by don't stop and gawk.

"So, I talked to my mom on my lunch break today," Oliver announces after a long, comfortable silence.

"How'd it go?" I lean my head against his shoulder.

His fingers tighten against my right biceps. "Tense, at first.

I'm still really angry." He takes a deep breath. "But we talked about my writing, and the bookstore, and Maisie. And you."

I snap my gaze to his. "Me?"

Then he smiles and says, "Yes, you." And I think the heat his words send through my body will be enough to keep me warm for the rest of my life.

"We didn't talk much about *her*. Actually, I realized she was steering the conversation very deliberately away from herself. It was like she was starved for details of my life."

I remember how my mother had done the same thing, desperate to restore our connection. "I actually know exactly what you mean."

Oliver presses a gentle kiss to my cheek in answer. "So I think I'd like to keep trying. And I told her we'd come to her wedding." His eyes sweep my face. "Assuming you still want to, that is."

Any socially acceptable reason to see this man in a suit would be more than fine with me. "When is it?"

"October 19th." He must catch the hesitation in my eyes, because he continues hurriedly, "I know that's well after Maisie comes back from her surgery. I thought, even if you've already gone back to Boston, I could come out and meet you for the weekend? The wedding's on Cape Cod, so it wouldn't be too far for you. Maybe we could take turns visiting each other a few times a month, or something, even if you decide..." He pauses. "You know."

In this moment, I'm more certain than ever that I can't leave. How can I go back to Brookline without exploring the possibilities that are unfolding in front of me here, with Oliver?

"Count me in," I say, bending to kiss his shoulder. "On one condition, though."

He raises a speculative brow.

"Bring a book in your suit jacket pocket. Just in case the reception's boring."

Oliver laughs, pulling me closer to him. "I knew you were the perfect woman."

Something flares inside my chest, sending words shooting up my throat. Words I can't share; words I ruthlessly shove back down into the depths of my soul.

I knew you were perfect, too.

twenty-seven

When I check my phone after my beach run on Monday morning, I have a voicemail from an unknown number. I hit play while I stretch in a puddle of sweat on my bedroom floor.

"Hello, this message is for Ivy Parker. My name is Brianna Marsh. I'm calling from the Freehold Community Library, over in Springfield, about the position you applied for. We were impressed by your résumé, and we'd love to set up a time to do a virtual interview. Give me a call back at your earliest convenience and let me know when might work for you. Have a great day!"

It's a good thing my phone is sitting on the ground, or I'm certain I would have dropped it. I hadn't expected to hear back from *any* of the jobs I applied to, but especially not the Springfield position. It's an inner-city library with a huge tax base and lots of children's programming. There will never be a dull moment for whoever gets that job, and I imagine it's going to be a competitive candidate pool. The salary's nothing to sneeze at, either. As librarian compensation goes, that is.

The idea of a challenge—of endless book orders, staffing tasks, program planning—is beyond appealing. Working at a library like Freehold would definitely be the next logical step for my career. There'd be plenty to do, and so many kids who could benefit from my work. It's exactly what I've been dreaming of, as I wither away in the shadows at Farnsworth.

Maisie's smile flashes through my mind. So does Oliver's, and that one hurts a little more. Something like Freehold is what I'd wanted before, no question. But now I'm not so sure.

That said, I'm not certain Shoreline can pay enough to make a permanent move to Ogunquit feasible for me. In all the heady rush of figuring out what I want, it hadn't occurred to me to ask Maisie about benefits or how much she could offer if I went full-time.

I shake my head rapidly, trying to clear the sudden fog from my mind. There's no need to rush into any decisions. But I *do* need to take this interview.

I call Brianna back, and it takes a few minutes to get transferred to her line. "So sorry," she says breathlessly when we're finally connected. "I'm running a teen book club today, and we are beyond swamped."

She's running the book club? Is she the current children's librarian?

As if my thoughts are being transmitted directly into her earpiece, she continues, "I'm actually head of adult services, but I'm filling in for our current head of children's. She's going to be leaving us once her third child is born next month, but she's been put on bedrest, so we're short-staffed a little sooner than expected."

"Well, it's a pleasure to speak with you. And I'd love to set up an interview."

"Perfect," Brianna says, all business. "Can you do next Monday? Ten o'clock?"

I close my eyes, trying to picture the calendar on my phone where I've plugged in my shifts at Shoreline. Monday is also the day before Maisie leaves for her surgery. But I should be home at ten; I don't have to work until noon. It really would be the perfect time to do the interview. "That sounds great." Laurel will have to let me use her laptop for an hour or so, but I'm sure she won't mind.

"Wonderful!" Some sort of crash echoes through the phone. "I should go; I think some of the kids just knocked over a display. But I'll send you the details later today. Looking forward to it, Ivy!"

"Likewise. Thank you so much!" I hang up, then lay the phone next to my outstretched leg, staring at the screen when it goes black. I've gone from a path so narrow it makes me claustrophobic to an intersection that looks like something out of a Dr. Seuss book, colorful possibilities snaking off in every direction. Taking a steadying breath, I remind myself that these are just that: possibilities; options. Nothing is set in stone. Ultimately, I still get to decide.

All of these decisions are beyond overwhelming, though, and my heart is pounding in my chest like it can run away from making any choices at all. I've dealt with anxiety (and my psychologist mother) for long enough that I know my body's just reacting to the stress. That doesn't mean I enjoy feeling like I'm having a heart attack, though.

I need to get out of here. Oliver's working a closing shift today, and Laurel's back at it with her own peculiar spin on the

British Invasion (heavy metal plus nineteenth-century artists). Before I can talk myself out of it, I'm dialing Simon's number.

"Hello?" He sounds surprised to be receiving a call. Guilt etches a notch under my ribs.

"Hi, Simon. This is Ivy Parker."

"Oh, hello, Ivy. Is everything okay at the house?"

Of course he would assume this was a tenant issue. Because we barely know each other, despite the family connection, so why else would I be calling?

But he's the last tie I have to my grandparents, other than Janie, and she's two hours away. I've never had a stronger urge to talk to Eleanor; to let Charlie tell me everything's going to be okay. And I can't have that, now or ever again. But Simon is here, and he knew them better than anyone.

"I wondered if you might be up for that visit we spoke about?" The desperation in my voice rings louder than the vaguely musical screeching flowing out from under Laurel's door.

"Well, that would be lovely, Ivy. It's so rare that I have guests."

The guilt digs in deeper. "I'd love to come by. Two o'clock?"

"Absolutely. I'm up at the retirement community in Wells. Do you know the place?"

"I can look it up," I offer.

"I've no doubt your grasp of technology is more than sufficient to get you here," he says with no shred of mockery, just admiration. "I'm in room 412. I'll see you soon."

"See you soon, Simon."

When I hang up the phone, it occurs to me that my heart rate has returned to a completely normal rhythm.

. . .

I SHOW up to the assisted living facility in Wells with a bouquet of flowers. It seemed inappropriate to come empty-handed, though it felt equally ridiculous to bring what was essentially a housewarming gift to an octogenarian in a glorified nursing home. The rental of Beach Haven further complicated matters for me; was it weird to bring a gift to your landlord?

But Simon was sort of like family; he'd been so close to my grandparents for so many years. And he'd repeatedly hinted that he's lonely. For that reason, my visit felt more like a social call than a business appointment.

But I struggled deciding what to bring. It's always challenging to gift food to the elderly; who knows what they're allowed to eat, or if their teeth can hold up to things like hard candy or nuts. I figured flowers were a safe choice, and also the least I could do.

Simon's room sits at the middle of a long hallway disguised with cheerful wallpaper and bright carpeting, as if to say, "Hey, I'm not a nursing home. You could still return to your life—this isn't the end." He has a wreath of faux hydrangeas hung on his door, and a small placard above the doorbell reads "Simon Foster, Esq." I swallow a laugh. While I realized Simon was a lawyer, the inclusion of the honorific in this setting strikes me as more than a little silly.

I experiment with several ways to hold the flowers while I wait for Simon to come to the door. Out in front feels too expectant; to the side, too disinterested. I settle on shoving them in the crook of my elbow just as the door swings open.

Simon is grinning broadly, eyes surrounded by laugh lines. His white hair is combed gently to one side, and his orange polo shirt has clearly been ironed. His khakis are equally well-presented, not even wrinkling against the edges of his wheelchair. I do remember Simon as a very good dresser, but it's surprising that he's kept at it now when there's no one to impress.

"It's great to see you," I exclaim, holding out both the flowers and my hand at the exact moment he swoops in for a hug.

"Ivy, it's been too long," he says, something like wistful joy echoed in his voice.

"It really has." I think I see his hand swipe a tear away from the corner of his eye.

Simon collects himself, as if he'd been lost in a memory. "Come in, come in."

I follow him into his small apartment, which is outfitted entirely in white microfiber and nautical prints. "I love the aesthetic here," I tell him honestly. "It's perfect for the coast."

Simon smiles proudly, wheeling himself over next to the sofa. "If I'm going to be stuck in a home, it absolutely must feel like home." He surveys the space. "I had all of this brought over from Beach Haven. Apologies if what's left isn't quite up to snuff."

I don't have the heart to tell him that the house smells like decades-old mothballs and could desperately use a facelift. And a solid cleaning. "It's perfect," I offer. Because honestly, for what I need at this moment in my life, it really is. In so many ways.

"I brought these for you." I hold out the bouquet of dahlias, lilies, and vibrant wildflowers that I picked up at the corner market on my way out of town. "Do you have a vase? I can put them in water for you."

"Thank you, Ivy, they're lovely. Yes, there's a vase up in that cupboard there." He gestures to a cabinet near the door.

"So, tell me how you've been," I say. While he talks about his injury and the subpar food the residents get, I busy myself with finding the vase, filling it with water, and arranging the flowers. When Simon finishes giving me his update and asks how I've been, I'm not even sure where to begin.

I'm even less sure when I set the vase down on the end table next to Simon and am startled by a photo of my grandfather staring up at me.

Grandpa's eyes are vibrant, crinkling at the edges. He must be in his 30s here. He still has all his hair and the long, lithe frame that he lost when he got his desk job after my dad and uncle started high school. I recognize the shirt he's wearing; it's one I saw on him in so many of the photos my dad pulled for the funeral slideshow. It must have been one of his favorites.

I don't have time to puzzle through why Simon has this photo in such a prominent position before he notices me gawking at it. "Handsome man, your grandfather." He gives me a pleasant smile. "You have his kind eyes."

The Venn diagram of people who know both my grandfather and me well enough to notice we have the same blue-gray irises, the same lashes several shades darker than our hair, is pretty simple to imagine. Simon's the only person in a 100-mile radius who could land squarely at the center.

"I've always loved that he shared them with me." I try to smile gracefully, even though my mind is reeling from both the photo and the memories it conjures.

Simon looks down at the photo, too, and something melancholy clouds his gaze. He blinks it away as quickly as it appeared.

I try to imagine losing my best friend; try to figure out who I even love this much *now*, much less after the countless decades of friendship Simon and Charlie had. Maybe Laurel. If life hadn't taken us in such different directions, maybe Amie could have made my list. Now, though, I'm unsure if I'll ever see her again. We haven't so much as texted in six months.

It occurs to me that, if my heart continues crying out for Oliver like it has been, maybe losing him would be like this for me. But of course, that's a different kind of love.

And I really don't want to think about losing Oliver.

"So tell me, Ivy." Simon's face betrays none of the sorrow it was just reflecting. "What do you do for work?"

I perch on one edge of his immaculate sofa and explain that I'm a librarian; that I'm looking for a new job. "I actually got a call for an interview this morning," I hedge.

"Well, that's wonderful." Simon's smile is so effortless; he has the casual charm most businessmen spend their lives chasing without much success.

I shrug. "I suppose that it is, yes."

Simon tilts his head and pinches his lips. "Something about your tone suggests it's anything but."

A small chuckle escapes my throat, not because anything is funny, but rather because he sounds so much like Charlie that I can't quite believe it. "If you'd asked me six months ago if I'd want this opportunity, I would have offered a resounding, even desperate yes. But things have changed for me. And now I'm feeling a bit stuck."

"Does this have anything to do with your work for Maisie?"

Simon can see through me, I'm fairly certain. There's nothing but kindness in his face, but it's as if he's riffling through my thoughts as they occur.

"Yes, I think so. And there's...someone, here." My cheeks heat as the essence of Oliver swirls through my mind. His smile; his faint cedar and vanilla scent. The brush of his hand against mine; the way he tastes like the future.

I clear my throat, not wanting my thoughts to stray too much in a place that feels decidedly devoid of sensuality. "Not to mention, this has been my favorite place on Earth since childhood." My lips turn up. "There's just something about how dominoes are falling for me this summer. Ever since I got here, really. It's making me feel like the path has never been more apparent."

Simon nods, slowly at first, then with more conviction. "When the universe clears a path for us, we owe it to ourselves to follow."

I'm not sure how he manages to sound so wise. Most lawyers I've met are decidedly less profound. "You're probably right. I'm just not sure how it will all work. The money, for one thing. And with...someone."

Simon looks like he wants to laugh at me, but, to his credit, he refrains. "Well, maybe those dominoes just haven't fallen yet."

"Could be."

"And," he continues, "for what it's worth, you can rest assured you'll have a place to stay, for as long as you want to be here."

"That's so kind of you. But I'm sure you could get more money from vacationers. Wouldn't it be better for you if—"

He shakes his head vehemently. "You're family, Ivy. You're Charlie and Eleanor's family, so you're mine. I don't care about the money." Simon casts his eyes to the photo at his left. "There's nothing I wouldn't do for Charlie."

Something tugs at the edge of my mind, vying for privilege of the floor. I try to ignore it, but it whooshes in regardless. Was Simon...*is* Simon...*in love* with my grandfather?

I rush to clear the shock from my face, but I'm sure it's too late. Simon smiles at me gently, as if acknowledging the elephant in the room. "Don't walk away from love, Ivy. There's nothing more important."

"Of course," I whisper, thinking of Oliver, thinking of Simon. Thinking of Simon pining after my grandfather all those years, staying close because they were best friends, yes, but also because his feelings offered no alternative.

I wonder if Charlie knew. God, I wonder if *Eleanor* knew. She was always so kind to Simon; they both were. I have to imagine, if they knew, they were okay with it. That the three of them had found some sort of balance, where they could live around the edges of the truth and just be happy with what they each were able to give one another.

"So, tell me about working at Shoreline." Simon's eyes are rapt on my face, as if he didn't just divulge what must be his deepest, most intimate secret.

"It's really wonderful," I say. I'm sure my eyes light up, because my heart does. And I tell him all about it, from the thrill of finding the perfect book for each customer to the soothing rhythm of shelving books to the way Oliver and Maisie and I all get along so beautifully. But the whole time I'm talking, a little part of my mind is aching, throbbing like an open wound, at the realization that Simon lived his whole life with the person he loved most just out of reach.

. . .

"IT'S JUST SO TRAGIC, you know?" I lift my head off Oliver's chest, fresh off a frenzied fit of passion in absolute silence so as not to disturb Laurel, who already went to bed.

He pulls my hand to his lips and presses a kiss against my fingers. A thrill goes through me that I get to be here with him. That our very divergent paths happened to cross this summer.

"It does feel like a very unfortunate set of circumstances," he agrees. I've been telling him about my afternoon with Simon. I'm not sure I can discuss it with Laurel; she doesn't even know I went to see Simon in the first place.

"I just can't imagine it," I breathe against his skin.

"Can't imagine what?"

I love feeling his voice vibrating against me. I settle further into him, wishing this moment could stretch on long past September. "Not having *this*," I reply. "When it's so close."

His breath stills beneath me. "Are you likening your feelings for me to the unrequited, decades-long love affair of your grandfather and his best friend?"

A chuckle rises to my throat. "I suppose I am."

"Well, let me be the first to tell you how flawed that comparison is."

I think my heart stops. "What do you mean?" Is it possible I've massively misunderstood what's happening here?

Oliver shifts onto his side and looks right into my eyes. "Because this," he says, taking my other hand and pressing it against his heart, "is very, very much requited."

My heart swells until I feel it might burst out of my chest. "Oliver," I breathe. Then my lips are on his, and his hands are threading through my hair, and I'm pressed against him as tightly as humanly possible, wanting with every fiber of my being for this moment to stretch on into an infinite future.

And maybe it's because of how he's making me feel, or the distraction of Simon's big reveal earlier, but when I remember I haven't told Oliver about my interview, I decide not to bring it up. At least not today.

twenty-eight

Oliver leaves straight from Beach Haven to head to Shoreline in the morning. "I hope you don't think I'm being presumptuous," he'd said with a wicked grin the night before, showing me the change of clothes and toothbrush that he'd brought.

"Please sleep here every night," I'd replied, pulling his face to mine. Maybe these butterflies are going to fade someday, but they've shown no signs of settling down yet.

Laurel and I have pancakes for breakfast (I cook this time, so the process is much neater than when she made waffles our first week here), then she retreats to her room (or, as she's taken to calling it, her "study") to write. I'm working a closing shift at the bookstore today, so I have plenty of time to read and relax before I have to head out.

I'm finding it hard to focus on my book, though. There are so many emotions taking up space in my mind that I find myself reading the same page over and over again, until I dejectedly resign myself to a bookmark.

Perhaps it was the visit with Simon yesterday, but looking out at the waves that have watched the rise and fall of the House of Parker is making me feel more than a little homesick. Not so much for Brookline itself, but more for the people that make it home.

My mother's words flash through my mind: "You can call your dad, too, you know." A pang of guilt hits then; Dad's probably been lonely and depressed, dealing with work and estate stuff all alone. I should have called him sooner.

My father is a self-employed web developer, so he's always at home. Or, these days, at his apartment. I hesitate to refer to that as his home, and I'm sure he'd be even more reluctant. Grabbing my phone, I hit his number on speed dial.

Dad picks up on the third ring. "Ivy Bean!" He greets me with the nonsensical nickname he bestowed upon me at birth. "How's it hanging, kiddo?"

I suppose some women about to turn 30 might be bothered by the childhood nickname or the "kiddo" diminutive, but, in my heightened emotional state, I'm finding it oddly heart-warming.

"I'm doing pretty well, Dad. Reading on the beach right now, actually. How are you?"

I can practically hear the longing in his voice. "Ahh, that sounds perfect. I wish I were there with you."

Swallowing hard, I remind him, "You could be." But I think we both realize that maybe being here would be too much for him. At least for right now.

"Hopefully soon, kiddo. So tell me, what have you and Laurel been up to?"

"Well," I chuckle, "Laurel's basically been sequestered,

working on her dissertation. And occasionally wreaking havoc back at school."

"That sounds like Laurel."

"You're not kidding." Without stopping to consider whether it's a good idea, I barrel on. "I visited Simon Foster yesterday."

In that moment, the world goes utterly silent, save for the gentle crash of the waves on the shore. It must be at least five seconds before Dad says, "Oh, really?"

"Yep. I was feeling guilty that he's all alone in assisted living. He hurt his leg, did you know?"

"Oh, I think maybe Greg told me that." His voice sounds lightyears away now. Disinterested, or maybe sad. Does this mean he knows about Simon's feelings for my grandfather? I suppose that could be a little hard to navigate; knowing that someone besides your mother loved your dad so much, but couldn't have him. Doubly hard when that person is someone you looked up to; someone your whole family loved like one of their own.

"Other than his leg, though, Simon seemed great. Well-dressed, as always."

"Of course." I hear the smile creeping back into Dad's voice.

"I'll probably try to get up to see him again before I head home," I say. The word "home" sounds hollow to me all of a sudden; the idea of going *there* at the expense of being *here* like a cold bucket of water thrown over my head.

"Hey, Dad. Did you—" I hesitate, not sure if I should continue; sure that I'll regret it if I don't. "Did you know Grandma kept a diary?"

This time, the silence stretches a good 15 seconds at least.

"She did always like to dabble with her writing," he says finally. "It doesn't surprise me that she'd have a journal."

I can't quite put my finger on the specific reason—is it his tone, or the pause, or how acutely jovial he suddenly sounds—or maybe all three—but I know in an instant that he's lying.

"Right." I kick the sand with my toe. "Well, I should probably let you go."

"Sure thing, Ivy Bean. Thanks for calling. Let's talk again soon, okay?"

"Absolutely. Love you, Dad." The words stick in my throat, and I suddenly feel like I'm going to cry.

"Love you too, kiddo."

After we hang up, I lay back on the towel and cover my eyes with my forearm, desperate to keep the tears from falling. The ocean continues its relentless pursuit for the shoreline, crashing to the rhythm of the truth that won't stop pulsing through my head. I wonder how many times the Atlantic has watched things fall apart—for Eleanor, for Charlie. For Mom and Dad. For me. All I wanted to do was put some of them back together. But maybe it's already too late.

THE WEEK FLIES BY. Shoreline has never been busier, thanks to Ogunquit being at the height of its peak season. Oliver's largely occupied helping Maisie get things in order ahead of her surgery, so working the register and helping customers falls largely to me.

I'm loving every minute of it. I feel like a matchmaker, a go-between for readers and their perfect stories. This is why I became a librarian, I realize—to proliferate my love of reading and help others find theirs, too.

During my lunch break on Wednesday afternoon, I finally summon the courage to call Becky Green, my boss at Farnsworth. Maisie hasn't brought up me staying, and neither has Oliver, but I know I owe them both an answer. Simon also needs to be kept abreast of my plans so he can rent out Beach Haven after my departure.

Hell, I owe it to myself to firm up my plans, too.

Becky's clearly in summer mode, answering the phone with a cacophony of splashing and children yelling in the background. *Excellent*, I think. *She'll be distracted by her kids and more likely to say yes.*

I surprise myself by how aloof my explanation is. "I might need to take a brief leave of absence at the start of the school year," I tell her.

"Stop that right now, Zachariah," Becky shouts over the din of two screaming children. "Leave your sister alone. I'm sorry," she says closer to the mouthpiece of her phone. "These kids; I'm telling you. Can you repeat that?"

This time, I eliminate the uncertainty in my request. "I need to take a brief leave of absence at the start of the school year."

"Oh." Her voice drips with disappointment. I guess this might not be so easy after all. "Well, do you have PTO you can use?"

I'd anticipated this question. "I do; two weeks. But I'll need at least three off. I'm prepared to take that unpaid," I rush.

"Have you looked into family leave?" Becky sounds distracted now, like her attention has shifted back to whatever is causing the marvelous thudding sound in her yard.

I'd prefer not to tell her that I wouldn't qualify for family leave because Maisie is, in fact, not a relative. It feels like that would cheapen my case, somehow. "I'll have to check," I reply vaguely.

"Well, please do. I'll be honest, Ivy, the beginning of the school year is just about the worst time for you to be out. I don't have time to find a temp, and you'd miss all the first-week intro sessions for the computer lab. Those are important."

Tears fill my eyes, the hallmark of an inveterate people pleaser. I don't even like Becky all that much; she tends to swoop in to micromanage at seemingly arbitrary moments after having ignored her staff for months on end. In that regard, she's the worst kind of boss, really. Pretending not to care, then suddenly having a strong opinion and being flabbergasted that things haven't been run exactly her way in all of the time she's been paying no attention whatsoever.

Regardless, I don't want to upset her. "I'm sorry; I can try to make other arrangements." The words are out before I realize I *have* no way to make other arrangements, short of running out on Maisie and Oliver.

"No, no." Becky sounds like she has her head in her hands. "You have the PTO; it's your right to use it. Look into the family leave, and if you can't get it, you'll have to take that third week unpaid. We'll just run the intro labs when you get back."

"Thank you. I appreciate your flexibility."

She barks a laugh. "I'm not sure anyone has ever referred to me in those terms before, but you're welcome."

"Well, I appreciate it. This is...important. I can't get out of it." In that moment, I'm feeling like this is the truth.

"Send me an email with the details, please. I'll get it situated with HR."

"Thanks, Becky. I'll do that." I make a mental note to commandeer Laurel's laptop when I get home from Shoreline. I need to check the meeting details from Brianna at the Springfield library, too.

Once I hang up with Becky, I head straight to the office to talk to Maisie. She and Oliver are sitting at her desk, several piles of spreadsheets laid out before them. They look up expectantly when I enter.

"I'm sorry to interrupt. I just wanted to let you know, Maisie, that I spoke with my boss at home." The word still rings hollow. "I'll be able to stay here an extra three weeks to cover your leave."

I can't decide who seems happier to hear my announcement. Oliver's eyes are crinkling at the edges, and he looks like he wants to jump out of his chair and hug me. Maisie speaks first, though. "This is wonderful news, Ivy. Thank you so much for doing this for me."

"It's nothing." I roll off the praise. "I'm happy to do it." Unlike Becky, Maisie is a boss I don't have to lie to.

Maisie nods. "We'll have to meet later this week to discuss plans for my absence. All three of us." She looks between Oliver and I. "Although I have the utmost faith that the two of you could handle it without any guidance from me whatsoever."

I might be blushing now. "That's really nice of you to say."

"Well, it's true," she replies matter-of-factly. "You're a good pair, you know."

Oliver's cheeks look a little pink, too. "Ivy and I can put together a schedule and some high-level plans tomorrow when you're off," he offers, looking at me to confirm. I nod.

Maisie's gaze darts back and forth between us, one brow raised. She buries a smirk, but she just thanks him. The bell on the shop door jingles then, so I head back to the front of the store.

Only when I'm safely ensconced in the confines of the register counter do I process the reality: *I get to stay here.* Not forever. Not yet. But I've just bought myself another three weeks to figure things out. Relief floods through me, soothing pressure points I didn't even realize I had.

My mother used to give me strategies for managing my anxiety, including sitting on a couch and trying to focus intently on relaxing every last part of my body, one by one. It always shocked me just how tense I was before I started; how fluid and weightless I felt at the end, sinking into the cushions beneath me like there was no stress left to give me shape.

That's what this feels like. Except instead of just solving a problem, I've also handed myself an opportunity this time. An opportunity that feels an awful lot like my wildest dreams.

twenty-nine

On Sunday, Oliver is taking me out on his dad's boat. The sun is high in the sky, baking the land with warmth uncharacteristic for even this time of year. Still, I know the breeze off the coast will be brisk, so I bring a hoodie just in case. I also stop at the market down the street for sandwiches, chips, and an assortment of seltzers and sodas on my way to meet Oliver.

As I drag a cooler I found in Beach Haven's attic down the dock, it occurs to me how dating looks much the same for me as it did for Eleanor, even six decades later. Picnics, it seems, never go out of style.

Upon reaching the water, I immediately notice Robert Clarke has named his boat the *Orca*.

"Is this because of *Jaws*?" I ask, watching Oliver's tanned arms work the ropes.

He chuckles. "Oh, absolutely. My dad has quite the morbid sense of humor."

The boat is about 20 feet long, with an open back and a winch for hauling nets or traps. Even though it's been a good 15 years since Robert's fished for a living, the *Orca* is in excellent shape.

"So, who kept the boat up all this time?" My eyes sweep over Oliver's hard lines, and I already know the answer. His body wasn't built in the gym; it was honed through sweat equity: taking care of his dad, and the boat, and Maisie and her bookstore.

Oliver grins at my transparent ogling. "I did what I could."

"It looks great," I say honestly. Because it does. How had he ever found the time?

He offers a hand so I can hop aboard. "My father always made it very clear that the boat was our insurance policy. Even if things fell apart with his disability payments, or the bookstore, I could always run tours or register for a fishing license. Or we could sell the boat for a quick influx of cash." He shrugs. "I don't know how accurate that is, but I've always kept it shipshape, just in case."

I roll my eyes. "Again with the boat puns."

He wraps his arms around my waist, dragging me closer. "You know you love them."

My eyes flick up to his in surprise, because I do think the word "love" is hovering in the ether between us, but it has nothing to do with the puns. I'm not sure I'd admitted that to myself until now, though.

"Mmm," I murmur. "You're very clever." I let our faces drift together, our lips brush. I get lost in the feeling of being completely connected, of his arms around the small of my back; his chest against mine. Here, in the sun, sparkling waves spread out before us, my mind goes utterly blank, save for the feeling of being alive in this very moment.

I can't remember the last time I felt so present.

When we finally break apart, Oliver finishes getting everything ready and then turns the engine over. I stand beside him as he guides us cautiously out of the harbor, under the drawbridge and beyond the cove.

The wind starts whipping through my hair almost immediately; the waves bobbing us up and down as we skip across the surface of the Atlantic. I'm grateful for my sweatshirt, which I slip on about two minutes into the trip. Oliver shoots me an amused grin.

"What? I like to be cozy."

His arm slips around my waist. "You're cute, that's all."

"Likewise," I return, pressing a kiss to his cheek.

We trace the outline of the coast all the way down to York, where Oliver docks the *Orca* so we can have lunch. He stretches out on the bench across from mine, considering me over his sandwich.

"What's going through that brilliant mind of yours?"

"Have you thought anymore about staying past Maisie's leave?" His eyes don't leave my face.

I have to squint to look back at him, thanks to the position of the sun. I slide my sunglasses down, a guard against the intensity of both the light and his question. "I have," I admit.

"And?" The breeze blows his hair in time with the waves.

I shake my head. "I don't know. I would love to stay." In fact, the idea of leaving him makes me feel like I'm suffocating. "But I'm not sure I can afford it. Maisie isn't able to pay nearly as much as Farnsworth." I'd finally asked her for full-time salary and benefits information when we met to talk through the plan for her time away, and it wouldn't leave much wiggle room in my budget.

Granted, if I were to move here, I would either have to rent or sell my condo back in Brookline. It's in a decent neighborhood, though it is very small and rather out-of-date, so I'm not sure how much it would fetch on the market. I could probably live off that income for a while, but it would run out eventually, and I'm not sure what would happen then.

I don't intentionally avoid mention of the Springfield opportunity, at least at first. But, watching Oliver gaze at me from across the boat, I'm struck by how badly I want to extend this magic. I can't bring myself to ruin it with a much dimmer reality.

He nods his understanding, more quickly than I'd have expected given the nature of our conversation. "I think you should talk to Maisie. There might be options you're not considering."

My brows wrinkle over my nose. "I'm not sure what you mean."

Oliver crosses to me and takes my hand. "Just talk to her, okay?"

"Okay," I promise. "I will."

AFTER OUR AFTERNOON on the boat fades to evening, Oliver and I stop for ice cream so I can get a blueberry pie cone of my own. He orders one, too. "What is life without this ice cream, Ivy?" he jokes.

"Are you ripping off George Harrison lyrics right now?" I shove him playfully with my hip.

He smiles guiltily. "All artists borrow from one another."

"Do you fancy yourself a Beatle?" I tease.

"What can I say; you set my lyricism in motion."

For a response that sweet, I can't think of a clever retort. So I just insert myself between Oliver and his ice cream cone and kiss him, as if my lips can channel the ever-growing warmth in my chest straight into his. As if I can make him understand how much this means to me.

Then, we grab a six-pack from the convenience store at the top of Shore Road. We disobey the strongly worded sign banning alcohol from the beach and sit directly in the sand with our feet in the water, sipping hard lemonade and watching the sun set over the horizon.

"I love it here," I tell him, swirling my fingers through a frothy wave that swooshed higher on the beach than I'd expected.

"It loves you," Oliver replies, reaching for my hand. Before I can take it, he cups a handful of water and splashes me right in the face.

"Are you serious?" Setting my bottle down, I round on him. He's laughing manically, like splashing me just now was the highlight of his life.

"You're already all wet," he reasons, catching my wrists where I'm trying to splash him back. He lets gravity push us backward until he's lying down and I'm leaning over him, our arms still locked together.

I take in his blue eyes, still bright even in the twilight; the hair curling against his forehead in the evening humidity. The smile playing on his lips; a smile just for me. I'm pretty sure I've never wanted anything so badly in my entire life as to make him look this happy.

There are those words again, threatening to force their way

out of my throat. I silence them by leaning down and fixing Oliver with the world's sloppiest kiss, courtesy of the two hard lemonades I've downed since we got to the beach. Time slides away then, becoming merely a suggestion of a thing. Instead, it's just Oliver and me, caught in an infinite moment here on the wet beach sand, surrounded by the deepening sky.

It's not until a disapproving "ahem" sounds from behind us that we're ejected from paradise. I look up to see an elderly couple out for a stroll, arms linked, glaring down at us like our makeout session is the most offensive thing they've ever seen. After reading Eleanor's diary, I have a pretty good idea what the elderly might have been up to in their youth, so I don't let their disgust get to me. I do sit up, though, shooting the couple a polite smile and grabbing Oliver's hand. "Come on," I say. "Let's get back to Beach Haven."

We run up the sand like this is some sort of delightful movie montage. The second we're inside the house, he's pressing me up against the back of the door, parting my lips with his tongue, and sending me back to that faraway place only Oliver seems capable of taking me.

A second "ahem," this one significantly more amused, disrupts us a minute later.

"I didn't want to intrude," Laurel says, smirking at us, her purse slung over her shoulder.

"Then why did you?" I narrow my eyes petulantly.

"Sorry," she replies. "I'm going out. You're blocking the door."

Oliver pulls me to the side. "Sorry."

"No worries." Laurel skirts around us and turns the knob.

"Wait a second." I reach for her wrist. "Who are you meeting right now? Isn't it, like, nine o'clock?" It occurs to me I have absolutely no clue what time it is. The day flew by in a wholly otherworldly way.

This is now the second time in a week I've seen Laurel embarrassed. "Porter?" She says it like it's a question.

"Laurel! What about Nick?"

Oliver's eyebrows go up. "Who's Nick?"

Laurel shakes her head. "It's a long story."

"Is it, though?" I tease.

"Look, Porter's been asking me to hang out," she rushes. "I'm just meeting him for a drink, and I'll tell him about Nick. We can just be friends."

I nod slowly. "You *can*."

Laurel rolls her eyes. "That's all we're going to be, at least for now. Why don't you worry about your own...escapades." She looks furtively at Oliver, then back at me. "I refilled the toiletry bag."

Now it's my turn to blush. I'm trying to think of a clever retort when Oliver holds up his wallet. "I've got it covered, Laurel. But thank you."

I whip around to face him. "Oliver!"

He paints an innocent expression. "What?"

Laurel snickers. "You two are something else. Have a good night, okay?"

"You too," I reply as she turns to go. "But not *too* good, if you know what I mean."

"Screw you, Ivy!" Laurel cries out in a singsong voice as she departs.

"I can't wait to watch the sitcom about you two being old maids in an apartment together someday," Oliver says in a low voice, shutting the door behind Laurel.

"Wow." I feign offense. "Thanks a lot. But I'm not planning to spend my golden years in tight quarters with my cousin."

He throws his arm around my shoulders. "Good plan. You should spend them with me instead."

My eyes flick over to his, which are twinkling at the joke. But it kind of looks like he's serious? I swallow hard, and I think he notices.

"Come on," I pull him down the hallway, desperate to change the subject simply because I'm not sure how to respond. I love the idea of our future together, but I can't tell how serious he is, and I don't want to be the one to make things weird. "I want to see what you brought in your wallet."

He laughs. "I thought you might."

Once we're in my room, with the door shut in case Laurel comes back, it only takes a minute for us to shed our wet clothes. Grains of sand fall everywhere as we toss them aside.

"Sorry," Oliver says, eyeing the mess, then my pink lace bra.

"Don't worry about it. I'll find a vacuum tomorrow." I run my pointer finger down his chest. "I have a feeling this might be well worth a little cleanup."

His mouth tips up. "What is 'this,' exactly?"

"Oh, I think you know," I tease, walking him back toward the bed.

"Mmm," he murmurs against my mouth. "I might have an inkling."

Then his hands are at my waist, my hips, between my legs, pulling my underwear to the side and sending my heart racing. I gasp as his fingers slip inside me, fumbling at his hips to return the pleasure.

He turns us around and eases me back onto the pillows,

then comes to kneel inside my thighs. "I've been thinking about this all day," he whispers.

"I'm always thinking about this," I answer, looking straight into his eyes.

He smiles, then takes my breath away when he says, "I'm always thinking about *you*."

We're a jumble of limbs and hands and kisses after that, moving together in a perfectly beautiful mess of two selves that are losing sight of their edges. His body and his poetry and his words—I didn't know what I was missing until I found him, but now that I have, I don't think I can do without.

When we finally collapse in a pile of satisfaction atop the comforter, Oliver runs his hand gently across my forehead, pressing a kiss to my temple. "You know," he begins quietly, "for someone who loves words so much, I'm left with precious few every time I think about how lucky I am."

I turn to face him, pulling myself against his chest. "Lucky how?" I ask coyly.

He grins. "Lucky to have met you."

My heart overflows with joy. "I feel lucky, too." I run my hand down his forearm contemplatively. "You know, I hated you at first."

"I could tell," he chuckles.

"But I'm glad I got over that." I lace my fingers through his. "In fact, I don't hate you at all anymore."

"Oh, no?" he quips.

I lean over to kiss him. "Not even a little bit."

Oliver's eyes come to rest on mine as I pull away. "As much as I enjoy our banter, I don't want to dance around the truth, because I feel it's important that you hear it." The earnest expression on his face might be the most adorable thing I've ever seen.

My heart starts pounding in my chest. "Oh?"

"I need you to know..." He inhales deeply, like he's nervous. I've never seen him this nervous before.

I squeeze his hand. "It's okay, Oliver." I don't want to make him uncomfortable.

"No," he shakes his head. "I want you to know; I can't not tell you anymore." He tucks my hair behind my ear, so tenderly I think I might melt. "I...I love you, Ivy."

Hearing those words from his lips sends warmth to every corner of my body; to places of my soul I didn't even know existed. "I love you, too," I reply without hesitation. At the release of the words I'd been holding against their will at the base of my throat, I feel my heart take a deep breath.

Oliver wraps his arms around my waist and rests his head on my shoulder. "To be honest, I think I've been in love with you since the moment you made me read *Ella Enchanted*."

"Seriously? That was, like, the day after we met."

He wrinkles his nose at me. "Yes, and?"

"I didn't know I'd made such an impression," I tease, running my fingers through his curls.

Yeah, well," he begins, "there was something incredibly attractive about your insistence that I read this book." He shrugs. "I might have a thing for bossy women."

"Hey, now!" I pretend to pout.

His hands play a gentle symphony on my back, lulling me back into complacency. "You yourself said giving book recommendations is the thrill of your life."

"This is true," I allow.

"So I don't see the problem," he grins. "Besides, you were

right about *Ella*. So I knew immediately that I needed to ingratiate myself to you as much as possible."

I quirk an eyebrow. "For my book recommendations?"

He nods, then starts kissing my neck in an exceptionally distracting way. "Exactly. For your book recommendations."

"You know, you didn't need to fall in love with me to get those."

"Too late," he grins. "You're the best book I've ever read."

thirty

I could never be a criminal. It occurs to me all at once as I sit in a shaky, sweaty, anxious mess on Monday, waiting for my interview to start. I have no poker face whatsoever, and even if I could somehow develop one, the rest of my body immediately betrays me whenever I try to do anything I feel even vaguely guilty about.

And I'm feeling guilty today. Incredibly so. Because I'm interviewing for the job in Springfield, which by all accounts is perfect for me, and I haven't told Maisie. Or Oliver.

I've wanted to bring it up with both of them countless times, and I think, at least superficially, they would both understand. Maisie would, certainly. Oliver, I suspect, would pretend he did, but he might crumble internally the minute I mentioned it. And seeing that heartbreak on his face is something I'm not sure I could handle.

I've moved Laurel's laptop to the living room, positioning myself in front of the fireplace, which is hugged on each side by a floor-to-ceiling bookshelf. Simon's left some of his personal collection here for renters to enjoy, and I've added the books I brought and purchased this summer to flesh things out a bit. My muddled feelings about whether I should be doing this aside, it seems like being surrounded by books is the right move for an interview with a library.

Brianna signs on to the meeting precisely on time, wearing a broad smile. "Good morning, Ivy," she greets me. "It's a pleasure to meet you."

"Thank you for taking the time to speak with me. The pleasure is mine." I try to covertly box breathe to ease the queasy feeling swirling through my stomach.

Brianna's pen is poised above a stack of papers on her desk. "Can you tell me a bit about yourself?"

I run through my experience: my Master of Library Science, working at the Brookline community library as a page. My job at Farnsworth. And, hesitantly, I mention that I've spent the summer picking up shifts at Shoreline.

Brianna seems most interested in the last bit. "Oh, really? How do you like that?"

My mind flashes over moments: the woman who reminded me of Eleanor and wanted a new Kristin Hannah book; Maisie's joy at the author event; Oliver's secret smile while he scribbles in his poetry notebook. How it feels to match someone to the right book; the way my olfactory system delights in the bibliosmia the moment the door jingles shut behind me.

But I can't relay most of that in this interview. So I just say, "It's very satisfying to help people find the perfect beach read."

"I would imagine so."

"And," I add, trying to pull the conversation away from

Shoreline, "I love staying busy. Much like in a library, there's no shortage of things to do in a bookstore."

"Well, you're in luck." Brianna's eyes light up. "We are excruciatingly busy here, too, as well as beyond understaffed. It's a lethal combination, but you'll never be bored."

The future tense sends my heart racing, but I manage a polite smile. "That sounds wonderful."

Brianna describes the job duties, and I offer standard interview answers about my skills and career aspirations. Before I know it, an hour has flown by.

"Do you have any other questions for me?" Brianna sets down her pen and looks expectantly into the camera.

I shake my head. "I don't believe so. You've been very thorough."

"I try," she grins. "When would you be able to start?"

"The first week of October." My skin crawls with self-reproach.

"Perfect. By the time we get our ducks in a row, that's probably the soonest I'd have any time to train you, anyway. I'll reach out to you very soon, okay, Ivy?"

"Sounds wonderful," I repeat. "Thank you so much, Brianna."

She ends the call, and I remain motionless on the living room couch. I feel as if I've slipped out of my body, and a shimmering specter of Ivy is forging ahead on a path I don't particularly want to be on. Meanwhile, the shell of my actual human form remains here, despondent at Beach Haven. Hologram Ivy is out and about in the world, making decisions I'm not sure I'm okay with. And once they're made, it may be too late.

. . .

MY GUILT only worsens when I get to Shoreline. As soon as he sees me, Oliver looks over his shoulder, then pulls me behind a bookshelf and kisses me like his life depends on it.

"Hey," I manage breathlessly when he finally pulls away.

"Hey." His eyes are intoxicating; I think I could swim in them for the rest of my life. "Just wanted to make sure your Monday got off to a great start."

I return his smile. "You'll get no complaints from me." My cheeks are hot with shame for the secret I'm keeping, so I rush off to hang up my sweater before he notices.

Maisie's in the office, finalizing last-minute administrative tasks ahead of her pre-op appointment tomorrow.

"I'm glad you're here," she announces when I walk in with my cardigan. "I wanted to talk with you about something."

I slide into one of the chairs facing her desk. "Can I help you get ready for tomorrow?"

Maisie doesn't seem nervous at all, but I'm sure the many unknowns of a major surgery at her age are weighing heavily on her. She certainly looks more fatigued than usual.

"I actually wondered about a longer-term sort of help," she says, laying down a file folder she'd been flipping through.

My chest tightens. "Oh?"

"As you know, I'd been hoping to scale back my hours so I can enjoy some semblance of retirement eventually. And then with the departure of my other employee earlier this year, I had to invest more time here, rather than less."

I nod. "It was very unfortunate timing."

"Yes," she continues. "And I'm so glad you happened upon us. You've really done wonders for Shoreline this summer."

I feel my face flush. I don't deserve this praise. Not now. But I murmur my thanks.

"The surgery has put some things in perspective for me." Maisie's kind eyes well up with tears. "I think all of this," she gestures around the room, "might be a bit too much for me at my age."

"But you have the energy of someone 30 years your junior," I protest. "Easily."

Maisie laughs. "I appreciate the compliment, dear. But I think I'm ready to revisit that scaling back I mentioned." She takes a deep breath. "Would you have any interest in coming on full-time and running the shop? It would be a significant pay increase from the amount I mentioned the other day. Double, in fact."

My world screeches to a halt. When she started talking, I expected Maisie to offer me a full-time role continuing with what I've been doing this summer. I absolutely didn't anticipate anything beyond that. Certainly not an offer to be in charge of Shoreline.

"I...I don't know what to say," I stammer. "I'm flattered. Beyond flattered."

She inclines her head. "But?"

"No but. At least, not yet." I rifle through thoughts as quickly as I can. Double a clerk's salary would certainly change the equation. Would it make a move here feasible? And what about Oliver?

Oliver. Wouldn't *he* be the logical choice for this role? For about a million reasons? He's practically family to Maisie. He's been working here for years; he knows Shoreline inside and out. Plus, he needs it more than I do, if that's a consideration in any way. And he has no reason to be leaving town in a few weeks. If ever.

I debate how candid I can be with Maisie. We've grown quite close as the summer's flown by, but she's still my boss, and I certainly have no right to her innermost thoughts, or the numerous reasons she might have for making this offer.

But how could I accept a job that would rip the rug out from under the only option Oliver has for vocational growth? Even if I leave, even if we don't amount to anything, I couldn't do that to him. He means too much to me.

"Wouldn't Oliver be the better choice?" I ask quietly.

Maisie blinks twice, looking like she wants to say something specific, but she just shakes her head. "I'm asking *you*," she replies gently.

I think about Oliver helping me out of his truck; steering the *Orca* around the Nubble Lighthouse. Licking my ice cream; shirtless beside me in the morning. I want nothing more than a reason to stay here with him. But I can't do it if that reason strips him of the best opportunity he'll probably ever get in this town. Because he can't leave Ogunquit, and me taking this job away would leave him even more trapped than he already feels.

"I really, really appreciate the offer," I say, feeling the ground retreat beneath me with every word. "But I have to decline. I'm so sorry."

"Is there anything I can do to change your mind?" Her earnest expression just about kills me. I want this so badly.

"Can I have some time to think it over?" Maybe I can come up with a solution that will work for both me *and* Oliver if I mull for a while.

Maisie nods as if she understands. "Of course you can. I don't need to know until I get back from surgery."

"I really appreciate it," I reply.

"I love having you here, Ivy. But I see great things ahead for you, no matter what you choose." Her smile is full of pride.

I swallow back my feelings. "Thank you, truly, so much."

Then I head to the bathroom and splash cold water on my face for a solid 15 minutes, until my skin is just as numb as my heart.

thirty-one

M aisie's surgery goes well, and Oliver and I stop by to visit her at the hospital once she's in recovery. She looks overjoyed to see us.

"Oh, my two favorites!" she practically shouts when we walk in.

Oliver holds out a vase of pink hydrangeas, which he'd told me while we shopped together are Maisie's favorite. "For you."

"They're beautiful, Oliver. Thank you."

He puts his free arm around my shoulder. "They're from both of us."

Maisie shoots him an amused smile. "Thank you, also, Ivy."

My eyes slide quickly to Oliver's, questioning. He blinks back at me, as if saying, *"What? She already knew."* The expression is as clear as if he'd spoken aloud.

I hadn't realized she knew we were together. Or whatever you'd call being in love and most likely about to be torn completely asunder. I guess it doesn't matter anymore. I just smile to acknowledge her gratitude.

"How was your surgery?" I ask.

"I can't say for sure," she jokes. "I was asleep."

We all chuckle, then Oliver says, "You look pretty good, all things considered. Are you in a lot of pain?"

"They've got me on all kinds of drugs. I feel nothing right now, aside from a deep fear that my rosebushes might need to be pruned."

Oliver's gaze doesn't leave her face. "Already taken care of."

I look to him in surprise. When did he have time to garden for her? He and I have been working almost nonstop.

Maisie closes her eyes, a contented smile falling over her face. "What would I do without you?"

"Fortunately," he reassures her, touching her hand affectionately, "I'm not going to put you in a position to find out."

If I thought I loved him before, dear reader, let me tell you: in this moment, I find I love him even more.

We visit for a while, then a doctor comes in to discuss physical therapy options. Oliver and I rise to our feet to head out.

Before we go, Maisie orders us to close the shop on Wednesday. "It's always a slow day for sales anyway," she assures us. "I want you two to take a break. With pay." She points a demanding finger at Oliver.

"Noted," he says, mirth glinting in his eyes.

"WHAT DO you want to do with all of our free time?" Oliver asks when we wake up in my bed on Wednesday morning.

"Hmmm," I muse, throwing my arms around his neck. "I have a few ideas."

"I like the way you think," he murmurs, leaning down to brush a kiss over my shoulder.

"Actually," I say, tracing his collarbone with my pointer finger, "I had a call from Simon the other night. He's hoping I can bring some of his books over. There's a box in the attic that he's after, but he said it might be heavy."

"Is that so?" Oliver laces his fingers through mine and kisses the back of my hand.

"Mmhmm. I racked my brain trying to think of who has precisely the skillset for carrying large boxes of books around, and you came to mind."

He smirks. "You just want to watch me lift heavy things."

"Maybe," I shrug coyly.

"You definitely do," Oliver teases, dragging my hips against his. "It turns you on."

"So what if it does?" I retort. "That's to your benefit, as well."

"I suppose it is," he reconsiders. "Fine, I accept your offer. I'll help you bring the books to Simon." He slides his hand between my thighs. "For a price, of course."

"Wow, I didn't have 'book slut' on my vocational bingo card."

"Oh, please," he laughs. "You are the quintessential book slut."

"Only for you," I murmur against his ear.

WE FIND the carton of books shoved against the far wall of the attic, just two boxes away from the photo albums. "I don't think I ever showed you this." I grab the 1953 album and hold it up.

"No, you didn't." Oliver leans against an old dresser. "Are there pictures of your grandparents in there?"

"Yep." I flip to the page with Eleanor. "This is my grandmother."

"Wow. You have her smile."

I look up at him as he gazes back down at me adoringly. If I weren't afraid to flood the attic again, I think I might melt into a puddle, right here on the floor. "You think so?" Because Eleanor was startlingly gorgeous, so I take this as the highest form of praise.

Oliver nods. "Absolutely."

I flip to the photos of my grandfather on the beach. "And this is Charlie. It looks like he might have been helping Simon test out his new camera."

Oliver tilts his head, but he doesn't reply immediately. I sweep my eyes back over the photo, trying to discern what he's picking up on. Instead, I'm hit all over again by the expression on my grandfather's face. It's so familiar, but I just can't quite place it.

"Anyway," I say, clearing my throat. "We should probably head out. Simon has pinochle in a couple of hours."

That makes Oliver chuckle. "I look forward to the day when hours of card games are the most pressing thing on my schedule."

I watch him heft the box into his arms, both my heart and libido appreciating the visual.

He offers a mocking grin. "Enjoying the show?"

"So very much." I press a kiss to his cheek and follow him down the stairs.

. . .

SIMON AND OLIVER really seem to hit it off, and it's almost 12:30 before I realize that Simon's missed his chance to play cards today.

"I'm so sorry; I lost track of the time!" I apologize.

Simon waves his hand in the air. "Losing track of time is half the point of living. There'll be plenty of other opportunities to play cards. I'm just enjoying chatting with you young people."

God, he really is the nicest man.

"So, tell me how things are going at Shoreline," Simon segues.

I nod, slowly at first, then a few more times with greater conviction. "It's been tough without Maisie, but we're managing."

"What's 'managing' to Ivy would probably be considered 'thriving' by just about anyone else," Oliver teases. "She's a powerhouse in front of a bookshelf, really."

I blush. "That's awfully generous of you," I reply.

"There's no question that you were born to do this," he says quietly. I'm trying to decide if he means work with books or banter with him when I hear Simon chuckle.

"I recognize that look." Simon inclines his head toward Oliver.

Oliver's eyes are overflowing with warmth, his lips tipped up into a genuine smile, like the person he's looking at is the center of his entire universe. And all of that enraptured glow is directed right at me. It's breathtaking, honestly.

And then, in a world-shattering instant, I realize I recognize that look, too.

I've seen that exact expression before; just today, in fact. In a photograph. A photograph of my grandfather. And he was looking at...

Simon smiles. "A look of love if I've ever seen one."

My jaw drops, but I don't bother to close it. *Simon was taking the picture.* He's the person Charlie was looking at. The person Charlie loved.

All of a sudden, pieces that had seemed like they belonged to separate puzzles start to fit together in my mind. "Haven't you, though?" I ask gently.

Simon appears startled, then understanding settles over his face. "I suppose I have." He smiles sadly. "But maybe you already knew that?"

Oliver's eyes are darting back and forth between Simon and me; a puppy watching a televised tennis match in the living room. He looks lost at first, but it takes only a few rallies for comprehension to dawn. "Are you okay?" he mouths to me.

I nod, then address Simon. "Does anyone else know?"

He closes his eyes tightly as if holding back tears, then bobs his head. "Janie. Janie knew."

My breath is ragged. Janie knew. Of course she did. Because she was there when it all started.

Something's still not adding up, though. If my grandfather and Simon were in love, why did Charlie marry Eleanor? I know it was virtually impossible to be out in the 1950s, but surely Simon and Charlie could have carried on a relationship behind closed doors.

Unjust though that arrangement would have been, I think it was fairly common for the time. I can't pretend to understand how hard it would be. Looking at Oliver now, I consider a lifetime of sneaking around for fear of being caught; never being able to hold his hand on the street, proclaiming that he was mine. The air leaves my lungs bit by bit. I shudder to imagine what it would be like to have to hide from a love like that for fear of public scrutiny. Or worse. God, it was so much worse, for so many couples.

I know in a heartbeat that I'd do it, though. For Oliver. And if Simon and Charlie had something similar together, I'm surprised it survived my grandparents' marriage.

And then there's Eleanor. What must it have been like for her, knowing that her husband was in love with someone else? It's just a heartbreaking situation all around.

"I don't know what to say," I offer. "I'm so sorry." Because, at the end of the day, Simon's lost the love of his life. A man who I've just now realized loved him back, wholly and completely.

Simon's eyes are misty. "I got everything I ever wanted. I have no right to complain."

I rather think he does, all things considered, starting with the social injustice that necessitated his decades-long love affair be clandestine, but I just reach for his hand.

"I'm so happy to know the truth."

Simon looks like he wants to say something else, but his gaze is drawn, as if by a magnet, to the photo of my grandfather. "He would be glad for you to know."

I'm scrambling to retain my dignity, but it's a losing battle. I'm about to start ugly crying, right here in the middle of Simon's room.

Fortunately, Oliver sees the distress written all over my face. "Say, Ivy," he intones apologetically, "we should probably get going. I need to pick up a prescription for my father."

I'm not sure Simon's under any illusions about the true reason for our abrupt departure, but he handles the announcement with grace. "It was lovely to see you both." He turns his wheelchair and heads for the door. "I really meant it, you know." He puts his hand on mine as I pass him. "Charlie and Eleanor's family is my family. I'm always here if you need me, Ivy."

The tears fall then, despite my best intentions. I know it's not the same, but, just for a moment, it's almost like having my grandparents back.

"Thank you," I murmur, stooping to give Simon a hug. "I'm so grateful for the opportunity to know you, Simon."

He raises moist lashes and soothes me with a smile. "Your grandparents would be incredibly proud of you."

I nod through tears, unsure how to respond without unleashing further waterworks. "I'll visit again soon, okay?"

"Absolutely," Simon agrees.

Oliver sticks out his hand. "It was a pleasure to meet you, Simon."

"Likewise. Take good care of each other, you two. What you have doesn't come along every day."

Oliver squeezes my shoulder. "It certainly doesn't."

THE RIDE back from Wells is quiet. Oliver reaches for my hand at a traffic light. "I really need to start carrying some staff pick notecards so I can get your two cents wherever we go."

I shoot him a wry smile. "You always know just what to say."

He returns my expression. "I am a poet, after all."

The light turns green, and I shift my hand to his knee so he can 10-and-2 the steering wheel. "I wasn't expecting today," I say finally.

"Neither was I."

"It does make a lot of sense, though. When you think about it."

He nods slowly. "I suppose it does."

"Right? Like why would Simon just sit there and pine for 60 years if my grandfather wasn't actually interested?"

I watch Oliver's eyes in the rearview mirror. "I'm not sure you can necessarily just turn that off. That's why they call it 'falling' in love—it's out of your control."

"Poet indeed," I hum.

Oliver grins. "What can I say? I like to impress you with lofty talk."

"Of that I've no doubt." I squeeze his leg tightly, willing the gesture to convey the depths of my affection. "So, do you actually have to pick up a prescription for your dad?"

"Oh, absolutely."

"Really? Because we just passed the pharmacy." I point out the window.

"Huh. Oops." He shrugs nonchalantly.

"Thanks for taking care of me back there."

His voice slides into a more serious register. "Always."

OLIVER OFFERS to drop me off at Beach Haven, but I don't want to box up my feelings right now. I need fresh air; I need to be one with the horizon—to feel endless.

I suggest a walk on the Marginal Way, and Oliver agrees readily. We walk hand in hand, meandering along the gardens and the cliffs, speaking very little, but feeling so much. Every step echoes in time with the beat of my heart, goading me further along the path to healing.

When we get to the bench from Eleanor's diary, I ask if we can sit down. I close my eyes and breathe in the salty air drifting up the cliffs from the Atlantic; comforted by the fact that it's the same air my grandmother breathed when she sat here with the man she loved.

"That's the piece that's still missing," I say aloud.

"What is?" Oliver runs his hand through my hair.

"Why did my grandmother marry him?" I ask desperately. "How did she stay, all that time, knowing he didn't love her like that? And what happened to the man from her diary?"

In the light of day, Oliver's eyes blend right in with the ocean. They both sparkle the same brilliant blue in the sun. He blinks slowly. "I know Simon said that Janie knows. But I think there's someone else."

He's right. I know he's right. I inhale sharply. "I need to call my dad."

EVEN THOUGH I know what I have to do, I'm dreading it with every fiber of my being. I suggest dinner in Perkins Cove, then a long stroll back to town. We stop for blueberry pie ice cream, then watch the sun set over the waves. I never want my time with Oliver to end, but there's another reason I don't want to go home tonight. I know the minute I'm alone, I'm going to feel compelled to dial my father's number.

Eventually, the sky glints black on the ocean, and I begrudgingly admit it's time. "I need to check on my dad," Oliver says after he kisses me goodnight. "Otherwise, I'd stay." I'm sure he's telling the truth to an extent, but it's obvious the real reason he's heading home is to give me the space to make this call.

I stand on tiptoe and wrap my arms around his neck. "I love you."

He pulls me tight to him. "I love you back."

thirty-two

After Oliver leaves, I key in the door code. Beach Haven is dark, save for the moonlight lilting in through the living room window. Laurel had texted me earlier to say she was going to a party with Porter and his friends, and not to expect her back for several hours.

I haven't had a chance to ask her how things are going with her attempts at a platonic relationship with Porter. Admittedly, I've been rather distracted recently. I'll have to make time for a heart-to-heart with her soon.

Plopping down on the couch, I warily drag my cell phone from my pocket. I feel stuck in a bit of a duality right now; a Schrödinger's box in which my life both is, and very much isn't, what I've always known it to be. But with the revelation about Charlie out in the open, I don't see any option other than to press on. I have to know the whole truth.

The phone rings twice before my father answers. "Ivy Bean!" He sounds excited to hear from me.

"Hey, Dad. How's it going?" I aim for as gentle a tone as possible. The rest of this conversation may not be easy.

I hear papers shuffling in the background. "Just going through some things here in my office," he replies. "A great way to spend a beautiful summer night."

"Tell me about it," I chuckle, as if I'm doing the same thing. My chest is thick with anxiety. I'm not thinking particularly clearly, and it's starting to impede my ability to form coherent sentences.

"So, what's new with you?"

I know that Dad's really asking why I'm calling him. I decide to cut to the chase. "I learned something today. Something I think you already know."

"Oh?" His voice rings with trepidation.

I take a deep breath. "Dad, your father was in love with Simon."

Complete and utter silence, just like when I first mentioned the diary to him.

I try again. "But you knew this, didn't you?"

It seems like my dad is going to leave me hanging again, but at last, he responds. "I knew."

My voice starts to shake then, because somehow, hearing the truth from my father is making the whole thing hit all over again. "What about Grandma?"

"What about her?" Dad asks quietly.

"Why did she marry him?"

"Ivy."

I try for a different approach. This is too important; I can't let him shut down. "Is it because of whatever she wrote about in her diary?"

"I think you know that it is," he answers, defeated.

"Dad, what happened? It couldn't possibly have been that bad."

He laughs then, a ragged, bitter sound that I didn't know he had the capacity for. "It wasn't. That's the thing, it really wasn't. But it broke me completely, and that's why I've kept it from you. That's what drove your mother away. I couldn't bear to let it take you from me, too."

A muffled sob echoes through the phone. *Jesus*. Now he's *crying?* And what does any of this have to do with Mom?

"Look," I hesitate. "I really didn't mean to—"

"No, no. You're right. You should know." There's a long pause while he collects his thoughts, then he begins slowly, as if deliberating with every word whether this ice is safe to tiptoe across. "I didn't know about any of it until your grandfather died. My parents were wonderfully warm and welcoming, but they were very private people."

"Truer words have never been spoken," I joke, attempting to divert the negative energy from this conversation.

Dad doesn't acknowledge my play for levity. "When Grandpa Charlie passed, your grandmother needed my help getting his affairs in order."

"Right," I say. I remember my dad going to his parents' house every night after work for months to help Eleanor through the loss of her husband, and to deal with some of his accounts so she could focus on healing.

"Right. So one of the projects she needed me to handle was getting a certain bank account that was in just his name switched over to hers, with Greg and me as the beneficiaries. She wanted things to be all set for when something happened to her." He sniffles a bit. "It was a mess, Ivy. The bank was disorganized; they kept losing our paperwork, and every time I thought they finally had everything they needed, I'd get a call saying something else was missing."

"I think I vaguely recall you mentioning this." He mostly complained to my mom, but I'd heard loud mentions of "the damn bank" in tandem with various other profanities during the months immediately following Charlie's death whenever I visited my parents.

"One of the things they needed, which wasn't conveyed to me until about two months in, was my father's social security number. Something about reporting interest earned on his account to the IRS."

"Okay," I say, not understanding how any of this pencil-pushing relates to some earth-shattering secret.

"I didn't have the number handy, and Mom was too distraught to remember it. So I went digging through her file cabinet, trying to find his social security card. It was a lot less organized than I would have expected, given how particular my parents were."

I think back to the perfectly wrapped Christmas gifts Eleanor always gave us, the immaculately mowed lawn Charlie was so proud of. "That *is* a surprise."

"I know. As it turns out, my disorganization came from somewhere. Greg's, too." He chuckles. "Yep. Greg and I are definitely their kids."

I'm still not understanding where this is heading, but then my Dad speaks again. "Her kids, that is." He pauses as if for emphasis, but I've definitely missed the punch line.

"What are you talking about?"

Dad sighs. "When I was looking for the social security card, I found something else. My birth certificate."

"Okay?"

"Charlie wasn't my father."

The words are dense, suspended in the air for a moment as if to threaten their weight. Then all at once, they fall all around me, and I succumb to an avalanche of understanding.

"The man in Grandma's diary—she got pregnant?"

I can practically see him nodding, all the way in Brookline. "His name was George. George Marlowe."

"But I don't understand. Had you never seen your birth certificate before? Surely George's name looks nothing like Grandpa's." As the words leave my tongue, it strikes me that Charlie is not, in fact, my grandfather. My stomach twists into a knot.

"Believe it or not, I hadn't. My parents got Greg and me passports when we were kids so we could travel to see Mom's aunts in London. They always renewed before the passports expired, so I never had cause to look at my birth certificate. And when I married your mother, I just used the passport as proof of identity."

"Wow." I don't know how, given all the information I'd had at my disposal, I wasn't able to figure this out. I wonder if Oliver had; if this scenario was one of the plausible conclusions he'd drawn when I'd told him about my family drama.

I wonder also if I would have come to the same conclusion, were I less afraid to look closely.

"'Wow' is right," Dad agrees. "I didn't know what to do when I found out. At first, I didn't want to rock the boat. Your grandmother was still reeling from losing her husband, and I didn't think it would do her any good to add a son demanding decades-buried truths."

He sounds so much like Laurel, there's no question that the nurture side of the equation is strong in our family, regardless of the genetics behind it all. Although I guess Grandpa's the only odd man out, in terms of DNA.

"I laid everything at your mother's feet. I didn't know what else to do. And I became a burden to her. She wanted to help me move past it; to reconcile with the past. She kept insisting it didn't matter if Charlie was my biological father or not; he was my father in every way."

"I would tend to agree with her there," I admit. "But I doubt you were a burden."

"Yes," he sighs. "I agree with her, also. But I couldn't let it go. I never got to meet my father, and I didn't know why my parents hid it from me. I looked him up, and he'd died ten years earlier, so I would never be able to meet him, either. It was a lot to absorb all at once, you know?"

It's a lot for *me* to absorb, and I've been getting it a little bit at a time. Plus, I'm another generation removed from it all. I can't imagine what it's been like for my dad. "Of course it was," I say softly.

"I didn't handle it well," Dad continues. "I was depressed; I shrunk inward while I tried to process everything. I barely spoke to your mother for weeks, but it was nothing she did—my thoughts were just so wrapped up in everything I'd just learned."

"I'm sure Mom understood," I offer.

My father exhales sharply. "She did, at first. And she tried so hard to help. But my inability to deal with the situation drove a wedge between your mother and me. Eventually, it became clear I was hurting her by being so withdrawn. I couldn't let that stand; you know how much I love your mother, Ivy."

"I know," I say quietly.

He's definitely crying now; his emotions running every

which way with this confession I secretly suspect he was dying to get off his chest. "Six months after Grandpa died, I went to your grandmother, and I asked her to explain. I just wanted to understand, so I could start to heal and fix things with your mom. Eleanor was so nervous; it was hard for her to open up to me. Even then, when I had half the truth already."

Dad takes a deep breath. "She handed me her diary; told me it was all in there. So I read it. Her entries from that summer explained about George: about how he got her pregnant, then wanted nothing to do with her. She'd really loved him, she wrote. She wanted to marry him. But he left when the summer ended, and she didn't know what to do. She knew her parents would be mortified. Janie was the only one who knew the truth. But Janie encouraged her to tell Charlie; she said he'd definitely think of something."

"I guess he did."

My father laughs. "Charlie was always the smartest guy in the room. He'd just met Simon, and they were covertly seeing one another, but obviously they couldn't go public with it back then, society being as horrific as it was."

"It's heartbreaking," I interject. "It really is."

"I know." Dad's voice reflects his sorrow. "Whatever I'm telling you now, Ivy, I need you to know that your grandfather loved my mother. He loved her deeply and truly. They were best friends and soulmates, albeit platonic ones. And he felt that all the way back in 1953 when he proposed, and every day until he died."

Hearing this warms my soul a bit. All the recent familial revelations have been casting doubt on everything I've ever known, including the way my grandfather treated my grandmother like she was the most precious thing on the planet. "I'm glad to hear that," I reply honestly.

"Anyway, my father talked to Simon, and they came to an agreement. And then he came to my mother with his plan."

"He'd marry her and raise her children as his own," I whisper. "And she would keep his secret. And they'd travel to Ogunquit every year so he could see Simon, and no one would be the wiser."

"I knew you were a smart kid," my father jokes affectionately. "You get that from your grandfather."

Even though this has all been so heavy, I smile at the idea that I inherited my wit and strategic thinking from Charlie. While we might not have shared genes, he's no less my grandfather. The shared eye color is a bit of a head-scratcher, though, now that I think of it. Perhaps just a divine coincidence?

"Anyway," Dad continues, "That was it. The diary laid it all out. And I read it, but I couldn't handle the truth. I was heartbroken for all of them—for my mother, living a lie all those years, sacrificing herself at the altar of propriety. For Simon, who had to be at arm's length from the love he deserved. For my father, assuming the responsibility another man abandoned, kept away from the love of his life except for a fleeting few weeks every summer. It killed me," he sobs.

"I'm so sorry." I don't know what else to say.

"Your mother tried so hard," Dad continues. "She really did. But I was broken. I couldn't even acknowledge any of it with your grandmother. I never gave her back the diary; I never tried to discuss it with her."

It hits me all at once. "You're the one who ripped out the pages." It isn't really a question.

"I am. After she died, I couldn't take it. I brought the

journal back to the house; I was going to see if anyone else wanted it. But first, I pulled out everything surrounding the pregnancy and Charlie's love for Simon. I assumed Janie already knew, but I couldn't bear to think someone else might uncover the truth. I wanted to protect my parents' secrets. Protect anyone else from having to work through the trauma like I was."

"How did it end up in the trash?" I ask.

"Walking into their empty house did something to me," he explains. "I was so lost. So angry. I don't know why, Ivy. I just couldn't deal with it. I was afraid someone would want the diary and would ask about the missing pages, and I didn't know how to explain that. So I decided to just throw it out."

"As it turns out, that's exactly what happened regardless," I say wryly, remembering the feeling of my car's floor mat against my fingers as I shoved the diary under the seat.

"I'm sorry for keeping the truth from you; I wasn't in a good place. I wanted to understand what made it worth it to them; how it didn't break all three of them completely over the years." He pauses like he's shaking his head. "I'm never going to understand. Not entirely. And now there's no one left to explain it to me."

"Simon's still here," I offer quietly. "He still loves your father."

"I know," my dad says.

"Dad, what happened with Mom?" Hearing this story, I'm still not understanding what drove them apart. Not really. He was sad? I know my mother too well to think she'd abandon him just because he was depressed.

"Like I said, I couldn't handle it. It was eating me up inside, but I wouldn't get help. I didn't know how. Your mother tried so hard, and I just retreated, further and further away from her. Away from you both."

I think back to the countless nights when I came over for dinner and Dad worked late, blue light glinting out around the closed door to his office. To the look on my mother's face when I bid her goodnight after our meal, not having seen Dad at all. And I begin to understand.

His voice shakes. "It was years, after Grandpa Charlie died, before your mom left. She tried so hard. But all that time, I was struggling; I was pulling away from her. There was no 'us' anymore. She said we had nothing left; that she'd given me everything she could. That I needed to work through things on my own for a while." There's a long pause. "She said she'll be there waiting for me, whenever I'm ready to come back to her."

My eyes overflow then. The split had never made sense to me; it was hard not to vilify my mother for taking off right after Eleanor passed. It felt cruel and unusual, leaving your spouse in their time of greatest need. And maybe it was. Maybe that was the mistake my mother made in this situation.

But if she was doing all the emotional work in their marriage for years on end, trying desperately to help him, but running up against a wall, time and time again? Especially as a psychologist who is perfectly equipped to help others in their time of mental trauma, being unable to reach the person she loved most? I understand why she might have felt she had nothing left. She'd done all she could, and it still wasn't enough. She probably thought she'd failed him. And I can imagine how hollow that might feel. Especially if he had nothing left to give her, either.

"I'm so sorry, Dad." I don't know what else to say. What

solace could my consolation offer him, really? I wish Oliver were here; he always manages to find the words.

"Don't be. Don't be, Ivy. Thank you for pushing me on this. You deserved to know the truth. I would have told you sooner, but it was so complicated; the truth was wrapped up in your memories of Eleanor; your memories of Charlie. And it became entangled with Mom and I, and then I was afraid telling you could shatter the only stability you had left. I know you've been struggling with your job and your breakup with Kyle. I just couldn't throw another wild card into the mix for you."

Hearing Kyle's name is like a bizarre throwback. I haven't thought of him in weeks, since the night Oliver wore his old sweats. And, thanks to what happened next, my brain sort of overwrote the Kyle part of those memories.

"Thank you," I say earnestly. "But I don't want you to have to bear this alone anymore."

"Love you, Ivy Bean."

"I love you, too, Dad."

thirty-three

I'm reading the last book in my stash on the porch at Beach Haven when my phone rings. Glancing at the caller ID, I see it's Brianna.

All the air rushes out of my lungs. I'm not sure I can handle this right now, on top of everything else. But my anxiety dictates I do what's expected of me, no matter how it destroys me inside, so I swipe to answer the call.

"Hello, Ivy." Brianna sounds both chipper and completely overwhelmed. I hear shouting behind her. Maybe she isn't at the library?

"Good morning. It's great to hear from you."

"Sorry about all the noise," she whispers, like she doesn't want to be overheard. "The kids are doing a STEAM lab that involves building roller coasters out of cardboard, and it's gotten a little rowdy."

My heart pangs. That sounds like exactly the sort of program I'd love to run. The type of thing that would actually make a difference for kids.

"Oh, no problem." I want her to rip off this Band-Aid.

"Let me cut to the chase," she replies. *Thank God.* "I was really impressed by your interview, and I'd love to offer you the head of children's services position."

The air hangs heavy with opportunity, like humidity over the beach. It's so heavy, in fact, I think I might be suffocating.

"Wow," I manage. "I really appreciate that. Freehold seems like it would be a perfect fit for me." As soon as the words are out, I mentally curse them with every profanity in my repertoire. Because it does seem perfect, and I hate that fact with every fiber of my being.

"Is that a yes, then?" Brianna's voice rises eagerly.

I take a deep breath. "Would it be all right if I took some time to think it over?"

"Of course," she replies, any surprise at my hesitation immediately glossed over with consummate professionalism. "Can you let me know by the end of the month? I honestly won't have time to prepare for your arrival until the local kids are back in school anyway; our summer programs are keeping me so busy."

Without meaning to, she's just condemned me to three and a half weeks of cold sweats and sleepless nights. "Absolutely," I agree brightly. I've been a nervous wreck for so long, I have my fake enthusiasm down pat. I'm not sure even Laurel could see through it.

I think Oliver could.

Shoving thoughts of his face when I tell him about the job from my mind, I thank Brianna profusely.

"I need to go attend to these roller coaster tycoon wannabes," she jokes. "I'll talk to you soon."

"Good luck! Thank you again."

When I hang up the phone, I imagine Hologram Ivy swiping her employee badge at Freehold, a big grin upon her face. My body watches from a dark room, glimmering strings of my soul pouring out through the gaping hole in my chest.

I HAVE to get out of this house, and I need someone to talk to who can offer unbiased advice. There's nothing I want more than for someone else to tell me what I should do.

There's only one person I can think of who won't hesitate to do just that. Hitting the beach, I dial my mother.

"Ivy?" Mom asks, like she forgot how caller ID works.

"Hey, Mom. It is indeed me, your only child."

"Funny," she says drily. "What's up?"

Maybe she's just distracted with work. I guess it *is* only 4:30; she might still be doing her notes. "I need your advice."

I picture my mom sitting up in her chair, eager to do the two things she loves best: mothering and psychoanalyzing. "Shoot."

"Okay. So, I got two different job offers, and I'm struggling to decide which is the right fit."

"Of course you did! Tell me about them."

A wave splashes over my sneakered feet, but I don't care. That's what I get for rushing out of the house without changing. "One is a management position here, at Shoreline Books. The owner is stepping away and asked me to run the shop."

"Wow, Ivy! That sounds incredible."

"I know, right?" I swallow my excitement. I need to present both options in the same tone so I don't sway her opinion. "It would be a really great opportunity. A new challenge, but a bit of a departure from what I've been working toward."

"How about the other job?"

"That one also seems pretty perfect. Head of children's services at a library in Springfield. Much more in line with my degree and my experience."

"Hmm." My mother considers. "Well, from a location perspective, you'd have to move either way."

"I would," I begin slowly. "Springfield would be a new adventure, but I'd be on my own. Here, I wouldn't be."

"How much time do you think you'd be spending with your boss if you took the bookstore job?" She sounds awfully amused.

It occurs to me that I still haven't told her about Oliver. "I've actually been seeing someone here this summer." I'm not sure how much detail to offer.

"Ohhhh really? My, my, my." Mom might as well be singing the k-i-s-s-i-n-g song for how childishly she's reacting.

"I'm an adult, you realize." This conversation is significantly less helpful than I'd expected.

She laughs again. "Sorry. Anyway. So you met someone?"

"I did. His name's Oliver." I hesitate, more than understanding Eleanor's aversion to writing George's name in her diary, lest her mother find out and mock her. Or worse, track him down and giggle like a 12-year-old.

"And how did you meet Oliver?" Mom's clearly trying to return to my good graces, because she sounds artificially formal.

I decide to go for it. She might need the whole picture if she's going to tell me what to do. "He works at Shoreline, too."

My mother's gasp is anything but formal. "Oh. My. God."

"Mom. That's not productive."

Now she's laughing again, which makes me want to hang up, but I stay the course. Fortunately, she clears her throat and assumes a more serious tone fairly quickly. "Sorry, sorry. I just would have thought, after what happened with your last workplace relationship...but never mind."

She doesn't even know half of what happened with Kyle, or she'd probably be even more shocked. "It's different with Oliver. It feels like a risk I have to take." I realize it's true as the words leave my mouth.

"I see," she replies, her tone suddenly far more receptive. "So, in Springfield, you'd be starting fresh. And in Ogunquit, you have Oliver."

"Right."

"How about pay and benefits?"

"More or less the same," I answer. But it isn't really about the money. What I really need from my mother, I think, is permission to turn down the Springfield job. I realize, deep down, that's what I'm asking for.

"What would make you happy?"

"Either, in different ways."

Mom's voice is quiet. "Ivy."

"Mmm?"

"What do you want me to tell you?"

I breathe sharply. "I want your opinion."

"My opinion is this: I think you already know what you want. I can hear it in your voice," she offers gently.

And she's right. I do know what I want. But I don't think I can have it without hurting the person who's my reason for wanting it in the first place.

. . .

OLIVER TEXTS me after his shift and asks if he can come over. I don't want to see him.

I also want nothing more than to see him.

It occurs to me that forcing Laurel to hang out with us might be a good way to walk the line between the disparate desires battling it out in my mind right now.

"Hey," I chirp with false levity, sticking my head through her doorway. She's hunched over her laptop, where I'm starting to think she is going to spend the rest of her life.

"What's up?" She sighs and turns toward me. The circles under her eyes are even darker than they were yesterday, when I last saw her outside her room.

"You look like you could use a break. Want to go grab some drinks with Oliver and me?" I'm fully expecting her to say no, but I have to try.

Laurel nods slowly, as if convincing herself. "Okay. I suppose I could use some time away from this mess." She closes the lid of her computer. "Let me just get changed, okay?"

"Sure thing."

I text Oliver. *Want to meet us in 45 minutes at the dance hall? We can grab some drinks.*

Sounds good. Wear your curtain dress.

He immediately follows up with a winking smiley face, which makes me smile, too. Then, my chest caves in—how can I see him and act like everything's fine? How can I take an opportunity away from him? Alternatively, how can I leave town next month and walk away from the way his words have rewritten the song on my heart?

I draw in a shaky breath. I just need to work harder at finding a solution. There must be a way to honor both my feelings and Oliver's needs. Silently berating myself for not having an answer yet, I shut my eyes to keep the tears at bay. I just need to put one foot in front of the other. I'll do my hair and wear my green dress and let Laurel be the buffer tonight. Like Scarlett O'Hara, I'll push my worries to another day.

WE DON'T KEEP Oliver waiting this time, because Laurel is so tired, she doesn't seem to care about primping within an inch of her life. He's reading *Sherlock Holmes* outside Harbor Lights when we arrive, though, so he's been waiting at least a few minutes. My heart stirs in my chest.

"Hey," he says, drawing me to him and kissing me deeply.

"Seriously?" Laurel feigns disgust.

"Oh, please. Like you wouldn't do the same," I mutter.

"Let's just get inside. I need a drink or three." She marches toward the door, and we follow, hand in hand.

A few minutes later, we're each sipping a Jack and Coke, leaning against the bar.

"How's your dissertation going?" Oliver directs his attention to my cousin.

I shoot him a glare. "We're trying to offer her some escapism," I whisper.

"It's fine, Ivy. My work is never far from my mind." Her eyes slide between us as her lips tip up. "As I'm sure is the case for both of you, but for different reasons."

My heart skips a beat when, for a moment, I wonder if she knows my secret. But I haven't mentioned either job offer to her, and I don't think my mom would have shared my dilemma with Laurel or her parents.

I fall out of my paranoid cloud when it occurs to me that Laurel probably just meant that Oliver and I like to think about work because we get to be there together.

Now my heart palpitates, but for an entirely different reason. Because soon, we may not get to work together anymore.

I tighten my grip on Oliver's hand, which he's resting on my knee under the bar. He shoots me a questioning look, but I shake my head. I'm not ready.

Laurel surveys the assembled crowd. "I wonder if this is what it looked like the night Grandma met that guy. It feels pretty blasé in here, but she made it seem so romantic."

"Could be," I shrug noncommittally.

"Well, whoever he was, Diary Guy sounds totally dreamy." Laurel swigs her drink.

"I don't think we can assume that," I bite out before I can stop myself.

Her eyes flick to me in surprise. "Okay, geez. I didn't mean to upset you."

Oliver squeezes my fingers, as if to reassure me. But between the mantle of family trauma I've recently taken up and the fact that my plans for the future are swirling into an opaque haze, I'm feeling anything but calm.

"Grandpa was the real prize," I babble, letting my mouth roll with my emotions. "And Grandma knew that. She got dealt a bad hand when George left, but she loved Grandpa, and he loved her. They made it work."

Laurel raises a brow. "Who's George?"

My mind slams into a wall. Hard. "Oh. Um, that's just what I've been calling Diary Guy."

Oliver's fixing me with a look hovering somewhere between

concern and shock. I avert my eyes from his. I don't need him worrying about me. That's just going to add to my guilt about what I've been keeping from him.

Laurel clearly doesn't buy my fib. "I thought you were going to drop the whole Harriet the Spy thing."

"What?" *Play dumb, play dumb, play dumb,* my brain sings.

She narrows her eyes. "You were going to let the past stay there, Ivy. We talked about this."

Now she's pissing me off. "I don't recall agreeing to that."

Her mouth falls open. "I don't even believe this. What the hell did you do, Ivy?"

I glare at her. "I didn't *do* anything. The truth made its way to me."

"And what truth is that?"

Oliver puts his hand on my forearm. "I think we should talk about something else."

I shake my head. "No."

"Ivy—"

"Oliver, *no.*" I pry his fingers off me and turn toward my cousin. "George is Diary Guy. He got Eleanor pregnant. And Charlie married her so no one would find out."

I've definitely never seen Laurel look so shocked. "Okay," she begins, like the words are shards of glass. "So...Charlie's not actually our grandfather?"

"He's not," I snap. "And there's more."

"Ivy!" Oliver's voice is desperate now. "Why don't you and Laurel talk about this when you've both had some time to calm down?"

I ignore him and barrel on. "Charlie was gay. He was in love with Simon."

All color has disappeared from Laurel's face, a gaunt addition to the bags under her overworked eyes. "That can't be right."

My vitriol fades as awareness of what I've done seeps in. She'd made it patently clear that she didn't want to dance with old ghosts. "It is," I say quietly.

"Oh my God." Her eyes fill with tears as she processes all the family secrets that I had weeks to learn in one fell swoop.

"I'm sorry to tell you like this," I offer, as if apologizing will take it all back. But am I actually sorry? I don't even know anymore.

Where my anger has faded back into guilt, her tears are now escalating to fury. "Then why did you? Why did you push this? I made it so clear that I didn't want to unearth old secrets."

"I know. I'm sorry."

"It's been a shock for Ivy, too," Oliver adds, putting a protective arm around my shoulders.

Laurel glares at him. "Well then she should have left well enough alone, and she wouldn't have had to deal with any of it."

"I—"

"Save it, Ivy. I'm going home." She downs the last of her drink and grabs her purse. "It might be better if you found somewhere else to sleep tonight. I want to be alone."

As she stomps away, Oliver pulls me against his chest. "I think you're well within your rights to ignore her. But you're also welcome to stay at my house."

The thought of sleeping over in Oliver's bed would have been beyond enticing even a week ago, but the reason for its necessity is making the whole thing seem dismal.

"Okay," I say quietly. A soulful Van Morrison song comes

on, and the lights over the dance floor dim. "Can we dance? I really need you to hold me."

Oliver's look of concern sends my guilt skyrocketing. "Of course. Come on."

He grabs my hand and pulls me toward the center of the floor, then hugs me to his chest. "It's going to be okay," he murmurs against my hair.

I'm not so sure that it is, but I just nod. It takes every ounce of fortitude I have not to burst into tears right now. I've ruined everything—created a mess with Laurel, forced my dad out of his comfort zone, and put myself in an impossible situation with work. And Oliver doesn't realize it yet, but one way or another, I'm about to hurt him.

The tears spill over without waiting for my permission. Oliver starts at the sensation of one hitting his cheek, and he pulls back far enough to search my face. "Ivy, what's wrong? I'm sure you and Laurel will be able to work things out."

My head shakes back and forth of its own volition. "It isn't just that."

His bright eyes rush to find the source of my sorrow. "Then what is it?"

I absorb all of his perfection, committing it to memory. Knowing that in a matter of seconds, this will be the before, and I'm not ready for the after.

"I got a job offer this morning," I manage. His brows go up like he's about to congratulate me, so I rush out with, "It's in Springfield."

Oliver's face falls. "Oh." He smooths my hair away from my face. "Why didn't you tell me at work?"

"I—" Why didn't I? Because I didn't want him to ever look

at me like he is right now. Like I'm breaking his heart. I draw in breath sharply. "I couldn't."

"What about working at Shoreline?" he asks, like my answer could shatter him.

"Maisie offered me the manager job," I say quietly.

His expression remains stoic. "What did you tell her?"

I don't understand why he isn't reacting to this. I shake my head. "How can I take that job?" I search his eyes for comprehension.

"How can you not?" he whispers back.

"It should be yours," I reply against his cheek, settling back in to the warmth of his body. "How can I take that from you? You feel so trapped here, but you can't leave. At least a promotion would give you some way to move forward."

Oliver's gaze sweeps my face, sending a warm breeze straight into my heart. "I don't feel so trapped anymore."

But you will someday, I want to shout. *You'll resent me for taking your opportunity, and it will drive a wedge between us. Look what happens when people sacrifice too much for those they love—they separate and one of them has to get an apartment ten minutes away. Or they spend an entire lifetime in a sexless marriage, quietly pining for something they can't have.*

I draw a shaky breath. "I would never feel right taking something that's rightfully yours."

"Ivy, I don't care about that." His voice is louder now; filled with desperation. "I just don't want to lose you."

Tears prick the backs of my eyelids. "I don't want to lose you, either."

We sway back and forth to the blues, clinging to this moment like we're both about to lose everything. After Van

Morrison fades away, we spill out into the darkness, two points of light bobbing about on a black sea.

"Do you want to spend the night?" Oliver's words beg me not to extinguish his hope.

Being with him is excruciating, knowing how things are playing out. But being without him doesn't feel like a good alternative, either.

"Okay," I nod. I take his hand and let him lead me further into the night.

thirty-four

It's Tuesday. Today's the day I was supposed to leave. In less than a week from now, I'd be back at school, setting up for the new year. Instead, I'm leaning behind the register at Shoreline, lost in a trance.

"I hope the distant look in your eyes means you're thinking about how good I look shelving these hardcovers." Oliver's voice pulls me out of my musings.

In fact, I'd been caught in a loop of resolution and despair. Every time it seemed like I had a solution to the conundrum we've found ourselves stuck in, I'd think of a hundred reasons why it wouldn't work.

But I don't want to tell Oliver that. He's been so wonderful; going out of his way to be gentle and supportive and not push me in one direction or the other.

And he's right: he does look exceptionally attractive today.

So I force a little smile that I hope conveys my appreciation for his tight white t-shirt and hides the fact that my heart feels like it's been put through a blender. "Fishing for compliments is a good look, too."

He feigns shock. "And I thought you hated the nautical puns."

I shake my head. "That one was an accident."

"Sure it was." Crossing the room to stand before me, he leans down until our noses are almost touching across the front desk. "I happened to notice that you look amazing today yourself," he says low enough that none of our 14 current customers could possibly hear him. "And I was thinking, maybe I could take you out to dinner tonight? Italian?"

"Well," I say coyly, "I suppose your flattery deserves a reward."

His brows go up. "I'll take that, too."

"Oliver!" I toss a bookmark at him. "I meant the date."

He snickers. "I see how it is. Well, even if that's all I get, this place has free bread, too. Definitely worth it."

"It's not actually free if you're paying for the meal. They work that into the cost."

"You're an oracle of economics, Ivy."

"And you," I say, poking his shoulder with my pointer finger, "are a huge dork."

It feels good to be bantering again. Regardless of what happens in a few weeks, this feels right.

OLIVER PICKS me up at Beach Haven at seven o'clock. "It's just out of town," he'd explained to me earlier. "A bit too far to walk, given how full of bread we're going to be when we head home."

"I think you underestimate my self-control," I'd told him.

"Huh." He'd raised his brow. "Because you never seem able to control yourself around *me*."

That's when I'd pursed my lips and pretended to swat him away.

The restaurant is like something out of a fairy tale, with twinkling white lights coiled around exposed wooden beams and floating candles at every table. The bread is incredible; warm and fresh from the oven, with just the right amount of crust. Oliver orders a chicken sorrentino dish, and I pick the penne alla vodka, which has always been my favorite.

"So," I say, swirling a glass of pinot, "how was your day?"

He snorts. "Oh, you know. It was fine. Pretty busy; reset some displays. My coworker was a little annoying at times, but I've learned to just tune her out."

"Ha!" A laugh erupts from the top of my throat. "You think you're pretty clever, don't you?"

"*You* think I'm pretty clever," he retorts, grinning.

"This is true," I shrug.

He takes a sip of his water. He'd insisted that I order the wine I wanted, even though he was abstaining since he'd be driving us home. I study his features in the glow of the string lights: his dark eyelashes, stark above the blue of his irises; his lips, which always seem like they're hiding a smirk. His shoulders, which have borne the weight of so much; his hands, smooth like his poet's soul, despite how hard he works.

I can't hurt him. I just can't.

He's been desperate to escape this town since his mother left. And now he's stuck here, probably forever, looking after his dad. When his father is older and requires more medical attention, Oliver will either have to provide that care himself or hire someone. He'll need time off work, or more money, depending on which approach he chooses. If I accept Maisie's offer, I don't think Oliver will get either.

I still don't understand why she offered the position to me. Deep down, I'm a little frustrated about it, honestly. That she picked me over him; that she put us in this position in the first place. Why couldn't she have just given Oliver the job and let me stay on as a clerk? Maybe I could have taken another job in town, waitressing at night, or something, to make ends meet. I could have made it work. But she'd said, *"I'm asking you."* And it's her store. I didn't feel right questioning her motivations.

My grandparents sacrificed so much for each other—Eleanor, the romantic love she craved. Charlie, a lifetime of love with Simon. At least they lived peacefully together. My parents couldn't even do that much when things got tough. I just don't see how Oliver sacrificing his needs so I can stay is going to work out in the long run. It's not what's best for either of us.

"What?" He catches me mid-rumination again.

I shake my head. "Nothing."

His gaze sweeps my face. "Didn't look like nothing."

My heart is thumping almost painfully in my chest. I don't want to ruin this lovely evening. Whatever time we have left together. But he's clearly seeing right through my attempts at closeting my feelings. It wouldn't be fair to keep things from him.

I take a deep breath. "I think I have to accept the Springfield job."

Water flows in at the corners of his eyes, but he blinks it back almost as quickly as it appears. "I understand."

I nod several times, as if convincing myself that this is for the best. "But it'll be okay. It's only two-and-a-half hours from here." Reaching for his hand, I force another smile. "We can visit each other whenever our days off line up. It will all work out."

My brain immediately rebuts that suggestion; Oliver works almost every weekend at Shoreline, and the Springfield role is Monday through Friday. But I have to stay positive. "We'll make it work," I reiterate, as if bringing the words to life will manifest their reality.

Oliver doesn't look convinced, either, but he squeezes my hand. "We'll make it work," he agrees. His lips tilt in something resembling a smile, but his eyes remain ringed in sorrow.

AFTER DINNER, Oliver invites me to spend the night at his house again. Laurel is still licking her wounds, and I've been trying to give her as much space as possible.

"Are you sure your dad won't mind?"

"Nah," he says, starting the truck. "He likes you, remember? Besides, he'll probably be busy reading or watching TV. We can just do our thing."

As it turns out, Robert is finishing the last chapter of his novel right as we walk in. "Oliver! Ivy!" He has the excitement of someone who's been trapped in quarantine for several weeks and is finally allowed to return to civilization. "How about a game of cards?"

Oliver shoots me a nervous look. "Oh, I don't know, Dad. It's been kind of a tough day. We may just go to go to bed."

Robert's face falls faster than a broken elevator. "Sure thing."

"I'm getting a bit of a second wind, actually," I offer.

"Maybe we could play for a little bit?" I glance to Oliver in question.

This time, his smile goes all the way to his eyes. "Okay, let's."

I'm starting to think that cards are the official state pastime of Maine. Granted, my sample size is just three: Simon, Robert, and Maisie, who mentioned offhand that she belongs to a bridge club. I suppose there aren't many alternative activities in the winter months in northern New England. The beach is still gorgeous, but it loses its status as a way to spend a fulfilling or safe afternoon the minute the snow hits.

We start with poker. "Has Oliver warned you how good he is?" Robert asks, dealing out the deck.

"It hasn't come up."

Oliver flashes me a bright grin. "Did you ever consider that might have been intentional?"

"Sorry to have divulged your secret," Robert jokes.

"Eh, it's okay." Oliver shrugs. "I'm still going to win."

We all laugh, but after a few minutes, it's beyond clear that Robert was right. Oliver is an exceptionally good poker player. He wins every hand we play but three, of which I take one and Robert the other two.

After we wrap up, Oliver makes a vanilla tea that tastes like dessert.

I take a deep sip. "I'm not usually a huge tea drinker, but I'll make an exception for this."

"I'll make it for you anytime," Oliver offers sweetly.

"Consolation prize for losing at cards?" I joke.

He grins. "Of course."

"Well," Robert says, finishing his tea and rising from the

table with what appears to be deep effort, "I think it's time for me to hit the hay. Have a good night, you two."

I half expect him to add something like, "But not *too* good," with a suggestive wink, but thankfully, he refrains.

"You tired?" Oliver asks when we're alone.

"Kind of," I answer apologetically. I feel guilty, somehow. Like maybe I should be spending every last second with him that I can, given the interstate that's readying itself to tear us asunder.

"It's okay. Let's go to bed." He reaches for my hand. When his fingers close around mine, I feel tears prick the backs of my eyelids. I don't want to lose this.

After I've brushed my teeth with the toothbrush Oliver bought for me to keep here, I slip into his room and shut the door gingerly.

"There are some pajamas for you on the dresser," he offers.

I pick up the shirt first. "This is your Kafka tee."

"I had the sense you liked that one," he teases.

"Mmm." I slip my dress over my head and unhook my bra, letting both fall to the floor. "It was more how it looked on *you* that I enjoyed."

Oliver meets me at the center of the room, hands skimming up my bare ribcage. "I think it's going to look even better on you."

"Oh yeah?" Our faces are inches away now. It's so easy, being with him. And even though the mood is tinged with melancholy given current circumstances, there's definitely a more urgent need growing deep in my belly.

"Mmhmm," he murmurs, drawing me to him. "But I think we can wait to find out."

I'm all over him then, a moth drawn to a flame. I want

everything, always. We're a jumble of arms and legs and bleeding hearts, and I can't get enough. I'll never have enough.

I think the term "lovemaking" was invented for nights like these; for the way Oliver's looking at me in the dim light like I'm something precious. Everything feels heightened: his kiss, the way he moans when he slips inside me. The way we linger over every touch, savor each other like something decadent, because we recognize how fleeting these moments are.

Afterward, I fall asleep curled against him, feeling content in every way, other than the ache in my chest that's throbbing to the beat of my broken heart.

Much to my chagrin, when I wake up in the morning, I realize I never got around to putting on his Kafka shirt.

thirty-five

I f I'm moving to Springfield in less than a month, I need to
do some serious organizing of my condo. It's increasingly
harder to spend time around Oliver, anyway—my chest aches
whenever we're together, anticipating the wound to come.

I broach the subject with him while we're unpacking a
shipment of picture books. "Would it be okay if we rearranged
our schedule this week? I need two days off in a row."

He looks at me quizzically. "Sure, but why?"

I cast my gaze downward. "I need to get some things sorted
at my condo. To prepare for Springfield."

"Ah." He looks away. "When do you want to go?"

"Maybe Thursday and Friday?" That will get me back in
time for the weekend rush. I don't want him to have to deal
with that on his own. Plus, the grad student who's subletting
my condo this summer is going on vacation later this week, so
I'll have the place to myself.

"Fine," Oliver says, with a bite I wasn't expecting.

"Is everything okay?"

His eyes narrow. "No, Ivy. Everything isn't okay."

"I don't know what I'm supposed to do," I say quietly. "No matter what choice I make, I hurt you."

"See, but that's the thing," he says, words laced with a bitterness I'm not used to from him. "I've explained to you repeatedly that I'm okay with you taking the manager job. I don't want it. Not if I have to give you up to get it."

My voice quivers. "I don't understand why you're angry with me."

He closes his eyes, as if he can blink them back open to a better outcome. "I'm not. I'm not angry with you. I just hate this."

"I hate it, too."

He reaches for my hand. "Then stay."

I shake my head slowly. "I can't."

Oliver nods, but he doesn't look at me. "Thursday's fine." Without another word, he crosses the bookstore and walks out the door, the jingle of its bells echoing hollow through the empty room.

AT 5:30, I head home alone. Oliver's working a closing shift, and I haven't been to Beach Haven in a day and a half. I need to do some laundry, and possibly shower with body products that don't smell like vanilla cedar. And besides, we barely spoke to one another for the rest of the afternoon. I'm not sure that we're fighting, exactly, but things definitely feel a lot shakier than they did last night.

Laurel's working on a bowl of cereal at the kitchen island when I walk through the door. "Hey," I call out, far more cheerfully than I feel.

"Hey." She doesn't even look up from her phone.

I want to make things better, but I'm not sure how. Without considering the gesture too thoroughly, I slide onto the stool next to her. "How's the dissertation going?"

She sighs. "I think I'm going to go home."

"Oh. To see Nick?" I still haven't gotten the low-down on whether she and Nick are still a thing.

"No. I mean for the rest of the summer."

All the air leaves my lungs. "What?"

Laurel shakes her head. "I'm spending all my time working anyway; we've hardly spent any time together. And honestly, the way things have been going, I think maybe I need some distance." She considers the shock on my face, then adds gently, "And maybe you do, too."

I want to yell that I don't need space; that I'm going home for a couple of days, anyway, so she doesn't need to feel like she has to run away and hide. I want to ask her what I even did wrong; why she's so upset with me for sharing a truth that someone else hid, many decades ago. I could have approached it differently, sure. But I didn't write the reality she's been so hesitant to acknowledge.

Deep in my gut, I know I don't have the energy to fight this battle, though. So after pinching my eyes shut for a moment, I just say, "Okay."

And then I stand up and stride out of the room before the tears can fall.

AS I'M SHOVING clothes angrily into an overnight bag on Wednesday evening, I'm overcome by the urge to cry, but it's like my soul is too exhausted to muster the energy. Beach

Haven's quiet; Laurel left this morning. Oliver had to take his dad to several medical appointments today, so I ran the shop alone for 12 hours straight. And, though we'd talked about getting together tonight, I have a horrendous migraine. I'm thinking of telling him I just need to go to bed.

So much for my restorative vacation. So much for finding hope, and clarity, and regaining the sense of joy the beach used to bring me. Things started off auspiciously enough this summer, but they've quickly devolved into a ruinous mess largely of my own creation. The worst part is that it's somehow managed to sweep up everyone I care about and make things harder for them, too.

I end up falling asleep before texting Oliver, so I wake up to a series of increasingly worried texts the next morning. *I'm so sorry*, I reply as soon as I blink in a few hits of the daylight. *I passed out after I finished packing.*

No worries, he shoots back a few minutes later. An image of Oliver standing behind the counter at Shoreline breaches my mind's best defenses, and I'm torn between giving in to guilt or sorrow. He's probably just finished opening the shop all on his own, mentally spent already after a long day of caretaking.

I'm sure he's working through my impending departure in his own way. I hate myself more than a little bit for running scared right when I should probably be staying, so we can deal with the hurt together. It's the least I should do, really. But for some reason, I just *can't*.

My drive back to Brookline almost doesn't happen, because my Toyota Corolla, which has been parked in the driveway of Beach Haven for several weeks in the hot sun, resists my request for transport. After several attempts to turn the engine over, throughout which I try desperately to remember everything my dad ever taught me about flooding engines with gasoline, the car finally starts up.

"Thanks," I whisper to it, like it's a person doing me a favor. I truly think I'm going a little bit insane.

It's an hour into my trip before I even remember to turn on the radio. I'm so distracted by all the noise in my head that it doesn't occur to me to add more sensory input. Flipping the station to find anything other than ads, I can't help but wonder if I'm focused enough to drive safely right now. But given the choice between pressing on and stopping to have a panic attack at a rest stop, I settle on the former.

An oldies channel playing Van Morrison stops my restless spinning of the frequency dial. It takes a few bars of sultry brass for me to realize it's "Days Like This." My heart is exceptionally needy right now, but I'm quite certain the *last* thing it needs is a very poignant reminder of romantic moments with Oliver.

Angrily, I turn the radio off. And I spend the rest of the drive filling the silence with increasingly despondent thoughts.

I'm almost at full panic attack level by the time I get back to my condo. I've managed to work myself up beyond the point I can box breathe my way down from, but I don't want to take any of the benzos my doctor gave me for moments like this. Ironically, I'm too anxious about getting addicted to them to benefit from their use.

I don't think I should be alone right now. I don't *want* to be alone right now.

I don't want to be alone, period.

That's at the crux of this whole issue, really. Taking a deep breath, I back out of my parking space before I've even gone inside to see how my fiddle leaf fig fared during my absence, then I make a sharp left and head toward my parents' house.

It occurs to me all at once that it isn't my *parents'* house anymore. Not really. But I manage to block the panic that sad fact almost adds to my current rolling boil before it cascades over.

It's about a half hour to the Dover house. My heart's cheered more than a little bit to see how little has changed here. It looks like Mom has swapped out some of her petunias for mums, but otherwise, the exterior of the house looks exactly as it did the last time I saw it.

Taking a deep breath, I smooth my hair in the rearview. I force myself to make eye contact with panicked Ivy in the mirror; it's a trick I learned from my mother. Sometimes, seeing the terror in my eyes as if it's happening to someone else is all it takes to break the hold my anxiety has on me, if only momentarily. I realize it's a strange concept, needing to humanize yourself; to separate *you* from what's happening inside your body. But that's the effect it often has on me. And, thankfully, it works this time, too.

I grab my purse and head for the front door. Ringing the bell, I'm puzzled to hear muffled voices inside. One is a male voice, from the sounds of it. *Oh, God.* Is my mother *dating* someone?

Mom answers the door, her face slipping from surprise to joy to concern in a matter of seconds. "Ivy!" She wraps me in a tight hug. "I wasn't expecting you. Is everything okay?"

It's there, wrapped in the arms of the person who's always kept me safe, where I finally let go. Tears fall, and my shoulders are wracked by sobs. I don't even know where to begin explaining why I'm here; what's happened to lead me to this place of utter heartbreak. But that's the beautiful thing about finding solace with your safe person—you don't have to say anything. Even when you've pushed them away, time and time again, they're standing by, ready to offer a warm hug whenever you need one.

"Why don't you come inside?" Mom pulls me into the foyer and shuts the door behind me. She casts a furtive glance over her shoulder.

"Who is it, Rach?"

My brain screeches to a halt. "Dad?"

He comes into view behind my mother. "Hey there, Ivy Bean."

"Seems like we all have some things to talk about," I say wryly.

MOM MAKES some tea even though it's 80 degrees outside, and we sit around the dining room table to catch up. In this instance, "catching up" means me talking rapidly about everything under the sun other than the reason I came here.

"So, Dad," I ask during a lull in the conversation, "what are you doing at the house?"

The quick glance he exchanges with my mom doesn't escape my attention. "Just came over to get some things."

I raise a brow over my mug. "Uh huh."

"I needed my tool kit!" He's trying so hard to look incredulous rather than guilty. It's adorable, honestly. "There's something up with the washer at my apartment, but the super's taking ages to get out and fix it."

"I already told you that you can just do your laundry here," Mom says quietly.

"I don't want to put you out," he answers, giving her a look I can only think to describe as effusively affectionate.

I take a sip of tea to hide the smile growing on my face.

"So, Ivy. Care to explain what brought you here in tears today?" Dad rests his chin in his palm.

"I wasn't in tears when I got here."

"So it was your mother's fault, then?" His eyes twinkle.

"Excuse me?" Mom pretends to hit him. "I've been nothing but accommodating."

"Hey," he shrugs, "you're the one who answered the door."

A chuckle rolls out of my throat. "There's been a lot happening in Ogunquit this summer." My gaze sweeps to Dad, who suddenly looks very serious, and Mom, whose expression has shifted to therapy mode. "You both already know bits and pieces of it. But I think I should—I think I *have* to tell you the rest." I look down at my hands, curled tightly around the tea cup like it's the middle of winter and I've just been skiing. "It's gotten to be a bit more than I can handle on my own."

"We're here for you, kiddo," Dad says.

"This is a safe space." Mom nods encouragingly. "You can tell us anything."

And so I tell them everything.

I SPEND the night in my childhood bedroom, full of pizza and wine and the satisfaction that only several Scattergories victories can bring. My parents had listened to my plight with empathy (Mom) and the occasional joke (Dad), but getting everything off my chest did wonders for my emotional wellbeing.

Even though everything isn't okay just yet, I'm starting to

realize that it's going to be. I don't know when, or how, but things are going to work out the way they're supposed to—because I'll continue relentlessly striving until they do.

The next morning, my father makes pancakes. I don't bother asking where he spent the night; I don't want to damage whatever fragile peace my parents seem to be establishing by prying.

Especially if they've been spending time together in a romantic way. I'd prefer to know absolutely nothing about that.

After breakfast, Dad rolls up his sleeves. "Why don't we go to your place together after I tackle these dishes?"

My mom raises an amused brow. "Dishes, Steven?"

"What?" He accepts the faceoff. "You might remember that I'm great at keeping a home in order."

"Hmm." Mom barely gets the sound out before snorting into her coffee.

"Anything for my girls," Dad adds.

Mom reaches out to squeeze his arm. "Well, thank you. That's very sweet."

I've never seen my dad blush before. Usually, he's all puns and feigned masculine bluster. But pink edges up his cheeks now.

"Well, that's my cue." I sweep my plate off the table and head to the sink. "I'm going to get going. I have a lot of packing to do."

"I mean it, Ivy," Dad insists from the table, where Mom's hand is still on his forearm. "I'd like to help."

"I can help, too," my mother adds, looking at me like nothing out of the ordinary is occurring here in her dining room. "Let us just get some chores done, then we'll be right behind you."

I'm simultaneously amused and appalled, so I hustle to the entryway and grab my keys. "See you in a bit," I call back to them. "Enjoy your...chores." Shaking my head at how awkward my unintended pause just made things, I let the door swing shut roughly behind me.

My parents, flirting like teenagers right in front of me? This life just gets curiouser and curiouser.

thirty-six

I 'm sorting through a collection of what some might consider three times as many t-shirts as a person needs when my phone goes off. Glancing down to the spot next to my right knee where it's playing an Andrew W.K. playlist, I see that the message is from Oliver.

Mr. Romance Reader is back in the café.

I wasn't expecting to hear from him; it seemed like he was still dealing with my departure in his own sullen way. And I *definitely* wasn't expecting our next interaction would have anything to do with the customer he'd told me about. A chortle escapes my lips. *Oh my God! What is he reading?*

Something by Nora Roberts, he texts back.

I cross my legs and toss a pile of shirts to the side, leaning back against the bed. Before I can stop myself, I dial the Shoreline number.

"Shoreline Books." Oliver sounds only slightly more enthusiastic today than he did when I'd called the night of Rachel and the beach stroll.

"You need to get that man something else to read," I say by way of a greeting.

"Hey, Ivy." I can hear his relief.

"Hey yourself." I'm relieved, too. I didn't realize how starved for his voice I'd been. "Listen: Nora Roberts is fine, but romance novels have come a long way in the last decade. I want you to casually drop some Christina Lauren books on the table next to this customer. He deserves something that doesn't use phrases like 'hard as steel.'"

Oliver chuckles. "Even when you're not at work, you're working."

"I might care just a *smidge* too much."

"What would we do without you, Ivy?"

I think he's joking, at least somewhat—continuing the bit for the sake of a laugh. But I know another part of him is serious, too.

"How's it going otherwise?" I try to keep the mood light.

"Oh, it's been fine. Pretty busy, but nothing I can't handle."

"You *are* exceptionally capable."

He lowers his voice. "You're a terrible flirt."

"Only with you," I reply.

It's then that my doorbell rings. My eyes flick up to the clock on my desk—it's 1:30. My parents certainly took their sweet time with their "chores."

"I should go," I tell Oliver. "My parents just got here to help me pack."

There's the briefest pause, during which I wonder if he's trying to hold back a twinge of sadness. I know I am. "Sounds good," he says afterward.

"I love you," I remind him.

"I love you, too." My heart needed to hear that more than ever today.

"WHO WOULD HAVE THOUGHT my daughter would grow up to be a hoarder?" Dad says a half hour later, attempting to sort through the sky-high stack of papers on my dining room table.

Mom fixes him with a withering stare. "You're joking, right?"

"Why would that be a joke? I'm a minimalist." He grins.

"Oh, Dad." I shake my head. "I lived with you for 22 years. You're not fooling anyone."

"I see how it is." He feigns offense. "While I know the theme of the day is cleaning and decluttering, I actually brought something over to add to your collection."

"Helpful, Steven." Mom rolls her eyes, looking slightly less charmed than she did this morning. Maybe they're not completely over their issues after all.

"This is for Ivy," Dad replies. "Feel free to excuse yourself. You're good at that."

My brows shoot up my forehead, watching this standoff between my parents. "Kids, be nice," I beg after a moment of awkward silence.

Mom looks like she might cry, but she shakes her head. "I'll go box up some books in your bedroom." She walks away before I can respond, and the door clicks closed behind her.

"Seriously, Dad?"

His expression hovers somewhere between ashamed and guilty. "Sorry. We're not quite over the trauma of what's gone on."

"You'll apologize to her?"

He nods quickly. "Yeah. I'll talk to her in a bit. I want to give her time to calm down. She'd probably bite my head off if I went in there right now."

"Oh, indubitably."

My father sighs deeply. "I always manage to screw things up."

I squeeze his shoulder. "It'll be okay."

"I hope so."

I need to change the subject before he submits to the cycle of worry and despair that typically makes him shut down completely. "So, you said you brought me something?"

"I did." He sounds a bit nervous.

"Am I allowed to see it?"

Dad reaches into his pocket and pulls out a small pile of folded papers, yellowed with age. I recognize the script on the top page immediately.

"Are those—"

He nods. "The pages from Mom's diary. I...I'm really sorry for taking them."

"It's okay. I understand why you had to." I don't want to make things any more challenging for him than they already are.

Dad reaches out a shaking hand, and I take the pages from him. "Is it okay if I read them?"

He nods. "Of course."

I sink into a chair at the dining room table and spread the papers out in front of me, running my thumb along the crease to flatten it back out.

July 31, 1953

He took me to our place on the cliffs again tonight. It was so romantic. At one point, we were surprised by a tourist out for an evening stroll, and we had to scramble to make ourselves decent —definitely not my proudest moment.

August 6, 1953

I'm struggling a bit today. I invited my gentleman friend out tonight, but he said he had a family commitment. Janie and I went to Harbor Lights instead.

On the way home, though, I saw him walking arm-in-arm with a young woman. I recognize her from the beach; her family must vacation here, too, because she's been in town for weeks.

I wanted to confront him, but Janie urged me to wait. Maybe it was his sister, she suggested. Maybe it was a misunderstanding.

I don't understand how it could be a misunderstanding. I've given myself to him completely, and he led me to believe he had plans to propose. I'm either the most gullible woman in New England, or perhaps he's just a master at tricking women into sleeping with him.

My eyes flick up to my father, who's taken the seat across from me at the table. He's watching me read the pages, a look of nervous anticipation on his face.

"I hate this guy," I say.

"Me too." He purses his lips. "Unfortunately, it gets worse."

I turn the page.

August 15, 1953

I saw him again tonight. I've been avoiding him since the night he was out with Sarah—that's her name, I discovered. I've wanted nothing more than to approach him and demand answers, but Janie continues to insist that classy ladies don't do that—they just act haughty and superior and stop seeing the man forever.

I suppose my mother would suggest I'm no classy lady, given my behavior up to this point. I'm so ashamed.

August 19, 1953

It occurs to me that not long ago, I was concerned about my mother finding this diary and learning something as basic as my paramour's name. Lately, I've been describing all sorts of lewd things.

I laugh out loud at the notion that anything Eleanor's been writing is particularly lewd. If only she knew how culture would change over the next six decades. I read on.

In any case, this next bit is something I really shouldn't be committing to the page, but I need to get it out. Maybe that will help me to feel better.

My monthly courses are later than usual, and I'm starting to grow worried that my nights on the cliffs might have a more lasting impact than I'd hoped. I've only told Janie so far, but she wasn't much help. We're not anywhere near our doctor, being on vacation, and I don't have the money to pay for an appointment regardless.

I've started keeping this little book under my mattress, wrapped inside an old pillowcase. If my parents were to find it, I can't even imagine what would happen.

August 25, 1953
Charlie saved me today. My body is changing; I can tell. The signs are becoming more clear with every passing day.

I met him after his shift at his family's store and broke down completely. He held me while I cried, then kissed my hair and promised he'd help me. That I wasn't alone.

I don't know what I've done to deserve such a true and loyal friend, but I am forever grateful for his kindness.

August 27, 1953
Charlie brought me to a doctor in town today. He made sure to wait in the lobby the whole time so I didn't feel so alone. He also paid the fee and refused my offer to repay him when I was able. "You're my best friend, Ellie," he'd said. "I'm here for you always."

In any case, the doctor confirmed what I already feared. He even suggested it might be twins. I have no idea what I'm going to do. I suppose I'll have to track down the man who's broken my heart and tell him the truth so that he can make this right.

August 29, 1953
Today was the worst day of my life. I found him; he was with Sarah again. I asked for a moment to speak with him privately.

She cast daggers at me the whole time, but eventually he agreed to talk with me.

I tried to make the situation sound like an opportunity. We'd had so much fun together, I reminded him. We could have a great life together, and raise our child in a loving family.

He wasn't interested. He apologized for putting me in this situation, but he said he couldn't be tied down. I asked if this was because of Sarah. When he said no, that's when I knew.

I was never anything to him. Neither is she. He's just using young women for a good time, then going home to his real life, whatever that is. I'm so ashamed that I was misled to such a great extent.

The conversation didn't go well. I burst into tears when he refused me, then I resorted to begging. He just repeated over and over again that he can't be a family man.

Finally, he offered me $50. I took it, then threw it into the ocean while he watched.

I guess that's all I was worth to him in the end. $50 and a good time.

I'd gone to Charlie after that. "I don't know what I'm going to do," I'd told him. "There is no other way to fix this."

He'd held me while I cried, whispering against my cheek, "It will be okay, Ellie. There's always another way."

August 30, 1953

Charlie and I had a long talk today. He's revealed a big secret about himself, too—he and Simon are in love, but they're forced to hide it for their own safety. Not to mention, Simon is studying to become a lawyer like his father. He loves what he's learning, but he would be disgraced, or possibly even jailed, if anyone knew that he was breaking the very laws he's promised to uphold. It tears my heart in two to think that they cannot be together.

Charlie thinks he has the perfect solution to our problems. He will marry me and raise my child as his own. We'll be happy together, he says, because we already love one another in the way that's most important—as soulmates.

I cried when he offered. I told him I couldn't ask this of him, but he begged me to think it over. "I love you, Ellie," he'd insisted. "I want to protect you, and I promise to love your child. No one ever needs to know the truth."

"But what about your happiness with Simon?" I'd asked him. "No matter how much you love me, it isn't the same."

"It isn't the same," he admitted. "But I can love you in this way and him in another; they're not mutually exclusive. Perhaps we can move to your hometown to keep suspicion low, then vacation to Ogunquit each summer to visit Simon?"

"Would that be enough for you?" I'd asked. I didn't see how it could be.

"This would be a sacrifice for us both," he'd said. "Though if you ever fell in love with another man, I'd do whatever it took to ensure your happiness. We could divorce, or you could see him secretly. I'd be okay with any of it."

"This is too much, Charlie," I'd said. "These are huge sacrifices you're proposing."

"But if the sacrifices make us each whole," he'd replied, "then they're worth it."

He gave me time to think about it. As much time as I needed, he promised.

But I don't have all that much time. Soon, my secret, at least, is going to be out in the open, whether I like it or not.

November 2, 1953

Charlie and I are getting married tomorrow. My parents are over the moon, because they've loved him like a son since we were children. He's always been the best companion to me.

Janie knows the truth, as does Simon, of course. My mother has made a few comments about how I've been putting on weight, and that maybe I should stop enjoying the chocolates Charlie brings me from his family's store, but I don't think she suspects the real cause.

It's taken me some time to come around to this ruse, but it's felt less and less like a ruse as the wedding planning has moved

forward. Charlie's secreted me away to my doctor's appoint-
ments and helped pick flower arrangements. His parents are
paying for the whole wedding because they know mine can't
afford it, though my father insisted on covering the cost of my
dress.

It's a gorgeous white boat-necked gown that flows just to the
ankle. I've embroidered flowers along the hem—one for every
flower Charlie's brought me since he proposed. He's been
visiting us in our hometown every weekend, and he's already
found a home for us to buy just a few blocks away from my
parents.

Truly, I couldn't ask for anything more in a husband. I've
thought a lot about what he said—that a sacrifice is worth it if it
makes both people whole. And while our union wasn't what I
anticipated, I'm actually excited to spend my life with him. I
love him, and he loves me, and this sacrifice has made us each
more than whole.

"Wow." I look up from the pages and see that Dad's eyes
are misty. I can't tell if he's reacting to my own tears, or if he's
reading Eleanor's words from across the table.

"Wow is right," he says, sniffing back his grief.

"I can see why you hid these," I offer. "But I'm also so glad
you shared them with me."

"Yeah?"

I nod. "Yeah. Because Eleanor's words have given me what
no one else could—the assurance that this life they chose truly
was the best choice for both of them."

"Well, given the circumstances," my father adds.

"Right. I've really been struggling with that, since I started to unravel the truth." I run my thumb absently over the torn edges of the last sheet of paper. "The *why*. Why it was worth it to them—to all three of them—to make this kind of sacrifice for each other. But I suppose that embracing the complexity of the situation, their vulnerabilities, helped them all to heal and ultimately find exactly what they needed."

Dad's eyes well up again. "That's such a beautiful sentiment, Ivy Bean."

"And I think that they did something right. Something you and Mom haven't been able to figure out just yet. And something I've done wrong with Oliver."

"What's that?"

"They didn't hide from the truth. Or react poorly to it, or try to bear it on their own. Doing that destroys relationships. Instead, they took the truth and found a way to work within its confines." My mind flashes to Oliver, back at Shoreline, missing me, and me, here in Brookline, aching to be by his side. I hid the truth from him for too long.

And rather than try to find a solution to our current situation together, I resigned myself to the fact that there *was* no solution and didn't even discuss it with him. I know, deep down, that kind of unilateral decision-making is going to destroy us eventually.

And then there's my parents: my dad couldn't handle the truth about his family; my mom reacted poorly to his distress. Rather than work through it together, they both turned inward and ultimately decided they'd failed the other.

"Your grandfather was always very solutions-oriented," Dad jokes, a twinkle fighting its way back to life in his moist eyes.

My heart skips, thinking of Oliver, always joking about being solutions-oriented, too. "I think," I tell my father, "I'd like to be more like Charlie in that way."

Dad's face fills with love. "You have no idea," he says quietly, "how proud he'd be of you."

thirty-seven

I leave Brookline first thing the next morning, a pile of cardboard boxes standing next to the front door of the condo. There's more that needs to be done, but I need to get back to Maine for work this afternoon. And before I go there, I have a stop to make.

Laurel grew up just a few minutes down the road from me, and we were together constantly. When I pull up to her parents' house now, I'm hit with a flood of memories. Playing tag in their front yard; countless summer picnics out back. Christmas parties and Thanksgivings, play dates and sleepovers. Uncle Greg and Aunt Bea's place was basically my second home.

Today, it feels more than a little intimidating.

Because inside is my cousin, who prior to this summer I'd have said was one of my best friends in the world. As she'd suggested, we were essentially sisters. But in disrespecting her wishes where long-buried family secrets were concerned, I'd messed up. And as much as I don't regret chasing down the information, I should have listened to Laurel when she told me she truly didn't want to know.

I'm hoping it's not too late for me to apologize.

My heart's racing while I wait on the front stoop, but, fortunately, Aunt Bea comes to the door with a gentle smile. "Hey, Ivy," she offers kindly. "I didn't know you were in town."

"I had to pack up some things. I'm going to be moving to Springfield."

Bea's brow wrinkles, but she nods. "I hadn't realized you'd decided."

I guess my dad must have told her about the library position. Doing my best to look like I know what I'm doing, I paste on a smile. "I think it will be a great opportunity."

My aunt pulls the door open further. "I assume you're here for Laurel?"

"I am," I hedge. "I was hoping she might be open to a conversation." I don't see the point in burying the lede; I assume Laurel's already thoroughly vented to her parents about my transgressions.

"Come on in." Bea steps back. "She's working on her dissertation, but I think it would be good for her to take a break."

"Ah, if that isn't the theme of the summer," I quip.

Walking to Laurel's bedroom on the second floor is so familiar, I could probably do it in my sleep. I knock quietly when I get to her door.

"Yes?" she calls from within.

I take a deep breath. "It's Ivy."

There's a long beat, then she replies, "Come in."

Relief washes over me. I wasn't even sure I'd get this far. Easing the door open, I see Laurel hunched over her laptop, a notebook and pen to her right.

"Just working through some edits." She indicates the note-book and spins in her chair to face me, crossing her arms as she does. "What's up?"

"I was in town for a couple of days, and I thought I'd be remiss if I didn't come by to talk to you."

She stares at me blankly, waiting.

I try again. "I wanted to apologize."

Her gated posture seems to relax just a bit. "Thanks."

I step further through the doorway. "I mean it, Laurel. I don't regret learning the truth. I couldn't not know. But I *am* sorry for dragging you into it. You made it clear that you didn't want anything to alter your impression of the past."

Laurel drops her hands to her lap. "I really didn't. It's been hard enough to work through losing Eleanor this last year. It doesn't matter to me what her secrets are; I loved her, and so did Charlie. Their love story was true, regardless of the nuance."

"You're right." I inhale deeply. "You are. Nothing we've learned changes who they were or how they loved us. Or each other. And I'm sorry for weaponizing that information to hurt you. I was...I was having trouble processing. I was hurting, both because of these secrets and for...other reasons. And I lashed out at you. It wasn't fair."

"I may have been a little harsh with you, too," Laurel says softly. "I knew you were struggling, but I didn't bother to ask why. I let you help me through my issues with my advisor and Nick and Porter, but I never extended the same courtesy to you."

My mind flashes back to our chat the first night in Ogunquit as we sipped our coffees near Shoreline. "You did, though. You're the one who convinced me it was okay to leave Farnsworth." I shake my head. "I don't think I would have pursued anything else if you hadn't given me permission to be happy."

Laurel smiles sadly. "You don't need anyone's permission to be happy, Ivy. Least of all mine."

"Yeah," I concede. "But you said it yourself. You're the closest thing I have to a sister. And your opinion matters immensely to me."

I can practically see her anger melting in her chest. "I think that's why this all hurt so much. I really don't want to fight with you."

"I know. I'm sorry."

"I'm sorry, too." She closes her laptop. "How long are you in town?"

"I actually have to get back. I'm working this afternoon."

Laurel nods. "Were you visiting your parents?"

"In a manner of speaking," I agree. "I also needed to do some packing at my condo."

She tilts her head. "Oh?"

"I got the Springfield job. I'm going to be moving."

Her expression doesn't change. "I see."

Now it's my turn for confusion. "I thought you'd be happy for me."

"I am happy for you," she replies. "It's just..." She shakes her head rapidly. "Never mind."

"You can't do that. What were you going to say?"

"I'm just surprised, that's all. When you said you were moving, I kind of assumed it was somewhere else."

"I can't stay at Shoreline." I think my face reflects the sorrow in my heart as I say it, because her expression falls, too.

"Why not?"

I take a deep breath. "Because. Maisie offered me a promotion, but I'd basically be taking away the only opportunity Oliver has. And he doesn't seem to care, but I can't do that to him."

Laurel surveys me carefully. "I know the genetics aren't there, but you're Charlie's granddaughter, Ivy."

"What do you mean?"

Her lips tip up into a gentle smile. "He found a way when it seemed like there wasn't one. I know you have it in you to do the same."

"I don't know," I start. "I'm not so sure there's some magical compromise this time."

"As your almost-sister," Laurel continues, "I feel compelled to call you out when you're being stupid."

"Hey!" I retort.

She grins. "I've seen the way you look at Oliver. You'd never forgive yourself if you gave that up."

A wave of longing crashes through me. She's right, of course. Now that I've gotten a taste of life with Oliver, I can't imagine my life without him. I don't *want to* imagine my life without him.

"But I don't know how," I admit.

"Think outside the box," Laurel suggests. "You know what Grandpa would say."

I nod. "There's always another way."

AS I PULL in to a gas station a few miles away from Beach Haven, my cell phone starts ringing. It's Maisie. She never calls me; I hope everything is okay.

I answer immediately, anxiety rising in my throat. "Hi, Maisie. Are you all right?"

"Oh, I didn't mean to worry you, dear." Maisie sounds fine. My heart rate starts to slow. "But Oliver's working today, and I desperately need someone to grab my pain medication from the pharmacy. I took my last pill early this morning, and there's no chance I'll make it through until he clocks out without another."

"I'd be happy to get it for you. I'm actually just outside of town."

"Oh, thank you! I knew you were coming back today, but I wasn't sure when. Did you get everything sorted at home?"

Home. The word rings hollow in my ears. I'm not even sure what home means anymore.

"I think so. Thank you."

"Well, I'll let you go. Bring me a receipt for the medication so I can reimburse you."

"Absolutely," I reply. "I'll see you shortly."

I get to Maisie's house about 20 minutes later. It occurs to me when I ring the bell that she may not be able to get up to let me in.

"It's open!" she calls from inside.

My brows wrinkle over my nose. I'm not sure she should be leaving the door unlocked all the time, given her current physical incapacity.

Maisie's stretched out in her armchair, leg up on an ottoman. A table beside her is piled high with glasses, mugs, novels, and several television remotes.

"Ivy!" She's always an exuberant person, but I'm wondering if the pain meds are making her loopier than usual. My arrival doesn't typically elicit this much enthusiasm.

"It's great to see you, Maisie. How are you feeling?"

"I'll be better when I get some of those." She nods toward the bag in my hand.

How much codeine is she taking, exactly? I make a mental note to talk to Oliver about her prescription later. I don't want her getting addicted during her recovery.

"How about I get you a glass of water for your medication, then straighten up for you?" I offer, gesturing to the table.

"That would be very kind of you. I've been trying to keep up, and Oliver's been coming by twice nearly every day, but it's been hard to stay on top of things." She looks embarrassed, and I hate that for her. She's alone here for most of the day and can barely get around. The fact that her house isn't a complete mess is, frankly, shocking.

I collect all the dirty cups and mugs and head toward the kitchen.

"Could you also grab me some applesauce from the refrigerator?" Maisie calls in after me. "The codeine upsets my stomach a bit without something to accompany it."

"No problem." Pulling open the fridge, I notice that it's fully stocked. I'm certain I know who's responsible for that.

My eyes slide across three takeout containers, a carton of milk, and a bottle of lemonade before they come to land on a large Pyrex. "Chocolate raspberry cheesecake. Take one slice per day, with or without food," reads a note in Oliver's handwriting that's taped to the front. My chest swells, a surprised chuckle slipping out before I can stop it. Of course he would do this.

I find the applesauce, spoon some into a bowl, and grab a fresh glass of water. "Here you are," I say, handing them to Maisie when I get back to the living room.

"Thank you, dear. Have a seat."

"Oh. Well, I shouldn't stay long." I grin conspiratorially. "I do have to work this afternoon."

She smiles, too. "Your boss won't mind you being a few minutes late."

I laugh. "Tell her I appreciate that."

"Consider it done."

Maisie works on the applesauce, then shoots her pill with a familiarity that puts a dark underline and several exclamation points on the mental note I made to discuss her possible narcotics addiction with Oliver.

She closes her eyes, leaning back in her chair. "I knew you were a good egg."

"Aw, I appreciate that."

"All things considered, I understand why he did it."

I tilt my head. "Why who did what?" She is *definitely* loopy from these pills.

"Why Oliver turned down the manager job," she replies, sitting up again. She picks up a jumble of orange yarn from the arm of her chair and starts to do something vaguely approaching crochet.

My heart starts galloping in my chest. "What do you mean, when Oliver turned down the manager job?"

Maisie smiles gently. "It was the Monday before my surgery. I'd been talking to him about taking over Shoreline for quite some time, and he'd seemed interested. We'd discussed him buying me out, or managing the day-to-day and me taking a backseat to handle just the administrative aspects. We hadn't quite firmed things up yet." Her crochet hook dances across the yarn in her lap, generating a series of increasingly sloppy loops. "In any case, that Monday, he came in and told me he didn't want any of it. That he was going to just keep working in the shop."

My eyes must be as wide as saucers now. "But why wouldn't he want it?"

Maisie's looking at me with such sympathy, I can hardly stand it. "I think you'd be better off asking him, dear."

Oliver, who has so little outside of his work at Shoreline, would have so much to gain from a promotion. Even more to gain from buying the shop, if he were somehow able to swing it. It makes no sense to me that he would step away from something that Maisie has almost certainly been grooming him for since she hired him. He's the closest thing to family that she's got, and I know he loves her like a grandmother. This transition makes all the sense in the world.

But he turned it down. Something gnaws at the edge of my brain, but it can't be right. Can it?

The day she's talking about was right after Oliver took me out on his dad's boat. When he'd asked me if I wanted to stay on as a clerk at Shoreline, and I told him I wouldn't be able to swing it because the pay wasn't enough.

The day he'd carefully considered my answer, then nodded with finality as if he'd come to a decision.

The day he told me he loved me.

With one shuddering jolt, the truth comes into focus. I don't even need to ask Oliver. I know exactly why he stepped away from the opportunity.

He did it for me.

After all, it was later the same day that Maisie offered me the very job Oliver walked away from.

Oliver turned it down so I could take it, so the money would work out and I could move to Ogunquit. So I could work at Shoreline, which he knew I wanted. So I could be with him and build a life here, in this beautiful place by the sea.

Thoughts are racing through my brain at breakneck speed, but one rises above the rest, echoing over and over against every edge of every other thought.

Oliver did this for me.

"I...I don't know what to say." I can barely think right now, much less form a coherent response to Maisie.

"You don't have to say anything." She sets her crocheting down and reaches out to pat my hand, which she misses by several inches. "I realize this might be a lot to process. But I do think, when you're ready, it's something you and Oliver should discuss."

I nod wordlessly. She's right, of course. And I think I want that conversation to happen sooner rather than later.

I'd thought walking away from the bookstore was the right thing specifically so the job could remain open to Oliver. I hadn't realized he'd done the same thing for me.

Looking at the breakdown of my parents' marriage, I'd been desperate to avoid a similar scenario—two people who loved one another but were deeply unhappy. My parents' separation had nothing to do with each other and everything to do with bringing their problems into the marriage.

My dad couldn't deal with the fact that he never met his biological father, who was apparently a horrible person. The fact that the parents who raised him essentially went to their graves withholding the truth. The fact that his mother lived in a platonic marriage; that his father could never be with the man he truly loved. And surely, all of that would be a lot to process, especially in the wake of my grandparents' deaths.

No one modeled healing or working through loss for him.

All he saw was a picture-perfect marriage. Eleanor and Charlie did a lot right, but by keeping the truth from their children, they withheld important lessons about sacrifice and compromise, and how you have to fix your own problems before you can ever hope to be there for someone else. To be an active partner in your own relationship.

And my mom tried. She tried to help my father through his grief; his confusion. But at the end of the day, she didn't feel like my dad was present in their marriage anymore. He wasn't willing or able to do the work of healing, and he lost himself in the process. He lost the ability to connect with her, and she was crying out in pain.

Where I'd once blamed my mom for what seemed like abandonment, I now understand was something else entirely: self-respect and a desperate attempt to preserve her own mental health. To give my father the space to work through his feelings, in hopes that he might come back to her someday when he was able.

It wasn't her fault, and it wasn't his. They were both doing their best with an incredibly challenging set of circumstances. But the deterioration of their marriage had felt cautionary.

I hadn't wanted to take an opportunity away from Oliver, because he had so little else. Even though he would have loved for me to stay here with him, I didn't want him to resent me deep down for holding him back. He already felt trapped here, like there was no future for him anywhere else. I could see that future playing out for us—if he continued to shove down what he wanted, then someday, he'd be a shell of his former self, and neither of us would have anything left.

But it occurs to me now that two people sacrificing for each other only works if both people want it; if both people are served by the compromise. Charlie was right about that.

Oliver and I tried to protect each other, and it came from a good place. Like my grandparents, we both wanted to make the sacrifice. But ultimately, the offerings we placed at the altar of good intentions would never make either of us happy.

With Maisie's revelation sparking through my mind, lighting up every corner such that the reality hits me again and again, I realize that Laurel was right. Charlie was right. There's always another way. And when I look back on my life, I don't want to remember this moment and know I didn't try hard enough to find a solution. To know that I walked away from love.

Suddenly, an idea blooms all at once. I have no idea where it came from; it's like the answer was sent to me on the breeze. But I'm so grateful for it, whatever its provenance, because now I know exactly what I have to do.

thirty-eight

"I think this is the last box." I nod toward the carton labeled "Books" sitting by the front door of my Brookline condo.

"I'm not sure you have enough to read," my father jokes. He's right; we've dealt with 15 other boxes with the same label already.

"Hey, I learned from Grandma."

"You sure did. I'll bring this one out to the moving van, okay?"

I nod. "Thanks." As the door shuts behind him, I survey the empty shell of my life in Brookline. Memories are flying like sparks from a campfire with each pass—the pride I'd felt when I signed the closing papers; the kitchen where I'd made (and burned) my first Thanksgiving turkey; the living room where Kyle kissed me on a Tuesday night. The table where I'd read the offer letter for Farnsworth; the little balcony where I'd sit and cry in the months following the loss of Eleanor. Even though it was late fall then, the cold air helped keep me grounded. It reminded me that I needed to go inside, to come back to reality eventually.

Yes, this place has seen me through many an up and down. And now it's time to let it go.

I follow my dad outside.

"You know," he remarks when he sees me, "after hefting all these books of yours into this truck, I have to say—your new job is lucky to get such a well-read young lady."

The back of the truck slams shut. "You have no idea how lucky," Oliver says, walking toward me with a huge grin on his face.

My father smiles, too. "You're both pretty lucky, I think."

"You've got that right," I agree.

Dad's driving the moving truck to Ogunquit for me. He'll stay at Beach Haven for a few days and work on unloading everything. I feel horrible that I can't be there to help him, but Oliver and I have somewhere we have to be this weekend, and my father insisted that he didn't mind.

"I think I need some time at the beach," he'd admitted. "It's been calling to me."

I'd nodded my understanding. "It'll be good for you to be there."

"Ready?" Oliver asks.

"Ready." We say goodbye to my father, and Oliver helps me up into his truck.

"So, are there any particularly frightening relatives I should know about ahead of this wedding?" I joke when we pull away.

His smile starts. "Oh, did I not warn you about my Aunt Marcy?"

"No...why?"

He shakes his head in feigned disgust. "Let's just say you'd better brush up on your political conspiracy smalltalk."

"My what now?"

Oliver's laughing now. "I hope you're ready to discuss the bunker where JFK's being kept. It's apparently the same one where they store the government cheese."

"Alternatively," I retort, squeezing his knee between my fingers, "you could just not leave me alone with this person."

"What's in it for me?"

"Ha! Fine. What do you want?"

He makes a big show of thinking it over. "Hmm. Well, actually. Now that we're co-owners of Shoreline, I was thinking maybe we could explore a couple of those fantasies you shared with me last night."

My cheeks heat, remembering the scenarios I'd outlined for Oliver when we cuddled in my bed together after a marathon evening of packing up my condo. Several took place in the bookstore after it was shut down for the night.

"I think that can be arranged," I agree.

After Maisie had admitted that Oliver turned down the opportunity to manage Shoreline, I'd asked her if the offer to buy her out was still on the table. She seemed like she might still be a little high on her pills, so I waited a few days and then asked her again. Both times, she gave an emphatic yes.

Then, I'd mustered every ounce of courage I could find and told Oliver I had something to discuss with him.

"I don't want us to make sacrifices that will break us in the long run," I'd explained that night on the porch at Beach Haven. "I want you, and I want to stay here. But not if it means you feel trapped, and certainly not if it means me taking an opportunity away from you."

"So what do you propose?" he'd asked me, eyes bright under the stars.

I'd outlined my plan. I would move to Beach Haven and sell my condo in Brookline. I'd use the money from the sale to buy a majority share of the business from Maisie. If it wasn't enough, I could take out a loan; I had excellent credit.

"I'll cover your share," I'd told Oliver. "We can work out the details later. But we'll proceed like we're co-owners. And by keeping Maisie as a minority owner, she won't lose what she's worked so hard to build. And she'll still have some income."

"I love it," Oliver had said, squeezing my hand. "But I think I can do you one better."

"I convinced my dad to sell the boat," Oliver told me the next day. "He knows it's time. And with that money, I'll be able to offer my half right away. It should keep you from having to take out a loan."

And that's how we ended up on the steps of Shoreline a month later, doing a ribbon cutting for the bookstore and its new ownership team: me, Oliver, and Maisie. The local news-paper came to take a few photos, and Maisie raised her crutch in the air jubilantly in most of them. She's been really enjoying showing off her ever-improving mobility.

My parents drove up for the party, seeming to have found a gentle balance between their flirtation and aggression, and helped us toast our new venture with champagne and cupcakes.

"We're going to hire some new clerks," I'd explained when I showed them around the store. "And Oliver has amazing ideas for upgrading the pastry offerings in the café. Ooh, and I'm going to add some new shelves over here," I'd gestured to the front wall, "and really build out our recommended reading area, plus lots of couches for folks who want to make an afternoon of it. We may not take much of a salary for a while," I'd added with a chuckle. "But it'll be worth it."

Maisie had been beyond supportive of all the changes we wanted to make. She said she'd been so happy tackling administrative tasks from home during her leave that she wanted to go on doing that. "I'll still pop in from time to time," she'd promised. "Nothing can keep me away from my books for too long."

Oliver and I had exchanged a small smile. In buying the majority share of the shop, our biggest concern was that Maisie still feel like Shoreline belonged to her. I was so happy she was still referring to them as "her" books. No matter what the future holds, this place will always be hers.

I WEAR my curtain dress to the wedding, and Oliver's dark blue suit surpasses even my wildest daydreams. "You like it?" he asks, standing in front of the mirror in our Cape Cod hotel room.

"Mmhmm," I reply, stepping closer to whisper in his ear. "Very much so."

He laughs. "Well, you know I like your dress."

"I do." I put my hand on his arm. "Are you ready?"

He nods slowly. "As ready as I'll ever be."

We sit in the back at the ceremony, which is brief, but lovely. Oliver's mom reads tearful vows to her new husband, Jeff, and he reciprocates with even bigger waterworks. I sneak glances at Oliver throughout the ceremony, trying to gauge how much support he needs from me at any given moment. I keep my hand on his the entire time.

After the recessional, we find Oliver's mom in the church lobby.

Her face positively glows when she sees him. "Oliver," she breathes.

He stiffens beside me, but he keeps walking toward her. "Hi, Mom." The air is thick with the substance of this moment. They haven't seen one another in well over a decade. I can't imagine what this is like for him. For her. He's her only child.

"Mom, this is my girlfriend, Ivy. Ivy, my mom, Michelle." Oliver gestures between us, and I reach out to shake Michelle's hand.

"Oliver's told me so much about you, Ivy." Michelle's smile is warm. "Truly, only good things."

I'm not totally sure how to respond, because he's told me all kinds of things about his mother, most of which aren't very positive. So I just return her smile and say how lovely it is to meet her.

"It was a beautiful ceremony," Oliver offers.

"You think so?" Michelle drinks in his approval. "I wasn't sure, at first. I didn't know if the flowers would be too much."

"The flowers were gorgeous," I add.

Oliver's mom seems overcome with emotion. "I'm just so grateful to you both for being here." Her eyes well up. "It...it truly means the world to me, Oliver."

As she radiates love to him, I feel the tension in his arm, which my elbow is still linked around, start to dissipate.

"Thanks for inviting us," he finally replies.

"Tell me about your bookstore." Michelle's eyes light up. "I want to hear everything."

I let them volley tentative questions back and forth, building a hesitant connection that I suspect they've both waited years for. Nothing can right the wrongs of the past, but I'm so glad that the future is looking a little bit brighter.

THE RECEPTION IS HELD OUTDOORS, overlooking the ocean. The dance floor is under a tent, filled with revelers and pink roses. Oliver introduces me to what feels like three hundred of his relatives, to the point where I think my face might freeze with a permanent smile.

As it turns out, he actually undersold the lunacy of his Aunt Marcy, but I manage to escape that conversation when a fresh batch of hors d'oeuvres is set out.

"So, how do you think it went?" I ask him from a quiet corner of the tent. We've been sipping champagne and watching the sun set over the Atlantic.

He smiles, pressing a kiss to my cheek. "I think I'm glad we came."

"Yeah?" My brows rise in anticipation.

Oliver nods. "It doesn't take away everything that happened. But I'm ready to set it down." He takes a deep breath, fixing me with a poignant glance. "It's time to move on."

My heart dances around in my chest. "I know exactly what you mean."

Just then, a very familiar brassy melody picks up from the bandstand. It takes me right back to that night at Harbor Lights, when Oliver told me it was his favorite Van Morrison song and held me for the first time.

Oliver reaches for my hand. "Want to dance?" His eyes

twinkle, like they want me to know he's the one behind this musical choice.

Before I can respond, he leans over and kisses me deeply, then whispers, "They're playing our song."

thirty-nine

"Wow, I love what you've done with the place," Dad says, hefting two enormous blue duffels onto the new white sofa in the living room.

"Thanks," I reply, glancing with pride at the nautical artwork I bought to match Simon's. I wanted Beach Haven to be faithful to its roots.

My father moves closer to inspect the shelves by the fireplace. His gaze stops on the three framed photographs I've added above the mantel.

On the left is the portrait of Eleanor at the beach in 1953, grinning at the camera. On the right, a candid shot of Simon sitting on the porch out front. And in the middle, the photo of Charlie beaming love out to Simon, his eager photographer.

"They're beautiful." Dad's voice catches on the words.

My mother steps closer and rests her arm around his shoulders, then rubs his back comfortingly.

I blink back tears. "I wanted them all to be together."

My father clears his throat. "It's perfect."

"What time is Oliver supposed to get here with Simon?" Mom asks.

I peek over my shoulder at the microwave clock. "Should be any minute. Want to put your bags in your room, then we can meet them on the beach?"

I help my parents bring their luggage to the bedroom Laurel and I never touched during our trip last year. The bedding is new, and I even rented a carpet cleaner to rid the space of its musty smell.

"You've done a lot for the place." A smile comes to rest on my father's face. "Simon's going to be thrilled."

Even though I'm a grown woman, hearing praise from my parents still makes my chest swell with pride. "Thanks, Dad."

"Ready, my loves?" Mom presses a kiss to Dad's cheek.

"Ready," he replies with a grin.

Ever since so many truths tumbled out last summer, my parents have been going to couples therapy.

"It's sort of unfair," Dad always jokes. "She's a therapist already, so she's going to win no matter what I do."

"It isn't a contest, Steven," Mom will retort, but she lets her amusement show. "And I'm not a therapist; I'm a psychologist."

"What's the difference?" he'll quip.

"You're the worst," Mom often replies. "But as long we're together, I think we're both winning." A lot of the time, they'll be all over each other after that, and I'll step out of the room.

It's both heartwarming and kind of disgusting when your parents rediscover they're attracted to each other.

We're sitting on the porch when Oliver comes around the corner of Beach Haven, holding an arm out to steady Simon.

"It looks just the same," Simon remarks, holding a hand above his eyes as he gazes out at the sea.

I can't tell if he's joking, because of course the ocean never really changes. I mean, over centuries, of course, its constant nudging eventually reshapes the land according to its whims. But more abstractly, the ocean doesn't change. Instead, it changes us.

Just then, I catch a glimpse of Laurel and her parents striding toward us through the sand from the direction of their rental cottage. She raises her hand in a friendly wave. I run and tackle her in a hug.

Uncle Greg and Aunt Bea look amused. "I've missed you," I murmur. Ever since I moved to Ogunquit and Laurel successfully defended her dissertation, we've both been pretty busy—me, running Shoreline with Oliver, and her, teaching about 8,000 classes a semester at her alma mater, which snapped her up immediately.

"Me too," she answers. It took effort, but we've more than gotten past our disagreement from last summer, and we're in a much better place. Laurel even decided to read Eleanor's diary in its entirety. She just needed space to process everything in her own time.

So did Uncle Greg, but he snapped back pretty quickly. "I always thought there was something special about Simon," he'd said. "I'm so glad to finally know how important he really was to Dad."

When we're all gathered in front of Beach Haven, there's a strange energy hanging in the air—like we all know this is one of those moments we're going to remember for the rest of our lives.

"Are we ready?" I hold out Eleanor's diary. I've taped the missing pages back in their rightful place at its center.

Oliver wraps his arm around my waist and presses a kiss to the top of my head.

"Ready," my father says confidently. Everyone else follows suit, a syncopated chorus of voice.

Simon's eyes brim with tears. "Let's get Eleanor back where she belongs."

We work together to dig a hole in the sand 20 yards in front of Beach Haven. "So she can feel the sun," Simon suggests.

Then, Uncle Greg holds out a small metal lockbox. Hands shaking, I place the diary inside. Laurel turns the key, then hands it to her father. Greg raises an eyebrow in question, and my dad nods, taking the box and lowering it into the hole on the beach.

We take turns throwing sand on top of the box, swapping stories about Eleanor and Charlie all the while. Aunt Bea pulls a bottle of champagne out of her bag, and we pass it around, sipping and reminiscing beneath the cotton candy sunset.

When my father first suggested we bury the diary, I wasn't sure what to think. But we all discussed it and decided it was time. Perhaps even more than time. We'd learned the truth, and while it had brought us clarity, and closure, and Simon, we didn't need it anymore.

The diary had almost destroyed us, and now we'd done the hard work of coming back together. We agreed together it was time to leave Eleanor and Charlie's secrets in the past, and let her words live forever on the beach she loved so much.

By the time we've finished shoveling sand back over the box, the sun's dropped most of the way behind the horizon, hitting the water with a last glint of light as it goes. "Anyone want to take a dip?" Laurel asks.

It's a strange feeling, heading to the water en masse with

my entire family, its members both old and new. It's somehow simultaneously incredibly familiar and startlingly novel, as we venture out in our freshly sculpted way for the first time. The group looks different on its face than when we were last here. But I think where we've changed the most is on the inside.

Because we've lost Charlie and Eleanor, but now we have Oliver and Simon. Laurel and I are even stronger, having overcome our conflict, and my parents have loved and lost and found their way back to each other again.

There's a certain fatigue we all share now. We've been through the wringer and have finally made it to the other side, but to grow, we've had to leave bits of ourselves behind. After all, we wouldn't have room to carry new joy if we refused to set things down.

It's like that daydream I'd had, of the ocean carrying a new shell to shore for me. How could I put it on if I was still wearing the old one?

We troop into the waves in the dying light to a chorus of predictable gasps at the cold water and jokes from my father about it being refreshing. Laurel giggles and splashes her mom. Greg helps Simon wade further away from the shore. My parents move off to the side, their arms around each other. Oliver slips his hand in mine. It's warm in every way.

"Thanks for helping bring her home." I channel my gratitude through our linked fingers.

"I rather think I should be thanking her," he says.

I snuggle against his chest. "Oh yeah? Why's that?"

His voice is velvet against my soul. "Because she's the one who brought *you* home."

The waves roll in. The waves roll out. The ocean distracts us with its beauty as it wears away at our shorelines, molding our edges over time. I wonder how the coastline of my family might look in another generation.

But I don't want to wish it away. For now, I'm content to enjoy this beautiful place with these wonderful people, all of whom I'm proud to call my own.

I press a kiss over Oliver's beating heart. "There's no place I'd rather be."

author's note

I was in Ogunquit when I became an author. Like Ivy, this picturesque town on the coast of southern Maine holds a special place in my heart. It has been one of my family's favorite vacation spots for generations, too. Also just like Ivy, I grew up visiting Ogunquit Beach, oftentimes accompanied by my grandparents, aunts, uncles, and cousins.

I don't think I realized how special this place was to me until I was grown and had the good fortune to see even more of the world. I've been to so many wonderful places, but something always keeps me coming back to Ogunquit. I'm sure part of it is the memories, but it's also the kind people, the gorgeous, clean beach, and the breathtaking Marginal Way, which offers some of my favorite vistas anywhere I've traveled.

The year I ended up writing my first novel, which was completely unplanned, my husband and I took our family to Ogunquit on a summer getaway. I'd heard that a new bookshop had opened up in town, and I made sure to save time for a visit. Though I didn't base Shoreline Books in *Beautiful Place by the*

Sea on this real-life shop, it also changed my life, just like Shoreline changed Ivy's.

I'd finished all of the books I'd brought on our vacation, and there was some rain in the forecast, so I knew I'd need more to read. I purchased a hardcover from a bestselling author I'd been hearing a lot about. I devoured it in one day, and then a story crept back into my mind: the story of Esperanza, which I'd tried to write several times over the preceding decade. This time, though, more of the story's scaffolding coalesced for me, and I started working on *Ghost Writing*, my debut novel, on my iPhone from our hotel room.

Over the remaining few days of my trip to Maine, I wrote the first 10,000 words of the book. It poured out of me like nothing I've ever experienced in my life. I've hesitated to share this because I realize it might sound untrue or cheapen the accomplishment somehow, but I actually finished the entire novel in only 36 days. When I got home from Maine, I did little else—and even when I was doing other things, my mind was on my story.

While I was sitting on the beach during that trip, my back to the ocean, I caught myself looking at the row of covered chairs at the top of the hill that leads down to the sand. I remembered a family story about my great-grandmother sitting in those chairs, working on her embroidery. And then I had an idea. Wouldn't it be wonderful to set another novel here, in this truly magical place, where the place itself is a patient, ever-present character in a family's story over many generations? I was focused on *Ghost Writing* at the time, but I made a mental note to dream up something big to take place in Ogunquit for my second book.

Ghost Writing was an exercise in character for me, and,

without fully meaning to, I've written *Beautiful Place by the Sea* to be an exercise in setting. The way the ocean calls to Ivy, and her frequent musings about it witnessing the collapse and rebirth of her family, both make it a character in its own right. I only hope I've done it justice.

I am so grateful to this beautiful place by the sea, both for the generations of memories, and for inspiring me to take the leap to write. It's been my dream since childhood to be a novelist, but the dominoes never quite fell for me until that pivotal trip to Maine. I don't know what it was about the atmosphere that August by the coast, but it put me in exactly the right creative headspace to begin. And once I began, I knew it was what I was born to do.

Thank you for reading this book, which is far less autobiographical than *Ghost Writing*, but which, in some ways, is even more personal. This is my love letter to Ogunquit, which feels like the least I can do after all it's done for me. If you're ever looking for a place to vacation, I highly recommend it—there's definitely magic in the air.

Danielle Smyth

about the author

Danielle Smyth has dreamed of being a writer since childhood, and seeing that dream realized is the ultimate happy ending. When she's not writing, Danielle runs a small business. Her favorite days are spent traveling, eating tacos, and reading with her family.

* * *

Also by Danielle Smyth
 Ghost Writing
 Ghosts of Christmas Presents